CLASH OF EMPIRES
THE GREAT SIEGE

Also by William Napier

Julia
Attila: The Scourge of God
Attila: The Gathering of the Storm
Attila: The Judgement

CLASH
OF
EMPIRES

THE GREAT SIEGE

William Napier

First published in Great Britain in 2011 by Orion Books,
an imprint of The Orion Publishing Group Ltd
Orion House, 5 Upper Saint Martin's Lane
London WC2H 9EA

An Hachette UK Company

1 3 5 7 9 10 8 6 4 2

A CIP catalogue record for this book
is available from the British Library.

ISBN (Hardback) 978 1 4091 0531 2
ISBN (Export Trade Paperback) 978 1 4091 0532 9

Typeset by Deltatype Ltd, Birkenhead, Merseyside

Printed in Great Britain by Clays Ltd, St Ives plc

The Orion Publishing Group's policy is to use papers
that are natural, renewable and recyclable products and
made from wood grown in sustainable forests. The logging
and manufacturing processes are expected to conform to
the environmental regulations of the country of origin.

www.orionbooks.co.uk

To Sebastian, Sacha, Emma, Andrew, Charlotte, Jack and Tom

It was on this occasion that Catherine de Medici asked, 'Was it really the greatest siege? Greater even than Rhodes?'

She was answered by Knight Commander de la Roche, of the French Langue: 'Yes, Madam, greater even than Rhodes. It was the greatest siege in history.'

—*Jurien de la Gravière*

Malta of gold, Malta of silver, Malta of most precious metal,
    We will never take you, not if you were protected by no more than the skin of an onion!
    No, for I am She who drowned the galleys of the Turk,
    Who destroyed all the heroes of Constantinople and Galata …

—*Sixteenth century ballad*

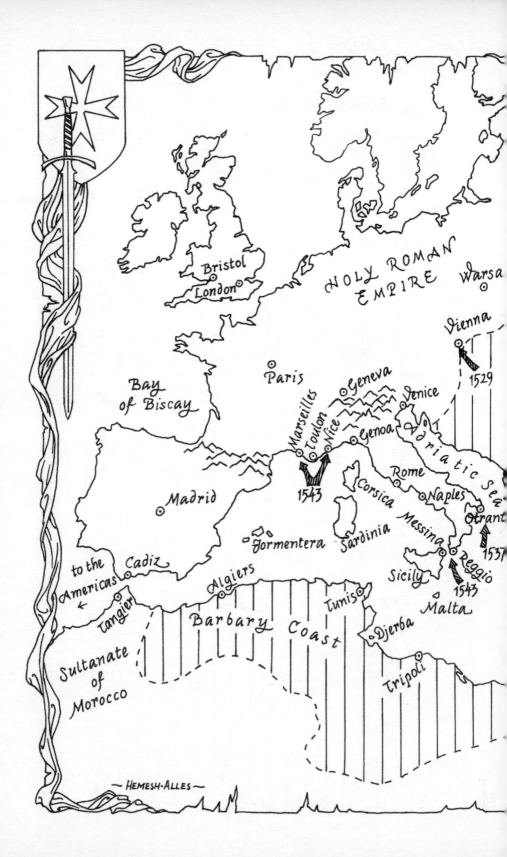

HOLY ROMAN
EMPIRE

Warsa

Vienna
1529

Bristol
London

Bay
of Biscay

Paris

Geneva

Venice

Marseilles
Toulon
Nice
Genoa

A d r i a t i c S e a

Rome

Madrid

Corsica

Naples

Otrant

Formentera

Sardinia

Messina

1537

Reggio

1543

to the
Americas

Cadiz

Algiers

Tunis

Sicily

1543
Malta

Tangier

B a r b a r y   C o a s t

Djerba

Sultanate
of
Morocco

Tripoli

— HEMESH·ALLES —

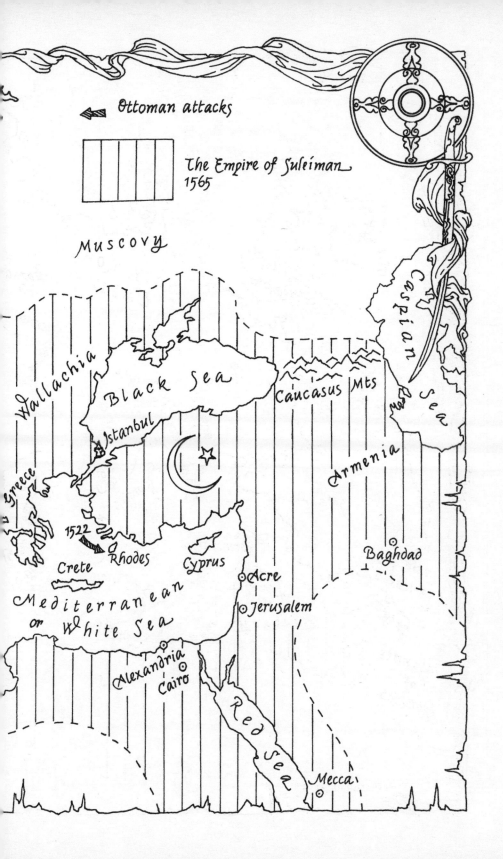

Ottoman attacks

The Empire of Suleiman
1565

Muscovy

Wallachia

Black Sea

Istanbul

Greece

Caucasus Mts

Caspian Sea

Armenia

1522

Crete

Rhodes

Cyprus

Baghdad

Mediterranean
or White Sea

Acre

Jerusalem

Alexandria
Cairo

Red Sea

Mecca

Gozo

Comino

Mellieha Bay

St. Paul's Bay

Mediterranean

Ghain
tuffieha
Bay

Malta

Grand
Harbour

Mdina

Zabbar

Zeitun

Dingli

zurrieq

Jilfla
Island

Marsasirocco

Marsamuscetto

Fort St. Elmo

Ottoman
Trench

Gallows
Point

Ottoman guns

Is. Salvatur
chain

Fort St. Angelo

Kalkara
Creek

Mount
Scriberras

Galley Creek

Birgu

boats dragged overland

St. Michel

Senglea

Turkish
Camp

Corradino
Heights

French Creek

Santa
Margherita
Heights

The Grand Harbour

— HEMESH . ALLES —

PROLOGUE
Rhodes: Christmas Eve, 24th December, 1522

One last arquebus shot cracked out from the battered walls of Rhodes, followed by the angry shout of a Knight Commander. Then there was silence.

Spread out beyond the city lay the vast army of the Ottomans. The horses of the Sipahi cavalrymen waited in line, snorting and tossing their plumes. The Janizaries rested their hands on their sword hilts, gazing steadfastly out across the wreckage of the plain. The fanatical Bektaşis stood crowded close behind, in the eyes of every one of them a grievous disappointment that the battle was done and they were still living, while their slain brothers were even now with the Prophet in Paradise.

Seated on a magnificent white stallion of Cappadocia, shaded from the mild December sun by an immense, tasselled palanquin of yellow satin, sat the Caliph of the Islamic World. Suleiman *Kanuni*: The Law Giver. The young Sultan moved not a muscle, never blinked. He waited for the inevitable surrender of the Christians with all the implacable patience of the Drawn Sword of Islam. For it was written that the whole world should finally bow to the religion of the Prophet, and even he, Suleiman, son of Selim, was but a slave of Allah and his purposes.

The fall of Rhodes to his numberless armies was just the beginning.

At last the splintered gates in the Eastern Wall of the city creaked open, and a slow procession emerged.

They raised banners of the Virgin and of the warrior archangel

1

St Michael for protection. First of all came the men, women and children of the city, for whose sake the Knights had surrendered. Barefoot, dusty and half-starved, four thousand of these wretched islanders made their way down to the harbour to beg for a boat to take them ... who knew where? A new life, without possessions, without hope. But still alive.

The Turks watched them go. These wretches would have earned a handsome sum indeed, four thousand souls, in the slave markets of Istanbul, even half-starved as they were. Especially the younger girls and boys. But the Sultan had shown himself as merciful as ever, and his soldiers' only booty would be what they could plunder from an almost unpeopled city.

Not one among the departing had not lost a father, brother or son in the bitter siege.

A young widow, in black from head to toe, stumbled and fell by the roadside. Her small son moved to help her, a child of no more than four or five years, face already scarred and wizened by hunger and disease. A Turk stepped forward to help her. She glared up at him ferociously, and pulling herself to her feet with the fragile aid of her child, she hissed at the Turk,

'Keep back from me, demon-worshipper.'

The Turk stood back and let her walk on.

After the long and mournful procession of islanders came the knights, some limping, some carrying their brethren on stretchers and litters down to the harbour, and their great carrack, the *St Mary*, riding at anchor in already choppy waters. Others carried the records of the Order, or its most holy possessions, the right arm of John the Baptist in a gold casket, and the Icon of the Virgin of Phileremos, painted by St Luke himself.

At their head walked the Grand Master, tall, lean, white-bearded, some sixty years of age. Philippe Villiers de l'Isle Adam, son of the highest French nobility, silent and grave in defeat.

He stopped before the Sultan and bowed his head, in acknowledge-ment of the Sultan's mercy, and as one fighting man to another.

Close by the Grand Master stood another, much younger Knight of St John. Like the rest he wore a long black gown sewn with a white cross, the habit of peacetime. Yet his eyes now fixed on the Sultan with an implacable spirit of opposition.

No man looked directly at the Sultan, least of all an infidel. A Janizary stepped forward instantly, vine stick grasped tight in his right hand, ready to strike.

'Lower your eyes, Christian!'

Outrageously this young knight continued to stare full in the face of the Sultan. At last Suleiman himself turned his head slightly and returned his gaze. The Knights of St John had been defeated, their fortress home destroyed. And yet in this one's eyes, there burned an emnity as deep as the Pontic Sea.

A brother knight, of the English Langue, limping badly from a wound to his left thigh, a rust-red bandage bound tightly about it, clapped his hand hard on the shoulder of the first. Yet still the young knight stood staring, like a hound fixed on its prey.

Then a commanding voice rang out from the head of the column.

'La Valette! Walk on, sir!'

It was the Grand Master himself, looking back angrily.

Chastity, poverty, and – hardest of all – obedience. For the knights were as much monks as soldiers. The young Frenchman dropped his gaze from the Sultan, Lord of the Unbelievers, as the Master of his ancient order had commanded, and moved slowly on. His English brother knight fell in behind him, a faint smile on his lips.

'We will fight again, Fra Jean,' he murmured. 'Do not doubt it.'

The knight called La Valette said nothing. Eyes staring ahead at emptiness, jaws set like iron.

The knights could have fought on at Rhodes.

Many times before, over five long centuries, they had fought the Armies of Islam to a standstill, and to the death. In 1291, at Acre in the great Crusades, they had fought and died almost to the last man. When the armies of Al-Ashraf Khalil finally broke into the city and began the steady slaughter, the last of the Palestine Hospitallers took their stand in a single dungeon. Just seven brothers were left, each still swinging his sword though mortally wounded, drenched in his own blood, white-faced. All died there. Seven knights, fighting in a tight circle, back to back. And perhaps another twenty or thirty jihadis, strewn around them.

These Knights Hospitaller, these Knights of St John – they were the Bektaşis of Satan.

They were the mad dogs of Christendom.

But at Rhodes, it was not only their own lives they would sacrifice, but the islanders' too. Fishermen, farmers, merchants and priests, wives and children, infants in arms. What right did the knights have to condemn the whole island to death? None. Not when Suleiman had promised them safe passage to leave, and merciful treatment of any islanders remaining.

Besides, Villiers knew that the fighting was done.

For six long, desperate months, the knights and the people had known nothing but the deafening roar of cannon, the crack of handguns, the hiss of seething, bubbling pitch on castle walls, the ring of steel, the hollow clubbing sound of shield on skull, the stench of blood and burning oil and ordure, the haw of mules, the squeal of pigs, the half-crazed barking of dogs.

Finally there were so few men left to fight. There was no more gunpowder, not a sword left unblunted or a shield undented, and there was the Sultan of the Ottomans offering safe passage.

With grieving and grace, Villiers de l'Isle Adam accepted the terms of surrender.

As the old knight and his men limped away down the stony road to the harbour and Suleiman watched them go, he was heard to murmur, 'It is with some regret that I drive this valiant old man from his home.'

But they were destroyed as a fighting force. Without a homeland, with not a single fortress to their name, they who once commanded a chain of mighty forts and commanderies right across the Holy Land, the fiercest defenders for Christ – they were no more to be feared now than a toothless old dog.

'They are out of their time,' said Suleiman that evening, addressing his vizier. He placed his bare feet in the silver bowl for the slavegirl to wash. 'They are ...' The scholar Sultan searched for the right word, and found it in the Greek. 'They are an *anachronism*.'

The vizier looked nonplussed.

Suleiman would have smiled, if smiling had not been inappropriate for one of his dignity.

'They belong to the ancient world, the old centuries. In these days, the new kings and rulers of the Christians have no sympathy for such – *heroics* as theirs. The Knights of St John are an embarrassment to them. The Genoans, the Venetians, the French – they would rather trade with us, buy our silks, sell us their grain.'

'And their armaments,' the vizier murmured.

Suleiman paused to admire the slavegirl. The softness of her hands, the falling curtain of her hair.

'Quite so. Though the knights themselves remain our enemies, they are powerless now. The wider Christian world has moved on. It has lost its appetite for war with Islam. It prefers silks, and spices, and gold. It is also bitterly divided against itself, these *Catholics* and *Protestants* endlessly fighting each other over the intricacies of their barbarous faith.'

'Yet we ourselves wish them nothing but peace.'

'Of course.'

Suleiman allowed the slavegirl to dry his feet. He looked up at his vizier, eyes smiling.

'Nothing but peace.'

In the city, the Bektaşis were celebrating the triumph of Islam.

First they attacked the Church of St John. They gouged lumps of plaster out of the brightly painted walls with their crescent yatagan daggers, they spat and urinated and heaped curses on these foul images of the idolatrous Christian dogs. They had confused a Jewish prophet with the unspeakable, the immeasurable, all-seeing, all-knowing Divine. What blinded slaves of Shaitan and his deceits!

They overturned the altar and smashed it to fragments; they flung outside all the relics, ornaments and crucifixes and burned them in a heap in the square. Happily, their religious zeal coincided with their love of lucre, a coincidence often found among men. For some of the Christian ornaments and reliquaries abandoned by the fleeing townsfolk were of finest silver and gold, and readily taken as booty.

They smashed open the ancient tombs of the Grand Masters in the crypt of the church, hoping to find treasure. In vexation at finding nothing but plain wooden crosses and old bones, some seized these crosses and bones and ran about the streets, using them as clubs. Some especially in the grip of religious fervour found the hospital where a few sick still lay, too ill to be moved, and beat them to death in their beds, raping the women first before killing them.

At dawn on Christmas Day, Suleiman himself rode into the city, sending word that order should be restored. His men had had their reward for victory. He approved of the cleansing of the Christian church, and ordered it to be turned into a mosque, with prayers to Mecca to be said five times daily from tomorrow. But the others had betrayed his own promise of fair treatment. He ordered those who had attacked the hospital to be disembowelled and beheaded, all stray dogs and pigs to be killed, and the streets to be thoroughly cleaned.

He gave another order, which caused surprise among his Janizary guards, but could not be disobeyed. He ordered that the magnificent carved stone escutcheons of the Hospitallers, all along the principal thoroughfare of the city known as the Street of the Knights, were not to be destroyed or damaged in any way.

At the moment that Suleiman rode into Rhodes on Christmas Day, it was said that Pope Hadrian was celebrating Mass in St Peter's, Rome. As he raised the chalice, a cornerstone fell from the roof above him and smashed to the ground close by.

They said it was an ominous sign that one of the key bulwarks of Christendom had been lost.

From the tilting decks of the *St Mary*, rolling through unforgiving winter seas, the knights looked back not only at lost Rhodes, but at the snow-capped Taurus mountains beyond, the whole of the Levant, the ancient heartlands of Christianity. So many knights, Hospitallers, crusaders, had fought and died to regain those lands for the Cross, over nearly five long centuries. Now all of it was lost.

They sailed west, and three weeks later, Villiers stepped ashore at Sicily with his handful of faithful knights, and all the islanders there to meet him knelt bare-headed in honour of fallen greatness. The knights knelt too, giving thanks to God that they had survived the dangerous winter voyage.

It was a cold day, and the January wind ripped at a tattered banner the knights brought with them. At one point the wind seemed about to tear the banner free altogether and hurl it contemptuously away, until one knight stood and planted the staff more firmly in the wet sand.

It was the knight called La Valette.

The banner showed the Holy Mother with her crucified Son. Weather-beaten, salt-stained and torn, it bore the motto,

Afflictis spes uniea rebus.

In adversity our only hope.

Part I
THE JOURNEY

1

Istanbul: October, 1564

'All present, bow the knee!'

'Bow the knee and bow the head, before the Sultan of the Ottomans, Allah's Viceroy on Earth, Lord of the Lords of this World, Possessor of Men's Necks, King of Believers and Unbelievers, Emperor of the East and West, Majestic Caesar, Seal of Victory, Refuge of all People, the Shadow of the Almighty, the Destroyer of Christendom!'

Any who did not bow his head would lose it. All bowed.

Now almost seventy years of age, Suleiman the Magnificent, ruler of the most powerful empire on earth, turned carefully on the high dais and sat back upon the richly gilded, crimson cushioned Throne of the Caliph. Before him, more than a hundred courtiers, viziers, eunuchs and pashas bent low in obeisance. He waited for some time. It was at his word, his whim, that they might arise again, and none other. Let them remain bowed until they stiffened and ached. Let them remember.

At last he gave the nod, and the assembled commanders of his empire stood upright once more.

He surveyed the Hall of Audience, hushed with soft Persian carpets, lit with fine silver filigree lanterns, hung with silks and tapestries. He knew almost everything, but let them think he knew all. His great dark eyes rested on many a face in turn. His once handsome features now sagged, riven with lines of care, and more private sorrows. But he was Sultan and Emperor still.

In the past four decades, had he not conquered from the Pillars of Hercules to the Black Sea, from the heart of European Christendom to the shores of India? Tomorrow he would have his crier give out his list of conquests once again. Let none think this ageing Emperor was finished yet, or ripe to fall. Let them remember.

'By the will of Allah, the compassionate, the merciful, Conqueror of Aden, Algiers, Baghdad, Belgrade, Budapest, Rhodes, Nakshivan, Rivan, Tabriz, and Temesvár!'

His kingdom stretched from Austria to Egypt, from Algiers to Tartary and the debatable lands beyond. His galleys ruled the seas from the Mediterranean to the Persian Gulf. Only once, in 1529 before the walls of Vienna, had his army been halted. But he was young and foolish then, and had learnt much about the arts of war in the intervening years. Now in his last decade – for a dream of the Prophet had told him he would rule for another ten years yet – he would complete the task appointed to him. He would turn back upon the ancient enemy, Europe, now so weakened and divided. He would at last avenge the shame at Vienna, the insult of the Crusades, and complete the destruction of Christendom.

At the start of next year's campaigning season, as soon as the first signs of spring appeared, he would march his army to their final victory upon the plains of Hungary, and beyond. Meanwhile the Muslim inhabitants of Spain would rise up in revolt, tying up the greatest of Christian powers in internal civil war, and his allies in Tunis and Algiers, the North African corsairs, would fall upon Sicily, the heel of Italy, and before long, Rome itself . . .

But first to business, and the afternoon's tiresome petitions.

All the women departed, being unfit to hear or understand the business of rulership, and all the men except the day's petitioners and Suleiman's chief officers.

Today, one petition was different, the news both better and worse.

It was Kustir Agha, Chief of the Black Eunuchs, who approached the throne.

'Kustir Agha, loyal servant. Speak.'

'Gracious and Imperial Majesty, may you live a thousand years, and leave a thousand sons.'

Suleiman made a gesture of sharp impatience.

'Gracious and Imperial Majesty,' went on Kustir Agha, 'we have suffered a grievous loss.' His breathing was tight, and not just owing to his girth. 'The *Sultana,* a rich galley, the richest I owned. With its cargo it was worth 80,000 ducats.'

'Allah afflicts us all with his storms.'

'Majesty, it was no storm. It was Christian pirates. It was … our ancient enemy. The Knights of St John. '

Suleiman's eyes hardened. Kustir Agha must tread very carefully indeed.

'It was the Sultan's clemency that allowed the Knights to survive and live on after Rhodes,' said Kustir. 'An act of clemency in perfect obedience to the teachings of the Prophet, peace be upon him. Yet these Christian savages showed no gratitude. They took to that barren rock of Malta and grew again in power. This latest insult is only one of hundreds. It was the galley of the Chevalier Romegas that committed the insult.'

Suleiman nodded almost imperceptibly. He knew all about this Chevalier Romegas. Perhaps the most dangerous sailor on the White Sea.

'And with this 80,000 ducats, what will they do?' Kustir rolled his eyes and held his arms wide. 'They are celibate men, they have no families, they buy no luxuries. They do not live in fine palaces, nor wear pearls and silks. They live for one thing only. To wage war. With these 80,000 ducats stolen from us, they will only buy new weapons, more powder, build higher the fortifications of their island home. Commit ever greater depredations on your Majesty's subjects. While the captive master and crew, our Muslim brothers, shiver with prison fever in their rock-cut dungeons, or are driven at the end of a whip to man their galleys.

'Most Gracious Majesty, there is only one response to such provocation.'

Suleiman allowed a long silence. The deep red sunset of an October evening began to illuminate the slender minarets and high crescents of Istanbul. Then he called forward another man.

'Mustafa Pasha!'

From the crowd of courtiers and petitioners stepped a tall, lean man with a face darkened by the sun. Old and yet anything but infirm, he strode forward like an arrogant young Janizary, black robe billowing. Others hurriedly made way for him.

Veteran of wars from Persia to Hungary, Mustafa Pasha had been captured once by the Christians, and served an astonishing four years as a galley slave in the fleet of the great Genoese admiral, Andrea Doria. Most galley slaves were lucky to survive a year, before their exhausted bodies were tumbled over the side of the ship for the fish. *Four years.* Of any man who has served as a galley slave, they said, something hard and hate-filled enters into his soul. And Mustafa Pasha already had a heart and a soul of iron on the day he was born.

He escaped the galleys of Andrea Doria by beating the one-legged bosun to death with his own wooden leg, while still chained to the bench. He then levered off his own manacles with the leg, smashed open the heads of four more overseers, strangled a fifth with his whip, jumped over the side and swam ten miles to the Albanian coast. Forty-eight hours later he was scouring the Adriatic in his own warship. He found the galley he'd served on for those four bitter years and sank it, not rescuing even his former fellow slaves from their chains.

He was said to have killed over two hundred men with his own hands, fathered more than fifty sons, daughters too (though they had never been counted), and amassed a private fortune of more than a million ducats. Now seventy, the same age as the Sultan, he fought with the sword every morning for two hours against the finest Janizaries. Only last month he had sliced off a man's hand. The Janizary, now retired, displayed his stump at the gates of the city to passers-by, with mingled sorrow and pride, saying that he had lost his hand to none other than Mustafa Pasha. People gazed in awe and gave him silver pennies.

Mustafa Pasha stopped abruptly before the Throne of the Caliph and bowed low. Stood swiftly again. A grey moustache and pointed beard, deep-set eyes, and the great hooked nose of a bird of prey, so that many whispered that Arab blood ran in him. He did not look directly at the Sultan, naturally, but he held his head high and haughty nonetheless. His face was deeply lined, and there were sword cuts and gunpowder burns visible on his strong, thick-veined right hand.

'You are keen to share with us your view of the Knights Hospitaller?'

Mustafa needed no further encouragement. Nor did he trouble with Kustir Agha's grandiloquent flatteries. His voice sounded deep and harsh, filling the great audience chamber.

'The Knights we know of old. And this accursed rock of Malta, their new base, stands between you and your rightful possessions. From this rock with its great harbour – the finest in all the White Sea – their lean galleys come out like wolves to attack our ships, enslave our brothers, steal our cargoes.

'Your Majesty plans the conquest of Christendom. But you will do nothing unless you first capture Malta, and exterminate once and for all these dogs of St John. It is time to wipe the Knights off the face of the earth, as you would wipe out the rats in your barn.'

There was an uneasy silence. Mustapha had come perilously close to criticizing Suleiman's previous clemency. But if anyone was permitted such lèse majesté, it was this ancient warrior.

Suleiman stroked his trim beard. 'Tell us more.'

Mustafa gestured widely, his robe filling like a sail. 'This barren rock is the key to the western Mediterranean. You cannot mount any naval operations beyond it with safety.'

'Our galleys have sailed many a time beyond Malta and returned.'

'Many more have never returned. Like Kustir Agha's precious, though under-defended ship,' his lip curled, 'the *Sultana.*'

Kustir Agha blinked furiously but said nothing. Mustafa Pasha had a foul temper. None crossed him, all meekly accepted his sneers.

'The island of Malta dominates those narrow straits between Sicily and Africa, only sixty miles from coast to coast. An Ottoman galley might pass through, but an entire armada, such as will be needed for the final conquest of Christendom – no. Those sea wolves would wreak havoc upon us. Their flagship, the *Great Carrack,* is the most powerful warship in the White Sea. With my own eyes I have seen it. Alone it could destroy a dozen of our galleys.

'The Sultan will never conquer the rest of Europe without first conquering Malta.'

Suleiman's eyes were old and haunted. 'Forty-two years ago I drove the Knights from Rhodes. They fought bravely, and in my munificence I let the survivors depart with honour.' His voice became steely again, he sat straight-backed. 'Yet it is in the book of Ibn Khaldun, the book of prophecies, that the armies of Islam will come by sea, and ultimately the lands of Christendom will fall to them. For all men in time will bow the head to Mecca.'

He turned to a slave. 'Bring me the map of Ptolemy.'

In a trice, a wide table was brought and a great map spread out.

It was a map made by the Greeks, centuries ago, and many a time Suleiman had traced its outlines with rapt attention to detail. Here would be a good place for a new city, a new Ottoman capital of the West. Here was a fine harbour, here an enchanting island in the ocean stream, fit for the palace of a conqueror. Everywhere he saw dreams of conquest and glory. He, Suleiman, Padishah of the White Sea, the Red and the Black. Now he narrowed his eyes upon the tiny island of Malta. They said you could walk across it in three hours. This speck of grit in the Ottoman oyster.

He raised his head again and addressed the gathered crowd with inimitable authority. Every word was heard, to the back of the vast chamber.

'Allah has prepared this for us: that the Christian idolaters should fight against each other and never come to alliance. The Franks have treated with us in secret, they will not lift a finger to save Italy, Spain or Austria. These territories are ours for the taking. Soon the cry of the muezzin will sound in Vienna, and then in Rome. That great charnel house of saints' bones that they call *Saint Peter's,* we will make into a mosque, as Hagia Sophia is now a mosque. We will bring even France under our sway, Paris will bow the head to Mecca – the French willingly obey a conqueror, for the sake of peace and wine. And finally England, which is ruled by a mere woman, and the cold islands beyond. All this will come to pass during our reign. All will be ours, submitting to the law of the holy Koran.

'One empire, one faith, one leader.'

The hall was filled with the murmur of war.

'But first,' he raised a hand, 'as I have always said – first, we shall conquer Malta. It is written.'

2

By candlelight that very evening, a much smaller meeting took place. Around a marble-topped table in an upper room, the map of Ptolemy again before them, just three men sat in counsel. Suleiman on a raised chair, to his left Mustafa Pasha, and to his right, Piyale, admiral of the grand fleet. Where Mustafa was a cunning Anatolian peasant risen to the heights by ruthlessness and ability, the aristocratic Piyale, little more than half Mustafa's age, smooth and charming, had been raised in the Imperial Palace itself. He also made the cunning move of marrying Genhir, one of the Sultan's granddaughters.

Mustafa was speaking, sharing his limitless knowledge of the White Sea.

'It will be a distant campaign. The island is almost a thousand miles away' – he traced a bony finger over the blue-tinted sea of the map – 'and has no resources. Not a timber, not a stick of firewood. We must take everything.

'Aside from the harbour, dominated by the Castle of the Knights, San Angelo, Malta is no more than a bare sunburnt rock, some ten miles across. A wind-scoured mountaintop between Europe and Africa, its roots on the bed of the White Sea. A merciless desert of thorn scrub, a few carob trees, no rivers. Other inlets on the east side, a small harbour to the south, shallow bays to the north, but to the west, towering, impassable cliffs. A handful of wretched villages, and an ancient city in the heart of it. Note well this city's name: Mdina.'

'The Arabic for *city*,' murmured Piyale.

'For three hundred years,' nodded Suleiman, 'this island was under Islamic rule. And as Islamic law teaches, a land that has once been under Islam, is always under Islam.'

He waved his hand for Mustafa to continue.

'Rainwater is collected in cisterns. Now it will be raining, but by March the rain will stop, and not fall again till autumn. The island lies further to the south than even Algiers or Tunis. In summer the sun can kill a man in armour.'

'We know the number of knights?' asked Piyale.

Suleiman knew everything, from the name of the French king's new mistress to the private finances of the Pope.

'There are some four hundred knights now stationed at Malta,' he said. 'As many again might answer the call from Italy, Spain, France and Germany. The Hospitallers still have commanderies and estates across Europe. But many of those "knights" are farmers in all but name. We will face eight hundred knights at most.'

'And our Army of Malta will number forty thousand,' said Mustafa.

Sultan, general and admiral contemplated these figures with satisfaction.

Mustafa resumed. 'The inhabitants other than the knights are a decrepit and ancient Maltese nobility in Mdina, and an ignorant village peasantry, devoted to Christian idols. Raids by the North African corsairs have only made them more ardent in their un-belief.

'A harsh and worthless land, then, but for those dogs of St John who must be destroyed, and the great harbour, which must be taken. It will be our base for the southern conquest of Europe. The war requires planning and supplies, yet its course will be simple. First the harbour will be captured, then the knights destroyed, and the population slaughtered, enslaved or exiled. Slaughter is satisfying, but slavery enriching.'

Suleiman almost smiled. A typical maxim. 'We should seek to rupture the island's water cisterns,' he said.

'Majesty.' Mustafa nodded. 'Cannon will be needed for this, and to reduce fortifications. Dragut's knowledge of the island would also be useful.'

Suleiman looked up.

'Dragut?'

Mustafa smiled. 'Dragut. The very sound of his name is a weapon of terror in Malta.'

3

Shropshire, England: Autumn, 1564

Father Matthew was saying Mass when they heard the horses' hooves approaching.

The priest had been about to bless the bread – *hoc est enim corpus meum,* that holiest moment. But he stopped and instead prayed silently that the hooves would pass on.

There was a frightened silence in the small oak-panelled room, lit only by candlelight. Father Matthew with his head bowed, lips moving, beside the table spread with the bread and wine. Sir Francis Ingoldsby, white-haired, broad-shouldered and bow-legged, with his four children behind him. The eldest, Nicholas, and his sisters Susan, Agnes and Lettice. The servants behind them. The October wind moaning in the chimney, the flames in the fireplace dancing in torment, the thin rain pattering against the leaded windowpanes. Ironshod hooves on the road.

The listeners barely drew breath.

Then the horses' hooves clattered to a halt outside.

At once there was movement in the room. Father Matthew took up the silver chalice and drained it and wrapped it up in a cloth along with the bread. The servants licked their fingertips and snuffed out all but one candle. Nicholas flung open the door and looked down the hall. At that instant the studded front door seemed to shake on its hinges at a mighty knock from sword hilt or musket butt.

'Quickly, Father,' urged Sir Francis. But the gaunt and bony Father Matthew was not of an age to move anywhere quickly.

The other three Ingoldsby children stood back in the shadows, white-faced, the younger girls trying not to cry. A servant named

Hodge, an expressionless, solidly built youth, was hauling back a section of linen-fold panelling. Another, louder knock came at the door. The wind moaned.

'They'll not knock a third time!' said Nicholas in a desperate whisper.

'That door has stood for four centuries,' muttered his father. 'It'll stand a while yet.'

'Patience, patience,' muttered Father Matthew, with his bundle and missal under one arm, clambering slowly and stiffly into the tiny priest's hole beside the fireplace. 'Unto everything there is a time and a purpose and so forth.'

There was no more violent knocking, only a curious grating sound from around the huge old iron lock. Then to Nicholas's horror, a part of the mechanism moved as if at the hand of a ghost. The lockbar went back and the door swung slowly inwards. At first the others didn't even realise it had happened. Father Matthew was still settling himself down in the hole, muttering about the dignity of the priesthood, Hodge standing by holding the panel.

Only when they heard the rising howl of the wind and felt a gust of chill air from the hall and saw the solitary candleflame lean and flutter did they freeze and stare.

His father cried, 'What the devil?'

Nicholas could only stare back aghast, as if it were somehow his fault.

In the open doorway stood two hulking, thuggish men, their hoods concealing their faces, the wind whipping their travel-stained cloaks about their legs and mud-spattered boots. One had a sword already drawn from the scabbard, the other held a storm lantern. He raised it high and both were eerily illuminated. The one with the lantern pushed back his hood to reveal unkempt fair hair and a beard the colour of old tallow, and high ruddy cheeks. The other did likewise, showing a much darker, more threatening appearance. Black beard and black burning eyes, the whites bloodshot, making him look like a bull of dangerous and evil temperament. His sword hung loosely from a great right hand.

'No, sir, no!' cried a voice from behind Nicholas. It was Hodge. He even put out an arm to restrain his master, but old Sir Francis would have none of it. He would die defending his household if need be.

'Out of my way, boy!' he roared. He pulled down the sword in its scabbard that hung above the fireplace and strode out into the hall. Or strode as best he could, with his aged joints, his left leg crooked from an ancient wound.

The tallow-headed ruffian smiled to see the old warrior.

'We have interrupted you at some game?' he said. 'Or perhaps some more spiritual exercise? Have you a visitor?'

Nicholas glanced back in terror to see if Father Matthew was hidden yet.

A mistake.

The fairhead said, 'Ah, so he's in there.'

Blackbeard beside him said nothing. He was not one for talking, it was clear. Killing was more his temper.

'Please,' said the first ruffian. 'Pray continue, Sir Francis.' And both of them took a step forward into the hall out of the rain. Blackbeard kicked the door shut behind him and lazily, insultingly, sheathed his own sword. They seemed even bigger now, infernal figures, lit only by their own lantern and the single flickering candle of a servant. The girls whimpered in terror. The youngest, little Lettice, held a tiny white handkerchief up to her eyes so she couldn't see. Nicholas groped at his belt and found he wasn't even carrying his dagger. Beside him, Hodge was slowly reaching out for a horsecrop that lay on the oak chest. Much good would that do him against two such men. Yet even at that slight movement, Blackbeard's gaze turned on Hodge and his reddened eyes burned like coals in the night. Hodge froze.

'God damn you,' muttered Sir Francis, standing protectively before all his household, still powerfully built despite his crooked leg. 'Coming to my home with weapons drawn. Whatever my offence may be, I have the same right to a trial as any freeborn Englishman. You are no agents of the Queen or of the Church, you are nothing but low criminals. And if you take one step further into my house, your guts will feel my sword.'

The fairhead smiled pleasantly. 'The weapon looks rusted in its sheath.'

Sir Francis growled and pulled hard at his sword hilt – and sure enough, the scabbard leapt with it.

The fairhead gazed keenly at Sir Francis, eyes gleaming. Raindrops ran down his cheeks and beard, and water puddled on the flagstones round his battered leather boots. When he spoke his voice was strangely softened, cracked with emotion. He said words that none but Sir Francis himself could have understood, tenderly, with not a hint of sarcasm. At the sight of the old man's dauntless courage, trying to pull a rusty sword from its scabbard in solitary defence of his ancestral home, the fairhead murmured, 'Ah, Brother Francis. The Religion hath need of thee, and such as thee.'

Then he pulled his cloak down at the throat to reveal a brilliant silver cross on a chain. A cross with four equal arms and eight points.

Sir Francis let go of his sword. 'My brothers!' he gasped.

Nicholas stared rapt at the blazing silver cross, and it seemed to burn into his eyes forever.

The strangers locked the door again behind them, using the key this time. Nicholas wanted to know how they had unlocked it from without, what mysterious trickery they had used. The fairhead seemed to sense his burning curiosity, but only smiled and tapped the side of his nose.

'My brother and I have travelled far and wide, and learnt much in our travels,' he murmured infuriatingly. 'From the locksmiths of Germany, the alchemists of Alexandria, the gymnosophists of India ...'

'If you come as friends,' said Sir Francis, 'why pick the lock of my door?'

The fairhead grinned. 'Had you peered out of your window and seen two such figures as us – on such a night as this – would you really have let us in?'

Sir Francis guffawed. 'Not till the crack of doom.'

'And besides – we are in a hurry. It is better we were not seen by any others.'

Nevertheless, the two visitors insisted that the family resume the Mass. They would willingly join them.

As Father Matthew intoned the solemn church Latin, there was a chance to study the newcomers sidelong. They smelt of horsehair and leather and sweat, and somehow, distant and exotic lands. The ruddy cheeks of the fairhead were really burned a reddish brown, Nicholas now saw, as were Blackbeard's, and their massively powerful hands too. The deep, deep brown of a hot sun.

After Mass, Father Matthew rode away into the night on his Welsh pony, and the children and servants were sent early to bed. Some lingered on the darkened stairs, peering down. This was the most exciting thing to happen in the village since the miller fell down the well.

'To bed with you!' bellowed Sir Francis, and they scuttled away to their rooms.

In his library, Sir Francis poured three cups of Portugal wine. His unexpected guests stood before the fire, their wet cloaks hung over the backs of chairs and steaming. Hodge still lingered in the doorway, eyes wide. Blackbeard glanced back, and then strode over and pushed the door shut in his face.

'Along with us, Hodge,' said Nicholas.

'But how'll I sleep, Master Nicholas? With them foreigners under the roof?'

Hodge thought anyone who came from across the millstream was a foreigner.

They went upstairs.

Once he had heard all the bedroom doors shut, Nicholas slipped out again, burning with curiosity. What a hypocritical villain he was, to be sure. He crept down the stairs in darkness, keeping close to the edges so as not to creak, and knelt outside the library door.

There he heard confused snatches of urgent conversation. About The Knights, and the island of Malta, the Great Sultan, war galleys, and of a Grand Master of St John, called Jean de la Valette, who was 'dauntless'. Yet some vast and terrible threat hung over them all, and there was desperately little time left.

The two strangers continually addressed his father as Brother Francis, which baffled and intrigued Nicholas at once. As if his father was a monk or a friar! His father never talked about his own early life. It was a mysteriously forbidden subject. He married late, a much younger girl, the daughter of an old friend of his, and they were blissfully happy for nine years, until she died in childbed.

24

Nicholas was eight when she died, and even now could not think of her and speak at the same time. Her golden hair, her radiant smile . . .

He made no sound now, hardly able to hear himself breathe. Yet the strangers knew he was there. The door was abruptly flung open and Blackbeard seized him by the collar of his jerkin, hauling him inside and slamming the door again behind him.

His father rose up from the table with a thunderous expression.

'How dare you, boy! How dare you eavesdrop like some petty sneakthief on a private conversation, and one of such consequence. I'll give you such a beating, you disobedient wretch!'

Blackbeard let the boy go and he slumped, head bowed in shame.

Sir Francis was just raising his fist to strike him when the fairhead murmured,

'Ay, I was young too once, and thrilled by tales of voyages and adventures.' And he laid his hand on Sir Francis's arm.

Sir Francis scowled at him, then slowly, very slowly, the thunder subsided from his face and his arm fell.

'You are a confounded disobedient dog, and obedience is one of the truest virtues. Have you learnt nothing in all your schooling?'

Nicholas's face was red with shame. 'I am heartily sorry, sir. My curiosity was greater than my judgement.'

'Hm.' He stumped back to his chair. 'Prettily said, if not done.'

'Is the boy discreet, brother?' asked the fairhead.

'Is he?' His father glared at him. 'Well, boy? Are you?'

'Have you ever known me not, sir?'

Sir Francis rubbed his white beard. 'You mean we let him stay and hear?'

Blackbeard spoke for the first time, his voice a bearlike growl. 'If only all stayed to hear what we say. All of Christendom. Our news is bitter, and time is damnably short.'

'Very well.' Sir Francis nodded. 'Sit, boy. Listen and learn, and speak not a word. Not now, not hereafter, not to any living soul. Or countless lives will be sacrificed for it.'

Then the three men resumed speaking, as if Nicholas were invisible.

The fairhead said, 'If Christendom would stop tearing itself apart for just one moment – like a dog tearing open its own stomach – and stop, and look up towards the eastern horizon – then it would see a far, far greater danger approaching like a whirlwind. A danger that will make all arguments between Catholics and Protestants, Greeks, Calvinists, Anabaptists and whatever other sectaries seem lunatic in their pettiness. For this is a danger that will, if it is not faced and conquered, destroy all of Europe. It is a danger that has never ceased to menace Christendom since that damned Mohammedan creed first arose like a demon out of the sands of Arabia, a thousand years ago. It will never cease to threaten us. It is the religion of perpetual warfare. The religion of the Barbary corsairs, the Moors, the Saracens, of Saladin, of the drug-maddened Assassins in the Alborz mountains of Persia. It is the perpetually drawn Sword of Islam. Now that sword is wielded by the most fearsome enemy we have yet faced. Suleiman the Magnificent. He who calls himself the Lord of All Under Heaven.'

'And this single battle,' added Blackbeard, 'this one last, desperate stand against the numberless army of the Ottomans, will decide the fate of Christendom for ever.'

The fire gave a loud crack, and Nicholas jumped.

Blackbeard remained unmoved.

Sir Francis said, 'The Christian powers will send no aid?'

The fairhead smiled bitterly. 'They are too busy fighting each other, as usual. The German Protestant princes, and of course this fair realm of England, regard us as wicked Catholics. Why would they help us? Italy is torn apart by perpetual war, and the competing ambitions of the French, the Spanish, even the Papal States. The great republics of Venice and Genoa, their treasuries overflowing, still care only to amass more gold. If we receive any help at all, it will be from King Philip of Spain. But he has troubles of his own. The Protestants are stirring to revolt in the Spanish Netherlands. English privateers – as they are called – relentlessly harry his treasure ships. His mad son, Don Carlos, is a perpetual torment to him.'

'Mad ever since he fell down the stairs, going to a midnight assignation with a porter's daughter,' said Blackbeard.

'So there he sits in his gloomy palace of the Escorial and dithers. We cannot rely even on him. And so we wait, we four hundred knights, on our barren rock, for the wrath of the entire Ottoman Empire to fall on us. And soon.'

'And if Malta falls,' said Blackbeard, 'then you know what will follow. The Rock of the Mediterranean guards those straits for the whole of Western Europe. The war galleys of the knights plough those seas unceasingly, to the terror of the Barbary corsairs, and even Suleiman himself.'

Sir Francis nodded. 'But if Malta falls …'

'If Malta falls,' said the fairhead, 'and our Great Harbour is lost, then Suleiman is free to roam westwards as he wills. He can fall on the Italian coast, the Spanish, the French—'

'The French!' roared Blackbeard with sudden violence. 'The French deserve all they get!'

The fairhead nodded at his comrade. 'My Brother John here does not care for the French.'

'Those mincing treacherous milk-livered cotqueans! Only twenty years ago, that woman of a king, their Francis, made secret alliance with Suleiman, to spite the Emperor Charles V and the Hapsburgs. Do you not recall?'

'I remember it,' said Sir Francis. 'All of Christendom was disgusted.'

'The French,' concluded Blackbeard, and made an extraordinary noise, somewhere between a snort and a growl. Nicholas thought of the she-bear devouring the little boys in the Book of Kings. 'Don't speak to me of the *French*, nor expect any aid from *that* quarter. They are born cowards and collaborators all.'

'Is Grand Master Jean de la Valette not a Frenchman?' enquired Sir Francis.

'No,' said Blackbeard. 'He is a Knight.'

There was a silence, and then the fairhead resumed.

'The delicate matter of France aside,' he said with the lightest irony, 'if our island fortress of Malta should fall – as fall it surely will, without aid, in only a few days – then the Grand Fleet of the Turks will be free to pass westwards, even beyond Gibraltar. To roam the Atlantic, to capture the Spanish treasure fleets returning from the Americas laden with the silver and gold of the Indies. To sail onward to the New World, even, and plant the Green Banner of Islam on the American shore. It is only twenty-five days' sailing from Cape Florida to the Scillies on a good wind, after all. And northwards too, up the English Channel, the Scheldt, the Rhine ... the Thames? Before long, the minarets of the Mohammedans might soon appear in place of the towers of Christianity, in Antwerp, and Cologne, and London. The unearthly cry of the muezzin will be heard drifting over the spires of Oxford ...'

Sir Francis grimaced. 'You have a poet's fancy.'

'Perhaps. But you understand me? If Malta should fall, the balance of power in Europe will be for ever changed. Suleiman will have complete mastery of the sea. And he who rules the sea, rules the land.'

Sir Francis Ingoldsby brooded long and deep. 'It will take time for me to raise any small aid—'

'Time we do not have!' cried the fairhead in a sudden passion, stepping forward. 'Forgive me, Brother Francis. But day and night the forges of the Ottomans are ablaze, the great furnaces fed by the forests of Armenia and the Crimea. The waters of the Bosphorus glow red with their flames, the arsenals are stacked high with cannon, cannonballs, powder barrels. The greatest of their guns, the monstrous basilisks, could bring down the walls of Krak des Chevaliers!'

'War has changed,' murmured the old knight sadly. 'Oh to have fought and died at Krak des Chevaliers! But now guns and gunpowder reign over all, and chivalry is no more.'

'There is always chivalry,' growled Blackbeard unexpectedly.

'Suleiman's army numbers perhaps forty thousand men,' said the fairhead, 'and his corps of Janizaries – well, you know the Janizaries.'

'No warriors more ferocious under heaven,' murmured the old knight.

'They long to die for the faith, and go straight to their promised Paradise. They champ at the bit for war like maddened horses. Suleiman's navy is the greatest fleet seen on the Mediterranean since the days of Ancient Rome. And over this vast force presides Suleiman himself, seventy years of age, and not a whit more peaceable for his white hairs. Scarce one decade of his life has been spent at peace. And he is in a hurry now to finish the job. Before he dies. To destroy Christendom once and for all.'

Sir Francis's old face, battered and weather-beaten, furrowed with disbelief. 'You really believe he could do this?'

'I do,' said the fairhead quietly. 'He has planned all his life for it. Once he has taken Malta, then he will fall on the rest of Europe like a ravening wolf. And as we squabble and fight amongst ourselves, weakened and vulnerable, he will devour us one by one. The entire conquest could be achieved in no more than ... five years?'

A heavy silence oppressed the small oak-dark room. Suddenly it seemed as if even here, in this peaceful corner of a quiet English shire, the shadow of an evil power in the East was arising.

'His entire army,' resumed the fairhead, 'this numberless armada, will soon be sailing. As soon as spring comes, and the seas quiet, this army of fanatics will sail west, and descend on Malta. And you know how crude the defences of our barren island home, compared to our beloved Rhodes before. Or Acre—'

'Or Krak des Chevaliers.'

'And you know how many we are. Even with all our scattered European brothers, eight or nine hundred at most. Against forty thousand. Valorous we may be, but that is no fight we can win. We need all aid, brother. And we need it now.'

Ingoldsby looked from one to the other. Nicholas felt invisible. 'You are not men for wild exaggeration. And if Jean de la Valette has heard from his spies that the Turkish fleet is sailing soon, and the Sultan's evil eye has fallen on Malta – then I do not doubt it. But you know that I am no longer a knight, though a thousand times I have wished I were. You know that when King Henry, and the entire realm of England, broke from Rome, the Catholic Order of St John was suppressed throughout this kingdom. And you know that each and every Knight of the English Langue was forced to make the most dreadful decision of his life. To abandon the Order – or to abandon his country.'

His father trembled with emotion.

'My Brother Knights, you are my brothers no longer. I chose my country, for I am as proud and loyal an Englishman as any. You will understand the agony of that choice. I returned to my ancestral shire, and my family, I married and became a father. Infants on my knee, daughters kissing my old grizzled cheek, tearaway sons.' He glanced at Nicholas. 'A very different destiny from that of a warrior monk, you will agree. Yet in my youth I fought my way through the bitter Siege of Rhodes, shoulder to shoulder with Jean de la Valette himself, against that same devil's son Suleiman who now threatens Malta.

'After some happy years, my beloved young wife ... went to a better place. I farmed. I raised my children. And I worshipped my Lord and Saviour in the Catholic faith. Though this is now a Protestant country, it has been so for only six years, since Mary Tudor died. Her Majesty, Elizabeth, does not wish to pry too deeply into the private faith of her subjects, so long as they are obedient. In her own words, she does wish to *make windows into men's souls.* Here among our quiet Shropshire hills, we worship as we see fit, in secrecy but not in shame. Loyal to both the Queen of England and His Holiness in Rome.'

'And the knights are sworn never to draw their sword against a fellow Christian,' said the fairhead.

'Quite so. I have nothing but contempt for these damned plots to assassinate our Queen and have a Catholic monarch on the English throne once more. The People of England have ever gone their own way.'

Blackbeard drained his wine in a single gulp. The fire crackled. The wind was subsiding a little.

'Any aid you can send, brother,' said the fairhead. 'Gold. Guns. Prayers.'

They drew their cloaks from the back of the chairs, still heavy with rain.

'Stay one night under my roof, at least.'

The fairhead shook his head with a sad smile. 'Walls have ears, wells talk. We have put you in danger even coming to your door. And as I said – there is no time. I dream the same dream every night now. The vast shadow of an approaching army.'

'Well,' said Sir Francis. 'Tomorrow I will make contact with what few English brothers remain, and set about raising what aid I can for my old order.' He inhaled deeply, thrusting his chest out in pride. 'Nicholas, you are looking at two of the finest knights of the venerable Order of St John. Knights Hospitaller. Crusaders.'

The very words, so strange and antique, thrilled Nicholas to the bone.

'This,' he said, indicating the fairhead, 'is Sir Edward Stanley, Knight Grand Cross. And this is Sir John Smith, likewise Knight Grand Cross. Knights of St John of Malta, warriors of Christ, and among the most courageous and chivalrous soldiers in all Europe.'

Blackbeard – John Smith – remained expressionless. Stanley smiled faintly and looked at his boots.

'I speak the truth,' cried Sir Francis, clapping his hands on their shoulders like a proud father. 'The Last Crusaders in Christendom!'

They clasped hands, and without another word, the two rode away into the night.

Nicholas was nearly bursting with questions. He had never known half the truth about his father's long life before he was born.

Ingoldsby saw his youthful eagerness and gave a great loud bark of a laugh.

'Ha! So you never thought your rheumy, crabbed old sire was once a young gallant who fought like the Lionheart himself against the Saracens, eh? Eh? Ha!' And he took up his sheathed sword and began to thwack Nicholas on the back and legs with it.

'Ay!' yelped Nicholas. 'Ow!' The thwacks were hefty.

'Ha! Have at thee, thou swart infidel!'

His father was moonstruck, an aged knight suddenly thinking he was on the battlefield once more.

Nicholas ran upstairs.

'Tomorrow, boy!' his father roared after him, still swinging his sheathed sword dangerously around the narrow hallway. 'I'll tell thee more about the youthful battles and travails of your aged sire! There's tales will make your lilywhite ears burn!'

A door opened above and a female voice hissed angrily, 'Ssshhh! You'll wake the whole household with your noise and rumpus!'

It was Mistress Copstick, the housekeeper.

After that there was no more noise. Even old Ingoldsby himself, slayer of Saracens, was afraid of Mistress Copstick.

4

It was Hodge who came running, red-faced, saying there were soldiers riding down the hill towards the village. Nicholas's younger sister Susan, already something of a scold at thirteen, flicked him with her cleaning cloth and told him not to be such a clodpoll. What would soldiers want with a village like this?

She stared at her brother.

'Unless ... it's to do with those strangers last night.'

Nicholas froze.

His father was in his library.

'It's true I tell you!' cried Hodge. 'And that Gervase Crake riding at the head of 'em.'

'Crake?' said Nicholas sharply.

Hodge nodded. 'Lookin' as proud as a peacock too, the lubbock.'

Gervase Crake. Local landowner, sycophant and cheat. Tax gatherer, informer and liar. Of puritan tendencies, but careful not to let his private convictions get in the way of his ascent to wealth and power. With friends in high places, and correspondent even with Lord Cecil himself, down in London, it was whispered. Above all, he was Justice of the Peace and Lord of the Hundred, and thus responsible for upholding the law throughout the neighbourhood. And he held some ancient grudge against his father – as he did against so many.

Nicholas suddenly felt very, very afraid.

He ran up to the top field and peered over the hedge. In the grey October morning, there gleamed the breastplates of a dozen scruffy-looking mounted men. Not soldiers, surely, but armed hire-lings. At their head, lean and small, hunched and gimlet-eyed on his grey nag, Gervase Crake.

Nicholas dashed back down the hill.

'Hodge! You haven't – talked, have you?'

'I kept as mute as a mouse!' said the startled Hodge, flushing with anger.

He ordered Hodge inside with the other servants and was just knocking on his father's library door, when the farmyard was filled with the sound of clattering hooves on the cobblestones.

They died down, and a thin, nasal voice called out, 'Francis Ingoldsby, master of this house. You are a wanted man!'

His father burst out of his room and strode out into the farm-yard. He looked angry, and yet also … guilty. His father always was too honest a soul to be a player. He stood bow-legged and broad-shouldered before his front door.

'Crake,' he muttered.

Crake did not dismount, but looked down his thin nose at him, and coughed his usual little dry cough.

'To horse, sir. You are coming to the county jail, and perhaps thence to London.'

'On what charge?'

Crake's smile was as warm as the midwinter sun on ice.

'The very gravest. High treason.'

The villagers lined the lane that led out to Shrewsbury, silent and white-faced. Many of them had taken bread and wine from Father Matthew's hand. But among them was evidently one who preferred to take a silver shilling from the hand of Gervase Crake.

As Ingoldsby stepped onto the old, moss-grown mounting block, suddenly looking an old and weary man, Crake called out, 'Halt! This one knows how to handle a sword. Shackle him!'

It was then that Nicholas saw red, a furious tide of anger flood-ing through him. That his father should be treated like a common felon.

'No!' he cried out, and flew at the soldier who had dismounted to hammer the shackles onto his father's bony old wrists.

What happened next was a terrible, blood-dimmed blur.

Hodge was near, trying to restrain Nicholas. A soldier lashed out with the butt of his sword hilt, and struck Hodge, perhaps by accident. The sturdy servant fell back with a muffled grunt and lay dazed. Nicholas seized the bridle of the soldier's horse and wrenched it with all his might. His father was stepping off the mounting block again, shouting, trying to calm him. Two more mounted soldiers crowded round, and above the noise Crake's thin voice shouted orders. At last he drew a matchlock from his cloak and took a smoking fuse from one of the soldiers. He raised it in the air just as the powder exploded in the pan.

A horse whinnied and reared. A soldier rolled to the ground with a cry. Another swung his sword. Sir Francis tried to seize his son and drag him clear, as the rearing horse came down again. Even amid all the noise and chaos, Nicholas heard the hollow, sickening sound of an ironshod horse's hoof meeting human bone. His father reeled aside and crumpled to the muddy ground at the foot of the mounting block.

Everything went still then. The horses were pulled back, soldiers remounted, dropped their drawn swords down by their sides. Yet the still air screamed.

Nicholas knelt by his father's side. His skull was shattered, there was blood, mess, shards of white bone. Blood poured down over half his face. Nicholas gripped his hand.

'Father!'

His father could not see. The world was fading. It mattered not.

'Had I more hair,' he murmured, 'perhaps the blow had been less grave.' He smiled faintly. 'Grave indeed.'

A cold terror clutched the boy's heart. 'Father! Speak to me!'

The old man had some last sorrow for his children. Something dreadful had happened, he could not remember what … Yet God would provide.

He spoke the words of the Scriptures that he loved, the words of David to Solomon as he lay dying. Nicholas leaned close to hear him, his words a whisper on the wind. '*I go the way of all the earth. Be strong, and show yourself a man.*'

One last effort in this world. 'My son. Such tales I could have told thee, such things. But … Care for your sisters. Be just, be faithful. To the very end.'

Then the old man's hand no longer returned his grasp.

The boy's howls filled the village. His sister Susan stood near, so stricken with grief and bewilderment she could not cry. She pressed the faces of the two trembling little ones into her pinafore so they could not see.

The soldiers waited for orders to clear them away and collect the body, but Gervase Crake seemed strangely oblivious. He barely regarded the scene, which made even the soldiers' hard hearts ache.

Indeed it was as if some far more interesting thought had occurred to him. An expression of quiet satisfaction on his face suggested that he thought this day of clumsy tragedy had turned out really rather well. His eyes roved over the fine old farmhouse of the Ingoldsbys: the venerable oak timbers, the handsome stone mullion windows, the tall chimneys gently smoking in the autumn sunshine. The barns were pretty dilapidated, true. But for the rest . . . And then there were several hundred acres of hill and grassland, excellent sheep country. With the prices wool was fetching nowadays . . .

At last he looked back and coughed dryly.

'Pull the boy away.'

It took three soldiers to drag him free. One received a kick in the shins, and responded with a mighty backhand swipe of a heavy leather gauntlet that set Nicholas reeling. Susan screamed out. The little ones wailed. At last Crake lost patience.

'Drag them all here!' he cried, pointing before his horse.

All four children were pulled over and dumped unceremoniously before him in the mud. He looked sourly down at them.

'Now listen to me, you traitorous whelps. You are not of the age of majority, or it would be worse for you. Though God knows under the reign of Bloody Mary, Protestant blood as young as yours was wickedly shed. Bodies as soft and young as yours burnt at the stake in Smithfield market. But your father was a foul traitor.'

Nicholas rose up on his knees to cry out at this, and was once more violently cuffed into silence.

'He was a Catholic – though not yet a crime in this Protestant kingdom, alas! But I doubt not we shall find his library stuffed full of the latest Popish propaganda from Flanders. Above all, we know he entertained two knights of the most élite and dangerous order of Catholic warriors in all Christendom. Known assassins. Here, in this house,' he gestured angrily, 'only last night! You should think it lucky he died as he did – thanks to you!' His eyes bored into Nicholas.

'Nevertheless he will be declared a traitor post mortem, his entire property forfeit to the Crown, and the name of the Shropshire Ingoldsbys utterly erased. How many servants have you in the household?'

'Only one old retainer,' said Nicholas.

Crake moved with the snakelike swiftness of a small, lean man, and cut Nicholas across the face with his whip.

'Liar! Do not think you can lie to me, boy! You have seven household servants, *seven*. I know their names, I know their ages and their occupations, their religious practices. Damn it, boy, I know when they last changed their underlinen!'

Nicholas pressed his hand to the hot welt across his cheek. Tears pricked his eyes but he blinked them angrily away. His face burned, his heart ached, his whole world tilted.

'I will deal with your servants. As for you and your sisters, you are now penniless orphans.' Crake compressed his lips at the children's cries. 'Well, your dotard of a father should have thought of your fate before he entertained Knights of St John at his fireside, should he not? Your best course now is to quit this county, and throw yourselves upon your nearest relations, or else some charity or poorhouse. Either that or become mere hedgerow beggars, and join the great army of filthy vagabonds that infest this kingdom. It is no concern of mine.'

'You cannot do this! You are a heartless villain, you will never sleep easy in your bed if I—'

'Do not bring down the law upon your own head, boy!' rasped Crake, his small eyes gleaming.

'What care I?'

'Nor the dainty heads of your pretty little sisters.'

Nicholas scowled ferociously.

'Ay,' murmured Crake, 'there's the rub. You are head of the household now. But without a house, alas! So enough of your youthful fits of rage. You need to learn to govern yourself, boy. For it will not be easy to keep body and soul together, the four of you, in your new life on the road. As vagabond children of a traitor. A short life but not, I fear, a very merry one.'

He pulled his horse around.

'Turn them loose! Fire the barns!'

'And the house, Sire?'

'The barns would be sign enough. Leave the house.'

Some of the villagers looked mutinous as the barns and outbuildings of the Ingoldsby farm were put to the torch, and the four children were driven off down the street. Men clutched hoes and billhooks, women's faces were dark with anger. But what could mere peasants do against a dozen mounted men-at-arms?

Crake observed it all with cynical penetration. If only the children could have been finally disposed of ... But there were limits. Catholic priests on missions from France might be caught and lynched promptly enough, and night-time visitations from a foreign order of Catholic knights were certainly sufficient cause to argue treason. But you could not simply dispose of heretical Catholic children, as the Israelites slew the children of the Amalekites.

The law of England was harsh but fair. He would have to let them go. Penniless, without friends or family, they would not last long.

5

The children passed away down the lane and into the open country under the gaze of a hundred villagers. Smoke drifted overhead from the burning barns. Flames crackled. Rooks rose indignantly from the tall elms.

'Here!' called out Crake at the last moment. 'Something for your journey.'

To everyone's astonishment, he pulled a small but weighty leather purse from his cloak and tossed it down to the boy. Then he wrenched his horse around and trotted back up the hill. At the head of the lane, he turned in his saddle and watched them go.

The children stumbled on for they knew not how long. Perhaps they would wake up and find it had been a nightmare. The short October day drew to a close and the sky darkened over their heads. A wind came up and whipped the leaves about in maddened flurries beneath the trees. They did not wake up.

After a time, little Lettice said, 'What will we have for supper? Is it to be only bread?'

'We will ask at a farmhouse. Perhaps we can buy something more.'

He drew Crake's purse out and unknotted the strings as he walked and peered inside. Then he looked up.

Susan was observing him closely.

'Is it well?'

He re-tied the strings, he wasn't quite sure why, and stowed the purse away again.

'Very well,' he said quietly. 'If I had a sling.'

Crake had thrown him a purseful of pebbles.

'I know what is in it,' said Susan. 'It is a favourite jest of Crake's. He often throws purses of stones and pebbles to paupers, to see them run and grub in the dust. He finds their desperation amusing. But he says it is a parable, to teach them not to put their trust in gold.'

'The man is a monster.'

'God will make him pay.'

'*I* will make him pay. One day.'

'You cannot usurp God.' She hesitated and then added, 'It was not your fault. What happened to father.' She swiftly wiped an eye.

Nicholas said nothing. His heart was as locked up as a casket.

They came past a barn near a lonely farmstead, but a huge dog barked and tore at its chain as they approached, and Lettice and Agnes refused to go any nearer. Finally they made shelter in a small copse, Nicholas laying a row of sticks against a fallen treetrunk and then covering them crosswise with brushwood. They slept fitfully in this makeshift wooden tent, damp and desperately hungry, like shivering puppies.

Nicholas was lying awake in the bleak grey dawn when he heard footfalls in the leaves nearby. Someone knew they were there. He put his hand over Lettice's mouth. Her eyes flared wide. He put a finger to his lips, and motioned her to tell Agnes.

He peeped out of the shelter, just in time to see a burly figure step behind a broad oak tree, the glint of steel in his hand. A dagger.

So Crake had changed his mind, after all, and sent one or more of his hired henchman after them to finish the job. Perhaps ex-soldiers, ex-mercenaries, hearts like flint. Come from the late religious wars in France, where they would have witnessed, or enacted, the foulest massacres. What would it be to them, to cut four children's throats in this isolated copse, and bury them deep under the leaf litter? It would be nothing to them. And who would ever know?

Nicholas's heart raced fit to burst. His fingers curled around one of the half-rotten sticks above him. His only available weapon, to defend himself and his three sisters against hardened killers.

39

The henchman remained behind the tree.

Nicholas drew the stick free and crawled out of the shelter as silently as he could. Leaves rustled, a twig cracked, but it was soft and damp and made little noise. He was across the clearing in a trice, rounded the tree, and delivered the hardest blow he could to the broad leather-jerkined back in front of him.

The stick snapped in two.

The figure turned, hurriedly returning his privy parts into his breeches.

'Master Nicholas!'

'Hodge!'

Hodge thought Nicholas had struck him in indignation at his relieving himself so near to his sisters. Nicholas, babbling with joy and relief, said he thought Hodge might be a mercenary come from the late religious wars in France, which only baffled Hodge the more.

'And I saw you carrying a dagger!'

Hodge frowned and then pulled something from his jerkin, tucked in above the belt. It was a fire steel.

'We can have a fire!'

'Ay, sir,' said Hodge. 'Though I do have a small knife too. And a pannikin, and some eggs and mushrooms. I stole the pannikin and the eggs from the farm, under the very nose of that crookback dungheap Crake back there, God rot his stones. But since it was Sir Francis's pannikin anyhow, I thought he'd not mind.'

'No,' said Nicholas. His throat felt tight. 'No, he'd not mind.'

'Well,' said Hodge, trying to sound cheerful. 'Let's have our breakfast then.'

Soon he had a fire going, with hunks of bread warming on the end of twigs. He split open some beechnuts and squeezed out just enough to oil the pannikin, then got to frying the eggs and mushrooms. Field mushrooms and platter mushrooms and jew's ear and lawyer's wig. It was the time of year for them. They ate them straight from the pan with grimy fingers, and spirits rose a little.

Lettice wiped her mouth. 'Well done, Hodge. You are now promoted groom of the household.'

40

'Well,' said Hodge proudly. 'While you were learning Latin and Greek and double Dutch and whatnot, Hodge was about the fields trappin' partridge and hares and such, makin' fires and cookin' mushrooms. He don't speak much Latin now nor will he ever, it's safe to wager, beyond your hocus pocus in the Mass. But he knows how to fry a mushroom, even with no butter about him.'

He advised them to take down the shelter and hide all traces of where they'd slept. They bashed down the old sticks with noisy glee. He shook his head. That wasn't what he meant.

He went and stood at the edge of the copse, looking out down the road. He heard girlish shrieks of laughter behind him. Yet there was no sadder fate than an orphan's. He should know, he was one.

They had no chance. One small breakfast of eggs and mushrooms might lift their spirits for an hour. But their lives were ruined, and they were too grand folk in their laces and bodices and linen caps and nice neat shoes to know it yet. What to do? In the end, that verminous Crake was right. They would be best off in the poorhouse, even with the narrow wooden beds and the fevers and the gruel for supper.

It was their only hope.

Susan retired behind a bush, and when she returned, the others gasped. She had sliced off her fine long hair, that glowed almost red in the sun. Mere patches and tufts remained, with shining glimpses of white skull between. Like one committed to the asylum of Bethlem, head shaved to let out the heat of her madness.

She smiled at them. 'To stay neat. Easier that way.' And for some reason she sat down beside Nicholas.

Susan, always so organised and orderly. Her mother dying so young, she had been female head of the household since she was seven, and early bowed down with seriousness and responsibility. A cold fear gripped Nicholas's stomach. It was Susan who wasn't going to survive. The little ones would chatter on through – at least until they fell ill in winter. But Susan ... there was something in her eyes already, roving about the empty fields and the bare sky. A look of something lost.

'Come along now,' she said. 'Off to Shrewsbury we go, all sprightly and spry.'

Yet she stayed sitting where she was.

He took her hand and pulled her up. She had no weight in her at all. She drew her hand away from his and walked on ahead, alone, looking neither left nor right.

Later that morning he heard her softly singing a psalm under her breath.

'*I delivered the poor that cried, and the fatherless, and him that had none to help him ...*'

6

The blood-red sun went down below the horizon of the western hills and the afternoon darkened into twilight.

'I'm scared,' whispered Agnes.

They were walking down a long lane in a bleak country with hills to east and west. The evening star began to rise. They would have to find shelter soon.

Then they crested a rise and there was a small wood ahead. As they came near, Lettice's sharp eyes glimpsed an orange glow through the trees.

'Firelight!' she cried, and started to trot towards it.

'No,' Hodge whispered urgently, and actually dared to seize her grubby dress. 'Hold back, maid. You know not what kind of folk they may be.'

'And singing!' added Agnes.

They waited, hushed. And an old woman's voice, strange and low, sang in the darkening wood.

Nicholas and Hodge looked at each other uncertainly. The air was growing colder by the minute, they must find shelter, and where else was there? Yet there was something here that made their skins prickle with dread.

'Let go of me!' Lettice said, suddenly imperious. And she twisted and broke free of Hodge's grasp, and she and Agnes ran on into the wood before the boys could stop them.

The girls pulled up sharp in a clearing. Hodge and Nicholas came rushing up behind them.

There was a warm glow of fire, and something sizzling over it on a spit. There was a cauldron beside. And in the darkness beyond sat three, no, four people, backs against the trees, faces deep shadowed in the firelight. An old woman who smiled at them, black-toothed and nodding. Three men. And further off, a beaten-down donkey standing asleep, and a low donkey-barrow with frayed rope traces.

'Why,' said one of the men, looking up from the wooden bowl he was slurping from. 'Here's a pretty one. Come nearer, maid.'

He smiled, and the men looked at each other. Then they noticed Hodge and Nicholas standing behind them.

'What a tribe, is that all of ye?'

Hodge was just about to say that the rest were back on the road, a dozen or more, but Lettice blurted out, 'Five's all we are, and fearful hungry, mister!'

'Then come closer,' he said softly. 'And tell us your story.'

Agnes shook her head. 'We have none. Our father died!'

The second man clucked. 'You fell on hard times but lately though, I see from your boots and garb. Do any know you be here?'

Hodge again tried to speak first but Agnes's high pitched voice wailed above him, 'Nobody! Not a soul in the world knows of us now!'

Hodge shoved Nicholas in the ribs and they both stepped nearer the fire, close by the girls.

'*Stand tall*,' he whispered.

The men slurped more broth. 'Ye'll sleep here?' said the first man, wiping his lips.

Nicholas said they would. What choice did they have now? Even the air on the back of his neck and legs was cold.

'But we two may lie awake a good deal,' he said pointedly.

There were only shreds left on the spit, but the vagabonds hung the cauldron over the fire again and threw on more sticks to reheat the last of the stew.

There was little enough meat, but big white bones floated in the thin broth. Hodge stared at the stew and wouldn't eat. He asked for bread but they had none.

'You must eat, lad,' said the old woman, but Hodge only stared at her woodenly and said nothing.

'Then ye'll sleep well enough, right down by the fire! Eh?'

Again the men looked at each other.

Nicholas felt uncomfortable. Something was wrong here. Yet if they went out onto the road now, it would be bitter cold, the hoarfrost settling, the poor creatures of the field limping through the stiff grass. Owls hunting. There were still wolves in the Welsh forests, they said. This was a good shelter.

He would stay awake, that was all.

The vagabonds gave them blankets that smelt foul. Or maybe it was just the air. The odour of poorly butchered meat. But perhaps he was wrong to be so mistrustful and suspicious. All they had done so far had been kindly and hospitable.

He drowsed then stirred. 'Hodge,' he whispered. 'Stay awake.'

Hodge nodded. 'My belly's too empty to do otherwise. Besides, I'd no more sleep here than at the gates of hell.'

In the small hours, Nicholas pushed his blanket off to go and empty his bladder. He had been fast asleep.

Hodge was snoring gently. The girls all lay in a row, huddled up to each other. The vagabonds lay the other side of the embers. He had been wrong to be so suspicious.

He went some way away behind a tree, and there was something there, half under the leaves. The moon passed behind a cloud. There was a foul smell here, even in this cold air. He stared down, his throat tight, and then up. Thin cold cloud raced past and the moon sailed out. Something hung from a branch above him, twisting with the wind.

With stomach knotted, ears ringing with terror, he turned and ran back.

In the clearing, two of the men were already on their feet, one looking over to where the girls lay.

'Hodge!' he yelled.

The sleeping servant was awake and on his sturdy legs in a second, squat dagger in his hand.

The men stood stock still.

One smiled his blacktoothed smile, lit by the eerie moonlight.

The girls were slowly awakening.

In the darkness behind, Nicholas heard the old woman cackling.

45

Then she shucked her rotten teeth and crowed, 'Well, a lively night for all!'

'What's with the dagger out, lad?' said one of the men.

Hodge held it out steadily before him.

'There's something in the woods,' said Nicholas, trying not to let his voice shake. 'Hanging from a tree.'

The man turned on him. 'There's lots in the woods, lad. Badgers and hedgepigs and—'

'I mean a body, half butchered.'

The man's face darkened visibly, even in the dark of night. 'So if we steal a sheep, well, what is that to thee? Mortal men must keep flesh and spirit together. You woudn't turn us in for sheep thieves and see us hanged at Shrewsbury assizes, would ye now?'

Nicholas couldn't speak. All he knew was that was no sheep back there.

'We're going now,' said Hodge, stepping back very carefully.

The girls were standing, rubbing the sleep from their eyes.

'To us, mistress,' said Hodge quietly.

In a flash, one of the men had seized Agnes and there was a gleaming blade at her throat.

'One step backwards more and the little one here will be drained of her blood like a hung rabbit, d'ye hear me? I'll not have you high-born whelps going out on the road and squealing to all and sundry of us. You're going nowhere, not now. You hear me?'

They froze.

Clouds covered the moon once more and in the blackness, a figure moved in silence. It was Susan. She swooped down and seized a brand off the dying fire, whirling it through the air to make it burn again. Then there was a hiss, a man's cry, a shower of sparks. A girl's sob, and scuffling in the leaves.

The moon was still dark.

'Run! Back to the road!'

In blind terror, the children stumbled away between the trees, scuffing up cold leaves rimed with frost, arms and faces scratched with holly and blackthorn. Girls weeping, men roaring close behind them, as in a nightmare. Nicholas shook his head furiously as he ran, trying to clear away the visions of Lettice or Agnes, seized in

46

the darkness and hung from the branches of trees, their throats open wounds ...

Somehow, they never knew how, the five children stumbled clear onto the road and ran to each other. They crossed themselves, shaking and sobbing, Susan muttering over and over again, 'Thank you, Lord Jesus Christ, thank you Blessed Mother Mary ...'

'Move,' said Nicholas. 'Keep moving, all night.'

They moved down the road as fast as they could in the dark, judging the closeness of the hedge from the sound of their footfalls.

There was sudden movement in the hedge to their left. Lettice clutched Nicholas in terror. A snuffle, an odour. Only a stoat or a fox, hurrying away from them.

After a time the moon reappeared. Unable to help themselves, they looked back as they walked.

On the road behind them, staring after them, stood a single figure. Something glinted, hanging from his right hand. A long-handled axe. He did not run after them, this watchman of the night, silent and motionless. They felt the power of a demonic hatred flow towards them. But it was as if they were not worth pursuing. They were damned anyway.

They walked all night. None would have slept.

'We will sleep in the day,' said Nicholas as they marched, exhausted.

But even then, they knew, the nightmares would follow them.

He could have spewed at the thought of what he might have eaten from that cauldron last night. But already he felt something inside him toughening in the face of hardship, and prayed an odd, halting prayer that his heart would not toughen beyond all pity too.

That day they found shelter in a tumbledown barn amongst some winter hay. The girls were so tired they slept deeply, hungry as they were.

'We cannot go on,' Nicholas muttered, almost to himself. 'We are not going to make it. We are already dying.'

Hodge said nothing.

'We must get food. Come nightfall, I'm turning thief as well as vagabond.'

Hodge nodded. After a while he said quietly, 'Some have an airy-fairy fancy of life on the road. But in truth, it's filled with the poor and desperate and savage. It's no place for us.'

'There *is* no place for us.'

Hodge looked hard at Nicholas.

'You mean … Shrewsbury. You mean the church, or the poor-house.'

Hodge took in a deep breath.

'There is a parson there, and a schoolmaster, and town parishes are rich. In the parish of St Thomas's, I heard of a girl that left her baby there on the doorstep. She was dying herself. I heard the parson and his wife were well known for taking the bairn in and caring for it as if it were their own. If not that, he'd be Christian and find them shelter at the very least. Serving maids in grand houses, perhaps …'

Nicholas tried to think clearly, in the pit of misery. Care for your sisters. His father's dying wish. Be just, be faithful. To the very end.

When he spoke his voice was thick with grief, tears welling in his eyes.

'We go back to Shrewsbury. The girls will find shelter there. But not I.'

He shook his head savagely.

'Not I. *I go on.*'

Grief weighed on him all that day as he tried to sleep. Too tired to sleep, almost, and sorrow searing his heart. He saw his father's body left lying in the village street. No decent church burial for him, but a traitor's hurried interment. The world was in ruins.

But as well as sorrow, anger burned in his belly like a knot of bright hard flame, and hatred as pure as fire. Anger, hatred – and an undying thirst for vengeance.

That night he stole bread and a ham from a poor farmhouse with a lazy guard dog in its yard. He felt wretched. How many children here would now go hungrier through the winter for it? Yet the poor stole mostly from the poor. The rich were too well protected.

They walked back north for two days until they came in sight of the town.

People hissed and clacked as soon as they saw them. Beggars, thieves, Egyptians. Let the constable thrash them out of town again, they'd only cheer him on.

The children huddled in St Alkmund's Place in thin rain. Stout citizens scowled at them as they passed by, muttering curses on them. Such as they belonged only in the open countryside, on the rain-lashed hills or in ghoul-haunted woodlands. Ditches for beds, dead leaves for coverlets.

'Look, master,' said Hodge, nudging him hard. 'There.'

Round the corner and into the marketplace came filing a column of the poorhouse children, going up to St Mary's church for morning prayer. They wore off-white linen gowns, much-washed and patched and frayed at the hem, yet clean enough. All wore bonnets, and all had boots, however crudely made. All were thin, but none were starved. He saw no sores, though several heads shaven for lice could be glimpsed beneath the bonnets. As they walked in pairs, hand in hand, with glowing red cheeks, they laughed and chattered like children anywhere, for all their poverty. And against the rain, they wore cloaks, though all of different colours, black, grey, brown and dun. On closer view they were hardly cloaks, mere large cuts of woollen worsted, yet worn round the shoulders and hooped over the head, quite enough to keep off all but the worst rain. Doubtless used again as blankets on cold nights. On the left shoulder of each cloak was sewn a small white lion, emblem of St Mark's Poorhouse.

'Wish I had a woollen cloak, at least,' said Hodge. 'They're better garbed than we are.'

Nicholas understood his point.

Susan hadn't spoken for two days, not a word, and now she pressed herself against the wall, head bowed, gazing into the running gutter as intently as a treasure seeker.

'Is she gone mad?' whispered Lettice, staring down the street at her.

Nicholas smiled weakly. 'No, not mad. She is very tired. We are all tired, aren't we?'

Lettice nodded. Her plump cheeks were already thinning away, and very grubby. Her left eye looked red and swollen.

'Now listen to me,' said Nicholas. 'I want you and Agnes and Susan to be very brave girls. Will you?'

She and Agnes looked up at him anxiously. They knew what being brave meant. Nasty medicine, bad news.

'Hodge and I must go away for a time.'

'No!' both girls cried as one, with such howls that even Susan stirred and looked up. 'You can't leave us! Never!'

'Never,' he repeated, hugging them both. 'I never will completely abandon you. I will know where to find you. It was the last thing our father made me promise. Would I dishonour him?'

'Then why are you going?' Lettice wailed.

'Just for a short time. Because ...' He sighed. He hardly knew himself. 'Because I must. Because you will be safe and well cared for, and I am too old, and cannot rest, nor ...'

It wasn't working. Too complicated. The little girls' eyes were filled with tears and resentment. He put it differently.

'You saw all those children, walking through the market square in their warm woollen cloaks? You are going to stay with them, just for a while. And I – I am going away, to seek my fortune!'

Their sobs slowly subsided.

'As a pirate?'

'Well, no, not exactly. But I shall travel over the sea, and bring back chests and chests full of gold, and—'

'We'll come with you!'

'You can't,' he said bluntly. Then, more subtly, 'Our father wouldn't want you to.'

They still looked miserable, but intrigued by the chests of gold.

'Will you come back?'

'Of course I will!' he laughed. What a player he was. 'Very soon, laden with treasure.'

'And donkeys?'

'And a whole train of donkeys.'

Little girls' minds were so hard to fathom.

'And monkeys,' he added, 'jewels, ostriches, and little blackamoor slaves, all sorts of things. But only if I go away first and seek my fortune. Then I will return, and find you, and we will all be happy as before.'

'In the farmhouse?'

'Yes. In the farmhouse.'

The girls wept and clung to him.

He was suddenly aware of Susan at his elbow. She still said not a word. She reached out and hugged her brother, one swift hug, and then took her little sisters by the hand, and led them away down the alley.

The boys followed at a distance.

They threaded through the old medieval streets of the city until at last they came to a low wooden door in a long wall. They knocked.

Nothing happened. They knocked again.

Eventually a bolt was shot, and a stern-faced woman appeared.

Susan tried to speak, they could tell from the heave of her shoulders, but not a word came out. The stern-faced woman looked her up and down without encouragement. Finally Agnes spoke, though they couldn't hear her words. The woman questioned them for several minutes, not smiling once. At last she jerked her head and stood back in the doorway, and the three girls went in. The door was shut and bolted behind them.

There was long silence until Hodge said, 'They will prosper there, master. Have no fear. They will be well enough.'

'Till I return.'

'Till we return,' said Hodge. 'You'd be lost without me.'

Nicholas looked at the stout servant lad and smiled faintly.

'Come on, then. Let's go and find that treasure.'

7

They walked south for days and weeks, begging and stealing. Still they grew thinner, the days shorter, the nights colder. Nicholas wondered if they would survive, even without the girls. Yet they must. They must make it to a port.

There was much to do before he died.

They survived through the winter, Christmas passing them by almost unnoticed. Thin and tough and cunning, they survived. It was early spring. And then they were caught stealing.

After a night in the pound, they were dragged aching and blinded by the weak daylight into a small cobbled market square.

Nicholas blinked and stared around, still feeling he might faint at any moment. If his wrists were not tied so painfully behind his back, he might reach up and touch the side of his head. His hair felt knotted, crusty with dried blood where the constable had clubbed him.

It was a grey morning, there was a light drizzle and it was bitter cold. Yet the market square was milling with people, as if for a fair. Some ate apples, keeping the cores in their pockets for throwing later. Children laughed and played with tops and hoops. A local butcher did a good trade selling hot roast pork. More people were leaning out from the upper windows of the handsome half-timbered houses that surrounded the square. Some of the finer womenfolk up there were already weeping and delicately touching handkerchiefs to the corners of their eyes. Others were sucking oranges.

A charcoal brazier smoked, an iron laid across it. A wooden wagon stood in the middle of the square, and nearby, a crude gallows.

Nicholas's blood ran cold.

Here was the end of the noble name of Ingoldsby. Hanged in a town square in the rain for common thievery.

Someone banged a drum and the crowd fell silent. Nicholas and Hodge were dragged forward. Beside the gallows there stood the hangman in a crude cloth mask, two constables, and a local parson, looking both sorrowful and grave, a small New Testament in his hand. The local magistrate, his back to the boys, addressed the parson. The parson listened and nodded.

The magistrate turned.

It was Gervase Crake.

He smiled.

'Bring forward the murderer!'

Another boy was dragged forward, filthy and in rags. They said he had murdered a little girl, drowned her in a ditch. They gave no reason. The boy said not a word. He might have been a deaf mute, or a dummerer, faking such. As he was dragged past them their eyes met, and Nicholas saw in those dead hollows a total indifference more terrifying than any savagery.

The parson stepped forward and asked the boy for his last confession of sins. The boy stood in sullen silence before him, saying nothing. Then he hawked and spat full in the parson's face. The parson stepped back and wiped his face with a cloth and bowed his head and prayed.

The hangman checked the knot in the rope one last time, glancing at the boy. Then the noose went over his filthy neck and he was hauled up. He didn't kick once. The beam creaked, the thin body twisted back and forth. The eyes still stared. He must have been about eleven.

Crake himself read out their crimes, in a voice that sounded like he was giving a sermon.

'The two villains here apprehended are guilty of idle vagabondage and thievery, to the just anger of Almighty God. They are of that kind which currently infest our kingdom, called sturdy beggars, who lack nothing in the way of limbs or faculties, as customary beggars, upon whom Our Lord himself looked kindly; but rather lack only the will to work, favouring a life of thieving and dishonesty practised on decent townsfolk such as are here present.'

There was a general self-satisfied murmur.

'Whereat it is decreed that these two shall be stripped and tied to a cart, and lashed through the streets of the parish until their backs be bloody, as the Law of England decrees. They shall then be branded on the chest with a V, to mark their chosen profession, in the hope that their souls be cleansed. And God have mercy upon them.'

Branded. Hence the brazier. They would be marked and shamed for life.

One of the constables drew out the lash. It was no schoolmaster's cane for switching backsides. It was a length of oxhide furled into a whip, purposely made to take the skin off a man's back, and more. Such a whip could cut through to ribs or backbone in only two or three lashes. It could tear the flesh away in chunks, like the jaws of a wolf. It could leave a man standing, or falling, in a puddle of his own blood. It could kill a man.

The two constables pulled their arms forward roughly and hooked the ropes over the stanchions at the back of the haycart and cinched them as tight as a tourniquet by twisting a strut of wood behind, until the two boys hung there, backs stretched, toes barely touching the ground.

'Want a stick?' one growled.

Nicholas shook his head.

'Yes,' said Hodge. 'We both.' He looked at Nicholas. 'Believe me.'

One of the men produced two short sticks and held them in front of the boys' faces. 'Open your jaws. Now bite down.'

Nicholas worked his jaws again, and spat the stick out at the man's feet. 'Have it to kindle your fire.'

The man grinned.

Hodge grunted through his stick. His high-mettled arse of a master. He'd be screaming soon enough.

The other constable flicked the whip straight behind them, not cruelly, but the slight crack made Nicholas clench in anticipation of pain.

Let it come, he thought. From heaven my father looks down on me now. Let him see how I bear it.

Crake himself was right behind them, and it was the Justice of the Peace himself, unaccountably, who slid a knife beneath their shirts and split the seam, and then tore the shirts from their backs.

Nicholas caught his gaze.

Crake raised a mocking eyebrow. 'Surely, villainous spawn of a traitorous father, you have some rude curse for me? As I go about the Queen's appointed justice?'

Nicholas's gaze remained fixed. 'Deeds, not words. You will know them in time.'

'How splendid.' He tore the last remnant of shirt off the boy's back. His skin gleamed white and pure. He tossed the scrap of linen into the cart beside him.

'To staunch the blood flow after. You'll need it.'

He turned away.

The last thing Nicholas saw before the lash descended was the boy still hanging from the gallows bar, shamefully still not cut down. Tongue garishly bulging from darkening lips. Eyes staring out of hell.

What he and Hodge did not see was two strangers riding into the square on big horses. Huge horses, like those thunderous destriers ridden by knights of old. Plough horses, presumably. Why did they ride such leviathans?

People instinctively drew back from them. They had an air about them, travel-stained and powerfully built, a distant look in the eye, and scabbards showing beneath the hem of their muddy cloaks. They pulled up their animals behind the expectant crowds. People glanced back at them uneasily.

One kept his hood up against the thin rain, shadowing his grim, darkly bearded face. The other dropped his back to reveal dirty blond hair and handsome, sunburnt, somewhat battered looks. Perhaps thirty years of age. The crowd had even more reason to step away and give them space when the fairhead drew his sword, faster than the eye could follow, and seemed about to run someone through. People swayed back like wheat before the wind. The swordsman reached forward and with the most delicate, fine-judged flick of his swordpoint, removed a horse-leech that was fattening on his horse's neck.

He sheathed his sword.

At the spectacle about to unfold at the cart's end in the middle of the square, he seemed merely amused. He leaned his elbows easily on the high pommel of his saddle, eyes narrowed, a flicker of a smile on his lips as he lazily chewed a stem of dried grass.

'Well a-day,' he murmured. 'Looks like these beggars hadn't the trick of begging for mercy.'

The lash flew high in the grey air, straightened, and bit down. It cut into the servant boy first. He arched his back and bit down on the stick with all his might, head thrown back, throat strained, eyes squeezed shut.

The second constable flicked his lash out and let fly against the bold one without a jawstick. To give the boy fair due, he reeled under the savagery of the lash but made no sound.

Then a voice roared out from the back of the crowd.

'Hold there!'

It was a voice of such deep strength that the constables stopped still and stared. Crake stepped forward and tutted, glaring over the people's heads and seeing the two dangerous-looking strangers for the first time.

The crowd parted before them and the two mighty riders came through, the hooves of their plough horses clopping on the wet cobbles like wooden dinner plates. They pulled up beside the cart where the half-naked boys were tied, blood already oozing from their cuts, and sat easily.

The fairheaded one said, 'Tell me, you are the presiding Justice here?'

'That I am,' snapped Crake, 'and these constables are appointed by the parish. You are?'

There was something horrible in the way the two strangers glanced at each other at this question, the fair one grinning, then turned back and gave no answer. Something indefinably threatening. Could they be the Queen's men? Yet they wore no crest, no insignia, nothing but their dirty riding cloaks. And beneath them, Crake now discerned – he swallowed – jerkins of chainmail.

'How many lashes are the lads to have?' asked the fairhead.

'Thirty,' said Crake. 'And that's merciful. Now I ask again, who—?'

'Thirty, on these skinny young backs?' interrupted the stranger. 'They won't have skin enough left to make a lady's purse.'

'That is their misfortune. They should have considered their fate before they took to thievery.'

'What have they stolen?'

Crake snorted. 'All that they eat, they steal! What can they honestly earn on the road?'

'What indeed? How came they on the road?'

Crake looked furious, white-faced and puritanical. 'I know not.'

The rider smiled equably. 'You lie.'

His hooded companion now tossed back the corner of his cloak, and there hanging from his belt was a very fine sword and scabbard indeed. Not the fine rapier of a court fop to impress his lady, but a weighty broadsword very much made for use. He rested his hand lightly on the gilded pommel, and with his other hand drew back his hood a little. His eyes were darkly bloodshot.

'I say,' said the first, 'the boys should be let loose, for the sake of Christian mercy. And the hanged one should be cut down and buried, for shame.'

The crowd stared agog, pressing closer – but not too close. An air of danger hung over the two horsemen like mist over a river.

One of the sturdy constables standing nearby must have tried some trick at this moment, but the response was so fast that none ever knew what it was. With a bull-roar that seemed to shake the windowpanes, the blackbeard neatly side-stepped his horse, slipped his booted foot from the stirrup and thumped it like a battering ram into the constable's chest. The fellow staggered back over the cobbles and then collapsed, desperately trying to suck air into his shocked lungs.

Blackbeard whipped out his sword and stationed his huge mount over the man's prostrate body. Like all horses it hated to tread on a living creature, delicately setting its vast fringed hooves on either side of the fellow. Blackbeard leaned over to his right and dangled his swordpoint above the constable's belly as he lay there winded and terrified, looking up at the huge beast that shadowed him.

'Now don't stir,' murmured Blackbeard. 'And the rain won't wet you down there. Though the horse may piss on you.'

In perfect unison, the fair one had also drawn his sword from his scabbard once again, and was holding the gleaming steel point an unwavering hair's breadth from Crake's thin white throat.

'I say again,' he said pleasantly, 'that the boys should be let go.'

Without further discussion, Blackbeard kicked his horse forward over the fallen constable, touching not a hair of his head. He slipped the point of his sword flat between the ropes and the boys' wrists. One false move and such a blade would have opened a red flood from their veins. But not this swordsman. A sharp twist and the rope was cut, then the next. The boys dropped and staggered back from the cart, shaking their numb hands gingerly. It was their backs that burned with pain.

Blackbeard speared their shirts in the carts with his swordpoint and tossed them over.

'You,' said the fairhead to Crake. 'Strip.'

'You will not live to see another—'

The swordpoint pricked his throat as delicately as a needle. 'I said strip. And let's have no idle threats to accompany your disrobing.'

Eyes black with hatred, Crake removed his cloak and his doublet.

'More. Much more.'

He removed his shirt and then his linen undershirt and showed his white body. Some women tittered, some looked away.

'Still more. As bare as a beggar on the heath.'

Eventually the shivering Justice was reduced to nothing but his underwhittles. Only the swordpoint at his throat prevented him from speaking his mind, coursing with direst promises.

The boys got up behind the riders, Nicholas behind Edward Stanley, Hodge behind Smith.

'This is going to hurt you,' murmured Stanley over his shoulder. 'But we need to shift. Hold on.' Nicholas gritted his teeth.

Stanley's voice rang out once more. 'Good people! You have a worm for a Justice. A white and trembling worm. Her Majesty's representative? Her Majesty deserves better. You should petition her in such terms. Meanwhile, you will see us no more. Our business is elsewhere.'

He and Smith pulled their giant horses around, and the crowd parted before them like the Red Sea before Moses.

8

They cantered out of town, the heavy horses needing whipping over the hard streets, the boys trembling with pain at the jolting. They crossed a wild range of rocky hills and put many miles between them and the town, finding cover in woodland before Stanley pulled up.

'Tell me,' he said as they sat on the sweating horse. 'How the devil did you become vagabonds? Nicholas Ingoldsby is a proud-sounding name for a beggar. I thought such kind had simple peasant names as Jack by the Hedge, or Bedlam Bill.'

Nicholas slipped off the horse's rump.

'Hey!'

Nicholas looked up. 'My father is dead.'

Stanley stared at him, and then dismounted more slowly. He had feared this, the moment he saw it was the young Ingoldsby tied at the cart's end.

'When?'

'The day after you left our house. Crake came – that Justice there. With armed men. There was a struggle and my father was killed by the kick of a rearing horse. I was responsible.'

'You?'

Nicholas could not speak.

Blackbeard rode into the glade nearby. He seemed to have heard every word from far off.

'You gave command for the horse to kick out, did you?' he growled.

Nicholas glared up at him.

'Well then. You were not responsible.' He dismounted, jerking his head at Hodge to do likewise. 'It was in the hands of God.'

'He speaks the truth,' said Stanley more gently. 'Do not punish yourself. As for your father, though I am damnably sorry for it – he is in a better place. Bitter loss though it is to the Order.'

Suddenly, to his shame, tears were coursing down Nicholas's grimy cheeks.

'He was the bravest of knights,' said Stanley, and laid his hand on the boy's shaking shoulder.

Nicholas felt a wretched weakling, weeping before them. But the fairhaired knight murmured, 'It takes a man of heart to weep, and a man of wit to know a matter worthy of weeping. I've seen a man weep over losing at dice – which was not so worthy. You are your father's son.'

He glanced around the glade. 'We wait here till nightfall. Get some sleep. We ride all night.'

'Cuts first,' said Blackbeard. 'Get in the stream over there.'

Hodge and Nicholas found the stream at the edge of the wood, shallow with leafmould, but knelt beside it and washed as best they could. After only one night they already had the sour staleness of prison on their skins – besides weeks of vagabondage. Their single cuts were deep and tender even to a splash of cold water. Thirty such cuts and they would surely have bled to death.

They came back freezing cold, pulling their ragged shirts on.

'Not yet,' said Blackbeard.

He pulled a battered flask from his leather pannier and turned them around.

'I don't need to warn you this will hurt.'

Whatever he poured from the flask went down their cuts like flame. Nicholas's ears sang with the pain of it. But they made no noise. A chaffinch sang happily overhead. The sky was blue and clean. The only evil in the world was the evil of men.

The knights gave them their bread and cheese and their blankets and they lay down gingerly on their sides. Blackbeard made them sleep on their backs.

'It'll seal the wound quicker.'

Voice already thickening with sleep, Nicholas asked, 'What was in that flask?'

60

Blackbeard spoke through a mouthful of bread. 'Finest French brandy and a good pinch of gunpowder.'

'*Gunpowder?*'

Blackbeard grinned. 'Gunpowder has more uses than blowing heads off Turks.'

When Nicholas awoke it was dark. Hodge still snored beneath his blanket, exhausted by all this travel in foreign parts.

A fire burned low in a shallow pit, and Stanley was turning two leverets on a spit. Blackbeard was quickly skinning a third, and then the mother hare. She was paunched and gutted, her legs and head cut off and skin pulled free and all buried in half a minute.

Stanley questioned Nicholas quietly. Where was his father buried? What was the cause of Crake's enmity? He could answer neither question, except to say that Crake was a Puritan. But there was more to it than that.

Where were his sisters?

Nicholas told him, and Stanley brooded.

'This will weigh on you. The responsibility of it. But they will be cared for well enough. One day, in time, you will return.'

'I mean to.'

'And where do you and your man make for meanwhile? Are there uncles, cousins?'

'There are,' said Nicholas, 'but none will want to take in the children of a traitor.'

'Your father was no traitor, and such would be hard to prove before a court.'

Nicholas shrugged. 'I'd not burden any distant kin, nonetheless. We make for Bristol.'

'Bristol?'

Nicholas looked at him steadily. 'To take ship for Malta.'

Slow, uncomforting smiles spread over Smith and Stanley's faces.

'Malta?'

'Malta of the Knights,' said Nicholas.

'Well.' Smith tore off a large chunk from the hare's thigh and chewed it slowly, savouring this childish fantasy as much as the sweet spring meat.

'Malta, you say. And how exactly do you propose, you and your steadfast manservant here, to pay for your passage to Malta? Do you imagine Bristol shipmen have charitable hearts? And once at Malta – I presume you're not going there to grow pomegranates, but to wage noble war upon the Turk – how do you propose to arm yourself? Do you have any idea of how much armour costs? A sword? Or perhaps you're taking your catapult – the terror of all the sparrows in Shropshire?'

Stanley coughed sharply. It wasn't right to mock the boy over-much. He had lost a father, his family estate, given up his sisters, taken to the road – and they themselves had some part in it. Young Ingoldsby had nothing left, but still this boyish dream. It was not so contemptible, though ludicrous.

But Nicholas needed no defending, and his voice was steady.

'We go to Malta with your aid or without. Your sneers cannot hurt me. The death of my father before my eyes, the lash of a whip, winter's hunger, dishonour, these can hurt me. But not your sneers and mockeries. Hodge is no longer my manservant, since I have no money to pay him. But he is my companion still, and goes where I go.'

He tugged free a shoulder of the roast hare, glistening with dark meat, and ate. The boy had self-possession, no question.

'You might help us on our voyage, but you cannot hinder us.'

Even Smith looked at the boy's set expression with a faint, grudging respect.

'Besides,' said Nicholas swallowing, 'here we will never be safe. This country is cursed for me.'

'Never curse your country, lad,' said John Smith. 'You might as well curse your mother that gave you birth and suck.'

Stanley stoked up the fire. 'Times are evil in all Christendom. In Holland they have slaughtered Huguenots by the thousand, and in France. In England they begin to persecute Catholics. The Body of Christ is divided and cut in pieces once again.'

'All the more reason to flee such troubles for Malta,' said Nicholas.

Smith snapped a thin bone and sucked at the marrow. 'We might as well lead you into an abattoir, boy. Into a firestorm, the mouth of a volcano.'

'Are there no women and children on Malta too?'

'Aye. That stubborn and mulish peasantry will never leave their barren rock of an island, not if all the Legions of Hell were sailing on them.'

'Well, if women and children are preparing themselves to face your firestorm and your terrible Turk, so can we.'

Stanley and Smith were silent. The boy was speaking some skewed sense, damn him.

Meanwhile the boy sounded ever more like a man.

'Do not mistake me. You came to my father's house, and I do not mean to ... to turn that into a weapon against you. Yet you will agree that your coming to my father's house was the origin of my misfortunes.'

'We owe you nothing,' growled Smith.

'No. Nor do I mean to blackmail you. My father would roar me out of the house for such a thing.' He smiled faintly. 'I can hear him roar now. Nevertheless, the start of our troubles was your coming. So could it be that now we are meant to go with you? What else has providence got for me? Beatings and beggary. What would my father wish from you?'

That was a sharp question. Like father, like son.

Nicholas kept them wriggling, like playing two trout at once.

'I am the only son of your brother knight, Sir Francis Ingoldsby. Is that how you requite him?'

Damn the boy.

Stanley looked at Smith. 'We have truly failed on this journey of ours into England.'

Smith grunted agreement. 'Which we were supposed to conduct with as little hubbub as possible.'

To Nicholas, Stanley resumed, 'We will find you some better protection before we go. Some position in an old Catholic household, perhaps? One of my own, in Derbyshire—'

The boy's voice rose in anger now and Hodge stirred.

'In the bitter winter I protected my sisters, I found them shelter. We have wandered the length and breadth of the shire, Hodge and I, under snow for a blanket. We have slept in barns and pigsties and bartons not fit for beasts. Yet I am no Prodigal Son, with father to run home to.'

63

'You have proved yourselves tough and cunning, I grant you.'

'We had no choice in the matter. Neither I nor Hodge have father nor mother nor inheritance. If you will not go with me to Malta, yet I will find my way, through every hardship. It is my fate. You came to our house, and my father died. Yet it was me you came for, though you did not know it.'

The fire crackled in the still night. A fox barked. The boy spoke with conviction and a sublime simplicity.

At last Stanley stirred. 'I do not agree with your interpretation, boy. But—'

Smith said brusquely, 'Have you shot a fowling piece?'

'Of course. And I can bring down a woodcock.'

'How is your swordsmanship?'

'Not so much. But I will learn.'

'It takes years.'

'Well then, I will learn in a month. The Turk is coming soon.'

Now Smith and Stanley exchanged a different smile. The boy was unstoppable. The son of Sir Francis Ingoldsby, Knight Grand Cross.

'*Malta?*' said Hodge. 'Where in the back-of-beyond the Forest of Clun is Malta?' He looked around, all three faces smiling now. 'You mean we're going to *Wales?*'

The moon was high when they rode out of the glade onto the frosty road, the night cold and clear. The sound of their hooves would carry, dogs would bark as they passed by.

'We need to move fast,' said Stanley. 'The whole country will be looking for two men and two boys on stolen plough horses.'

'Two boys?' pondered Smith. 'What day is today?'

'Near Lady Day. The twentieth in March, I think.'

''Tis a Monday. Washday.' He turned in his saddle. 'You are shivering, lads. But we will find you new garments, if some addled housewife has left her linens on a hedgerow overnight.'

Within a few miles they saw such linens cast over a holly hedge, gleaming in the moonlight. Smith made his choice, and hung a small purse of silver pennies from the gatepost in payment.

He tossed the clothes to the boys. They were stiff with frost.

Nicholas and Hodge stared down. Kirtle, pinafore and white lace-fringed mob cap for each.

'That's right,' said Smith. 'You're going to Bristol as girls, never mind what Saint Paul says against men dressing up as maids.'

'And your names shall be ...'

'Nancy,' suggested Smith.

'And Matilda,' said Stanley.

For some reason, this was so amusing that the two knights had to stifle their laughter on their sleeves.

'We also need a whore,' said Smith at last.

The boys looked startled.

Smith grinned and offered no explanation.

It was a party of five who arrived unmolested at Bristol docks a week after. Mr Edward Melcombe, man of law; his brother Simon. His wife, a somewhat raddled-looking older woman called Margaret, whom he had picked up only recently in a dubious alley in Ludlow. And their two daughters, Nancy and Matilda, regrettably ill-favoured maids, both being of strapping build and with a distinct foreshadowing of beard about the jawline.

9

In Bristol the boys lay overnight in the door of a warehouse, sleeping fitfully as sailors bawled drunkenly and sometimes tried to nudge them awake, thinking they were waterside whores, or catamite boys. Stanley and Smith said they had business in the town. Business best conducted by dark.

At dawn they were kicked awake again.

'On your feet!'

The two knights were now laden with bundles and bags over both shoulders.

'We sail in an hour,' said Smith, hulking dark against the red sunrise. 'Into many a springtime storm.'

The boat was called the *Swan of Avon*. It smelt bad.

It was something of a cross between a cog and carvel, having a triangular lateen sail on its mainmast and a full square-rigger on its foremast. A small, scruffy vessel, no more than a hundred tons and badly in need of a paint. Certainly it carried no gilding. Nicholas only hoped it was better maintained below the waterline, where it mattered. A crude swan had been painted on the flat face of the stern, looking more like an Aylesbury duck, and then a crucifix surrounded by flames, added for good measure as an afterthought. It bore no flag.

The master was a tall, lean, pockmarked fellow with a wandering gaze and two daggers in his belt. He was taking English broadcloth to Spain, and bringing back oranges and Canary wine. As for an island called Malta, he knew nothing of it.

He eyed Nicholas and Hodge, still in their thin disguise. 'Your daughters, you say?'

Stanley nodded. 'Nancy and Matilda.'

The captain sneered. 'What you runnin' from?'

'None of your business.'

He grunted, and told them they'd have to bring their own food and drink, and keep out of his mariners' way. Other than that, they'd not be molested.

'And remember to spew at the stern,' he added.

Nicholas and Hodge spewed all the way to the Scillies and beyond. But as they came in sight of France – Brittany, Stanley said – the sea began to calm, though the west wind was still biting cold. At least they were allowed to jettison their maids' clothes and return to their own.

Exhausted and thinner than ever, they lay against a coil of tarred rope in the weak sun, wrapped in blankets. Smith came and dumped a bundle on the deck nearby. He took a leather flask from his bag and handed it to them.

'A swig each,' he said.

Nicholas unstoppered the cork. It smelt of rotting seaweed.

'Scurvy grass soaked in ale,' said Smith. 'Drink it. It'll stop you getting the Dutch Disease. Your gums rotting and your teeth falling out.'

Stanley came by whistling.

'Ah,' he said. 'A draught of Dr Smith's sovereign anti-scorbutical infusion. The foulest concoction yet brewed this side of hell. So how are our young crusaders?'

Nicholas swallowed the liquid morosely. 'Not dead yet.'

'Well said, well said.' Stanley grinned broadly, his ruddy cheeks becoming ruddier daily in the sun and wind, his thick fair hair blown back from his fine broad brow, his whole appearance so powerful and leonine.

'Strange to remember you're a monk,' Nicholas blurted out.

Stanley gazed out to sea.

'When we were born, this ruffian here and I—' he indicated Smith, who ignored him – 'England was a Catholic country still, under Henry. Many younger sons of my family have served the

67

Knights for generations. It is the highest honour.'

'But – you can never marry.'

Smith grunted. 'There's another blessing.'

'Taking that oath, and swearing fealty unto death, lifts all trouble from the mind. It makes life simple. Such a Brotherhood,' said Stanley softly. 'Such a band of brothers.'

Feeling a little more alive, Hodge and Nicholas explored the ship, as far as they were allowed.

It was a thing of wonder, despite the frequent sighting of rats and the smell.

'You think that smells rosy,' said one old mariner, 'try opening the hatches of the bilges. 'Twill knock you senseless into next week.'

He was called Legge, and had but one. There were other mariners like Craven and Bloodisack, who barely spoke to them but to snarl. There were landsmen, apprentice mariners, and lowest of the low, pages: boys of no more than twelve or so, who emptied out the slop buckets, killed the rats, scrubbed the decks, and worked the bilge pump banded to the mainmast, hour by exhausting hour. They hardly dared speak, but looked at Nicholas and Hodge with fraternal pity.

There was Vizard, the blasphemous bosun, who sang obscene songs when not shouting, and Pidhook the helmsman, who treated them with a pinch less contempt than the others. He showed them where he stood on the upper deck called the bridge and swung the whipstaff left and right, turning the great rudder hanging from the sternpost likewise. He showed them his half-hour sandglass, which told the time and reckoned the watches in and out, and his dry compass mounted in a gimbel, a cunning device which kept the compass needle flat to the horizon, no matter which way the ship tilted.

Old crock though she was, the mariners seemed to have a sturdy confidence in the *Swan of Avon*.

At the end of the first eight-hour watch around dawn, the mariners took their breakfast. One tossed a slab of hardtack to the boys. 'Here. Test your pearly teeth on that, young sprat.'

68

Nicholas couldn't even break into it. They laughed. 'Ye'll have to soak it a while yet.'

To their surprise, the master came forward and said a Paternoster and an Ave Maria before his men were allowed to eat.

'Is this not a Protestant ship?' said Stanley evenly.

The master said in his gravel voice, and with a distant stare out to sea, 'For the Bishop of Rome and the Church of Italy I care not. And this newfangled Church of England makes my head ache, since I don't see how Christ could have founded such a church when he never came ashore on English soil.'

'Ah,' said Stanley, 'the pragmatical English mind.'

'And he lived and preached before England was even a kingdom, I heard tell, so how can he have appointed the Queen's forefathers as head of such a church?'

'A theologian ship's master,' said Stanley delightedly. 'And preaching what sounds like Popery!'

'Popes and Protestants,' said the master in a flat, bored tone and a wave of his hand. 'Such tangled arguments belong on land. We're not on land, we're at sea, and the law is different here. I decorate my ship and make my prayers as I see fit, and I will pray to God and his Holy Mother under any name I know, if he'll send us clear weather and plain sailing. When a man's fifty miles out in the Bay of Biscay, that's his usual religion.'

10

Istanbul: Winter 1564 – Spring 1565

All that winter Istanbul had been in a ferment, devoted to the coming war.

From the forests of the Crimea came timber, from the high plains of Anatolia came hemp and flax. Out of the vast Imperial workshops came coils of rope and bales of sailcloth, while in the naval dockyards, they said a new war galley was being built every week. Saltpetre for gunpowder came in from Belgrade, sulphur from Lake Van, copper from the mines of Kastamonu, and church bells throughout the conquered Balkans were melted down, turning the Christian's own iron and bronze against them.

Day and night there was the ring of hammer on anvil, the steady tapping of shipwrights and the hot stink of burning pitch poured over the caulking ropes, tamped down into the seams of the wooden hulls to make them watertight. Oxen drew carts bringing vats of tallow straight from the slaughterhouses, steering them carefully down to the dry docks where they would be used to grease the galleys' hulls, making them slip still faster over the waves of the White Sea.

Day and night, too, the great forges of the Ottoman arsenals on the Bosphorus glowed red, while within, shovelling charcoal into hungry cast-iron mouths, super-heated by giant bellows, the faces of the slaves dripped with sweat. The bellows roared, oil burned, the winter sky was filled with smoke, and at night the very moon and stars were obscured. Greek fishermen along the shore muttered among themselves, and clutched the evil eye amulets around their brawny necks, saying the red glow of the Sultan's furnaces was like the fires of hell.

Overseeing the frenzy of activity in the arsenals from a high walkway was a figure in a plain black robe, hook-nosed, deep-set eyes missing not one detail. From the huge casts, monstrous cannon of solid bronze emerged, each one requiring a team of forty or fifty slaves to move on iron axles and wheels. One basilisk, Ghadb-al Lah – the Anger of Allah – required its own galley. The destructive power of these monsters when unleashed would be unimaginable. They could hurl balls of marble or iron in excess of two hundred pounds. The roar would deafen any nearby, and their effect on walls of mere stone would be devastating.

'The whole island of Malta will rock about on the sea,' said the forgemaster, spitting out a mouthful of charcoal dust and swiping his sweaty face with the back of his hand. 'Like a fisherman's boat in a storm.'

Mustafa's eyes gleamed.

He interrogated provisioners and quartermasters, inspected warehouses filled with everything from gunstocks to biscuits to opium supplies to massive pyramids of cannonballs, surveyed acres of hundredweight gunpowder barrels. There were wooden frames for making speedy breastworks, hides for protecting siege towers, sacking for trenches, and crates full of double-baked biscuit that would last for ever, though they would also break your teeth.

There were stables full of horses and oxen, all needing to be transported and fed, so they could drag gun carriages and plat-forms at the siege. When their strength finally failed, they would be eaten.

He questioned the shipmasters, and looked in on the Christian slaves, waiting in their pens to be chained to the rowing bench again.

'Only a little while yet,' he rasped through the bars at the hud-dled wretches within. 'We must catch the spring tide, when there's war in the air!'

On a windy day in early March, Mustafa for the first time stepped aboard his fig-wood flagship with its high stern and its twenty-eight rowing benches aside. *Al-Mansour*. The Victorious. She would fly like the wind. From the mast above fluttered and snapped the green silk banner of Islam with its crescent moon and its verses from the

Koran, and at the stern was planted the standard of the Sultan: a golden globe with horsehair tassels, symbolising the globe of the world, which he was destined to rule.

Mustafa gripped the taffrail hard, his lips clenched, and glared back ferociously at the workshops and furnaces of the Bosphorus. *When?* It was time to sail. It was time to fight.

Cannons firing salutes, pipes wailing and cymbals clashing. Janizaries in their plumes of heron and ostrich feather, holy men in green turbans, great drums beating, marching in a slow stately rhythm out under Palace Point to the waiting galleys. The greatest naval venture in four centuries of Ottoman history. Wind batting the sails, salt tang on the air. The ground trembling under the weight of those sixteen-team ox-carts and their monstrous cannon, and the remorseless thunder of the drums.

All Europe knew of the frenetic preparations in the empire of the Turk. But where would his scimitar fall? Some said Cyprus, some said Sicily.

One man knew, and sent out word. Grand Master Jean Parisot de la Valette, of the Knights of St John of Malta.

He knew.

Across Europe, old men with bent backs and white beards shook out their time-worn tabards. White cross on red. The tabard of war. Elderly retainers oiled old-fashioned hauberks of mail and whetted ancient blades.

The sword of Islam was raised, pointing straight at the heart of the Christian Sea. And if Europe's kings and princes would not go to the aid of that small beleaguered island, then loyal knights might yet.

Let him laugh and mock, *l'uomo nuovo, l'uomo universale,* and count his ducats, and say that money and science, knowledge and advancement were now the thing. The Age of Machiavelli was come, the Age of Chivalry was dead. From the villages of Spain and Italy, Provence and Auvergne they still came, the old knights, the old brothers. Some on horses, some on donkeys, some on dusty mules.

Some sang the old ballad for company as they rode.

Then rising from a doubtful seat and half-attainted stall,
The last knight of Europe takes weapons from the wall,
The last and lingering troubadour to whom the bird has sung,
That once went singing southward when all the world was young.
In that enormous silence, tiny and unafraid,
Comes up along a winding road the noise of the Crusade ...

A song to keep them company on the perilous voyage to Malta, and into the eye of the coming storm.

11

'So, Matilda,' said Edward Stanley. 'What do you know of foreign parts?'

Hodge was whittling a stick. 'My name's Hodge,' he said woodenly.

Stanley bowed low. 'A thousand pardons.'

Hodge took a deep breath. 'Well. I know the country round Cambridge is a flat and sodden country, not fit for any but fenmen and fish. Men of Essex are turbulent and lawless and born cheats, and men of London the same, only worse. Further north they are coarse as farmyard swine and drop their breeches without shame and make their business in the middle of the street. Men of Lincolnshire are notorious dullards and villains, and men of Lancashire and Yorkshire are worse, so quarrelsome and stiffnecked they would find fault with a fat goose.'

'By foreign I meant ... out of England.'

'Ah, Wales,' said Hodge. 'They are barely of the race of men. They live in caves and eat raw mutton and speak in a tongue so barbarous it frightens the birds off the trees. Men of the south and west be Welsh too in all but name, idle and sly and deceitful from the first day out of their mother's wombs. 'Tis only in Shropshire you'll find honest men, and only in the parishes west of Shrewsbury. The rest are fools.'

Nicholas laughed. It felt like the first time he had laughed in months.

Hodge drew breath.

'Across the sea they are all foreigners. Sail to Scotland or Ireland

and you'll wish you'd stayed home, even with a witch for a wife, my old dad used to say. The Scots are nought but barbarians, they go naked all year but for animal skins. The Irish are worse, with hardly the wit to feed themselves and so starve often.

'The Germans are fat drunkards. The Danes, drunkards also. Dutchmen, drunkards and gluttons to boot, with huge swag-bellies and beards thick with grease from their last dinner. They skate over ice on cows' shoulder bones, though it's a wonder the ice holds 'em. The French are a vile race, slothful as swine and as evil-smelling, foppish, curtseying, arrant, vain, silk-dressed perfumed treacherous deceitful cowardly knaves one and all, forever bowing the head or bending the buttock to any who will flatter them.'

'Hear hear,' said Smith. 'The lad speaks some sense.'

'The Switzers fight well but stink of cheese, for they eat nothing else. Of the Austrians I know not and care less, also the Hungarians, the Polacks, and others to the cruel cold East. The Russians live in everlasting ice and snow and eat their own parents when they die. Your Spaniard is cruel and treacherous, conceited and a braggard, your Italian avaricious, shallow and malign, and as given to incest as any villain in Norfolk. The Greeks are swarthy and notorious fools.

'Beyond them they are not even Christian. The infidel Turks go circumcised and have four wives apiece and murder their own brothers, and "to turn Turk" is to turn evil and worship the Devil, who they call Mahound. Their brothers the Arabs ride camels and their evil and cruelty are almost beyond telling. The Jews we know of, wandering gold-hoarders and Christ-deniers, and then there's the Ethiop, who's barbarous and black as coal and couples with monkeys. Beyond him is the Parsee, the Hindoo and the Chinaman, all idolaters and devils. In the New World there are none but savage men who live in trees, often with tails, who some say are not truly human at all.'

'Well,' said Stanley. 'Though you have not gone far in the world, friend Hodge, yet you are as stuffed full of opinions as a puritan preacher.'

Hodge regarded him impassively.

'I think you will enjoy your foreign travels.'

'Enough bandying words,' said Smith, standing abruptly. 'Here. Take this.'

And he handed Nicholas a sword.

Of course Nicholas had many a time taken down his father's old sword above the fireplace, when his father was not about. It felt as heavy as a sack of grain, and as he well knew, was long-rusted in its sheath.

Now Smith handed him a very different article.

'An Iberian blade,' he said, 'finest Toledo steel.'

Hodge chuckled. 'Seems funny we're going to fight the Spaniards with their own swords.'

Stanley eyed him askance. 'The Spaniards will be fighting alongside us.'

Hodge's mouth fell open.

'Look down the blade,' said Smith. 'See the furrow that strengthens it. Is it straight?'

It was as straight as a rule.

'Now. Stretch out your arm and raise the sword to your shoulder height a dozen times.'

Nicholas began. At the seventh, his shoulder muscles were hot and burning. At the ninth, his arm failed. He angrily let the sword drop, nearly throwing it to the ground.

'Have a care,' said Stanley sharply. 'Never let the point fall, you'll only blunt it.'

'I'll be a bowman,' said Nicholas. 'I know a crossbow.'

'Very useful,' said Smith neutrally. 'But crossbows are for foot soldiers. The noble-born use swords, and you are the son of a Knight of England.'

'I'm not,' said Hodge.

Smith turned to him. 'What *was* your father?'

'Bit of everythin', really. Hedgin' and ditchin' mostly in the winter, shepherdin' in the summer. He could smith too.'

'Truly a man of universal talents,' said Stanley.

Hodge fixed him with a stare. 'I'll not have you make mock of my old dad, even if you are a knight and he was none.'

There was an awkward silence. Then Stanley said solemnly, 'Forgive me, Hodge.'

Hodge nodded.

'Here,' added the knight. 'You will learn to use a sword too.'

Hodge took the fine blade tentatively. Surprisingly, though of stockier build, his arm too tired quickly.

'You see what this means,' said Smith. 'A few times you will raise your sword to parry the enemy's thrust. And then one more parry, and you will fail, and you will die. In a battle, this will happen within the first minute.'

Nicholas hung his head.

'Despair,' said Stanley quietly but crisply, 'is not among the knightly virtues. Raise you head, lad, and attend. You too, Hodge.'

Smith reached for another bag, a lumpy hessian sack.

'Now we are past the coast of Brittany, it will be another two weeks of sail to Cadiz. Perhaps three, and certainly there will be more rough weather. But you will be too exhausted to fret over that.'

He indicated two barrels close by.

'Our small beer. By day five it will taste like horse piss, but you will drink it the same. You will need it.'

He held open the sack before them.

'Contents: sixty barley loaves, twelve flitches of bacon, four heavy cheeses, one flagon of vile wine. These are our rations until Cadiz, where we will take on more of the same. Also figs, dates, almonds, and oranges which will do the job of the scurvy grass until Malta. Spanish sailors get less of the Dutch disease. You will neither thirst nor starve, but you will have an appetite. Why? Because you will be working to put beef on your bones for the next four weeks. What we call your sword-muscles.

'Strip to the waist.'

Smith and Stanley then prodded their white torsos as they shivered in the wind, flesh like a plucked fowl. Hodge retained a bit of meat. Nicholas was as thin as a pikestaff.

'Saint John have mercy,' muttered Smith. 'Well, leave off your shirts. You'll heat up soon enough. Take these staves.'

For half an hour on the tilting deck, Smith and Stanley had the boys raising and sweeping the staves over their heads like swords, lifting them one-handed, and finally batting at each other, slash and parry. By the end of that time, the boys' arms were aching like fury and screaming for rest.

It didn't help that some of the brawny mariners had come to watch. Ears gleaming with gold rings, mighty forearms inked with strange devices of mermaids and anchors and random symbols of good fortune, they stood nearby laughing and hurling abuse.

'What ye doing, lads, swatting flies?'

'They couldn't fight off a pigmy with a straw!'

'That's a pretty couple of lilywhite lady's maids you've got with you there, sir knights!' called another. 'But pray, where are their bubbies?'

'You'll hear worse insults than that in the heat of battle,' grinned Stanley.

'Half an hour by the sun,' said Smith, scowling at the boys' exhaustion. 'When the Turks come to Malta, how long will they fight us? For a morning? For the daylight hours only? No. All day and all night, every day, every night.'

The boys drooped and panted, covered in sweat.

Smith gave them each a chunk of bread and a glug of small beer, and then told Nicholas to attack him with the stave. The boy flailed wide and at the perfect instant, the knight simply stepped backwards. The stave swept past him, Nicholas twisted after it, and Smith tripped him to the deck.

The knight glared down. 'Which corporeal part of me were you trying to strike, lad?'

Nicholas hauled himself up on all fours, his knees and left hand painfully scuffed where he had hit the planks. The mariners' uproarious laughter echoed in his ears, until drowned out by the master bellowing at them to get back to work or they'd feel his whip.

'My upper arm?' mocked Smith. 'Which would be armoured anyway. First lesson. A blade will get to your enemy ten times more often with a straight thrust than a wide slash. One step backwards is enough to avoid such a slashing blow, but a long thrust with your weight behind it ... Your man will have to take two, three steps backwards. That is far harder. If there's a wall, breastwork, another man behind him, it's impossible. You've got him.

'So what if you've got no sword? What if it's dropped or broken?'

The boys were silent.

'You use anything you can lay your hands on. Your sword is broken? Throw the jagged hilt in your enemy's face, and then come on after it. You inflict as much damage as possible, as quickly as possible. You go for his eyes, his throat, his stones. You want him out of the fight, and fast. For there will be many more of them coming on behind. You show no quarter, as your enemy will show no quarter.'

Nicholas felt as if his brain was already filling up, but Smith went on relentlessly.

'There is only one kick you will need. The forward kick, planting your foot square in your man's chest and shoving him back.' He demonstrated swiftly on Hodge, who grunted out air and tottered backwards. Stanley grabbed him to stop him toppling back over the rail.

'Any other kick, you will lose your balance, expose your side, end up facing the wrong way – and with a Turkish blade in your guts. Your feet are for standing on, not kicking. Mules kick. Once in a while you might stamp on a man's foot. That hurts him. But by that time you'll be so close to, you'll know what he had for breakfast.

'Never, ever, ever use your bare fist. A knight with a broken hand is useless. Guard your hand well. Never throw idle punches like a drunken varlet in the street. Here, boy. Punch me as hard as you can.'

Nicholas, knees still stinging from where Smith had tripped him, needed no second bidding. He punched out hard. Smith could easily have dodged the punch, but he took it full on the breastbone. Nicholas pulled back his bunched fist with a gasp of pain.

'See?' said Smith. 'It hurt you more than me. I'll have a small bruise tomorrow but no more. Why? Not because you've no more meat on you than a sparrow – though you haven't. But it's a very, very rare man indeed who can really throw a hard punch. Forget it. It's a fool's fighting. Whereas to seize a sturdy oak joint stool and clout a fellow in the sconce. That would show some wit.

'So: use an object. You hear me? Never, ever use your fist. Always—' his voice rose to a sudden roar – *'seize the nearest object!'*

And at the same time as he bellowed these words, Smith seized the wooden stave from Hodge's hands and charged at Nicholas like a maddened bull.

It happened in the blink of a bird's eye, the twitch of a wren's tail. The boy had time to glance about – fear did this, they said later, fear slowed the sun on the dial and gave you time. There was only one thing within reach, the corner of an empty hemp sack weighed down under a coil of rope. Nicholas saw the end of Smith's stave driving hard at his belly and knew Smith would not stop. He meant to injure him.

His only weapon of defence, a scrap of hessian, flew up in Smith's face. At the same time Nicholas twisted and the stave struck his bare flesh aslant, only lightly grazing it in passing. He fell on the stave and gripped it, until Smith wrenched it back with his far greater strength and left the boy's hands burning from the friction.

Smith said, 'See? You fought off an armed man with only a bit of hopsack.'

'Not just a man either,' said Nicholas. 'A Knight Grand Cross of St John.'

Smith cuffed him on the side of his head with a great paw.

The closest he came to praise.

All that day the rules were drummed into them. Never use your fists. Kick but rarely. Thrust, don't slash. Any hard object can kill a man. Care for your sword. Go for eyes, throat and stones. One backward step may be as good as a shield.

There were harder lessons the next day, and the next. Never leave an enemy merely stunned or injured. Kill him. Never go to the defence of a wounded comrade before one still fighting. He will do the same by you.

And there were the rules of chivalry. Never hurt a woman, always defend her. Nor child nor beardless boy. Never insult or spit on the enemy dead. Always honour and bury your own.

'Beyond that,' said Stanley, 'there are many oaths and vows that bind a sworn Knight. But if you still mean to fight with us at Malta—'

'We do.'

'Then you will fight only as gentlemen volunteers.'

'I will be a Knight of St John after.'

'It takes years.'

'I've got years.'

It was after dark with the ship sailing slow over a starlit sea before the boys finally devoured their evening ration of bread and cheese and bacon and fell asleep almost instantly. Smith and Stanley let them sleep for ten hours that night, they were so exhausted. They would be just as exhausted tomorrow night, but then they would have only eight hours. The night after, seven. By Malta, they would have learnt to live on five.

They murmured to each other of how they had gone to England for sacks of gold, for cases of guns, for knightly volunteers, and come back with a bundle of swords, a couple of purses, and two errant boys who had hardly raised a sword in their lives. A pretty success. They could guess the Grand Master's verdict all too well. His words stung in their ears like imagined hail.

Yet tonight the sky was clear and studded with stars, the wind gentle from the west, making hardly a sound in the sails. Only the gentle swish of the bow wave below them.

The knights prayed to God for wind, for storm, for tempest. Anything but this damnable pacific calm, anything to hasten them. For they felt it in their bones.

The enemy was sailing too.

The boys fought with staves, they did endless squats, they pulled themselves up ropes and rigging and climbed to the fighting top, the master's sour objections being silenced with gold coin. They ate their grim rations like young wolves, and on the fifth day they asked to do more sword-arm raises. Each did twelve.

After a week, Smith showed them how to wear a helmet. First he settled his own rounded morion on Nicholas's head without its wadding inside, and then struck him lightly on the crown. It rang, and hurt.

'Quite so,' he said. 'A helmet without good wadding or bombast is useless. Stuff it well.'

He packed it tight, set it on the boy's head again, and struck hard. Nicholas reeled instinctively, eyes tight shut – but barely felt discomfort.

'And if you've helmet on, don't forget you can butt the other fellow in the face hard enough to blind him. Two pieces of armour, and two only, protect you most. Helmet and breastplate. For the rest, 'tis better your arm or leg does not encounter a Turkish blade. For you know which will come off best.'

'The blade will come off best,' said Stanley, 'but your arm will come off easily also.'

'Spare us your labouring wit, brother knight.'

'My wit is mostly *'armless*. Like a knight careless in battle.'

'I beg you.'

'Like a dissolved Parliament, his *members* have departed.'

'*I beg you,*' repeated Smith.

Stanley sighed. 'Had I not been a knight, I would have made a royal court jester.'

There was silence.

12

Dawn, and the sun coming up to larboard.

'Out of France,' said Nicholas wonderingly.

'Out of Spain,' corrected Stanley. 'We sail south and west now. Look hard and you'll see the snow-capped mountains that stand sentinel behind the Spanish coast. The mountains of Cantabria.'

They were beautiful in the sun. And the very word, *Cantabria* ...

'From their oak forests are made the Spanish galleons at Bilbao, which sail all the way to the Indies and back. Noble mountains, are they not, Master Hodgkin? More wild and sublime than any of your Shropshire hills?'

Hodge grunted. 'Fatter sheep on the green hills of home, I'll wager.'

They were rounding Cape Finisterre. Stanley was indicating eastward where Santiago da Compostela lay, the great pilgrim city where St James was buried, when the master called out from the sterndeck, 'Storm coming in from the west. Hoist in sails!'

Sure enough, on the western horizon there were growing towering clouds, a dark and ominous grey, swollen with rain. The first gusts flurried across the sea, flinging up spray and flattening out the little waves. But the waves would be growing soon.

'Off the coast of Galicia too,' muttered Smith, and a look of genuine anxiety crossed Stanley's bearded face.

'Is that bad?' asked Nicholas.

'Bad?' growled Smith. 'It's worse than the coast of Cornwall.'

Only a few minutes later a wall of wind hit the little ship like a backhanded swipe from Neptune himself. Every timber creaked and the ship keeled hard to larboard in the blast. The sails cracked like musket shots and the blocks rattled in the rigging. Everything started to tremble, including Hodge and Nicholas.

'Pull her to starboard, head her into the wind!' roared the master to Pidhook at the whipstaff. 'She's a tilt to the north, bless the devil. We can bring her out from the coast, or at least keep her off it.'

In another instant the air was filled with icy rain driving into them almost horizontally, stinging their noses and cheeks and making them gasp. But it was fear, raw fear that overwhelmed them. Pain was nothing to that. The black, clawed coast looked horribly near through the murk. The boys hooded their faces with their cloaks, though not being able to see the heaving waters around them made them feel instantly sick.

'Pages, to the pump!' roared the master. 'Vizard, check anchor! Legge, wad up the water jars and lock down the hatches! Down below first, landsmen, ye're nothing but a danger up on deck! Down below now, and no spewing on our cargo either. If you see a sprung leak bigger than an infant's piss, give us the yell.'

Clutching on tight to rail and rigging, Smith moved aft to where the master stood bow-legged, holding on tight himself as the ship began to rear and buck over the growing waves. He said something, lost in the teeth of the gale, and the master stared at him, rainwater streaming down his face, and then shrugged as if he was listening to a madman.

Smith clawed his way back and loosened a pile of ropes tied round a capstan. He threw one end to Nicholas.

'Bind yourself tight, boy, round the chest, tight as if your life depended on it! Which it does!'

Shaking with fear, feeling himself white-faced and nauseous, his eyeballs aching, Nicholas tried not to see the size of the waves already running in from the west, like green glassy dunes. To the east, white water breaking on needles of black rock. The ship straining to sail outward, the deck already tipping steeply. He forced his cold, wet hands to tie the thick corded rope around his chest, just below his arms, in a double knot. It was momentarily a relief to have something else to think about. Then the knot was done, and

84

the ship gave a terrific lurch, timbers audibly screeching above the gale. He pictured nails twisting, boards springing loose … Terror gripped him again. He thought his bowels might empty.

'And you, Hodge, the other end!'

No less terrified than Nicholas, Hodge did as he was told.

'Now, about the main mast, both of you, two circuits. It'll not be used for sail for a while, not on this blast!'

Slipping on the drenched deck, the two boys clumsily circled each other until both were looped fast around the great spruce mainmast, slipping and sliding back and forth, scrabbling desperately with wet leather soles on the sea-darkened timbers of the deck. The ship rocked and reeled, briefly on an even keel and then over again with a sickening lurch, the larboard deck almost down to the water's edge. Yet they kept their balance and their panic under control, knowing they were bound to the ship with rope thick enough to tow another.

'Now!' bellowed Smith, and thrust the staves into their numbed hands once more. 'Fight! If you were Norsemen of old, you'd do this with daggers to the death!'

Smith and Stanley bound themselves to brass cleats on the deck, and took staves also. Suddenly Smith roared again, 'Now! Fight us!'

On the wildly tilting deck amid the teeth of the storm, faces dashed and eyes blinded with stinging salt spray, the two boys fought back desperately as the two knights belaboured them, delivering many a true hit to legs, arms and sides that would leave bruises for a week. Gradually the boys' fear receded as outrage and then anger took its place, and they returned blow for blow with increasing fury. Even if the ship did founder on those jagged rocks, not half a mile off, they'd outlive it. They'd out-swim the bastard storm!

The knights laughed and mocked them, goading them on, roaring out in the wind.

'Well named you are, Nancy and Matilda! You fight like maidens! Fight! Devil take you, *fight!*'

The rope clutching them securely round the chest, they spun and dodged and strained from the mainmast like bears tied in the pit and set on by dogs. Their blood was up, hair plastered to their skulls, soaked to the skin, yet they were wielding their staves and ducking and slithering and yelling too vigorously for the cold to touch them now. It was like galloping a horse through the rain, thought Nicholas. Your flesh was cold to the touch, yet your hot blood sang, your brain pulsed, your heart burned with an animal heat. He caught Smith hard across the hip with a side blow that had the knight bellow in his black beard and shake the water from his eyes.

'Blasted puppy, have at you!'

A return blow was only just parried, leaving Nicholas's fingers tingling with needles at the shock.

'Yell, yell into the storm!' roared Smith, coming at him again. 'Shout out that you love the storm! Say it!'

'I love the storm!'

'Hah!' Another painful blow across Nicholas's back as he turned too much aside. 'Again! Louder!'

'I love the storm!'

He fought back. He yelled. He screamed. The storm screamed around him, and he was one with it now, riding it, riding the little ship beneath his feet like it was a wild horse and he the rider, in command now of this bucking wild thing. He further called to mind scenes of torment from the past weeks and months, and the shipwreck of his life. It steeled him, and terror fled away.

The mariners on the rear deck squatted low to keep their balance, watching this crazed performance in disbelief. These four voyagers belabouring each other with longstaffs in the teeth of the gale, staggering back and forth, only kept from sliding clean of the canted deck and certain drowning by being bound to the mast.

'The storm has turned their wits!'

'Perhaps it's a cure for seasickness.'

A third simply spat downwind and growled, 'Landlubbers.'

At last Smith and Stanley dropped back laughing, even their mighty frames exhausted from fighting in drenched clothes on such a shifting ground, eyes stung red by saltspray, beards streaming water.

'Fight on! Fight on!' they roared at the boys, goading them to further furies.

What good practice this was – for they would soon be fighting in the heart of another storm. When the ground beneath their feet would be slippery not with saltwater but with blood.

At last Smith and Stanley looked at each other and nodded. They had it. Both boys. The Ingoldsby boy for certain, and his Hodge too. Both of 'em. That *furor martialis,* that battle fury, without which no amount of fancy swordsmanship is worth a fig.

Between the two of them however, the knights held privately that once at Malta, the two boys would fall to and become useful porters of powder and musket balls, provisioners, perhaps builders and ditchers. They had survived homeless through an English winter well enough, they might endure through the coming inferno of Malta. But not as fighters. Though the gentleman boy, certainly, had that knot of anger in his belly that drives the best warrior. Anger against what? Against the world that hurt him.

Young Ingoldsby had damnably little left to him in England, it was true. But at Malta, all this swordsmanship flummery would suddenly seem as nothing under that burning, unforgiving sun. They would have their uses, these stout-hearted boys, but not as fighting men. A certain Grand Master would not allow it. But for now, let it keep them busy.

The storm endured from dawn till dusk, but the ship was kept off the toothed coast of Galicia well enough, and at last the wind began to ease. The waves heaved and dragged at them all night, but by sunrise the following day, the sky was a pale washed blue, and the roll at last abating. Hodge and Nicholas had slept down below, curled up among the bales of English broadcloth, and never felt a hint of sickness. Before he slept, as every night, Nicholas prayed for the souls of his father and mother, and for his sisters.

In the morning they groaned and stretched and every muscle ached. Their breakfast rations were nowhere near enough. They fantasised about roast pork, sizzling on the spit. They dreamt of boiled beef and pottage, plum tart, green garden peas, apple duff and cream, frumenty, woodcock, duck roast, sweet rice pudding. But stale bread, mouldering cheese and tart small beer would have to suffice.

*

Smith had them raise the sword that day.

Each raised it twenty-two times.

'A fair promise of parry and thrust,' said Smith, trying to hide his pleasure in his beard. 'In truth, a good swordsman will only raise his sword three times before he kills. One parry – two parry – three thrust. The rhythm of meted death.'

Nicholas's voice rose with indignation. 'Then why—?'

Smith smiled, with little mirth. 'You will have more than one man apiece to fight, I fear. And you may just meet as good a swordsman as yourself. Then endurance is all. In Malta, if you remain steadfast to fight—'

'I do.'

'Then you will meet swordsmen of the very finest in the world. You will meet the Janizaries.'

There was one weighty bundle that Smith had not loosened yet. At sunset that day, he laid it on the deck and untied it and there were a dozen or more gleaming swords in their scabbards, sword-belts and whetstones with them.

Nicholas and Hodge stared. Though no soldiers, they knew what such a number of swords would cost. This one bundle was worth more than a ploughman or shepherd might earn in a whole lifetime. Now they knew what the two knights' nocturnal business in Bristol must have been.

There was a great hand-and-a-half sword, venerable but not so wieldy. And Smith said they would be fighting tight-packed, have no doubt. There were two most beautiful blades, both with richly patterned and gilded bronze hilts.

'Ours,' said Smith.

Finally he drew out a pair of Italian short swords, *cinquedeas*, with plain leathern grips about the hilt.

'These will serve you well enough. The Roman conquered his Empire with swords much like these. You will need to close up on your man to use it, and a shield is essential for that. But a stout thrust at the belly will finish any man.'

The boys took their *cinquedeas* with reverence, and Nicholas immediately began to buckle his about the waist.

'Not now,' said Smith. 'Store it down below, out of the salt. Time enough to flaunt it later.'

Stanley and Smith also had the boys hearing and learning their foreign languages. They would hear half a dozen at Malta. Hodge learnt grumblingly, but well enough when Smith threatened to withhold his rations. Nicholas's French and Latin were already good, and he knew a little Italian. He learnt more now, a few phrases of the difficult Malti tongue, and picked up Spanish too, an easy language and very mellifluous to his ears.

'*Está bien?*' asked Stanley.

'*Sí, es – es una lengua hermosa.*'

'*Es soberbia la hermosura.* Beauty is pride. Or pride is beauty. There is the Spanish soul in essence. Sometimes to your laughing, mocking, red-faced Englishman, Spanish pride will seem like nothing but unbearable arrogance. But it is more to do with honour than self-love. Remember that Spain is a hard country, far harder than gentle green England. Spain was born under a hard sun, out of seven hundred years of war against the Mohammedan, and every inch of sun-baked Spanish earth was bought with Spanish blood – and Spanish pride.'

For five days they sailed calmly south down the thickly wooded coast of Portugal, though moving too slowly for Smith and Stanley's liking. Nicholas felt a growing excitement. Who would have believed, when he lay shackled as a vagrant in that stinking pound only a few weeks before, or slept shivering in freezing barns with his orphan sisters, that he would soon be sailing south to war with two Knights of St John?

As for Hodge, he seemed to look out impervious on every coast they passed, and Nicholas knew he was already homesick.

'Don't be downcast, Hodge. You will look on the green hills of Shropshire again, I promise. I dream of it too – and my family. What remains of it.'

Hodge remained gloomy. 'Foreign parts don't suit all of us.'

'And imagine the tales you will have to tell over your ale down at the Woolpack.'

'Ale,' whispered Hodge longingly. 'Shropshire ale.'

Smith too stared out gloomily from the bow at the calm seas, the gentle wind only just filling the sails. The shadow of the mast on the sea like a mocking sundial, ever moving. His brothers at Malta, steadfastly waiting. The numberless Turk coming on.

Stanley nodded over at him. 'My brother knight is of a tragic disposition,' he said jovially.

He spoke loudly enough for Smith to hear. The gloomy knight's back stiffened.

'But then he has much to feel melancholy about,' Stanley went on. 'His unfortunate visage, for instance. And he was once disappointed in love, when the jade ran off with another. Very fair she was too. Rather long in the face, perhaps – but lovely long legs, a rich auburn mane, huge brown eyes like honey. Altogether the prettiest horse you ever saw.'

Smith turned and snarled over his shoulder.

'And you, Master Hodgkin. Do you pine for your native land because you left a sweetheart behind?'

'No,' said Hodge shortly. 'I'd just rather bide there, is all.'

'Ah, but the world has grown vastly of late.' Stanley looked out over the western sea with that faraway expression of his, eyes half closed. 'And whole new continents yet to be found, some say. The fabled antipodes, islands in the Pacific Ocean. Such travellers' tales.'

'Have you travelled much, then?' asked Nicholas.

Stanley twisted back suddenly, half hanging from a rope, eyes dancing. 'Have we? My brother knight and I, have we not sailed the known world in our time? Were we there when the Great Mughal rode into the battle on a mighty elephant dressed in scarlet silk? Have we seen the caravans pass in the shade of the palms of Mysore? Have we ascended the High Kashmirs? Have we wandered the bazaars of Bengal, seen Circassian slave girls as white as ermine pelts? Have we seen fiery macaws in the Island of Serendip, and the wooden houses of Yeddo among the Japanese lakes? Smoked Chinese opium in gold and jade pipes?'

Nicholas's eyes roved over Stanley's travel-stained clothes, his battered boots, his distant gaze formed by far horizons. He shivered. What kind of Knight of St John was he?

'Have we not raided the shallow inlets of the desert Libyan coast, and spun yarns of it for our supper in the city squares of Bohemia, people throwing silver pieces into our begging bowls? Have we not crossed over the high pine-clad mountains in the depths of a snowbound December, to fight in the hard-pressed marches of Hungary? And have we not seen the very flower of Hungarian chivalry fall beneath the curved blade of the Ottoman? Seen Christian skulls whitening on the great Hungarian plain? For Suleiman was there too. And will come again.

'Have we not gazed upon the ruins of Antioch, of Heliopolis, and the wondrous pagan temples of Isfahan? Slipped unseen through the Straits of Bab-el-Mandeb, beneath the bright Arabian moon? Breathed in the sweet odours of the frankincense trees of the Yemen? Walked in thick furs along the banks of the frozen Moskva, set eyes on the Czar of all the Russias himself, whom they call Ivan the Terrible? Perhaps we have even sailed the Atlantic, and seen the wild jungles of the Americas – they are only a month's sailing away! Hummingbirds and volcanoes, conquistadors in the deep green forest, the snowcapped mountains of the Andes. Did we fight alongside Pizarro and that terrible General Carbajal, still fighting in the saddle at eighty? When they finally hanged him, he went to his death with all his satanic pride and ferocity intact, disdaining to ask for pardon. *They can but kill me*, he sneered.'

Stanley shook his head softly. '*They can but kill me.* Now there's a motto for a man.' He fixed his wide-eyed gaze on the two boys. 'A *grave* maxim. And one to remember when we come into Malta.'

The boys pondered.

Then Stanley grinned his teasing grin once more. 'Were we sent by our Grand Master, La Valette, to league with the wild tribesmen of Daghestan against the Ottoman columns? Did they nickname us Blackbeard and Inglitz? Did we escape through the midnight streets of Trebizond from an evil Turkish jail, the manacles still on our wrists? Were we were there at the siege of Nakhichevan, when the monstrous Ottoman basilisks roared against the armies of the Qizilbashi in their red hats? Did we sail through the Straits of Hormuz, were we there at the siege of Surat on the spice-laden Malabar coast?

'The wind is blowing in the sails, boys. The horses' hooves are stamping, and a myriad new worlds wait to be discovered. The green hills of Shropshire are as lovely as May, and a man should know and love his native ground. But beyond the far horizon ... *aah* ...'

'What tripe he talks,' said Smith, stumping past to relieve himself over the stern. Yet as he passed by, he shot his comrade-in-arms
what looked like a warning glance. As if to say, *Hold your tongue,
brother knight. You talk too much.*

Then Stanley fell silent.

The master of the *Swan* was still adamant that he'd not go east
beyond Cadiz.

'Malta I know not,' he said stubbornly.

'Sardinia, then. You know Sardinia. You might pick up a fine
cargo of sweet wine there, much cheaper than in Spain, and yet sell
it back in Bristol for Spanish prices nonetheless.'

The master pondered Stanley's business advice. At last he said,
'Cadiz for fresh water and the best price for our cloth. Then
Sardinia, for four hundred florins more, or a hundred ducats.'

'A hundred ducats!' Stanley laughed. 'Twenty.'

'Eighty.'

'Ten.'

The master scowled. 'You mock me. That's no bargaining.'

Stanley hadn't time to bargain. He stood. 'Listen to me, man.
We sail to Malta to fight a Christian crusade against an invader
who will devastate all of Europe if he triumphs. One day he will
come to Bristol too. This gold coin in my wallet is to buy men and
weapons to fight him, not to pay you for your services. You take
us to Sardinia, and you will earn yourself twenty gold ducats, no
more, and the knowledge that you have done God's will.'

At last, the captain sullenly held out his hand. Stanley counted
out the heavy Spanish ducats.

It was common knowledge that you could not argue with a master on his ship, Emperor of his little wooden domain amid the sea's
boundlessness. Evidently, it was common knowledge that Stanley
did not have.

13

They rounded Cape St Vincent, passed by a flat, marshy coast to the north, the sky filled with elegant white seabirds, and finally into a great harbour, backed by an ancient city, gleaming white and pleasantly crumbling.

'You are now nearer the sun in his zenith than the north coast of Africa,' said Stanley. Hodge looked very uncomfortable. 'Mind your drink is clean and never go hatless, or your wits will fry in your skull. And this –' he held is arms wide – 'is the most ancient sea city of Cadiz, founded by the Phoenicians, three thousand years ago.'

'We're in Spain?' said Hodge disbelievingly, gazing round the harbour tight-packed with jostling boats and many coloured sails, a babel of barefoot seamen shouting, loading and unloading sardines and olives and wool. 'Will they treat us well? Are we English not enemies?'

The mariners were already lugging the bales of broadcloth up from the hold onto deck.

'*Negotium omnia vincit,*' said Stanley dryly. 'Trade conquers all.'

'Two hours,' said the master. 'Enough for us to make our sale to the Jew dealers, and take on water. We sail again before sundown.'

A crowd of fellows were drinking watered Jerez wine in the shade of a thatched and open-fronted quayside bodega.

Smith glanced back at the two boys following them and murmured, 'Practice is one thing. They need a real brawl, if they are not to shit and run at the first sight of the Turk.'

'Here's one,' said Stanley, nodding his head in the direction of a talkative drinker seated on a stool surrounded by listeners. The knights called for four cups of sweet wine and hot water and sat on a bench just out of the sun.

The drinker and braggard was bedecked in outlandish attire, plumes and silver bracelets and a necklace of shark's teeth along with his unbuttoned shirt and ridiculous wide galligaskins, to make it known he had travelled much in foreign parts. His listeners, hard sunburnt sailors all, listened to him nevertheless, some grinning, some agog.

Smith's great fist tightened round his wooden wine cup. The fellow spoke Andaluz Spanish, but his accent was French.

'What's he say?' asked Hodge, taking a sip of wine. Nicholas had already drained his and was calling for another. The pretty young barmaid was getting prettier with every cup. Her dark eyes flashed and glittered in the dark of the wineshop.

Stanley translated.

'He commends Russian wine and Cretan bread above all others. He says English beef is nothing, you should taste the roasted snake they eat in China, where he says manners are so much finer too. The Emperor is a personal friend of his. He says the moon gives off a burning white heat near the tops of the mountains at the equator, and fills half the sky. He says in the far north, men live in houses of ice, share their wives freely with strangers, and coat themselves with bear-fat instead of clothes. He says he has met a great hairy man whose beard nested birds, and gathered hogsheads of orient pearls from shallow lagoons in the tropics, in water as warm as a bath. There, naked maidens disport themselves wearing nothing but garlands of flowers about their pretty tawny throats, begging passing sailors to dally with them.'

'If there's one thing I cannot abide,' said Smith, looking meaningfully at Stanley, 'it's a fellow who brags about his foreign travels.'

The traveller tossed back another cup of wine in a single gulp. Nicholas did likewise. It was manly.

'Señorita!' he called.

She came over with a leather jug, her slim hips swaying. He held his cup out. She looked at him.

'Please,' he said. *Por favor.*

The girl arched her fine black eyebrows at Nicholas with just a hint of amusement, and then refilled his cup.

'*A borracho fino, primero agua y luego vino,*' she said as she turned away. For a fine drunkenness, first water and then wine.

'What did she say?' asked Nicholas.

'A compliment,' said Stanley. 'A saucy compliment indeed.'

Nicholas grinned goofily.

The great French traveller was telling of the island of Madagastat off Africa, ruled by Mohammedans as black as devils. On another island, mermaids and tritons swum inland and slept in the treetops at night, and there were owls the size of horses, and dragons with feathers as long as a cannon royal, and mouths like a castle gateway. There he had raked up carbuncles beneath the palm trees, diamonds and amethysts, and carried them home in sacks to his beautiful wife, the daughter of a duke.

'All this,' said Smith, 'from a fat braggard who never stirred beyond the stinking backstreets of Paris, except to cheat a few simple Spanish sailors for his dinner.'

'And before you know it,' said Stanley, 'your hand has bunched itself into a fist and punched the windy fool off his stool, sprawling on the flagstones, with blood pouring from his nose now flatter than an Ethiop's.'

'At which he says,' added Smith, his voice rising, 'why, manners are far superior to this in China! Then everyone in the tavern joins in belabouring him and tossing him over the quayside into the brine, wishing him hearty Godspeed back to China, and give the Emperor there a kick in the Netherlands for us!'

Nicholas laughed and stood a little unsteadily. He had taken too little water, as the barmaid had observed, and the strong sweet Jerez wine had already warmed his empty stomach and young head.

'I need to piss,' he said. 'All this traveller's talk has gone to my bladder.'

He made his way carefully outside.

Stanley just managed to catch the braggard's eye at that moment. He shook his head apologetically, murmured something, and gestured outside at Nicholas.

The braggard stopped talking and frowned. The crowd of drinkers about him fell abruptly silent and stared round. The braggard stood up. He was a good height and of useful build, full-bellied but broad-shouldered, his lantern jaw finished with a neatly pointed beard. He pushed one or two men aside, staring directly at Stanley. Then he came over, hand on his sword hilt.

'*Qu'est-ce qu'il a dit?*' snapped the great traveller.

Stanley replied in French, 'You didn't hear?'

The traveller shook his head impatiently.

'Oh, it was nothing,' said Stanley, looking beseechingly up at him. 'Really, nothing. I mean, not so terrible as it sounds.'

'*Qu-est-ce qu'il a dit?*' demanded the braggard violently, slamming his hand down on the table. Smith and Stanley both quailed abjectly before him. Nothing like fear to encourage a bully.

'He said,' Stanley murmured sorrowfully. 'My profoundest apologies for the discourtesy of my passing acquaintance out there, but ... he is young, and a little drunk.'

Nicholas was weaving his way back from the quayside, grinning foolishly, thinking of the lovely young barmaid.

The Frenchman drew his sword a few inches from the scabbard.

'He said, he said,' babbled Stanley in a high-pitched, whimpering voice, he and Smith both rising from the bench. 'He said, oh *mon Dieu*, he said ... that your mother was a filthy French whore, and you yourself were nothing but a fart-filled son of Sodom.'

With a great roar the Frenchman seized the edge of the table and overturned it. Nicholas halted and stared. Hodge remained seated, looking bewildered, Stanley and Smith both vanished abruptly, and there was the great traveller panting and staring at him with a very angry look in his eye.

'What?' said Nicholas. 'Wha—'

Racing up the cobbled side street, Stanley and Smith passed by three fellows talking French, and immediately accosted them.

'*Votre ami est là, dans la bodega là-bas?*'

'*Matthieu, oui, qu'est-ce qu'il y a?*'

'*Vite, vite! Une bagarre!*'

'*Et un salaud Anglais!*'

'*Ah, merde, allons-y!*' roared the Frenchmen, breaking into a run. '*A bas les Anglais!*'

'Four against two,' said Stanley thoughtfully, looking after them. 'I think that's fair.'

'Very fair,' said Smith. 'Very fair indeed.'

'Two minutes?'

'Five minutes. Time for a drink.'

'A celebratory potation. Excellent.'

Thumps, crashes and yells could be heard from the tavern below. Something burst suddenly through the thatch roof. A table leg, perhaps.

'A shame to pick on the fellow, in some ways,' said Stanley.

'Well,' said Smith. 'He *was* French.'

Coming down to the cobbled quayside again, Smith nudged Stanley. He looked along towards the town. Walking away from them was a slow quartet, arm in arm. Two had rough bandages round their heads, another's arm hung down motionless at his side, and a fourth was using a table leg for a crutch.

'They'll live,' grunted Smith. 'What of our comrades-in-arms?'

The tavern was deserted but for the pretty young barmaid and two forlorn figures, Hodge and Nicholas, sitting silently on a bench. The latter was being tended by the girl, no older than Nicholas himself. He had a badly bruised eye and a long cut across his skull. The girl scowled ferociously at the two troublemakers, and then Hodge was on his feet, shouting at them. He seemed to have suffered little damage.

'How dare you come back here, you pigeon-livered villains! Knights of St John, my arse you are, you're nothing but a couple of born cowards with no more fight in you than a peevish dove!' He was red-faced and bellowing and magnficently unafraid. He stood blocking Smith's way and shoved him angrily in the chest, shouting in his face. Smith stepped back and did not retaliate. This servant boy was a prince among scullions. He could have clapped him on the shoulder, but needed his fists free to block any incoming blows.

'Now get out of this alehouse and back in the shitten gutter with you, you leprous scum-sucking churls, or I'll kick your lubbardly arses from here to Bristol and beyond, so I will! I mean it, you shit-begotten worms! Step back now!'

Hodge's fist flew out hard and straight, and it was only with his best-judged step that Smith evaded it. A moment later he and

Stanley each had an unbreakable grip on Hodge's arms, and pinned him up against the wall. The boy struggled so wildly that they thought he might dislocate his own shoulderbones. Damn it. He was in a devil of a temper. They might have to knock him cold after all, valiant though he was.

'What did I say about never using your fists?' said Smith.

Hodge cursed him obscenely.

Then a voice spoke quietly behind them.

'Set him down.'

And Smith and Stanley each felt a hard jab over their kidneys. They glanced down. The Ingoldsby lad had come behind them and filched both their daggers from their belts simultaneously.

The daggers remained as steady as the voice. 'Do not doubt I mean it. Set him down *now*.'

They set him down.

'Step past 'em, Hodge.'

Hodge came round and stood alongside Nicholas.

Stanley began to turn, but the dagger point thrust so hard into him that he gasped. The lad might even have punctured his flesh through his doublet, damn him and praise him.

'I said do not move,' said Nicholas. 'Talk.'

'If you give us space.'

'I'm not moving, nor are these daggers, till you talk.'

The boy had them pressed so hard against the wooden walls of the tavern that they truly could not move, slide nor turn on him no matter how fast they tried. Their own daggers had them pinned, and the boy's voice was filled with that cold determination which told them not to attempt it. Once before they had got themselves trapped like this, pressed to a wineshop wall by half a dozen daggers, in an old town in Germany. On that memorable occasion, feeling the thin wall sway distinctly, they had both pushed with all their might and collapsed the planks forwards before them, rolling back on their feet in a trice to face their foe, with satisfactory consequences. But that was another time.

Stanley said, 'We caused you to be caught in a fight, it is true. That you might profit by it. We did not believe you would come to serious harm. We did not flee to save our skins, we stayed near. When we come to Malta, you will face far worse skirmishes than this, with a far deadlier foe. Then you will find the lessons of today useful.'

It was a long time before they felt the daggers' points soften.

They turned at last and leaned back against the wall. Stanley was not ashamed to feel his heart beating hard. The boy had truly meant business. He slipped his hand under his doublet and withdrew it. A small spot of blood.

The boy contemptuously dropped the two daggers on the earth floor at their feet and turned his back on them.

Now the knights could see better in the gloom of the tavern. Hodge was dusty and doubtless well-bruised beneath his clothes, but otherwise seemed hale. Nicholas's eye was already bulging like a Cyclops's, and would boast many colours before long. That must have hurt. The cut across his skull looked worse, still leaking blood down over his pale forehead and puffed eye. He also stood unevenly. It had been a serious thing, this brawl. To his dismay, Stanley also saw that the young girl had a short, deep cut on her chin.

'Maid,' he said, and knelt before her. 'Forgive us.'

She eyed him coldly and turned away, wringing out a cloth and then sponging Nicholas's skull again. The boy's face was white.

'On your feet, brother,' said Smith. 'You'll get no forgiveness here today.'

Stanley rose and set upright a fallen table. One leg was loose. He opened his wallet and laid down a handsome gold ducat with a heavy clunk. The girl sneered. She bathed Nicholas's wound one last time, and then pressed a clean linen bandage over it.

She said in Spanish, 'Hold it there. It will heal. You have a noble heart, English soldier.'

Nicholas understood little, though the tone of her voice was sweet and soft.

'Thank you that you came to my rescue then,' she said. 'The Frenchman swung his sword as elegantly as a peasant does his scythe.'

The knights, on the other hand, understood every word. They smiled faintly.

She gave them a withering look. The tone of her voice altered, her eyes burned, and a stream of furious, fearless Spanish flowed from her lovely lips. *Spanish pride,* thought Nicholas.

'As for these two sons of cold-hearted whores, these white-livered slaves and windy pox-ridden shitsacks, they are not worthy to travel with you, nay, not to share a wine cup with you. That they die soon and rot like the offal they are, I spit on them.'

And to illustrate her words, she hawked and spat full in Stanley's face. He wiped it away with his sleeve and bowed.

He looked at Nicholas. 'I think she likes you.'

'More than I like you.'

The boy stood again, still unsteady and white-faced, and not from the sherry wine.

'To Sardinia with us?'

Hodge began to protest, but Nicholas spoke over him.

'Against my better judgement. You villains.'

Hodge helped him limping back to the *Swan of Avon*.

As they drifted away from the quayside with just a foresail to bring them round, there was a girl there on the sea wall watching.

Nicholas held up his hand.

She shielded her eyes against the sun and then raised her other hand. '*Un corazón noble,*' she whispered.

The water widened between them, and the mainsail batted and filled above Nicholas's head. The ship gradually picked up speed. He hesitated too long. She would not hear him. At last he called out, 'What is your name?'

She did not hear or understand.

'*Cual es su nombre, señorita?*' murmured Stanley near him.

More loudly still he shouted, '*Cual es su nombre?*'

'Maria de l'Adoración!' she called back.

Maria of the Adoration.

'Nicholas!' he shouted back. '*Inglés!*'

She nodded, and he thought she was smiling. But it was hard to see over the sparkling water. Then he heard her voice one last time. '*Vaya con Dios, Inglés!*'

It wasn't only his head that ached.

'And he thinks to be a monk,' muttered Smith.

14

After the big swell of the Atlantic, they headed west and nor'west on an easy wind, into the more peaceful waters of the Inland Sea.

'More peaceful?' said Smith, squinting. They were skirting south of the Balearic Islands and Formentera. 'Then what's that ahead? Five, ten points to larboard.'

Stanley saw a long, dark line of rocks, an outlying needle of the island to their left. And almost hidden behind the rocks, he could just make out the low, lean shape of a black-painted hull, dismasted for concealment.

'If that's not a Barbary galley, awaiting us like a wolf,' he whispered, 'then I'm the Queen of Sheba.'

Smith looked him up and down.

'It's a Barbary galley.'

Stanley grinned. 'Does this ship have any guns?'

'One old petrier in the bow,' said Smith.

'A petrier.' Stanley shook his head. A crude stone-thrower. 'Noah had one of those on his Ark.'

They sailed closer to the concealed craft. Even now he could picture the rowing benches below, poorly covered in salt-cracked cowhide. Christian slaves chained and encrusted with sweat and excrement. The whip raised over their backs ready to fall, the drumstick hovering over the drum.

Stanley's blue eyes fixed on the motionless shape ahead of them like a hawk fixed on some unwary pigeon. Then he said, 'Time to charge our muskets, Fra John.'

Nicholas saw the two knights stride back from the prow and

begin preparations with astonishing swiftness and dexterity.

'What is it?'

They spoke not a word to him, to the master, to none. There was no time to explain.

Smith sent Hodge below for his baggages, and quickly unrolled one faded green canvas. He and Stanley turned their backs and strapped on each other's mail jerkins, and buckled on their swords.

'What? Where?' said Nicholas, almost beside himself.

The master aft remained oblivious, even his sea-eyes seeing nothing yet. His crazed passengers were yet again at their games.

Another fine oilcloth with three neat ties was unbundled, and there lay six muskets. Four were plain enough arquebuses, one was a longer weapon, and the sixth a thing of rare beauty. Nicholas whistled.

'That's a fine musket. Can I have a shot?'

'Afterwards, maybe.'

'After *what*?'

Infuriatingly, Stanley just grinned, busily preparing the guns.

'Not a musket,' said Smith, his attention likewise all on the weapons. 'A *jezail*. A Persian word, I believe.'

The jezail was richly inlaid with mother-of-pearl, its deep reddish-brown wood polished to a deep lustre, and with a patterned barrel so fine and long it would have to be rested on a bulwark or prop. It seemed almost too beautiful for use. Yet Smith treated it just the same, swiftly checking the barrel was clean with a prod, driving in a charge of carefully measured gunpowder in a twist of cartridge paper, and then tamping in a perfectly round, smooth sphere of a ball after it. It was a wheellock, not a matchlock. Nicholas had rarely seen one before.

'For a sword,' said Stanley, tapping a spit of serpentine black gunpowder into the pan of an arquebus, 'Toledo steel from Old Spain. For armour, the armourers of Germany cannot be beat. For small daggers, poignards, pistols, along with poisons, assassinations and corruptions of every sort, then of course you will go to Italy. But for a musket of the finest – though it shames me to say it – go east. Beyond the Ottomans. To Persia, or India.'

Nicholas remembered Stanley's account of his supposed travels.

The Great Moghul, and a trumpeting Indian elephant, its mighty ivory tusks raised in battle fury. Is that where John Smith's jezail came from?

Smith held up the long, elegant musket before him in both hands. 'The four-foot barrel is as smooth as slate within. Forged of finest Indian wootz steel. There is no musket to compare with it in all of Europe. Better yet, load it with one of these' – he held out in has hand a few curiously shaped musket balls – 'and you can fire through any armour known to man.'

'What are those?'

'They are called *stuardes*, made by a knavish and counterfeit Scotsman called Robert Stuart, who claims kinship with the Scottish kings. He lies. But he does make these musket balls that pierce armour, which no other man in the world, I believe, has the secret of. If the Knights only knew …'

He pocketed the stuardes carefully, set down the jezail with the muzzle propped up a little, and tossed Nicholas and Hodge a couple of matchcords.

'Get these lit. And guard them with your life. If they go out, you go over the side.'

Nicholas wound furiously at the tinder box.

'Oi!' yelled the master. 'No fire on my ship, not so much as a hot fart!'

Eyes still fixed on the guns before them, cleaning, priming and loading in a blur of speed, Stanley paused only to point an outstretched arm in the direction of the hidden galley. He added not a word of explanation.

The master stared north to the islands, and was heard to hiss, 'Suffering Christ! Man the sails, every man to the ropes! Move, you sons of whores, or your arses will be on a Mohammedan rowing bench by sundown. Move your poxy carcases, God damn you black!'

'If this ship is to be judged on its keeping of the third commandment,' murmured Stanley, working away, 'then we are surely doomed.'

Nicholas too saw the hull, and a moment later heard across the smooth waters the sound of a drum begin to beat out a dreadful, ominous rhythm, and a first muffled crack. The prow nudged forward, and then the black galley eased out from behind the rocks, as lean and lethal as a stiletto dagger. The prow was decorated with an evil eye talisman, and some Arabic lettering.

His blood felt thick and cold.

'Turks!'

'Not Turks, boy,' said Smith. 'Moors. Berbers. The coast of Algiers is but fifty miles south. But they are Mohammedans and unchristened infidels all.'

The sails slapped above them. There wasn't enough wind for flight. The rowing galley, immune to such vagaries, was now turning on its shallow keel and heading straight for them. Half a mile, less. A minute or two and they would be ...

'Bring 'em in!' Smith cried out to the master. 'Our appetites are up!'

'Bring 'em in!' retorted the master angrily. 'What do you mean bring 'em in, they're coming in anyway! There's twenty or thirty Mohammedan cuthroats on that damned galley!'

Smith said, 'Look as if you're fleeing—'

'We *are* fleeing!'

'—but keep your mariners on the end of the rope. The instant they close to, reef up for a fighting sail.'

The master looked as black as a strangled Moor. 'I am the king of this ship, and you, Sir Knight, or the King of all the Russias, are nothing here but damned peasants! You understand?'

Smith only smiled, a somewhat dark and unnerving smile. 'Do as I say. Those corsairs are ours, and their treasure may be yours.'

'Report, boy,' said Stanley. 'How many men?'

Nicholas and Hodge both squinted. The sea sparkled in their eyes. There were many heads, many dark shapes. 'Twenty? Thirty?'

No reply.

'Do we put on our swords?'

'How else were you planning to fight? By slapping them?'

Nicholas and Hodge buckled on their swords, trying to keep their hands from shaking. They had survived a couple of tavern brawls, it was true, the last one a true skirmish. But this was the real thing. Men would die.

'Draw 'em tighter!' cried the master, looking up at the listless sails in desperation. 'Swing her in from the wind! We can get in behind them and make for the islands!'

'No – we – can't,' murmured Stanley in a happy, sing-song voice, busily priming another arquebus.

Nicholas glanced down at him. He was loving this.

Then the two knights were on their feet, swords and daggers about their waists, and six muskets fully served and loaded, laid out on the oilcoth. There was also the biggest pistol Nicholas had ever seen. A petronel: a horse pistol, for putting old nags out of their misery. He wondered what on earth it would do to a man.

'You need a certain strength in your arm to fire the creature,' said Smith with a nod. 'But if you do it right, the effect is considerable. Now: if they've got a cannon, we might get a splash as they close in. You will see that not a drop of water touches the guns. Understand?'

Nicholas nodded.

'And if they fire up a cannon, and you see the sparks fly at the breech, then look where it's pointing and make sure you're not in the way. Remember you can move faster than a cannon on its carriage. But once the ball has left the cannon's mouth, and is coming straight at you – well then, it is too late to move. You will never see it, nor anything else before you see the gates of heaven.'

'But I can't see any cannon.'

The knights scanned the fast-approaching galley. The sea was calm, the sky clear, the sun warm. Good conditions for a shot. And no: no cannon visible. The corsairs would expect to come swiftly alongside this full-bellied, lumbering merchantman, and simply clamber aboard, scimitars whirling. Their usual technique. Some of the Christian dogs would be killed, the rest enslaved, and the cargo of broadcloth their reward in the markets of Algiers.

The master was still swearing furiously at his mariners, urging them to draw on every inch of sail.

'You cannot outrun, them, sir!' called Smith. 'There is not enough wind.'

'We cannot fight the villains either! Have you seen their numbers?'

Smith shrugged. 'We have no choice in the matter. Unless you wish to cry for mercy? I'd save your voice.'

'A good thing it looks like we are struggling to flee,' said Stanley softly. 'They suspect nothing.'

The master stared out over the water.

Now twenty or more corsairs could be clearly seen, eagerly lining the galley's narrow central gangway above the heads of the oar-slaves. They were stripped to the waist, skins every shade from coffee to Ethiop black. Most went shaven-headed – always easier at sea – except for topknots on their crowns, for the angels to pull them up to Paradise on Judgement Day.

Gold torcs and earrings gleamed. So too did scimitars, cutlasses, daggers and pistols. Smith and Stanley had taken up their guns and were crouching down below the bulwarks of the *Swan*. The high-sided little ship with its sterncastle and forecastle was something of a floating fortress, and evened the odds. But damn it, they should have instructed the boys in how to reload an arquebus by now. They never expected to meet corsairs this far out. Hunting so confidently, so close to the coast of Spain, the most powerful of all the Christian kingdoms. A sign of the times.

'When we pass you back our guns,' said Smith, 'you take them swiftly, lay them down there, and pass the next. With the muzzle pointing skywards.'

The boys nodded.

'You keep your heads down, and you keep those slow-matches burning. If you catch one of the swine climbing aboard, prick him while he's still coming up and over. Once he's on deck and it comes to hand-to-hand fighting – then God be with you.'

Nicholas felt cold to the marrow.

In the prow of the corsair galley, arrogant as a young god, stood the captain. A handsome, shaven-headed and moustachioed Moor, with flashing eyes and a ready smile. He wore an incongruous mix of grubby loincloth and startling red satin doublet, unbuttoned, showing his lean chest and hard stomach, twice scarred with deep swordcuts. He'd taken the doublet from a Genoese ship not a week before, the Christian's blood still staining the gold piping. A wealth of gold hung around his neck and arms and dangled from his ears. Corsairs tended not to trust their treasure to banks. Two fine ruby rings gleamed on his little fingers. He'd cut them from the delicate hand of a young Spanish bride, sailing off Valencia last summer. The rings were not all they had taken from her, he and his men. He grinned. Life was sweet.

Though the merchantman had shown no white flag, yet look how she wallowed and struggled on the windless sea. She was as good as finished, a goat in a net, with the lion approaching. He spat and then sucked in the clean sea air, his chest swelling, his heart pounding to the drum, his galley surging along through the small waves, face into the sun. Soon they would have the joy of killing again, the joy of victory, the joy of standing on their enemies' necks. Then the cargo, the cheers of his men, the triumphant return to Algiers. The dirty little whores in the waterfront brothels, and the white clay opium pipe. O, life was sweet.

John Smith and Edward Stanley carefully laid the muzzles of their guns on the top of the bulwarks of the forecastle, moving very slowly so as not to catch a corsair's eye. The galley was two hundred paces off now. One hundred and eighty. One hundred and sixty. Smith squinted down the barrel of his jezail, finger lightly on the trigger.

His target was clear. The corsair captain, standing plain at the prow. But not yet near enough.

The master and mariners had fallen still, waiting in terror. Some clutched boathooks or little-used blades, and Vizard and Legge both held useful-looking halberds. But they had no hope – unless these passengers of theirs proved of sturdier stuff than they seemed. Certainly they knelt now and cradled their fine guns with a steely determination. Yet the enemy were so many. Already they could feel the manacles round their ankles, the oar and the rowing bench grinding the flesh off their bones, and a slow death coming. Why in hell did they agree to sail beyond Cadiz, into these infested waters?

The corsair galley was a hundred paces off. Eighty. Sixty.

Nicholas's heart hammered, and his palms were so sweaty, he wondered how he'd ever keep a grip on his sword. Let it not come to that, he prayed with shame. Not yet. Perhaps they will turn away.

Forty paces off. The mechanical movement of the oars at top speed now, and they could hear the swish of the galley's bow wave from here, see every corsair aboard. The captain in his outlandish attire even grinned, raising his scimitar and waving it as if in greeting.

If only they'd had time to serve and load up the old petrier, that might have come in handy, despite its age. A 'stone thrower', blasting out a rough stone ball from a squat iron barrel, it hadn't much range but at short distances it could do business. And if you struck lucky, and the stone ball hit a piece of metal aboard the enemy ship, an anchor or cleat or even a metal band around a mast, it could splinter into a lethal spray of shards, hurtling in every direction, killing two or three men in an instant, laying low half a dozen more. But there had been no time, and the petrier sat untouched.

Smith breathed slow and steady and pulled the trigger. The steel wheel whirred and sparks flew, there was the powerful report, the smell of burnt gunpowder, a brief puff of dark smoke.

After having knelt so unearthly still, the instant the shot was fired Smith was all activity. Never taking his eyes from the corsair galley ahead of him, he dipped his gun, cleaned it with ramrod, cartridge of powder, ramrod, ball, ramrod, a modicum more powder into the pan, all with perfect smoothness and without once needing to check his actions. He was kneeling up to the bulwark and taking aim again within half a minute.

The galley had slowed and stopped, the oars were still. They could hear the small waves slapping against the sides. It was like a venomous snake that had suddenly had its head lopped off. For Smith's shot had sent the ball clean through the forehead of the corsair captain, and he was dead before he slumped to the deck.

'In truth,' said Smith, sighting down the barrel with a squint, 'I fire a ball like that only one shot in ten.'

'Twenty,' muttered Stanley, also sighting.

Smith grinned. A rarity. 'The curve of the ball from the barrel, even a barrel so beautifully smooth as this. The wind, the fall … But it looks mighty impressive when it works, does it not?'

Beside them, Nicholas felt his throat too dry to speak.

Another corsair, a tall lean fellow, ran forward and fell on the captain's body with a cry.

'Akhee!' he cried. 'Akhee!'

Stanley raised his head again from sighting.

'What does he say?' asked Hodge.

'He says, "*My brother.*"'

'As in my brother corsair, my brother Mohammedan ... or my blood brother?' murmured Smith. 'If the latter – then we may indeed be in for a fight.'

'From his grief,' said Stanley, 'I surmise the latter.'

'What does that mean?' stammered Nicholas.

'It means this is now a blood matter. It means they're not after our cargo. They're after our lives.'

Smith grunted. 'Take him.'

The lean corsair was just looking up again and across the water to the Christian swine, when Stanley pulled the trigger and the matchcord dropped and set the powder sizzling in the pan, and his arquebus erupted with a deafening bang, far louder than Smith's jezail.

The corsair's bare bronzed shoulder seemed to erupt in a spray of blood and he fell back with a cry. Then he stood again with his hand clutched over his wound, blood seeping through his fingers, and screamed back at them, unafraid.

'*Kul khara, kuffaar! Ayeri fi widj imaak!*

'What does he say?' asked Nicholas, whispering for some reason.

'Discourtesies about your mother,' said Stanley. 'You don't want to know. Next gun, lad, and quick about it.'

Smith was just sighting on the corsair to finish him when the rhythm of the drum changed, the oars moved swiftly in opposing directions and with astonishing litheness, the galley spun side-on. The corsairs dropped down below the gangway, out of sight, amid the fetid crush of the rowing benches. The oars moved back again in unison and the galley closed in below the sterncastle at full speed. The galley slaves were being lashed bloody over the last few dozen paces, the prow visibly rearing over the water.

'They're going to ram us!'

'The devil!'

'They've done this before.'

'Then we'll both go down together.'

'Fire!'

There came a terrible crash from below and a groan of timbers, as the bronze-headed ram of the galley tore into the side of the *Swan*. Then the air was filled with warlike screams and cries of *Allahu akbar! Allahu akbar!*

All hell broke loose. Shots erupted from the lean galley below, a mariner howled in pain. It was Vizard, dropping his halberd to the deck and crouching, cradling his wound. The master was shouting out, a pair of landsmen were still reefing up the mainsail as arrows struck the mast. Then at least half a dozen guns from the corsair crew fired in unison, balls tearing in through the bulkheads, holing sails, clanging off a brass stanchion on the deck, followed by a whistling ricochet. Nicholas risked a look, ducked down again. That volley was to clear them back so the corsairs could launch their grappling irons and shin up. The sides of the *Swan* were already swarming. He passed Smith his last loaded gun, Hodge served Stanley, and then they crawled back amidships. They huddled by the foremast, panting as if they'd already fought for an hour, and drew their short cinquedeas.

'For England and St George, eh, Hodge?' said Nicholas, his voice shaking.

'I can't bloody believe this,' said Hodge. 'We were better off in the pound with the lice.'

Smith stood exposed over the bulwarks and fired a sidelong shot, keeping his arquebus straight enough not to roll the ball out of the barrel, and blew a head clean off. But the corsairs had two grappling irons over the waist already. This was going to go hand-to-hand, and vicious. He took up the petronel and raced aft, swinging down the ladder to the waist of the ship without using the rungs, yelling to the terrified mariners to fight, damn them, fight!

'You, man, cut that rope! And you, take up that halberd. Prick 'em in the throat! You, Vizard, with the bloody arm, get it bound below and then back to the fray with you. The walking wounded fight well enough. You, boy, keep watch to starboard in case any rats swim round that way. There, man! Take him!'

Stanley also let loose his final arquebus, moving along the deck and leaning, firing – there came a scream and splash from below – then moving on again instantly, so there was no chance for enemy fire to be accurately returned. An arrow lodged in the rail near him. He drew his sword and hacked it off with a grand flourish.

A curved grapnel. Stanley seized it from the air in a huge hand and hacked until the leader frayed and split, the fellow below knocked back under a coiling cascade of rope. Stanley leaned down and caught another villain across the side of the head with the iron, then finished him with a short jab to the throat. An arrow glanced off his mailcoat and he dropped back behind the bulwark, taking in a sharp breath and resettling his helmet. That was close.

Nicholas had gone to help Vizard with his one serviceable arm to slither down the ladder to below decks. At the hatchway he felt a sudden dread and heard the weakened mariner gasp. He turned and there close behind him was a corsair, a black fellow twice his weight, scimitar gripped in a bulging fist, its blade already bloodied. His breeches dripped saltwater. Vizard gave a low groan and pulled free from the boy, kneeling exhausted in the hatchway.

'Run for your life, lad. Over the side.'

The corsair's teeth were white with a smile.

Every other man aboard was in caught in the mêlée, and Nicholas was alone. Over by the starboard rail lay the young landsman who'd been keeping starboard lookout, his head half cut from his neck.

Nicholas was pinned up against the sterncastle, hatch behind him, a wounded man at his feet. If he moved away, the corsair would finish Vizard. If he stayed, he would be trapped.

He gripped his cinquedea, stepped from one foot to the other. The corsair had killed over a hundred men, this was nothing to him. He waited. The fight raged behind him. Then he swung his scimitar swift and low to open up the boy's guts, giving him no room. But the boy dropped right down on his belly like a snake, fast like the young can, and was up again. The scimitar came back in a trice, lower this time, and Nicholas clutched at a brace and vaulted over it. Then he stepped away. The corsair turned with him, dark eyes fixed. This Christian was as hard to catch as an eel. He'd have to chop the wounded one after.

He made two cuts, one feint and one real. The boy moved wrongly, the second cut would have finished him, but an oar jammed down on the deck and blocked him. His blade stuck fast in it. He cursed. It was the wounded mariner, fighting one-armed with a short oar seized from the ship's longboat. He kicked out at the oar and freed his blade and cut down hard on the mariner's head, but the white-faced *kufr* backed up enough to miss it. Now the corsair was angry. They were humiliating him.

He sped up, moving much faster on the eel-boy. The boy tripped backwards and sprawled on the deck and he had him. No fancy wide sweeps now. He jabbed down hard with his scimitar's broad point to end it. It struck only wooden deck and the boy was rolling onto his feet again. Shaitan and Baalbub, these two would suffer for this.

Nicholas snatched off Vizard's felt cap, and the corsair hesitated for the blink of a bird's eye. What the devil? Then the cap flew and hit him in the face, he closed his eyes and turned his face instinctively, though it was but a bit of felt, and when he had mastered himself again, the boy's blade was deep in his side. He roared and twisted, but the boy managed to keep a hold of his blade, stuck between his ribs though it was, and pulled it free. Blood gushed down his side. From the corner of his eye he saw the wounded sailor with the oar moving behind him. So he would be killed by a beardless eel-boy and a half-finished mariner, filthy infidels both, porkmeat still stuck between their teeth. He swung again wildly, roaring, blood on his lips.

Nicholas snatched the oar from the tottering Vizard and jabbed it hard in the corsair's chest. He staggered backwards and suddenly knelt. That wound in his side was telling, his strength was gone. Nicholas stepped close, eye on the scimitar all the time, but it lay loose in the giant blackamoor's hand, and thrust his cinquedea straight into the fellow's muscular throat. He pulled it out, hot blood flooding over his hand, and the giant fell forward, his forehead thumping down on the deck with a bony clunk.

There was no one else now, there was just Nicholas and his short sword and the oar useful in his left hand, more corsairs coming at him. Vizard scuttling back to the hatchway, leaning to one side like a hunchback, and more killing to be done. He felt very cold and clear and moved very fast, never stopping. There was another corsair, dripping with the sea, and his scimitar seemed to move like a falcon's wing. The boy blocked it with the oar but the corsair moved just as fast. The instant his blow was blocked he switched his blade back and spun fancy on his heel in a wide swipe at the boy's other flank. Not fast enough. Nicholas stepped back and clouted him with the oar, not very hard. The corsair grunted.

In that fleeting moment – the moment that always comes if you wait for it, when your enemy can do nothing but struggle for breath and a clear head, and is exposed – in that one precious speck of time, you must kill them. The bloody cinquedea drove forward hard into the corsair's guts and he gave a horrible gurgling scream. His body fell far forward and Nicholas lost his grip on his buried sword. The dead man fell on top of it.

He stepped back, his arm coated with gore to the elbow.

He moved mechanically now, in a dream without emotion. Others moved around him watchfully, but they seemed to him to move quite slowly. At one point, beyond them, he saw Stanley surrounded by Moors, looking over in his direction, blue eyes wide.

Two more corsairs came. Never taking his eyes off them, he rolled the dead man off his blade with his foot and scooped it up and flicked the blood off it at his attackers. It flecked their faces, they spat. One cursed. What the devil was that?

Nicholas grinned. He felt the evil of it, the wide grin, the blood coating him. The corsairs circled, hesitant. A blood-fevered grinning madman here.

They caught him between them and a scimitar swept across his back and cut him open. It was nothing. He brought up his sword short in a fierce lightning jab when he should have been trying to save himself from the cut, and the unexpected strike went straight through the fellow's forearm, between one bone and the other. The corsair bellowed and snatched back his arm, and Nicholas held onto his sword tight this time. He was learning. He flailed the oar, the two gave him space, the first fellow's arm coursed with blood.

His ears were full of noise, of screams and explosions, yet they were very distant. In the foreground of his hearing was nothing but cold, murderous silence and slow time. He caught the second corsair an unexpected blow on the back of his head with the short end of the oar swiftly wielded, the fellow lurched forward, and ruthlessly Nicholas hit him again, and again, until his skull opened, bones splintering under the oar's weight. The corsair's eyes rolled up to the whites but he still stood, so Nicholas slipped near and then past him in a single move as smooth as a dancer, drawing his sword hard across the fellow's throat as he went. His throat gaped open like an obscene mouth and he slumped down.

The second corsair began to back away jabbering, glancing over his shoulder, then turned and dashed for the ladder up to the sterncastle. A third was behind him.

Almost without noticing him, certainly not thinking now, Nicholas spun and sent him reeling with the long end of his oar, the short end jammed tight under his arm. The fellow slipped and sprawled. Nicholas turned back and tripped the fleeing corsair at the foot of the short ladder, turned back on the first one and struck him once as he knelt up again, clean through his right arm. The fellow remained kneeling before him as if in prayer, or like a heifer about to be poleaxed, and with a third blow he struck into his neck. The fellow's head hung forward and he toppled sideways. Then he was standing over the corsair who had tripped, driving his sword hard down into his back, feeling the blade grating against his spine. The corsair spasmed crazily, arms out wide, slapping the deck, then Nicholas finished him with another stab in the back of the neck.

He stepped back. There was blood in his eyes, he didn't know whose. He wiped it away with his left sleeve as best he could. His right sleeve was drenched and sticky.

The gunfire dropped off, the fighting was done.

Stanley and Smith were staring over at him, panting, swords drooping.

Nicholas was breathing hard but felt calm.

Vizard too had appeared in the hatchway, arm in a rough sling, and was staring at him, with a look in his eyes almost like fear.

Stanley came slowly over.

'You killed five men,' he said quietly, his voice a strained mix of disbelief and admiration.

Nicholas could think of nothing to say. Then he said, 'They were trying to kill me.' He looked about. 'Where's Hodge?'

'How much blood is yours?'

'Just my back, I think. Where's Hodge?'

'Down below. He took a blow to the skull, but it's a thick Shropshire skull. He'll live. Though he'll probably wake thinking he's a Frenchman.'

'I doubt it.'

Stanley raised Nicholas's shirt with the point of his sword and clucked. 'A scratch. That constable's whip back in England made a deeper impression.' He dropped his shirt again. 'Truly your only injury?'

Nicholas frowned and felt about. 'Truly, yes.'

Again a look in the knight's eyes. Then he said, 'Find a clean shirt. We all need a cleansing today.'

15

The corsair captain and eleven of his men were dead. The captain's brother still lived, his shoulder wound roughly staunched.

Of their own, Stanley and Smith had taken a good few cuts and bruises, none to kill them. Smith's left ear was sliced so a portion hung down and flapped when he turned his head.

'Like a spaniel,' said Stanley.

Smith showed his teeth, rimmed with blood. 'Get your needle and horsehair out, mother dear.'

Eight corsairs still lived, variously wounded, in an abject state. They stood huddled on the slathered, bullet-pocked deck of the listing *Swan*, chained hand and foot. The mariners treated them cruelly as they chained them, stripping them of what gold and silver they wore. The tables were turned, the sun was smiling, and these Mohammedan dogs were theirs now. They would fetch a fair price in the slave market back at Cadiz.

One of the dogs muttered a curse in guttural Arabic. Faster than the eye could see, Smith's mighty fist shot out and hit the fellow's face like a battering ram. His head jerked back, blood spraying out in a circle from his flattened nose, and he slumped to the deck unconscious. The other corsairs bunched closer together, like nervous cattle, eyeing this glowerng blackbeard of a Christian.

'I thought you said never to use your fist,' said Nicholas dryly.

Smith's hammer-fist appeared unharmed. 'Quite so. But there was no time for otherwise. Besides, you did not understand what this one said.' He looked down at the battered fool. 'He may insult me, but not my Saviour.'

'You understand Arabic?'

'And speaks it,' said Stanley. 'As fluent as the Prophet himself, no peace be upon him. There was plenty of time to learn on the galley.'

'You were on a *galley?*'

Smith said nothing.

Stanley shook his head. 'Ask no more, lad,' he said softly. 'Only a barrel of troubles that way lies. None but a madman would reminisce about his time as a galley slave.'

Hodge came back on deck, barely able to speak, and desperate for water. His head was thickly bandaged. Nicholas greeted him with a bear hug and then stood back a little embarrassed.

'Well, Hodge?'

Hodge touched the side of his head gingerly. 'Unwell, Master Ingoldsby. Very unwell, in truth.'

'What is four times four?' asked Stanley.

'Sixteen.'

'Her Majesty's mother?'

'The Boleyn hussy.'

'What nickname did our Lord give to James and John?'

'The Sons of Thunder,' said Hodge.

'James and John *Boanerges*,' said Stanley, nodding. He clapped Nicholas and Hodge on their shoulders as they stood side by side. 'The Sons of Thunder.'

Hodge looked awkward, Nicholas proud.

'You fought valiant well, Master Hodgkin. You took a knock to the sconce, but I saw you deliver one heftier still that sent your fellow back into the brine like a dead duck.'

'I only hit him so you'd not call me Matilda again.'

The fair haired knight grinned. 'That I'll not. Well, not often.'

Vizard's arm was broken, but the flesh not cut nor ruptured. It should mend with a bit of splinting. The lookout landsman was dead, and a page had been beaten to death by three of the corsairs before being tipped over the side. His body was lost. The master himself had been shot in the hand, a minor wound, but pure agony. Smith went to him and did what he could with some oily stuff and some brandy. The master said, Couldn't he bind up his own ear first? He was dripping on him, and the sight was making him nauseous, and both men managed a bitter laugh then.

'I don't know whether to curse you for driving us on east of Cadiz, and into all this mayhem,' said the master, 'or show gratitude that you saved us.'

'You and your men stood by us,' said Smith. 'You did sufficient well, for mariners. Now here comes a measure of brandy. This'll hurt.'

The corsair dead were stripped of their bracelets and armlets, earrings and torcs, and rolled over the side with a splash. Then Stanley had the captain's brother lowered back onto the corsair galley and climbed down after him.

The smell that arose from the rowing benches was indescribable. The cramped wretches looked up from their filthy hold, many not with elation but with desolation and despair. Though they were about to be rescued, they showed nothing, no life at all. Some had been chained to the bench for so many days and nights, seen so many horrors, that to have freedom given them now was almost more than they could bear.

Stanley spoke to them one by one, hand laid on encrusted, sinewy shoulders. Some were naked but for a rag tied over their heads against the sun. The sores on their hands were abominable, the sores on their buttocks when they stood would be far worse. Some kept their heads bowed, not rejoicing, their faces lost in a mass of tangled hair and beard, eyes staring out like animals caught in a snare. Some greeted Stanley, some showed hope, but some had gone beyond that into madness. They had gone long ago into their own solitary worlds to survive, and now they could not re-emerge from that other world, nor ever again return to the everyday. They were galley-mad.

Behind the rearmost benches, almost hidden under the prow deck, were two emaciated boys of perhaps eight and ten. Too small to row, they had been simply chained there until the corsair galley should reach the next slave market. As Stanley squeezed his way in there, one of the rowers turned round and groaned.

One boy still sat, head bowed. The other lay on his side, so thin that his pelvic bone, his ribs and his arms showed like sticks of barkless ash.

Then Stanley understood that the younger one was dead. The older boy had sat chained to his dead brother for who knew how long.

He had the captive corsair unchain them all at swordpoint, rowers and boys, and then the boys' father, the rower who had groaned, crawled back and lifted up his dead son. The smell of decomposition was impossible to tell apart from the stench of the rowing deck.

'My daughter also,' wept the man as he looked down at his dead son, 'my daughter. What they did to her. She was but a year older ...'

Stanley laid his hand on the older boy's head and said gently, 'Your son.'

Under the rear deck was the captain's chest. Its contents were meagre, but included a silver crucifix. Stanley raised it to his lips and kissed it, as if to cleanse it of the filth around him, and of the unchristened hands that had stolen it from some sad isolated church or chapel. Some poor fishing village on the coast of Calabria or Sardinia, this silver crucifix all the wealth of a village now burned to the ground, its priest lying slaughtered on the church doorstep.

The rowing slaves were filed out, the sores on their backsides horrendous, the size of saucers, limping and bent double. But their hated oars, thirty foot long, were useless as crutches. They were carefully helped across and painfully raised up onto the deck of the *Swan*, along with the dead boy. Nicholas thought one or two might die at any moment. He grasped one rake-thin rower and the sun-dried skin slid loosely over the bones of his arms like an old woman's. Nicholas had a dread that if he pulled too hard, the arm might come off. These were the walking dead.

Then the captain's chest.

'This goes with us to Malta!' Stanley called up. 'Your reward is the infidels!'

The master nodded down.

Lastly he took a short manacle and snapped it closed on the wrists of the dead captain's brother. The man stared wide-eyed. He was tied to the mast housing with a rope rowlock, thick as his arm. He began to plead, but Stanley silenced him.

'You stay here. With your beloved galley.'

Then he called up to the *Swan* again, and soon they tossed him down a hatchet.

The captive began his prayers to Allah.

On the deck of the *Swan*, one of the rowers, not so near death's door as he seemed, suddenly swung his oar end at one of the chained corsairs. The man's head shot forward and blood spurted from his skull. Smith restrained the jabbering rower. He was half insane, eyes rolling, chewing his lip. The corsair had slumped down, dark red seeping over the deck, legs twitching. His fellows regarded him in silence. No point in pleading for mercy they had never shown.

Stanley knelt in the stern of the empty galley and dug out a strip of caulking rope from the hull timbers. The captive corsair twisted round to watch him work. Then he drove the hatchet into the seasoned hardwood with all his strength. After a dozen blows the wood was well split, and then a ragged medallion came loose. He tore it away. The wood below was thin now, dark with seawater. He aimed and delivered another blow with the neat blade, and a trickle of water seeped in. He struck once, twice more, and the trickle became a surge. He stayed kneeling, hacking and hacking. The noise of the water grew.

He stood and watched.

Someone called his name. 'Get off the boat, man!'

The water flowed strongly around his ankles. From his manacled captive came Berber and Arabic cries. The sea was rushing in now, pushing aside the nailed timbers of the creaking, weakened hull, collapsing like an arched bridge that had lost its coping stone. The sea was reclaiming its own.

There were more cries from above, but Stanley stayed watching the dark waters around his thighs a while longer, aboard the dying galley. How sweet it would be to die and go to bliss.

Finally he shook himself back to life, and bounded onto the prow deck, seizing the rope, planting the soles of his boots on the side of the *Swan* and walking up. He glanced back once at the manacled corsair.

'*Allah al-Qady,*' he said. Allah will be the judge.

The weight of the water in the stern of the galley raised up the prow, as Stanley had intended, and below, the mariners were able to push the evil brass beak of the ram free of the *Swan*'s hull at last, hurriedly wadding up the gash as best they could with swags of oiled wool and some hurriedly nailed planking. But they could not pump or bail her as fast as she was taking on water. They began to move the ballast and cargo to the starboard side. But they would have to limp in to an island bay for repairs.

The deck of the galley sloped back steeply now. The captive stood on the steep planking with knees bent, his lips moving furiously in prayer. His eyes were fixed on the Christians above him. Prayers and verses from the Koran, or ancient curses.

The sea rose higher up the deck. There was a deep, ominous groan from under water. The sea rose and surged around the corsair's bare shanks, over his knees, his thighs. He would not scream or cry out. Such men had hearts of stone for themselves as much as others. Let death come. Reach down from the golden walls of Paradise. Come, Lord Azrael, angel of death in thy midnight cloak ...

The galley gave a last tortured creak, and then very quickly and quietly slipped beneath the waves. A few small bubbles rose, nothing more.

'My Christ,' gasped Nicholas, suddenly choked.

Stanley turned around just in time to see one of the captive corsairs, the skinny one last on, dropping like stone off the side of the ship into the water, a red tide round his throat.

The master swiftly wiped his dagger on his breeches and returned it to the sheath on his belt.

Stanley closed his eyes.

'What did he do?' asked Nicholas desperately.

'Nothing,' said Stanley. He shook his head. 'He did nothing. That was a warning to the others, that's all. Not to rebel. It is sometimes done.'

Nicholas was all confusion. He had killed his first man himself, and his second and more, but that was in battle. Stanley himself had drowned a captive, and now the master had cut another's throat like he was a rat. Surely after the frenzied violence of the galley's attack, now there should be peace? But the violence went on.

What kind of burning hell was this inland sea?

Stanley saw his confusion.

'Bid welcome to the Mediterranean, the heart of the world between Christendom and Islam. Two worlds divided. The Mohammedans themselves divide the world into Dar al Islam and Dar al Harb: the House of Islam and the House of War. Though their faith is but devil-worship, and their Koran but the garbled, misshapen spawn of the Holy Scripture, yet they are right about this at least. The world *is* truly divided between Islam and War. Christendom will forever be the House of War to them, the house of opposition. That role is thrust upon us. What can we do but fight? This one sordid killing' – he indicated where the wretched corsair had fallen – 'is only a drop of blood in this sea.

'And the Mediterranean is a saltwater battle-line. Across this battle-line go atrocity and hatred and treachery ceaselessly, like spies in the night. It has been this way for a thousand years. It will be this way a thousand more, till Christ come again. You are right to feel sorry for it, lad. It is only Christian to do so. But the Mohammedan does not feel sorry for it. It is not his way. This is as it was appointed to be in his bloody scriptures. Welcome to the House of War.'

The *Swan* turned and sailed slowly and carefully into a shallow bay on the leeward coast of Formentera. Her shifted ballast and cargo and the westerly wind in her mainsail kept her keeled hard over for the most part, the hole in her larboard hull just above the water line. It was cunning sailing.

'We can make her fast enough here,' said the master. 'But then it's back to Cadiz, pumping all the way.'

'You have won yourself the value of those corsairs,' snapped Smith. 'That is more pay for our passage. Mend the hull, and then on to Sardinia and Sicily.'

'No. She needs a refit. Even here it will take three or four days.'

'We don't have three or four days.'

'Then take another ship.'

'There are no other ships, and you've been paid to Sardinia.'

The master looked uncertain, caught between a pragmatic seaman's wish to mend his ship well, and a grudging respect for these landsmen, who'd fought so hard and saved him and his mariners from the Mohammedan rowing bench.

'Two days then.'

'One day.'

'It can't be done in a day,' said Jackson, the ship's carpenter.

'A day and a night,' said Smith. 'Work by moonlight and lantern light. And work fast.'

'I say it can't be done.'

'There's half the corsairs' treasure in it for you.'

The master rubbed his stubbled chin.

'So now can it be done?'

'We'll work at it.'

They went ashore meanwhile and buried the landsman with a cross of sticks at his head, and also the dead boy from the galley. They left his father weeping beside the shallow grave, knees in the dust.

Hodge and Nicholas shared a hunk of barley bread. The sun was beginning to sink and lose its heat. Hodge broke off the corner of the bread where Nicholas had been holding it, as if to throw it away. As if it was bloodstained. Nicholas saw him do it. Hodge slowly put it in his mouth and chewed.

Nicholas walked out over the headland for some peace, and to daydream of a certain barmaid back in Cadiz. There was a goatherd boy sitting on a rock, wearing a goatskin and a felt cap, holding a crook. He must have been eleven or twelve. He stood and saluted Nicholas. He had seen the fight at sea.

The boy's native tongue was Catalan, but they spoke in crude Spanish, the goat-boy understanding a few French words too. Nicholas tore off some barley bread for him. The boy ate ravenously.

'Do you know Malta?' Nicholas asked him. 'War there? Guns?'

The boy shook his head. Then he said, 'If I have money, I buy a corsair slave off you.'

Nicholas smiled. 'Why need you a slave? To come and wash your feet, to watch your goats—'

'No,' said the boy. 'I buy him, I chain him down outside my hut and watch him die in the sun.'

The late afternoon sky was deep blue, the breeze tranquil, the colour of the sea below them an astonishing limpid azure. Little birds flitted through the thorn brakes. At a glance you might think it a peaceful and lovely island, sun-baked and thyme-scented, with its goatherds and goatbells and little rocky hills. But this goatherd boy was very thin, and in his great melancholy brown eyes there was an unspeakable loneliness. Nicholas could guess his story all too well, no need to ask. His family was gone, only he was left. One night, in one of those ceaseless slave-raids that Africa made upon Europe, his entire family had been stolen. They were gone to the Barbary Coast, to the rowing bench or the workbench, the kitchen or the quayside whorehouse. They would never be seen again. Now he lived alone in his hut, with only the murmurous bees in the thyme and the tinkling goatbells for company, in place of his sister's laughter, his father's call, his mother's voice.

Nicholas gave him the rest of his bread.

'We are sailing to Malta,' said Nicholas. 'We are going to fight the Mohammedan.'

The boy nodded, chewing hard. 'Kill them,' he said. 'Kill them all.'

16

'What a bloody baptism was there,' murmured Smith.

'He has no after-battle sadness at such slaughter?'

'But little.'

'He is a soldier to the bone. If not a soldier, he could have grown into a killer of the worst sort, this country boy.'

Smith said, 'He'd have survived on the roads of England too. Till he came to the hangman's noose and danced the Tyburn jig.'

They brooded a little on what was in part their creation.

'And to think, Fra John, that we provoked a fight back there in Cadiz to give them martial experience.'

'He fights like a devil. What do the infidel call it? A *fasset al-afrit*. A dust devil. One who moves like the wind.'

'There's no meat on his bones,' agreed Stanley, 'and the strength of his sword arm is no match for a knight's. Or a Janizary's. But his speed is astonishing. When he fights, he moves in a world where every other man in his eyes seems to move like an aged pensioner. He darts in and cuts 'em open before they even see him. I glimpsed him at work once or twice. An eerie sight.'

'Tell him nothing of this.'

Stanley shook his head. 'Didn't they say old Friar Bacon invented a potion which made him invisible, so he could pass among men and not be seen by them? This boy moves so fast in a fight, it's as if he has drunk this potion.'

They replenished their water jars from a source the goatboy showed them, and sailed again the following afternoon. They would have to sail and bail all the way. It would be three days to

Sardinia, three more to Sicily, and then a day south to Malta. Only a week more and it would begin.

Yet Lady Day was far gone now, it was well into April, and the Turk would be upon them soon. The knights had a dread of coming into Messina and hearing that the Turk was already on Malta, the island had fallen, and this time there had been no mercy for the Knights of St John. They pictured their severed heads already decorating the battlements of the poor fort of San Angelo, so meagre a successor to the great fortified city of their beloved Rhodes.

The six days to Sardinia and Sicily were uneventful, slow and tense. They called over to passing merchant ships in a macaronic mix of Latin tongues.

'*Les Turcs a Malta?*'

Mariners called back, '*No, signores. No escucho no armas de fuoco, no cannones. Todo paz. Paz e benevolenza.*'

All is peace. Peace and goodwill.

They grimaced and hastened on to Messina.

The ancient Sicilian harbour was a clamorous babel of voices, ships loading and unloading, gulls crying, crowds jostling. The master of the *Swan* got a good price for the Spanish merino wool that he had picked up in Cadiz. He would take nothing on to Malta but his troublesome, stout-hearted passengers. He would set them ashore in the Grand Harbour, and then hurry back west as fast as he could, leaving the mayhem of this holy war behind him. He and his mariners were already thinking longingly of the alehouses of Bristol.

Few other masters and shipmen around the harbour showed any interest.

'Malta?' they grunted. 'No trade there.' And no more.

No others were sailing south. Many quickly changed the subject, no keener to talk of the island than to bring a cat on board ship, set sail on a Sunday, or talk of a storm in fair weather. Malta had become a name accursed.

There was some small encouragement for them, regarding the one naval commander among all the Christians who was truly feared by the Turk.

'Is Romegas still sailing?' asked Smith.

A Sicilian gave a slow, guarded smile. 'Ay. Night and day, the Chevalier Romegas is still sailing.'

They had a short time before departure, while the crew laded the *Swan* with water and provisions, so found a hostel close by. A dark panelled interior, pleasantly cool, and four cups of wine.

'And none of your mindless belligerence this time,' Smith said to Nicholas. 'Nor making love-lorn eyes at any barmaid.'

Nicholas gave him a look.

At the rear of the hostel was a private room, though the door was ajar. A fruity, well-mannered voice was saying,

'Slay me, but if I had not spent so much time a-dallying with the Lady Maria, *or* her equally delectable sister, the Lady Catherine, I should have been at Malta a month ago. It is the story of my life, Don Luis.'

Stanley and Smith exchanged glances.

'That voice is familiar,' murmured the latter.

'I am ever torn between the burning of the flesh and the cool of the monastery,' continued the fruity voice. 'And then of course, the clarion call of war.'

'That will be for your brother to decide,' said the older voice of Don Luis.

'My brother,' repeated the fruity voice in a sarcastic tone. 'One might as well await the conversion of the Jews. And Malta will soon be under violent siege.'

Chairs were pushed back, and then there appeared in the doorway the venerable figure of an old Spanish nobleman in a fine black surcoat, a heavy gold chain around his neck. Yet he stood back to let his superior pass through the doorway first. And into the room where they sat stepped a startling peacock of a man. Only some twenty years of age, immaculately bearded, with a pale face and high cheekbones, he was clad in a pure white velvet suit with a small jewelled belt and dagger at his waist, and soft white leather top boots reaching to just above his knee. If you hadn't heard him talking of his mistresses, you would very much think that this was one of those gentlemen who preferred the company of other gentlemen.

He held his nose so high in the air that he would never have noticed the four scruffy wine-bibbers at their table, had not Smith and Stanley, to Nicholas's astonishment, stood up the instant this ridiculous coxcomb appeared, and bowed very low. Nicholas then saw, to his even greater astonishment, that the white-suited coxcomb was wearing a small silver Cross of St John around his neck.

He looked at the two bowed knights and arched one immaculate jet-black eyebrow.

'We do not recognise the crowns of your heads, gentlemen. Show us your faces, if you please.'

Smith and Stanley stood once more, and the coxcomb winced exaggeratedly at their appearance.

'Brother Knights, we see,' he said, and gave a minuscule nod. 'Greetings.'

'Majesty,' said the knights.

Majesty. Nicholas swallowed. The fellow was a prince, of royal blood! He had never set eyes upon one of God's appointed royalty before. Instinctively he and Hodge both bowed their heads, but they needn't have troubled. The Prince did not even notice their existence.

'You sail for Malta?' said the Prince.

'Yes, Majesty. Within the hour.'

'Then we sail with you. Our passage here has been damnably difficult, waylaid with the most *tiresome* distractions.' He drew off his white kid gloves once more and used them to fan his face. 'Pray, finish your wine before we sail.'

The knights drank fast. Nicholas and Hodge gulped theirs even faster. In the very presence of *royalty*.

The Prince turned his head, and wrinkled his nose.

'On reflection,' he said, 'we shall wait outside, in the purer air. Our noses will thank us for it.' He smiled beneficently upon them as he left. 'Pray do not hurry. Surely the Turk himself is coming but leisurely.'

Then he and the old courtier Don Luis were gone.

'Who was that?'

Smith stepped up to the door to be sure that the Prince that departed.

'That,' said Stanley quietly, 'was the natural-born brother of the King of Spain.'

Nicholas and Hodge gaped.

'Truly,' said Stanley. 'We step into the first tavern in Messina, and there he is. But not so remarkable, really, since he too is a Knight of St John.'

'Formally speaking,' growled Smith. 'A deal of use that fop would be when it came to war. And the meaning of the vow of chastity seems to have escaped him.'

'He is not the only knight to have erred there,' said Stanley. 'And by all the evidence, he is on his way to Malta to fight with his brothers.'

Smith sneered. 'You can well imagine what terror the sight of so gorgeous a creature would strike into the hearts of your battle-hardened Janizaries.'

'You mean,' said Nicholas, still digesting this magical encounter, 'he is the brother of King Philip of Spain?'

'Half-brother. His father, like Philip's, was the great Charles V. Philip's mother, of course, was Queen Isabella of Portugal. Our Prince's here was a certain German lady of playful disposition, called Barbara Blomberg.'

'So playful, indeed,' said Smith, checking out of the door once more, 'that some say there is no certainty whatever that her natural son, our friend here in the white velvet, is the son of Charles V at all. He could be the bastard offspring of two or three dozen kings or noblemen from any country in Europe.'

'What is his name?' asked Nicholas.

'His name,' said Stanley, 'is Don John of Austria.'

A moment later there came a terrific cry from outside. A cry that was almost a howl. Stanley and Smith were running in an instant, sword in hand. Nicholas and Hodge raced after them.

In the bright Sicilian sunlight, the white-clad figure of Don John of Austria at the harbourside was almost dazzling. He was in no danger. It was but a scrap of paper that had discomposed him. He read it over once more, hand held to his mouth in disbelief. Don Luis stood gravely by, and the message-bearer more awkwardly. All down the street waited Don John's retinue, his personal bodyguard, and the porters for his numerous chests of clothes, weapons and personal accoutrements. There were three wagonloads, piled high.

Don John turned on the two knights as they ran up, hardly aware of who they were, and said glassy-eyed, 'My *brother,* God bless him and save him and make his reign long and prosperous – my *brother,* has decided that it would not be *politic* for us to proceed to Malta at this time. We are summoned home to Spain, there to await his further pleasure.'

'It is understandable that His Majesty should—' began Don Luis.

But he was cut short by another infuriated cry, as the Prince momentarily lost his royal froideur, crumpled up the letter and dashed it the ground. Just for a moment, Nicholas saw him not as a ridiculous coxcomb, but as a passionate young man only a few years older than him, with all the same dreams of glory.

The Prince seized Stanley by the shoulder, his gaze still distant.

'I will fight the Turk, I *will* fight him. I will make my name a byword for war, and we will conquer. Fra, Fra ...'

'Fra Edward, sire. Fra Edward Stanley, Knight Grand Cross.'

'Fra Eduardo.' Don John released his grip, a little embarrassed, and patted Stanley's rucked shirt back into place. 'Damn it all, Sir Englishman, how I envy you your common blood.'

'Common as muck, sire. Descended merely from English nobility, and the Earls of Derby.'

Don John smiled faintly, a moment of fraternal warmth. Nicholas saw then that he was proud but not arrogant, of haughty bearing but not cold or unapproachable, and he looked upon the world around him with a bright sparkle of pleasure in his eyes. Then the mask of royalty snapped back on, and he was as formal as before. He clicked his fingers rapidly, and the message-bearer scurried forward, head bowed, and retrieved the crumpled letter from the ground. The boy wiped it on his own sleeve lest it should have gathered any dirt, folded it carefully, and handed it back to Don Luis.

Don John pulled on his white kid gloves again.

'We should give thanks to God for the wise caution of our dear brother,' he said crisply. 'Our brother the King, who is indeed so cautious that he will not relieve himself in his close stool before it has first been checked for *sharks.*'

He smiled around, and for the first time his gaze descended on Nicholas and Hodge.

'These are your squires?'

'We are gentlemen volunteers,' interrupted Nicholas firmly, breaking at least three cardinal rules of etiquette in a single blow. Don John merely raised an eyebrow. These were but red-faced, dusty-booted English churls, from a barbaric Protestant island famed for nothing but sheep's wool, heresy and fog. They could hardly be expected to know the intricacies of Spanish court etiquette. Besides, there was a fire in this one's eye that he liked. He had always loved the impetuous, the ardent-hearted – so unlike that watchful, wary, frosty-arsed throne-squatter that was his damned dear *brother*.

'Gentleman volunteers,' he repeated, and bowed to the lad. 'We crave your pardon.'

Nicholas could think of nothing to say. Stanley almost choked.

Don John sighed. 'We envy you. *Vaya con Dios*, my English volunteers.' He raised a gloved hand. 'You and all my brother knights. For this coming battle of Malta will be hard.'

'May it please your excellency …'

Don John nodded, allowing Stanley a question.

'Does the Court of Spain have any intelligence of the Grand Turk's progress?'

'The Turk left Stamboul three weeks ago. Twenty-ninth of March. He will be at Malta any day now. Any hour.' He smiled, but not unkindly. 'I should delay you no longer. You are needed there.'

As for him, it was back to the slim white arms of the Lady Maria, the stiff cold court of Madrid, and the waiting.

'But our day will come,' he murmured.

The English party had already bowed and gone.

'Three weeks ago! Jesu save us.'

'I expect to hear the roar of guns in the south at any moment.'

Smith said, 'Only thank God we have not heard them yet.'

'They sail into a contrary wind much of the way.'

'They will be here in less than another week, all the same.'

Racing after them, Nicholas instinctively dropped his hand down onto his sword hilt. It would come soon now.

17

They had only just scrambled aboard and were discussing urgently with the master when a deep, powerful voice roared from the high quayside behind them, 'So this is the leaking bucket going to Malta! I might have known only a gang of sunstruck Englishmen would sail on such a ship of fools!'

'I know that voice.' Stanley shielded his eyes and looked up, a broad grin spreading over his ruddy features. 'The Chevalier de Guaras. Fra Melchior! Do you seek permission to come aboard?'

The burly bearded figure swung himself down the iron ladder in the stone harbour wall. 'I need no permission!'

'Oi!' called the master. 'No strangers come aboard my ship without my word!'

Smith silenced him with payment. Stanley and the knight called Melchior de Guaras embraced.

'Brother, you look older,' said Stanley.

'And you look fatter. How are you planning to slay the Turk, suffocate him with your belly?'

'Ah, Fra Melchior, surely the greatest wit this side of Toledo! How near is the Army of Islam?'

De Guaras said, 'Beacon fires from Calabria tell that they have passed by. We may have three days, no more.'

Stanley beckoned. 'Master Ingoldsby, Master Hodgkin – I give you the Chevalier de Guaras, Knight Grand Cross. Our brother-in-arms.'

The Spanish knight shook their hands, eyeing them keenly. 'Your squires?'

'I am no man's squire,' said Nicholas quietly. 'I am a gentleman volunteer, and this is my comrade, Hodge.'

De Guaras's eyes twinkled. 'I am honoured. You come at a good time. All are welcome upon Malta. Even Englishmen.'

Hodge seemed about to say something, so Stanley asked who else might need passage.

'I will return,' said the Spaniard. 'There are more of us. Though never enough.'

Never enough indeed. The crowned heads of Europe sent no aid. Of all the ships in Sicily's busiest port, the *Swan* was the only one heading south. All others were keeping well clear, sailing along the coast for Palermo, or north for Italy. The port of Siracusa was almost dead, the Malta Channel empty of shipping. All had heard the news, and it was mere folly to sail into a coming storm.

A few minutes later De Guaras returned with some crates on a cart, and two companions. Fra Adrien, the Chevalier de la Rivière, a knight of the French langue, an elegantly attired and soft-voiced fellow, whom Stanley whispered to Nicholas was as fine a swordsman as he would ever see. And with him a young novice of the Order, a Portuguese lad called Bartolomeo Faraone, no older than Nicholas.

Smith considered him. 'And of the Holy Father's proclamation that no beardless boys should fight, for the sake of Christian mercy?'

'I am no beardless boy,' said Faraone, rubbing the backs of his hands over his cheeks. 'Perhaps your eyes are weak after a long voyage at sea.'

'Does your mother know you are here?'

'Peace, Fra John,' said De la Rivière, smiling. 'He is an earnest and devout novice, no younger than your – gentleman volunteers here. And besides,' his smile faded, 'every man is needed.'

'How many are the Order now at San Angelo?'

De la Rivière hesitated. 'The last I heard ... four hundred or so.'

'Four hundred?' said Smith.

'Four hundred of the finest in Christendom,' said Stanley.

'Pray that it prove so,' said De la Rivière.

There came one last passenger for Malta, a youth who seemed to be travelling alone. He stood and swayed on the quayside just as they were loosening the ropes and preparing to move off.

'Another for Malta! Hold there!' he cried weakly.

Smith muttered, 'Puppies in a sack, is he drunk?'

'Or badly fevered,' said Stanley.

The youth on the quayside was indeed an extraordinary sight. Very tall and lean, his face was long, thin and pale, adorned with a moustache like a bootlace stuck to his upper lip. He wore an extraordinary confusion of swords and daggers, none of the newest, and a much-dented breastplate in the ancient style with a huge crest in the centre, badly tarnished. He stood and swayed, eyes unfocused and brow sweating profusely in a manner suggesting extreme ill-health.

'You'll bring no fever on board my ship!' said the master bluntly. 'Now back off, we're full.'

''Tis no fever,' protested the youth, 'except it be the *furor martialis*, the fever of chivalry and noble war.' He clutched his stomach.

Smith said, 'Stand back, I think he's about to spew.'

There was an anxious moment, and then the youth regained his composure.

'Your name, sir?'

He bowed very slowly. 'My name is Don Miguel de Cervantes Saavedra, from the demesne of the Alcalá de Henares, in Old Castile. My father is the universally renowned Rodrigo de Cervantes, knight at arms and sometime apothecary-surgeon, in reduced cirmcum-stances. Through him I claim descent from the ancient kings of Castile, from Alfonso and Pedro, as well as Eleanor of Navarre, and ultimately from the Visigothic Kings themselves, Rodrigo being the name of—'

'Spellbinding stuff,' said Smith, 'but we are in some haste. Your ancestry later, perhaps? We sail to war.'

'Yes, well, quite,' said the young man. 'Now if you would just hold your craft still a while, I shall fetch my pack ...'

He turned away unsteadily.

'Sail!' called Smith.

They were some paces off the quayside when the tall, starveling figure of Don Miguel appeared once more, carrying a small pack and, for reasons unclear, leading a donkey.

'What ho!' he cried. 'For Malta, for our Saviour and Saint James! I say, what ho there! I require passage!'

And to their astonishment he began to descend the iron rungs straight down into the water, sack on his back, the donkey staring gloomily down at his master as if he had seen it all before. People gathered around, laughing down at the fevered madman. It was good entertainment.

'Hold there,' cried the young knight errant. 'I shall swim out to you!'

'The breastplate alone will drown him,' muttered Smith. 'What's the addlepate fool thinking of?'

'He's brain-fevered,' said Stanley. Then he shouted to the by-standers, 'Grab a hold of the puppy and bring him back! He'll souse himself!'

At that moment the youth slipped from the bottom rung into the water and immediately vanished beneath the surface, until a stout mariner swung a boathook down and collared him by the leather strap of his breastplate. Another climbed down the ladder to help, and he was hauled up like a sickly eel.

The moment he could speak again, the fellow was calling out across the water about the Moors, and King Boabdil, and the Reconquista; about El Cid, and the Lady Aramintha, whose love tokens he wore about his person, sewn to his breast, and whose unearthly beauty he could scarce—

Then he lost consciousness, and was laid none too gently upon the quayside like a dead fish.

'Brain-fevered, truly,' said Smith.

'A fellow of rare imagination,' said Stanley.

'Come,' said De la Rivière. 'To Malta.'

Smith tossed Nicholas an arquebus sidelong.

'Here,' he said, 'show me how you'd load it.'

Nicholas was unfamiliar with the weapon, but he followed what he knew of loading a fowling-piece, and the twenty-one steps needed to ready a gun. Aware of the eyes of Smith and Stanley and the other knights keenly upon him, he worked as fast as possible, taking pleasure in his own speed and deftness. Very soon it was done. He looked up triumphantly.

Smith said softly, 'Strike me but you're fast, boy.'

'Always was,' he said a little complacently. He handed the arquebus back to the knight. 'My father said I was always fast, at running, archery, everything. Once some bullyboys set on us in the lane, Hodge and I, not knowing I was gentleman-born. Hodge punched them hard enough but I got behind them – we were only ten or eleven, mind, they a year or two older – and I struck 'em all across their heads with a milkpail, ding ding ding like a set of bells. They never even knew I was there. I climbed trees fast, I went up like a cat, I swam fast even—'

He stopped abruptly and bit his tongue. He was boasting like a drunk Spaniard.

'Ay,' said Smith, not minding overmuch. The boy had earned a boast or two. 'You move like a Severn eel.'

He handed the arquebus to Hodge. 'You learn too. Master Nicholas: instruct him.'

'How do you make a Maltese Cross?'

'Is this another of your side-splitting puns, Ned Stanley?'

'Kick his Maltese arse!'

'You were a loss to the jesting profession, truly.'

'I have another.'

'Keep it.'

'How do you make a Spanish donkey—'

'I said *keep it*.'

It was then that Nicholas saw something, clinging halfway up the rigging. Other eyes constantly scanned the eastern horizon, on the lookout for an armada of numberless warships. But Nicholas's gaze was to the south.

'I see it!' he cried. 'I see it!'

'There she is,' said Stanley, vaulting onto the prow. And both Knights of St John felt a surge of unspeakable pride.

As they sailed closer, the little ship gently rising and falling, the boy saw it was so small a place, so dirt poor and tiny an island where this great battle would be decided. He had never realised before how pathetically small and poor. Suddenly a deep, clear calm possessed him. Just as Elizabeth's England was no more than a small, unregarded island off the shoulder of Europe, barely considered by the mighty continental kingdoms of France and Spain, Portugal and the Holy Roman Empire, so was Malta. A sunburnt rock in the far southern Mediterranean, far closer to Africa than Rome. Too insignificant for great kings and potentates to waste their armies on. Yet one Emperor had noticed it, and understood its significance.

Suleiman had bent his dark eye upon it, the whirlwind was coming, and an army of forty thousand men was about to fall upon this one small rock of an island. Nicholas felt the glory of it stir deep in his blood. Once at school there was a small boy being bullied by four bigger lads. They taunted him and then began to whip him with hazel sticks, as you would a cowering dog, for amusement. Then Nicholas had gone in with fists flying, only six or seven himself, and the bullies scattered. His father was proud of him that day, and in the evening he ate rice pudding with plums and as much sugar as he wanted, which was a lot.

He smiled strangely to himself, hanging from the rigging, sun in his eyes, the island drawing nearer. He thought of his father, the bullied little boy, and his sisters. The green hills of Shropshire. The little lion-tawny island shimmered in its heat haze on the sea, the sun beginning to set in the west, and he smiled to himself. Here was where it had all been heading, after all. Here was his destiny.

Part II

THE ISLAND

1

The little English ship rounded the point and turned into the vast Grand Harbour. The master had raised the flag of St George. The red cross on white may have looked like the emblem of the Hospitallers' ancient rivals, the Templars – but the Templars were long gone, along with the rest of the world of chivalry. Only the Knights of St John remained now, of all the Orders. And it was good to see the flag of St George today.

Nicholas stared around in wonder. High on the headland to his right was a crude little star-shaped fort of roughcut stone.

'Fort St Elmo,' murmured Stanley. 'Hardly Krak des Chevaliers, but it must serve.'

On the headland opposite was Gallows Point, and between them the entrance to the Grand Harbour.

The harbour itself was vast, surrounded by tall, majestic cliffs, and bobbing with brightly painted local fishing boats, fishermen busily passing crates of the day's catch along chains of hands. But no foreign merchant ships were anchored here, not for weeks now. None would dare. Stanley said that the very word *Malta* meant nothing more than 'harbour' in the ancient language of the Phoenicians. It was the island's very reason for existence.

'You see now why Suleiman might covet it,' he said. 'It is the finest harbour in the Mediterranean. God himself made it for sailors and shipwrights, surely.'

The deep harbour gave way southwards into several narrow but deepwater creeks, perfect for shipbuilding or safe anchorage. Kalkara Creek, Galley Creek and French Creek. At the mouth of

Galley Creek, the most important of them, a massive chain hung down into the water from a gigantic capstan embedded deep in the rock, made not of a single tree trunk but of seven, lashed together. Across the creek, the chain was attached to a huge old anchor, also embedded in solid rock. Loosened for now, the mighty barrier lay on the bed of the creek to allow ships passage. But the moment the first Ottoman galley was seen, the cry would go out, the mighty windlasses would be turned, the capstan would groan into action, and the chain would be hoisted, rising dripping from the depths.

'Hand-forged in Venice,' said Stanley. 'Each link cost ten ducats. Strong as adamant.'

Nicholas could believe it. The chain links vanishing from the capstan down into the water were as thick as his thigh. No war galley no matter how powerful could break through those.

'The galleys are out, scouring the seas, of course,' said Stanley.

'Under this Chevalier Romegas?'

Stanley grinned. 'You learn fast. The most savage sea-wolf of them all. Fortunately he is on our side. But you may admire the warship there in the creek. That is the *Great Carrack* of Rhodes.'

She was magnificent, a towering structure whose wooden walls rose like a fortified city, sides studded with gunports, forecastle and sterncastle rising yet higher like miniature castles.

'Will she be brought into play against the Turk?'

Stanley looked anguished. 'She needs work, and we need money for the work. Timber must be imported from Sicily or Spain. The *Great Carrack* is no longer young. But let us hope.'

Between each of the creeks rose narrow rocky promontories, small clusters of houses and churches crowning each one.

'Birgu,' said Stanley, nodding at the principal. 'The city. And the other, with its few houses and windmills, is Senglea.'

At the tip of Birgu rose a sterner fortification, its gun ports commanding a wide range over the entire Grand Harbour.

'San Angelo,' said Stanley. 'The fortress of the knights.'

People lined the walls of the small towns and cheered as the *Swan* dropped her anchor with a splash, and two longboats came out to unload her.

'No gun salute, then,' said Stanley.

'Keeping their powder for other arrivals,' said Smith.

They stepped up onto a narrow harbour wall, and a tall knight in black surcoat with a white cross came through the crowds of Maltese sailors and lightermen to greet them.

'The Chevalier Medrano, Knight of the Langue of Aragon!' said Stanley.

They clasped each other.

'In God's name,' said the Spanish knight, 'you are welcome at this time, Fra Edward. How many are you?'

'Four knights come to join you,' said Stanley cheerfully. Medrano did well to keep his expression from betraying disappointment. 'Some good silver, some arms. John Smith and myself, De Guaras and De la Rivière here. A novice of Portugal, and these two lad … these two gentlemen volunteers of England. I give you Master Ingoldsby and Master Hodgkin of the County of Shropshire.'

The Chevalier Medrano bowed gravely. 'You are young. I trust you are brave for your years.'

'Do not doubt them,' said Stanley quietly.

Medrano's eyes rested on them a moment longer and then he turned swiftly. 'Come,' he said.

A voice called from behind. It was the master of the *Swan*. He stepped off his ship onto Maltese rock, for the only time in his life.

'Well, master,' said Stanley. 'Our thanks for an eventful voyage. May God keep you on the return.'

'We pray likewise,' said the master. He gazed around at the towering walls of Birgu and San Angelo, and the vast stretch of the harbour, burnished copper under the setting sun. ''Tis a fine anchorage,' he said. 'But before God, a poor and waterless island that you fight for.'

'It is not the island we fight for, at the last,' said Stanley quietly. 'It is a greater cause than that.'

He and the master exchanged a handshake and a long look, and then the master said, 'My prayers go with you, and the prayers of my mariners.'

He leapt aboard his ship and glanced back one last time. 'For all that the prayers of such heathen dogs as my men may be worth!'

*

Medrano led them hurriedly through the crowd.

'The Grand Master has already demanded to know who arrives from England,' he muttered. 'And as you know, the Grand Master is not a man who likes waiting.'

Everything passed in a whirl. Nicholas shouldered his small pack with his sword and provisions at a jog-trot, as they filed up through busy streets between tall, sunless houses. Among the many voices he heard snatches of Spanish and Italian, though of strange dialect, the Italian of Naples and Sicily, not the schoolbook Tuscan Italian he had learnt. And then with a thrill he also began to pick out conversations in the native tongue: Maltese. A soft and slurring tongue, the language of Phoenicia, of Dido and Hannibal, and sailors out of old Tyre and Sidon. He felt a sense of unimaginable ancientness. As if he was in the East already.

It was a poor place, but like the poor the world over, the people had lavished on it all the care and love they could. As he followed the striding Medrano and his fellow knights, Nicholas glimpsed, through little doorways, courtyards exquisitely tended, filled with blue pots containing lemon trees, walls bright with painted tiles. Children playing and tethered goats munching. The warm aroma of a bakery, the fetid stink from runnels of greyish water flowing from laundresses' houses. And high above, grilles and porticoes and narrow stone balconies, and tantalising glimpses of women looking down upon the handsome chaste knights, jewelled rings on their fingers and smiles on their lips.

They were led into a high, gloomy hall. A few shields, swords and lances decorated the flaking walls, but otherwise bare. Medrano went on into an inner chamber. They waited.

Another fellow stepped in from the street. He was grimy and sweaty and his eyes darted nervously about.

'What news, brother?' asked Stanley.

'What news, what news?' He spoke rapidly, confusedly, with a Greek accent. 'I must see the Grand Master. Only his ears, only his.'

Medrano reappeared, holding open the tall doors. 'The Grand Master bids you enter.'

The inner chamber was only a little less spartan than the outer. A flagstone floor, a plain table with some papers, pen and ink. At a small desk in the corner, a pale, elderly secretary, peering over his record book. A splendid triple window of diamonded lead panes, looking out onto the sunlit harbour below. And silhouetted in the bright window, his back to them, a tall man, very tall, and of proud bearing. They knelt and bowed their heads and waited in silence. Then he turned.

Jean Parisot de la Valette, 48th Grand Master of the Knights of St John.

He must have been some seventy years old, but with a full head of white hair, a trim beard, and undimmed eye. He radiated power. His gaze burned into them. He said nothing. A man accustomed to the silence and solitude of the truly great, and of great responsibility, needing none other to lean upon. His frame was lean but powerful, his shoulders broad, his features extraordinarily handsome.

Then he spoke, in a voice deep and low, a voice to calm a storm. 'You honour the Order with your coming.' He lifted his hands and they stood again. 'Friend from the East,' he said, eyeing the nervous new arrival. 'Tell me what I do not know already.'

The Greek simpleton babbled for more than a minute of how the Ottoman fleet was already sailing, of how vast it was, how he had seen it with his own eyes.

The Grand Master interrupted. 'Numbers?'

The simpleton looked anxious. 'Many. More than I could count. As numberless as the sands of the sea or the stars in the sky. Every port was busy with provisioning and ship building, not just the Golden Horn but Bursa too, all the ports of the Ottomans. Soldiers coming down to join the fleet from inland and from the European frontiers, from Hungary, from Bessarabia, Karamania, paid levies from Wallachia, mountain men from Albania. Many columns of marching men, singing of a new jihad.'

'You paint a picture,' said La Valette crisply. 'But here is nothing new. Our other informants already tell us the Grand Fleet is only a few hours off the coast of Calabria. We thank you, brother. Go now.'

The simpleton stared and then hurried out.

'Everything is falling into place,' said La Valette. 'The Order will live or die in the coming battle. As God wills.'

He did not sound discomposed. It was as if his whole life had been building to this hour, when Malta and the Knights would stand alone against the greatest military power on earth.

'We have perhaps two more days,' he said. He smiled and walked over. 'Chevalier de Guaras, De la Rivière, and my last loyal Englishmen.' He clasped their hands. 'And the boys?'

They gave him Faraone, then Nicholas and lastly Hodge.

'Hodge,' repeated La Valette gravely. 'This name could only be English. It sounds stout.'

'They have already stood by us in a skirmish with the corsairs, Sire,' said Stanley. 'This one,' he touched Nicholas on the shoulder, 'bested five of them.'

La Valette looked at him sharply. 'Five? Five men?'

'Full-grown and ferocious, now in Hades. You knew his father.'

La Valette's eyes narrowed.

'The late Sir Francis Ingoldsby. He fought with you at Rhodes.'

Rare emotion swam in La Valette's eyes. Nostalgia and memory. He stood before Nicholas, towering over him, and laid his hands on his shoulders. 'The son of Sir Francis Ingoldsby,' he said softly. 'Lord bless you. Have you brothers?'

Nicholas shook his head. 'Sisters. They are cared for in England. My father died some six months ago. Our estates are forfeit, we are orphans.'

'This sounds like injustice.'

'It is. One day I shall right it.'

La Valette nodded. 'So you fell in with these knights of mine and sailed for Malta. In memory of your father?'

'Yes,' said Nicholas, his voice too quiet. Then 'Yes' again, more firmly.

'Two more nights of sleep without fear. Then the storm will break. I trust you will not think you have sailed too far from England.'

'I will not.'

La Valette addressed them all. 'Gentlemen, you know how perilous is our situation. The Turk is almost upon us. We hasten to build what defences we can until then. We pray that God help us. The French will not, they ally with Suleiman. Nor the German princes, nor England's Protestant Queen. King Philip of Spain remains our best hope, but so far he has sent us nothing, though

146

the Spanish possessions of Sicily and the Kingdom of Naples would be the first to suffer invasion should Malta fall. His Holiness the Pope sends us ten thousand crowns, to buy powder and arms. Yet it is men that we desperately need, and do not have. So it seems we fight alone. Brothers-in-arms. All four hundred of us.'

He smiled grimly.

'Eat well this evening, sleep well tonight. Tomorrow there will be work to do. This novice with you, De la Rivière. The English boys to be billeted.'

As they filed out, La Valette murmured to Stanley, 'This Ingoldsby will fight hard, I see. He fights not merely for glory, as other volunteers, but for his family honour, and his father's pride.'

The finest street in Birgu was the Street of the Knights, the auberge of each langue handsomely escutcheoned over the brightly painted doors.

Stanley spoke to a bread-seller on the corner. He jabbered in Maltese and pointed down a narrow side street. Stanley hailed the two boys and led them to the door, drawing out his purse as he went.

A dark, shy-looking woman answered the door, no more than twenty-seven or twenty-eight. Stanley spoke to her in Italian, she said little. Then he handed her a silver coin, and pushed them on in.

Nicholas and Hodge were given a small, windowless room off the tiny courtyard, with two straw pallets on the floor, and plentiful fleas. They dropped their packs and stretched out.

'Well, Hodge. What do you reckon to Malta so far? Hodge?'

He was asleep.

2

'Inglis! Inglis! Up stir your asses! Franco Briffa is returned home!'

Nicholas awoke, scratching. It was dark. A monstrous bull-voice was roaring in the tiny courtyard, just outside their thin door, his language a baffling polyglot mix of heavily accented Italian and snatches of Maltese.

'Franco Briffa is returned from the bastard sea, with his great friend the bastard Anton Zahra, bringing fresh fish for your Inglis dinner. Appear! Stand before us! Let us see these noble heroes of England!'

Hodge and Nicholas stumbled out of the door, dopey after only two hours' sleep. It was yet early evening, the air still as warm as an English summer noon, and the little town of Birgu was all astir once more.

Before them, seemingly filling the little courtyard from wall to wall, was a man of some thirty-five years. Of medium height, but barrel-chested, with mighty forearms, thick black hair, huge, black oiled moustache, and large, fiercely burning eyes. Strong white teeth gleamed as he grinned, but instantly vanished when he set eyes on the two skinny, weary, travel-stained young heroes.

'You are the soldiers come to defend us against the Turk?'

They nodded.

He braced himself and swallowed down his grievous disappointment. 'Well,' he said. Then, returning to his customary volume, 'Well! You are welcome into the home of Franco Briffa.' He shook their hands violently and clapped them on the back. 'I never meet an Inglis before now. You are no filthy Protestant like the fat Dutch?

But no, you are Inglis, and gentlemen I see from your hands, at least you are, not him. Now, come and eat sardines, gentleman and his peasant both. And meet my family.'

They emerged into the little courtyard and were seated on low stools. Nicholas couldn't believe how sweet the air was, scented with orange and lemon blossom – and how warm too. Yet it was night! What on earth would it be like in the day? And to fight in?

The door onto the street was left wide open and people went by, many carrying sacks and stones. Even at this late hour, when all good Englishmen would have been long abed. Some called in greetings. Life was lived in public here.

Franco Briffa lit candles and stuck them in niches. A small fire burned in a brazier, fed with animal dung.

'So that's what they use for firewood here,' muttered Hodge.

Franco Briffa indicated an ancient woman on a stool by the brazier, apparently feeling the cold. 'My beloved mother, Mama Briffa. My dear wife' – he seized the shy woman as she entered from the little room opposite, and turned her to face them, her face bowed – 'Mother of my two wicked sons. *Il bambino*, over there in the cradle. Here is my two young sons, very wicked, they are Mateo and Tito.' Two young boys, perhaps eleven and nine, stared up at the two foreign soldiers in their house, bursting with excitement and curiosity. 'And my daughter, my eldest' – he roared out – 'Maddalena!' He glared back at them. 'You will hearken to me now, yes? Franco Briffa does not lie.'

They nodded, bewildered.

A slim girl of fourteen or fifteen stepped into the courtyard, wearing a simple pale blue dress and a headscarf. He seized her as he had his wife, and turned her to face them.

'She is pretty, is she not? She is most beautiful, the most beautiful girl perhaps in all Malta?'

She was. Very pretty, her face aglow in the light of the brazier.

'She takes after her father! No, no, I jest,' and he pulled his wife to his side under a bearlike arm and crushed her to him. 'She takes after her *mother*. But she is pretty as a flower, and you are young men, and under our roof, and so I tell you this. If either of you Inglis approach nearer to her than the length of two arms, let alone God save us reach out and touch her – then I, Franco Briffa, will cut off your testicles and feed them to the pigs.'

Old Mama Briffa cackled on her stool. 'He will, he will!'

Mateo and Tito giggled.

Franco Briffa added an obscene gesture for illustration, glaring at the two boys fiercely, as if in anticipation, driving his forefinger hard through a ring made with his opposing forefinger and thumb. He seemed very concerned with his daughter's virginity. Nicholas wanted to protest that his host had no reason to fear that he, an English gentleman, would so abuse his hospitality. But he couldn't think of the right words.

The girl meanwhile was flushed with embarrassment, which only made her look prettier.

Franco Briffa pushed both wife and daughter firmly away. 'Now go, women! And you, children, it is time you were in bed.' Mateo and Tito began to protest passionately, until he roared in their faces. Then he called after the women, 'Bring us food. Sardines, bread, wine, the very food that Christ and his disciples ate to stay strong!'

The three ate heartily, the women scurrying back and forth to bring them more and more. Nicholas looked fixedly ahead whenever the girl appeared. She would give him dreams. His heart thumped, and he no longer thought back to the barmaid in Cadiz.

Franco Briffa ate most heartily of all, slapping his wife's bottom whenever she brought out more sardines from the cool dark larder to fry on the fire.

'Caught this very afternoon by myself and my great friend the bastard Anton Zahra. Are they not the finest you ever tasted? It is the dungfire that flavours them so sweetly.' He mopped his mouth and refilled their wine cups. Nicholas tried to avoid a refill but failed. The wine was very thin and pale red and not easy to distinguish from vinegar. But a cup or two certainly warmed the stomach. Franco Briffa drank some four pints.

The smoke arose slowly into the square of starlit night above them. Goats bleated, a dog barked. It seemed so peaceful. Yet none could forget the ominous shadow hanging over them, nor that this might be the last such night as this.

At last, nearly dropping off his stool for weariness, Nicholas managed to say, '*Grazzi. Hafna tajjeb.*'

Franco Briffa went silent, a hunk of bread halfway to his mouth. 'What did you say, Inglis?'

Thinking he had made some terrible mistake, Nicholas repeated the words uncertainly.

With violent abruptness, Franco Briffa leapt to his feet and bellowed, 'Why, it is an astonishment!'

Someone called in through the open courtyard doorway, 'Quit your shouting, Franco Briffa, you'll wake the dead from their graves!'

But Franco was impervious. 'Speak again, Inglis!'

Nicholas said the words once more.

'An astonishment, I tell you! The Inglis sits in my house for no more than a bat's fart, eats a little bread, drinks a little wine, and now he is talking already like a native Maltese.' He seized Nicholas by the arm and dragged him out into the street.

'Hear the Inglis!' roared Franco at anyone prepared to listen. 'It is an astonishment! Come hear him! Speak again, Inglis! Pronounce! Declaim! Listen to him, you fools, and hearken. It is a miracle! He has learnt to speak the ancient tongue of Malta in a half a minute. He is a *genius*!'

People nodded and smiled as they hurried by under their loads. Nicholas's head swam with tiredness and wine. A floor above, on a tiny balcony, a girl's faced peeped out. He glanced up. She vanished.

After the great performance, they went back inside and Franco Briffa insisted they had another cup of wine, while he told them how he used to be a bad man, a wild youth. He used to drink and chase whores, but now he was married to his beloved Maria, he drank no more, well, only a little. He drained his fifth pint of wine. Now he worshipped God with all the devotion of his heart, as devotedly as he once drank and chased whores.

'Not that whores need much chasing!' he guffawed.

His listeners nodded, half asleep.

'Well,' said Franco Briffa, wiping the wine from his moustache. 'Tomorrow, my Inglis friends, I would hear of your country, infidel and cold and full of red-haired women. After that, I fear, there will be little time for drinking and telling tales.'

*

Nicholas awoke to the sound of shouts and cries. He knew where he was instantly, and dread seized him. The Turks had come.

He kicked Hodge and ran out into the courtyard. Early sunlight touched the roofs. People in the street were calling. He looked out. But no, it was only a busy day, no one was panicking yet. His head felt cold and sickly from the wine. Everyone, men, women and children, was up and working. Poor they may be, this peasant people, but they were no idlers. And then cursing himself for a fool, he understood. This was not the ordinary business of the little town. Day and night, for days and weeks past, the people had been following the lead of the knights, and making preparations for war. These sacks of earth and sand, these rocks and stones – they were no innocent burden. They were the stuff of war, being carried to the walls.

He felt ashamed. He must go and join them at once.

'Come and eat first, Inglis!' cried Franco behind him, reading his mind.

He and Hodge sat on a step in the courtyard, and it was Maddalena who brought them bread and two cups and a jug of goat's milk.

She wore a red headscarf and this morning a thin gauze veil over the lower half of her face, so that only her dark eyes showed. Like a Turkish girl. Yet he could not avoid noticing the gentle swell of her figure as she leaned down to pour the milk, and as she breathed, the thin veil moved in and out on that tiny breeze, and he could see the full lips of her mouth. She kept her eyes from him all the time, until one last moment when she glanced at him, and he was looking at her, and their eyes met.

She snatched the jug away as if stung and almost ran back inside.

'The maids here,' said Hodge, chewing philosophically, 'are certainly more naturally maids than some of their kind back in England.'

The goat's milk tasted sweet, and the crusted white bread. This land so sun-warmed and earthy, where the blood flowed so hot in the veins – and yet so pious and restrained withal, the widows in black, the maids in headscarves and veils . . .

Then a church bell began to ring, a steady, insistent tolling. A call to remember why they were here, which was not for young girls in their pale blue dresses.

'They are mules, these Maltese,' said Stanley. 'Look at them. They have not always loved the knights, as we lorded it over them. But now look how they work. Like mules.'

He meant it as a high compliment.

It was only then that Nicholas understood the knights in their pitifully small numbers were not alone. Shoulder to shoulder with them would fight the Maltese people. He felt a lump in his throat. He thought of hurtling cannonballs, fragmenting stone, searing flame, and of Maddalena. Also a surge of pride in being part of this. Men, women and children would fight alongside the knights for their island home, against a fully professional army.

'Nor will they surrender, as the people did at Rhodes,' said Smith. 'They say, We are not Rhodian, we are not Greek, we are not Italian nor Spanish nor Arab. We are Maltese. And we do not surrender.'

They slung great blocks of limestone under wooden beams and hoisted them onto Birgu's old, battlemented walls to build them higher, or to brace them at weak points. They dug ditches and cleared away what little brushwood remained nearby.

The mighty voice of a foreman roared out, 'We shall starve them, they will find nothing here to sustain them!' It was the voice of Franco Briffa. 'Not a fig, not a twig, not a green leaf, not a drop of clean water, nothing will the worshippers of the devil Mahound find here to sustain them. This island will be to them as harsh and lifeless and lonely as the surface of the moon!'

An old man said, 'Some say the moon has lakes and seas on it, as you can see at night.'

'If I say the moon is lifeless,' said Franco Briffa, 'then it is lifeless.'

All the huts and dwellings beyond the walls of Senglea and Birgu were razed. The dirt-poor inhabitants, driving forth their goats, leading their children, infants in arms, did not weep or protest. They set down their infants and tethered their goats and went back and razed their huts and dwellings themselves.

'Well,' said one woman, looking over the blank landscape, face grim, 'a poor dwelling it was anyway, and will not not take much to rebuild. When the Turks are defeated.'

These people, thought Nicholas, hefting a load of timber on his shoulder and trudging back up to the city gates. They are made of the same rock as their island.

Word spread like wildfire that Don Garcia de Toledo, the Spanish Viceroy of Sicily, had sailed into the Grand Harbour under cover of darkness, spoken hurriedly with La Valette, and vanished again before dawn.

'Like a thief in the night,' said Smith. 'And did he bring any Spanish tercios with him?'

De Guaras laughed sourly. 'He left not so much as a perfumed fart.'

Yet Stanley said it was no mean thing for Don Garcia to make the crossing from Sicily to Malta, so late in the day. He was but a servant of King Philip, and Don Garcia would have reminded La Valette that even Spain, greatest of the Christian powers, could put to sea a navy of only thirty-five fully manned war galleys. The navy of Suleiman the Magnificent numbered an unimaginable hundred and seventy galleys or more. If Spain went up against the Turk face-to-face, it would be utterly destroyed. Even if all the Christian powers were to unite under a single banner – not a likely eventuality – they would still be hard-pressed to meet such a force. Philip must guard his own kingdom before he could save Malta. If it were possible, relief would be sent. But for now, the knights must fight alone.

Don Garcia de Toledo had offered to take away as many women and children and elderly as his ship could carry back to the safety of Sicily, though the people had refused in one voice.

'Wise decision,' said De Guaras. 'The people know well that if the Turk takes Malta, he will fall upon Sicily soon enough anyway.'

For a mile out of the city and more, the ground was stripped of cover and scorched black. Last year's wheat was brought into Birgu and Senglea, and carried down into cool dry underground storerooms, part of a labyrinthine system of tunnels hewn into solid rock beneath the city. They stored further food cargoes captured by the Chevalier Romegas on his ceaseless raids on Muslim shipping. It was not jewels and silks, spices and gold that would avail them now, but barley and raisins, dried fish and salt meat, and Arab medicines of the finest to treat wounds and fevers.

Quartermasters counted in ten thousand bushels of grain, huge rounds of Gozo cheese, dried tunny, olive oil, sacks of sesame seeds and Damascus dates. The vast water cisterns were still almost full from the winter rains, and there were several springs never known to fail within the walls.

All wells and springs without the walls were poisoned with a foul mix of hemp, flax and ordure. Though water was the very stuff of life, there was no hesitation. Nothing would be left for the invader but bare rock and burning sun. This was war. War to the knife.

Sometimes wells were even poisoned with arsenic, or a dead animal.

'That'll take some cleaning after,' said one.

'But we will have numberless Mohammedan slaves to work for us,' said another.

From the high battlemented walls of San Angelo, at the northern tip of Birgu, La Valette looked down. San Angelo would take a battering before it fell. Grim fortress walls topped by another, higher inner enclosure, thickly battlemented. It was good to let the eye roam over its massive proportions. Angled bastions, slanted parapets for deflecting direct hits, splayed gun ports, inner defensive lines – the new architecture of defence in the age of gunpowder.

He looked repeatedly towards the eastern horizon, and westward over the island. But he also looked north with a thoughtful expression, at Mount Sciberras, the great bare promontory that formed the opposite side of the Grand Harbour. There had been much talk of building a grand new city there, in a far more commanding position than the little huddled towns of Birgu and Senglea. Or at least an imposing new fort.

But it was all talk, and no money. Nothing had been done. Even the single modest building there now had not been rebuilt or strengthened in any way, and it was there that La Valette's gaze fell. The small, star-shaped fort of St Elmo. Unlike San Angelo, the little fort on Mount Sciberras was hardly of the latest design.

He sent across work parties to do what they could to strengthen the walls, and ordered them to build an outlying ravelin on its far side, in the unlikely event that the Turks should ever try to attack St Elmo overland.

He also allowed them a few more cannons, though Birgu and San Angelo were already cruelly short of firepower. The might of the Ottoman fist would of course fall upon Birgu and San Angelo. Yet St Elmo guarded the mouth of the Grand Harbour, and before the Turks could anchor their great armada there safely, it would have to be reduced.

Suddenly a cry went up.

'A ship! A ship!'

Nobody panicked, but many rushed to the walls and strained their eyes eastwards. It had begun.

But it was only a single ship, and it came from the north, from Sicily. A long, low galley with a hull painted blood red and glistening with tallow for more speed, and flying a matching red flag with a white cross. Even its progress around the headland and into the harbour was somehow dauntless, unhurried, unafraid of the hundred galleys coming its way.

A great cheer went up from the walls.

It was the Chevalier Mathurin Romegas, bringing in more supplies, more Muslim captive slaves to work in chain gangs on the walls, and above all, two hundred Spanish tercios: the finest infantrymen in Europe. Don Garcia de Toledo had persuaded King Philip to send reinforcements after all. An absurdly small number, against the approaching Ottoman horde. But spirits greatly rose to see them.

Romegas himself had a long fine nose, a straggly beard, deep-set eyes circled with dark rings, like a man who slept little, and as Nicholas observed him making his way up to the palace of the Grand Master, Romegas's hands shook badly.

Saluting the march past, Stanley said sidelong to Nicholas, 'Do not think that his hands shake for fear. Since he joined the Knights at the age of fourteen, Romegas has shown himself the most fearless of any. He is of the noble house of Armagnac – and a proud Frenchman.'

'A Gascon,' said Smith. 'It's different.'

'Once his galley was capsized and he survived underwater for twelve hours with his head in an air pocket. Something happens to a man who has looked death so close in the eye. He becomes more free. Romegas's hands shake only because of nervous damage. But he has destroyed more than fifty Ottoman galleys, liberated more than a thousand slaves. It was he who captured the Ottoman treasure ship the *Sultana* and set in train this great assault on our island.'

'Not that Romegas would apologise to anyone for that,' said Smith.

'No indeed.' Stanley smiled faintly. 'To have provoked Suleiman to outright war is probably his proudest achievement yet.'

The Spanish tercios followed Romegas, wearing their breastplates and tall morion helmets for show, and carrying their long, lethal pikes. They had a strange, almost sinister air, these hard-bitten veterans, sons of the high, bleak plains of Castile and Estremadura. Conquistadors, with faces darkened by a tropical sun, eyes distant and cold, and souls as hard as iron. They came from the New World, where they had been fighting the Christless Indians, seeing and committing who knew what atrocities there. Yet they would fight ferociously, these men, and even the heat of a Mediterranean summer might seem easy to them after the burning sun of the Peruvian Andes, or the humid jungles of Panama with its swamps, fevers and the cries of its nameless night creatures.

'This is a war that involves the whole world,' said Stanley softly, as if in slow realisation. 'A war of all four continents. These soldiers returned from the Americas, paid with Inca silver, to fight in Europe against an army of Africans and Asians, and an Empire that rules to the borders of Tartary and Persia.'

'And all focused on this tiny island in the sea,' said Smith. 'Like a glass focusing the sun, and burning a hole through parchment.'

La Valette promptly dictated the new arrivals their stations, and then had them help to arm the walls and bring up supplies. Not barley and dates now, but grimmer materials. Bandages and wadding, splints, flasks of alcohol. Spare recoil ropes for the culverins, arquebus balls in cases and cannonballs stacked in neat pyramids. Assembled pot guns that threw brass bombs full of Greek fire, clay pots of naphtha and fire hoops pasted with evil concoctions that would adhere to clothing and flesh and not cease from burning even underwater: pitch and tar, phosphorus and magnesium, even date wine and honey to make the stuff stick.

The knights knew every secret of siege warfare, and how to fight when hopelessly outnumbered, using the utmost aggression and every destructive martial device known to man.

The Spanish infantrymen and the knights set up high trajectory mortars to arc over the walls like arrows, needing no risky sighting or aiming. La Valette also gave orders for huge casks of water to be set up at regular intervals around the walls of Birgu and Senglea, both for drinking and for extinguishing the deadly fires that would soon be burning.

'Before long,' the soldiers joked, with the black humour of soldiers in all ages, 'we'll be tossing dead bodies down on 'em. That always causes a stink.'

La Valette disliked such jesting. They must all be worthy of their cause, even these rough-hewn soldiers. He had them go through the town and pick men of likely age, and give them rudimentary fire-arms training.

Their commanding officer was a Captain Miranda, a huge, powerfully built fellow with a great black moustache and lantern jaw, who looked like he might best even John Smith in a fight. He lined up his hasty citizen militia and told them,

'If one of my men gets his head blown off, and drops his gun or his sword in the dust, you're onto it in a trice. You hear me? Peasants and fishermen you may be, but you know how to spear a tuna. Well then, you can spear a Turk. We are short of everything in this coming battle. Have no respect for the dead. They will be past caring. Take up their weapons and keep fighting. It is your only hope. That and the mercy of God.'

La Valette heard the words of this Captain Miranda and liked what he heard. He ordered him to prepare a company of thirty of his soldiers to be sent over the water to St Elmo and join the station there, under the command of the stout Italian, Luigi Broglia.

'But not yet,' he said. 'There remains work to do here. The

moment the Grand Fleet is seen, your men will row over. You will remain here with the rest.'

He also asked for any volunteers among the knights. There was reluctance. St Elmo was a poor second to the main battle.

At last Stanley said, 'Sire, for St John and St George, I will go.'

'Then I too,' said Smith.

Nicholas and Hodge counted themselves in also, and La Valette addressed them gravely, as only he could.

'Be ready to cross over the moment the Turks are seen. It is the great battle between the Cross and the Koran which is now to be fought. We are the chosen soldiers of the Cross, and if Heaven requires the sacrifice of our lives, there can be no better occasion than this. Hasten to the sacred altar, my brothers, and be blessed with that contempt for death which alone can render us invincible.'

The waiting was the worst. No surprise it drove men mad. One hanged himself in the market square, with a note pinned to his breast asking for Allah to admit him to Paradise. Passers-by spat on the corpse of the traitor.

It made no sense. Even the Maltese people began to crack.

'Let it come soon,' murmured Stanley. 'Please God.'

The sun burned down on an empty sea.

In the town, rumours flew. Spies were widely suspected. A fellow walking on the walls at night was said to be signalling to the enemy. He protested that it was only the moonlight glinting on his belt buckle, but he was beaten anyway. The next morning a Jewish family were dragged into the street and accused of allying with the Turks. Some kicked dust in their faces, and one or two even picked up stones.

La Valette had been laying the keys to the city on the altar in the Church of St John, praying to the patron saint of the Order for their protection. Hearing the news he came running, as easy as a man thirty years his junior, face black as thunder. Without a word he fell upon a man raising a stone and cuffed him to the ground with a terrific blow. Others instantly dropped their stones and lowered their faces, stepping back.

'Ay, you cowards of men!' said La Valette. He raised up the

family of Jews where they knelt in the dust, still praying their Hebrew prayers.

'What is your name?'

'Isaac, Lord.'

'Father Isaac. Your family is safe. These scoundrels will not touch a hair of your head. Go home.'

To the mob already beginning to disperse, towering over them, he said, 'You fools! You look like none so much as those baying brutes who stoned St Stephen, our first martyr, so righteous in their own eyes. Any spies or traitors in this city are my business. Now depart!'

3

On the morning of the 18th May, Nicholas was on the walls with Hodge when a Spanish soldier ahead of them suddenly stood very stiff-backed, staring out to sea. He was as still as a hunting dog on the trace.

They raced to his side. 'What? What?'

He said nothing, still staring. He was young, twenty-two or so, and his eyes were good. They stared also. Nothing. No, but ... wait. The blue horizon there ... what was that? As if flecked with white. As if edged with white horses. But on so calm a day ...

Everything seemed to go silent, time stopped. And then they saw them. Sails.

The Spanish soldier crossed himself. 'They are coming.'

Nicholas couldn't move. He thought of a hare, frozen under the fixed, yellow-eyed gaze of a wolf.

Then there rose up over the horizon, some twelve miles distant, great sail upon sail. They stretched from left to right, from north to south, a myriad of sails, white and red, green and yellow. They came on slow and steady, the wind but sparsely with them, their lashed slaves rowing hard. More appeared. The horizon was nothing now but a huge crescent of sails and just discerned galleys.

'Sweet Jesu,' breathed the soldier. 'How many?'

'Hodge,' said Nicholas urgently, 'find Smith and Stanley, bring them here.'

Hodge vanished. Nicholas raced the other way, down the stone steps to the street.

An old woman caught the look on his face, and seized his arm.

'You have seen them?'

Nicholas pulled free. 'Yes,' he said.

The old woman dropped her bundle and covered her face with her hands and wept.

He raced on.

La Valette received the message without expression.

The church bells tolled and the startled pigeons flapped up into the blue air. Many citizens sank to their knees and prayed. From below the walls came a groaning and creaking of the mighty capstan at the mouth of Galley Creek, more than twenty men heaving at the windlasses, and the huge chain rose dripping from the seabed like some creature of the deep. Barefoot fishermen rowed out and pushed wooden rafts beneath it in the centre where it sagged, lashing them all together with smaller chains and the strongest ropes.

San Angelo with its moat dividing it from Birgu was a supremely defensible island, linked to the town only by a high arched viaduct. But now Birgu was cut off as well, an island surrounded by high walls, those on the Galley Creek side inaccessible anyway. Only the landward walls could realistically be attacked by infantry, though the massive Turkish guns might reach anywhere. It was infantry that took a town, and it was the landward walls of Birgu that must hold them.

Nicholas raced back up to the walls.

The different langues were despatched to their posts, the Spanish tercios being held in reserve. San Angelo itself was left virtually unmanned for now. The first knights would die fighting for the town.

The langues of Provence, Auvergne and France ranged up along the south-facing walls, looking out over the desolate and unpeopled country. Castile held the mighty bastion next to them, and Aragon, Catalonia and Navarre held the westward curtain wall running up to San Angelo, overlooking Kalkara Creek. The small number of Germans occupied the eastward walls over Galley Creek.

So few of them, stretched so thin.

The Grand Fleet had sailed out of the Bosphorus on 29th March, exactly as Don John of Austria had known. The embarkation of an armada this size could hardly be a secret. Spies raced ahead overland, travelling by relays of horses, beacon fires dancing from one rocky headland to the next.

Mustafa Pasha stood lean on the sterncastle of his flagship, *Al-Mansour*, stony eyes in the wrinkled sallow face looking westward. The more aristocratic Piyale Pasha, charming and black-bearded, might have seemed his junior, but Suleiman had commanded them to work together as joint commanders.

'You can only have one commander,' said Mustafa.

Suleiman looked at him keenly. 'Would you serve as second?'

Mustafa lowered his eyes. 'As you decree, Shadow of the Sun.'

Suleiman had viewed the departure of his fleet from the Golden Horn. He felt some regret that he was not commanding himself. But let Mustafa and Piyale first take Malta, then he himself would lead his victorious army on into the heart of Europe. How sweet it would be to ride into Rome.

His eyes surveyed the hundred and eighty-one ships, a hundred and thirty of them oared war galleys, with unlikely names such as *The Pearl* and *The Sun*, *The Gate of Neptune*, *The Rose of Algiers*, *The Golden Lemon Tree*. Thirty huge troop-carrying galliots, each carrying six hundred men. Eleven fat-bodied merchant ships laden with supplies. Six thousand barrels of gunpowder, thirteen hundred cannon balls. Six thousand Janizaries, acknowledged even by the Christ-worshippers as the finest fighting troops in the world. Four thousand Bektaşis, willing shock troops, longing for martyrdom. Nine thousand cavalry Sipahis, and many thousands of paid peasant levies, quite expendable.

As the fleet moved majestically down the Bosphorus, from the minarets came the ancient cry of the desert in all its stark certainty.

'There is no God but God, and Mohammed is the Prophet of God!'

As if in answer, offshore winds caught the sails of the galleys and they billowed eagerly forward, the green pennants with their embroidered gold crescents streaming likewise from the mastheads.

In time the armada's vast numbers had been swelled even further by thousands more North African corsairs. Even as they sailed south across the Aegean, outlaws and bandits joined them, slipping out from remote Greek or Levantine inlets, leaving unknown islands, the dens of thieves and robbers, to pursue a richer prey, matters of divinity far from their minds. Christian? Muslim? What did they care? They would sail with the devil himself if there was gold in it. They were cut-throats, opportunists, nationless men, who inspired fables among the vulgar of heroic deeds or fanciful freedoms upon the boundless ocean. They were savages to a man, without kin or country, honour or nobility, the dregs of mankind. They would latch on to the Ottoman fleet like fleas on a dog, bringing nothing but their knives and their murderous hearts.

From the walls of San Angelo they could now see the oars slowly rising and falling, unhurried, implacable. Stanley said they were fifteen miles away, not twelve. They would be here in three hours or so.

'We should go.'

Yet still they stood, even the two knights, as if fascinated by this vast armada of death that filled the sea from northern to southern horizon. The Grand Fleet of the greatest empire on earth.

'Your eyes sparkle, Master Ingoldsby,' said Stanley, glancing at him. 'As if this were a spectacle sent for our entertainment.'

'It is magnificent, for all that.'

'It is coming to kill us.'

The guns of San Angelo roared out three shots in quick succession. Only a moment later, St Elmo answered with three identical shots, and the standard of St John was raised over the battlements. A few minutes after the same volley came from five miles inland: from the ancient walled capital of Mdina in the rocky heart of the island, the small proud city on the hill, with its winding shadowy streets and its frigid nobility in their dark palaces. Valette had little faith in them. They would keep to their own.

The Grand Master understood well what the Turkish strategy would be. Direct attack on all fronts, by land and sea. With such numerical superiority that was inevitable. But the focus of the attack would clearly be the Grand Harbour and San Angelo itself. The Knights were far too few in number to oppose a general landing. It would all be about their resistance to siege from within the fortified town. Until relief came, from God alone knew where.

Nevertheless La Valette ordered the French knight, Marshal Copier, to assemble a small troop of cavalry and reconnoitre the coast. With an Ottoman force commanded by that most cunning of adversaries, Mustafa Pasha, there was no knowing what tricks and diversions might be planned. The Turks knew even now that their mission would not be easy. They knew the Knights of old.

Copier was ordered to harass any landing forces from a distance, but more importantly to glean all intelligence possible, and retreat to San Angelo in good time.

He took command of six mounted Spanish soldiers, and summoned knight volunteers before the Palace. Soon he was joined by his fellow countryman, the Chevalier Adrien de la Rivière, the Portuguese knight, Pedro Mezquita, sitting high and haughty in his decorated saddle as befitted a knight who was also the nephew of the Governor of Mdina, and the novice of his langue, Bartolomeo Faraone.

Nicholas begged Stanley to let him ride out with them.

'These are knights and veteran soldiers, boy. This is a cavalry sortie, and very fast moving.'

'I can ride as well as any in Shropshire.'

'You have no horse.'

'Your stables are full of them. I saw a fine white mare.'

'It is safer out there,' said Smith, hoping to dissuade the young hothead. 'This is where the fight will be.'

'I'll be back for it,' said Nicholas. 'But I want to ride out.'

'What of Hodge?'

Hodge looked unhappy.

Nicholas said, 'He can sit on a palfrey and fairly imitate a sack of mangels. Can you not, Hodge?'

'Me and horses don't get on,' said Hodge.

Stanley said, 'Very well, Hodge, you shall be my squire, and as they say in Rome, the *servus servorum dei*.'

'What's that when it's put in English then?'

'It means you'll do what you're told.' He turned on Nicholas. 'Well, get to the stables, lad. You'll have no armour, and you know nothing of turning a lance. Only your short sword, which is no cavalry sword. So make sure you choose a fast mount.'

Nicholas ran.

'Was that wise?' muttered Smith.

'He'll be back in a wink,' said Stanley with a grin. 'Grand Marshal Copier will never take him. Let him learn.'

Trotting down to the south gate, Copier reined in his troop of nine and glared back over his shoulder.

'That man at the back. Ride up, sir!'

Nicholas came up smartly on his white mare.

'Who the devil may you be?'

'English gentleman and volunteer, sir!'

'Good. Now back to your wall, and quick about it.'

'I was told I could ride with you.'

'Well, you can't. Who told you? The Grand Master?'

'No,' said Nicholas, 'the Chevalier Edward St—'

'I only take orders from the Grand Master and from God.' Copier heeled his horse. The troop moved forward.

Nicholas rode after them.

A few last refugees came in through the gate before Copier and his troop rode out. Infants and aged women, skinny dogs and scraggy chickens in wicker cages, pitiful possessions borne on donkeys and primitive carts, or in wooden wheelbarrows with creaking wheels.

They looked up at the squadron of cavalry with their lances and muskets, long swords and tall helmets, so fine in the sun. One old woman made the sign of the cross in the air.

Outside the gate, Copier looked back again and bellowed with anger. 'God damn you for a fool and a knave, I ordered you back inside!'

'I came to Malta as a volunteer,' said Nicholas. 'I am not under your command. I ride where I will.'

Just in front of him, Pedro Mezquita suppressed a laugh. This English boy had spirit.

'Then you are not under my command, and you are not under my protection!' roared Copier, red-faced and furious. 'The Turk lands on this island in two hours, and he will have your balls for his breakfast!'

He spurred furiously and his startled horse leapt forward. 'Troop, at all speed!'

They were just about to leave the walls of San Angelo and row over to St Elmo when Stanley paused. 'They're turning.'

'What?'

'Look. They're turning.'

It was true. The Ottoman crescent was sailing southwards, away from the entrance to the Grand Harbour.

'Why the devil?'

'They must be going south round to Marsasirocco. It's the only other bay will take 'em. Then coming back overland.'

Without another word, Smith went to inform La Valette. But La Valette already knew. Smith thought he even saw something like a smile play on the Grand Master's lips. A rare occurrence indeed.

'It will be harder for them, Sire,' said Smith, puzzled. 'To carry all those great guns overland.'

'Quite so. But several months ago, I had one of our double agents in Constantinople convince their Admiral Piyale that St Elmo was ferociously served with the best cannon, and that the *gregale*, our north-east wind, would play havoc with their fleet in the east-facing Marsamuscetto.'

'But the *gregale* barely blows in the summer months.'

Now La Valette was unmistakably smiling.

Smith said, 'Mustafa Pasha must know this. He knows every bay, every wind and current in the Mediterranean.'

'But Piyale does not. This tells us something of their command structure for the campaign. Clearly Piyale is commander of the fleet, as Mustafa is commander of the land forces.'

'You can only have one commander.'

'When Suleiman was younger, he would have commanded himself. But now he is old, and growing foolish. Dividing his command was the first mistake. Sailing for Marsasirocco, they have made two.'

Smith regarded his Grand Master with more reverence than ever, if that were possible. This great battle was one that La Valette had already been fighting for months. Years.

4

The cavalry troop rode south to follow the Ottoman fleet from the high cliffs. Nicholas rode a safe distance behind.

Inland Malta was a bare rocky tableland of stark pueblos, single-storey houses, white cubes glaring in the sun. Shelters for men and shelters for animals often indistinguishable. Many had fled for the safety of Birgu, but some stayed out in these villages, thinking it safer to hide away from the heart of the holocaust.

There were green melon patches, scratching hens, a goat tethered in the shade of a carob tree, nibbling a few hard leaves, its ribs straining beneath the skin. A dull iron bell clanged from a squat church tower. Then the bell-ringer appeared, a skeletal toothless priest in filthy gaberdine. He watched them pass without a word of greeting. There was another goat lying dead among the rocks, its belly bloated. Perhaps it had been slaughtered so at least the Mohammedan devils would not have it. Clouded with excited flies, its rotting stench mingled on the air with the sweet thyme.

There were olives and prickly pear and Fiori de Pasqua, but it was a hard, bitter landscape. Nicholas imagined High Spain and the Castilian plain was like this, only immeasurably more vast. What a land to fight for.

They rode down past the villages of Zabbar and Zeitun, and watched in bafflement as the Grand Fleet still sailed on, past Marsasirocco Bay and north again up the west coast, past the bird island of Filfla, haunted by the souls of the dead. They rode across to Zurrieq, and then north along the forbidding heights of the cliffs of Dingli.

'Perhaps they sail for Ghain Tuffieha Bay?' said De la Rivière.

Copier grunted. It was a poor anchorage compared to Marsasirocco.

Night began to fall, and on a millpond sea, the fleet dropped anchor. Nicholas thought of the fleet of Agamemnon off the coast of Troy. The ships rode serenely on their hawsers as if with nothing to fear. Ghain Tuffieha and Gejna were but small bays with golden sand, just enough for them to anchor, and very far from St Angelo. A two or three hour march for a man with a pack. But dragging the siege guns ...

'My fear is they will station between Malta and Gozo,' said Copier. 'That way they will cut off any hope of our relief from Sicily.'

De la Rivière hadn't thought of that. He looked grave.

Laughter and shouts in Turkish sounded over the water. *'Arkadaş! Akşam yemeği!'* Lanterns were lit, dinners cooked on the steady decks. Spirits were sky-high. *'Zefer!'* Victory! They would land unopposed.

Copier's cavalry troop unrolled their blankets and ate dry rations and slept. Faraone kept the first watch.

Nicholas had brought neither food nor blanket. He huddled against a south-facing wall, belly rumbling, and slept little. Vagabond again.

At dawn the one hundred and eighty galleys raised anchor and sailed south once more.

'Playing games,' muttered Copier.

'At least they're not anchoring off Gozo,' said De la Rivière. 'You think relief may yet come?'

Copier said nothing. Who could tell?

He despatched two of the Spanish soldiers back to Birgu to tell La Valette the fleet was sailing south again, probably for Marsasirocco.

'You know the Grand Master dislikes *probablies,*' said Don Mezquita.

Copier grunted. 'Very well. Just say they're sailing south.'

Copier was right though. The Grand Fleet returned to the broad bay of Marsasirocco and anchored and began to disembark. The Marshal led his troop right out onto the high promontory

169

of Delimara and looked down. They were perilously near the Ottomans, but like a gnat near a lion. The vast force would not trouble itself with them.

The Ottomans were landing on a flat, easy coast now, below the mysterious stone tombs of Tas-Silg, the burial chambers of a nameless people who had lived in the ancient past before Christ, before history.

Copier and his men could only look down helplessly from the heights as the army took shape.

The level of organization in this vast operation was astonishing. They watched longboats being lowered, men wading through the shallows with timbers and planking, ropes and hatchets, swiftly building a landing stage. Oxen driven ashore, wooden wheels bound in iron bands rolled up onto the planked sand, great gun carriages speedily assembled from beautifully carpentered parts, and the numerous guns themselves, sixty-pounders, eighty-pounders, and a few monsters of burnished bronze. Saltwater streamed from the sweating men, but not a drop touching the precious weapons, worth a small kingdom. Whole regiments of Janizaries and Sipahis came ashore, then waited patient and orderly under brightly coloured parasols, as if on a holiday.

It was the parasols that finally did it for Marshal Copier. Growling furiously into his beard about insolent swine, boy-lovers, nancying ashore with *parasols,* like *ladies of the court,* he quickly unshouldered his musket. De la Rivière's mouth twitched with amusement, but he said nothing about the waste of a shot. Copier loaded where he sat in the saddle, none too easily, and loosed off the ball at the forty thousand men below. They never even knew where it hit. A few looked up at the bang. Perhaps a few even smiled. None stirred a hair.

'Harassing the enemy,' said Copier, reading his brother knight's mind. He reshouldered the musket, the barrel hot to the touch. 'That boulder there. How many men could shift it?'

'Twenty? Thirty?'

'Ten,' said Copier. He turned in the saddle and glared back at Nicholas, still hovering some two hundred paces off. 'Boy! Move up your white English arse, at the gallop!'

Now Nicholas came close and looked down. The sight below

was awe-inspiring, beautiful. The Ottoman army. He had dreamt of it, but never in such richness. The plumes of peacock and white egret feathers, the tall standards of horsehair and beaten silver, the gold tassels and red fezzes and green pennants incribed with the names of Allah. *Ad-Darr, Al-Qahhar, Al-Mumit.* The Afflictor, The Subduer, The Bringer of Death.

Moustachioed Janizaries in trousers and long coats, cavalrymen in light mail, religious zealots in white or green, pashas in robes of apricot and gold, semi-naked dervishes in animal skins, conical caps in duck-egg blue, white headdresses with ostrich plumes, Janizaries shouldering long muskets inlaid with arabesques of ivory, circular shields of wicker and brass, pointed shields from Hungary, curved scimitars and compound bows from the Asian steppes, flags of shot silk decorated with evil eyes, scorpions and crescent moons, flowing Arabic characters, bell tents, music and drums.

Among the massing ranks of the soldiers, the armaments and the wagons, strode a tall dark figure in swirling black robes. Even from here, Nicholas could discern a master among men. It was Mustafa Pasha. He carried a short whip in his left hand, and in his right, a scimitar ready-drawn.

'Dismount!' cried Copier.

They were uneasily aware that if the Turks should make speed up the slope before them, they would be cut off from flight in a minute.

'Shoulders to the rock! Now *heave!*'

It was farcical. The boulder moved not an inch. Pedro Mezquita murmured something about Sisyphus and inspected a broken fingernail. And ahead of them, the Ottoman vanguard was already beginning to move inland, threatening to cut them off. Humiliated, the troop remounted and spurred their horses. The grand army of the Sultan had indeed landed unopposed, singing songs of victory, and there was nothing they could do. They were, as always, too few.

'Always outnumbered, always outgunned!' Copier bellowed into the wind as they galloped. 'Almighty God *damn* the Kings of Christendom for milk-faced pigeon-livered slaves!'

*

Mustafa Pasha sent out an advance party of unarmoured slave-runners to reconnoitre the country and identify resources. They returned shamefaced, to say they had seen some partridges, a few quail.

Mustafa's eyes gleamed like cold wet stones in his flat Anatolian face.

'You found no livestock?'

'No, Pasha. There was none. Everything slaughtered or gone.'

Pasha struck the slave-runner across the face with his short whip. The man remained motionless, the blood bubbling along the wound on his cheek.

'You found none. You did not look hard enough. And forage?'

The slave shook his head. 'They have destroyed everything and left us only a wasteland.'

Mustafa Pasha nearly struck him again and then his arm dropped.

'The first well we come to,' he said to a nearby Janizary officer, 'this cur drinks it.'

'Sire.'

He turned away. He was beginning to hate this island already. But the infidels' stubbornness and opposition would only make their punishment worse in the end. He watched the unloading. Coming up now were bundles of tied stakes for entrenchments. But they could also be used for the impalement and crucifixion of the Christians.

He took a deep breath. The omens remained good. It was the month of Shawwal, in year 972 of the Hegirah of the Prophet. For the Christians it was 1565, dated from the birth of the Jewish teacher Jesus, whom they worshipped in their blasphemous idiocy as Allah Himself. Surely they would learn. Surely his own scimitar would teach them the error of their ways.

The Ottoman army marched forth, the small band of Copier and his cavalry shadowing them all the way, sometimes no further off than half a mile. The Turks would only exhaust themselves giving chase, and the troop would soon be back within the walls of Birgu.

Yet they had to watch from a distance, in agony, as a five-hundred-strong marching Janizary vanguard, with the dark figure of Mustafa at their head on a nodding white stallion, ungelded and mettlesome, occupied each village in turn. They fired what buildings remained, cut down the last few trees and added them to their enormous store of siege materials in the following wagons. The precious rare timber of the island turned against it. Copier's rage grew.

They reined in beneath the flickering shade of a small lemon grove on a hill, no more than a hummock, and quieted their horses. Don Mezquita said with his aristocratic drawl, 'I'm all for a splendid cavalry charge. Grand Marshal?'

Before them on the burning plain, Mustafa and his Janizaries surrounded a cluster of village houses and a farmstead.

The inhabitants did not conceal themselves. Twenty or so, they came forward, neither fleeing nor bowing. The women in dresses, veiled, the men in high-belted white trousers, barefoot, their heads turbanned. The younger children standing staring at the approaching soldiers, flies settling round their mouths and noses, naked among the slain animals.

Mustafa pulled up before them.

'Where are your stores? Your fattest goats that you have hidden from us?'

A woman spoke for them, in the impudent way of Christian women.

'We only eat pork,' she mocked, and spat in the dust.

'You are a foolish woman.'

She laughed.

Mustafa struck her across the face.

Before him, Nicholas saw Copier lean forward in his saddle, hands gripping the pommel white-knuckled.

The Janizaries suddenly spread wide and began to encircle the settlement.

Mustafa said, 'Kill her. Enslave the rest. Burn the houses.'

The woman said, 'You will burn in hell.'

Mustafa turned his stony eyes on her. 'You will feel the flames of hell before I do.'

Copier drew his sword. The rest did likewise, Nicholas with

shaking hand, barely able to believe what was about to happen. Don Mezquita whistled a tune.

Five hundred Janizaries.

Copier turned to Don Mezquita. 'You, sir. You will not ride with us, but back to Birgu to report.'

Don Mezquita instantly flared with anger, but Copier quelled him.

'You are under my command, sir, and will follow orders. We will harry the enemy, but you will ride onward and report.'

Mezquita rose up on his stirrups, his mouth twitching with fury beneath his magnificent moustache, whipped his reins down hard on his horse's withers and rode off at a gallop across the plain, hallooing all the way, desperate for one or two of the Turks to pursue him so that at least he might taste a fight and win glory. None of them did. They simply glanced up and watched with screwed-up eyes as the Christian madman galloped away in a cloud of dust.

'I was thinking,' said the Janizary to his comrade, wiping the blood from his scimitar on the woman's grubby peasant dress and eyeing her headless torso. 'Since landing on this cursed rock, we've not met one coward yet. Even the women.'

The other Janizary looked up and said, almost amused, 'And now we are under attack.'

Nicholas's white mare galloped hard, her head straining forward, mane flying. He spurred her on and levelled his cinquedea before him, yelling wildly. The ten of them spread out into a natural line, the two fastest horses pulling ahead by half a length, a length. The Janizaries ahead of them still stumbling about in disbelief, without order and, more importantly, without pikes or halberds. This ghost troop, this small pack of scouts that had trailed them all the way from Marsasirocco, was now on the attack. It was barely conceivable.

Then they crashed into the milling infantrymen and with a locked arm, Nicholas swept his blade low and flat and cut a man deep across his face. He heard a screaming behind him.

Now they were within the circle of Janizaries, losing formation, pulling their horses round to ride back again, to keep free space and use their speed and be able to escape afterwards, after this lightning strike. The trapped peasants of the steading stared about bewildered. They had expected enslavement, beating, but not a battlefield. One or two impetuously ran to their tumbledown sheds for a pick or hoe. One was cut down by a big Janizary even as he ran. Another was pinned against a wall, sliding slowly, a red stain on the whitewash behind him.

A harsh voice was calling out in Turkish, Mustafa on his white stallion. Suddenly it came to Nicholas what his fate might be. He pulled around and made for the voice. Two Janizaries blocked his way. He tried to crash his horse through them but the terrified mare reared and he slipped back, scrabbling at the reins, dropping his sword. One of the Janizaries tried to cut his leg but he rolled off the other side and the beast took the blow. A horse's scream was a terrible sound.

Unarmed now, he rolled up from the earth with dust in his hands. *Use anything, throw anything.* Everything moved at slow speed. The Janizaries were onto him, yet he had time. With two handfuls of dust he would take them. He threw one, the fellow turned, thrust his sword at him, Nicholas took one swift step back and it was enough. It was a lazy thrust. At the same time he transferred the other handful of dust to his right for better throwing and cast it, all in one smooth movement, fast as a snake. It hit his man full in the face, he gasped and blinked, the back of his hand to his eyes.

There was a short shadow on the ground beside him, a Turk coming behind to finish him. The blinded man was standing still. Nicholas kicked out hard and caught the fellow in his stones beneath his flowing robes. A guttural grunt. He bent double. Away to his left galloped De la Rivière, hewing down a Janizary caught off guard, and then two arrows flew and thocked into man or horse, and he knew that De la Rivière had gone down. Now he would use his sword, that famous swordsmanship, the finest in France they said. How many Turks would he take with him?

Nicholas shoved his knee hard into the fellow's bended face and seized his scimitar. By Jesu it was heavy. He kept moving, moving all the time, his feet never still, never a steady target. Behind him was another, and he was cutting across Nicholas's back even as the boy moved aside without knowing he was there. The fellow he had kicked in the stones fell forward and his comrade Janizary's own scimitar cut him across the head. There was a moment of shock.

Nicholas had time in that still moment. He swung the heavy curved blade and cut deep into the fellow's side. There was an instant stench from his split torso, which the boy would learn in time was the stench of ruptured bowels, and the fellow collapsed as if cut in two.

He hauled the reeking scimitar blade free and turned again. Four riderless horses milled about. There were Janizaries bending over fallen men, kicking off tall Spanish morions and performing a couple of quick deft beheadings. They had become trapped. It had been a foolish escapade.

De la Rivière sat still in the dust, head hanging forward like a man in final exhaustion, an arrow in his shoulder. A Janizary stood behind him with his blade at his bare throat, but not killing him, not yet. Mustafa's harsh voice still rang out, and then Nicholas also saw the novice Faraone. They had stripped him naked. He was young and slim. They goaded him. He wept. Mustafa's voice came again, and they reluctantly roped him up and rolled him down in the dust beside De la Rivière. Nicholas saw also that Copier lay dead, the greatest loss. The four Spanish infantrymen were dead too, come all the way from the green New World to die here in the Old, the blood-stained Old, on the very first day of Malta's desperate struggle.

He was the last standing, he still clutched a Turkish scimitar, and he carried not a wound. And he was surrounded.

It was very still. Horses whinnied. His mare was led round the back of the line of troops and he saw that she carried a cut to the belly. It was not so bad. Hundreds of Janizary soldiers circled, and he was at the heart of them. Now he knew what would become of him. He was a boy. They were Turks. No, they would not kill him. They would keep him for recreation and amusement.

Mustafa stepped through the ranks and stood before him.

'I saw you. You were unhorsed and disarmed, and then you went on to kill one of my men and badly wound another. You are dangerous for so puny an infidel.'

Nicholas said nothing, fingering the sweat-soaked handle of the scimitar, bringing the point round to face his own heart.

'Ah.' Mustafa smiled. 'I see. And I saw you ride at me too. Well. Here I am.'

It took only an instant for Nicholas to choose how he would die. He thought he heard De la Rivière's weak voice cry out 'No boy!' as he charged at the smiling Pasha. And then his world went black.

5

For a while he thought he was in the pound with Hodge. It was dark, his head throbbed, his mouth tasted of steel.

'Is that you, Hodge?' he muttered, the words thick and clumsy on his lips.

'*Grace à Dieu*,' said a man's voice softly. 'Brother – I mean, English boy. Can you hear me?'

Nicholas nodded. His head throbbed worse with every movement. And he could see nothing. 'I am blindfolded, yes?'

'We three,' said De la Rivière. 'We are captured.' He sounded exhausted by these few words, and paused to draw strength. 'Do you have any blade left on you, boy?'

Nicholas shook his head, and then laughed weakly. The knight couldn't see him. 'No,' he said. 'None.'

There was a long silence.

'What will become of us?'

'It would be better,' said De la Rivière slowly, 'if we had a blade. It would be a better way out.' He gasped with sudden pain. 'Have you faith, boy? Do you fear to die, to go to Christ in heaven?'

'No. No I do not. Nor to join the souls that have gone before.'

'Then make your prayers.' He drew breath. 'I believe this battle is over for us now.'

A door was kicked open, there were heavy footfalls and their blindfolds were ripped off.

They were huddled on the beaten earth floor of the tiny bare chapel of the village they had fought for. It contained nothing but a plain altar table and one high window. Their hands were tied behind their backs. Faraone was still naked, curled up like a child, shivering, hiding his shame. De la Rivière seemed baptised in blood from head to toe, now dried black and crusted. The shaft of a broken arrow still protruded from his shoulder. He breathed with pain. Nicholas himself had a bad head, and his vision swam if he moved too quickly. But he could move little. He felt very tired and very afraid, and desperately thirsty.

Before them stood the Turks come to torture them, led by Mustafa himself. There was a tall thin fellow, naked to the waist, wearing a wolf's tooth necklace on a rawhide string, and with a simple bare curved yatagan dagger at his belt, and there were two senior Janizaries. Now Nicholas could see them close to and study them, they were magnificent men, with a far gaze, oiled dark hair, noble features. They wore broad billowing white robes beneath tight mail jerkins, high domed helmets, and immense curved scimitars at their sides. The weapons had beautiful damascened scrollwork along the blade, the tiny grooves still showing the dark rust-red of old blood. One wore a brass quill through the skin above his deep furrowed brow.

Mustafa's expression was of glowering anger at the insolent attack. He nodded at De la Rivière. 'You are a Knight of St John. These are acolytes, yes?'

'They are nuns,' said De la Rivière.

'If we put you to the torture, you may prove brave. So shall we start with torturing your acolytes? Or should I say, catamites?'

The knight said, 'The moment you begin to torture either of these, I will bite through my own tongue and spit it in the dust. Besides, they know nothing of worth.'

'So you do? Then tell us. What is the weakest point of Birgu?'

De la Rivière just smiled through broken teeth and split lips.

'Drag him onto that table there,' commanded Mustafa.

'It is called an altar.'

'How fitting.'

With their backs turned, Nicholas shuffled up close to the naked Faraone, now shaking like a leaf. It was the only comfort he could give. The boy was already far gone. Nicholas tried to warm him.

But it was not cold that made him shiver. Hearing the tortured screams would finally destroy his reason.

For a minute or two, De la Rivière made no sound. The torturer also worked in silence. Blood dripped, spotting the floor beneath the altar, and at one point there was a ripping sound, like fine leather being torn. Nicholas closed his eyes and hung his head. Faraone's eyes were wide open, staring wildly into the chapel's roof space.

'Be elsewhere,' whispered Nicholas. 'Think yourself another place, hear birdsong, the sea.'

But the other boy could not. He was trapped in hell.

Behind them, Mustafa said, 'Speak. Talk to us.'

They heard De la Rivière praying. He spoke the names of St John and the Blessed Virgin and his Saviour, Christ the Lord.

The torture continued, and then quite suddenly, without warning, the knight broke. He arched his back and screamed out, 'Castile! The bastion of Castile!'

He subsided and sobbed.

'Wash him down,' said Mustafa, already turning and striding for the door. 'And watch these two.' He bent an evil eye on Nicholas. 'Especially this one. He is a snake.'

Piyale asked, 'You trust the word of a tortured man?'

Mustafa said, 'Few men would suffer torture so long, only to lie. Nevertheless he is a Knight Hospitaller, our ancient enemy, and trustworthy as Shaitan himself. We will not send in the Janizaries. Not yet.' He turned to a senior officer. 'Call up the first division of the Bektaşis. We attack the bastion of Castile tomorrow dawn.'

'Where is Copier's scouting party?' demanded La Valette.

The lookout shook his head.

All day from the land walls of Birgu they kept their eyes on the southern horizon and the heights of Santa Margherita. The night watches leaned on the battlements and strained their eyes under the starlight. The land lay still. Not a dog barked. The stars wheeled silently in a velvet sky.

Then at dawn they heard the sound of a deep, distant rumbling in the earth. Citizens clutched tables, doorposts, thinking it was an earthquake. Some lay on the ground in the street.

'Little that will avail you!' cried a German knight, striding past to his post, clanking with armour.

People scowled at the arrogant knight. The Hospitallers had always looked down on them. One said sullenly, 'It is no *terramoto?*'

'No *terramoto*. The guns are coming.'

Stanley and Smith shared an eyeglass, looking out at the heights of Santa Margherita. There came another sound, of drums approaching. Cries rang out all around the walls, and immediately every man was donning his armour and seizing his weapons and running to battle stations, heart thumping. Above the drums sounded a braying brass horn. They were truly coming.

And then over the heights came line upon line of attackers. Gilded flags and waves of white silk robes casting long shadows, early sunlight flashing, dancing on polished shields and scabbards decorated with coloured glass, drums beating out a relentless dead-march rhythm.

Arquebusiers on the walls loaded and set their pans and checked their fuses. Crossbowmen stepped in their foot stirrups and ratcheted back and levered and set in the bolts and stood to the battlements again. They sighted.

The attackers stopped. An Imam pronounced the blessing of Allah on them, and they cried out with one huge voice,

'*Allahu akbar!*'

The sound of that roar of faith was more terrible than any battery of guns.

Then the ranks of men parted, and the black mouths of bronze cannon appeared in their midst. The infantrymen retreated a long way, giving the guns plenty of room. The Turks had brought up a battery of eight on wheeled carriages. Gunners moved busily about their beasts, wedging the carriages against recoil, priming and loading, while a gunnery master surveyed the walls, estimating trajectories with a superbly practised eye.

'Those are big guns,' said Stanley.

'But far from the biggest.'

'Testing shots. They seem to be ranging on Castile. I wonder ...'

Then knights along the walls were bowing low. It was the Grand

Master, bringing up the Spanish tercios in reserve, and come to take personal command of the south walls.

At a barked order from La Valette, seeing instantly that the attack was to be concentrated on Castile, the knights of Provence, Auvergne and France moved out onto their own flanking towers and walls in neat order, turning their arquebuses towards the bastion of Castile, ready for enfilading fire.

The Ottoman guns roared, almost in unison, a single, rolling thunder, and then hard cracks as the balls struck home against the sloped walls of Castile. Men ducked swiftly back behind the battlements as shards of stone flew up amid vast plumes of smoke and dust. They were using cannonballs of marble. Younger knights sprang up again too soon, but older hands dragged them back down and told them to keep their heads covered, faces lowered. Marble cannonballs fired with such force could send up burning splinters weighing a pound or more, hundreds of feet into the air. Then they came down again.

In the hot still air the clouds of dust formed great shielding curtains, impenetrable to the eye. And beyond the clouds of dust arose a fanatic howl, filled with madness, rage and longing.

'Bektaşis,' said Smith. 'Deranged with Allah and hemp.'

The Turks were only loosing one barrage. Now their infantrymen were already running at the walls with ropes, grapples and scaling ladders, still unseen beyond their own screen of dust, scimitars flashing and turning in the air.

La Valette raised an arm.

'Arquebusiers!'

His arm dropped.

At no more than fifty paces, the enfilading volley was devastating. The smoke roiled and the dust swirled, yet immediately La Valette had the second rank of arquebusiers step forward and loose their volley, though they could barely see their target. Another deafening roar, and many more screams below. There came a third volley, and then the guns were rested and the crossbowmen took over, loosing another three volleys of bolts into the ranks of Bektaşis, then cranking back and reloading a fourth time and waiting for the dust to settle.

'Free fire!' called La Valette.

They waited to aim clear and pick off individuals. Slowly the dust settled.

There were not enough attackers left standing for the fifty cross-bowmen to shoot. A single fanatic, his white turban dyed red, stood and swayed, waving his scimitar, eyes to the sun in the east already blinded, chanting the names of Allah. In a second he was stuck with more than half-a-dozen hurtling bolts, and went to Paradise.

'Hold!' said La Valette.

A waste of bolts.

The dust finally drifted away on the summer air.

All down from the heights of Santa Margherita, and below the bastion of Castile, lay a mown field of red bodies. Here and there came a groan, a twitching limb. An arm was raised. La Valette signalled to the crossbowman nearest and the wounded man was killed. After that, the defenders did not even bother to shoot the last few wounded. They would die soon anyway in this heat. They saved their bolts for later.

Not one attacker had come close to scaling the bastion walls. Emerging through their own blinding dust clouds, the Bektaşis had found the great walls of Castile barely grazed, let alone cracked or ruptured enough to permit an incursion. As Stanley thought, this was nothing but a test. Knights and soldiers looked down soberly on the field of tangled Ottoman dead. None celebrated. This was a very small beginning indeed. And if the Turk could be so prodigal with so many of his own troops, there would be many more to come.

Mustafa was incensed. There was no weak spot, or if there was, it certainly wasn't Castile. Birgu was a fortified town of grim strength in every yard of its towering curtain wall.

He wheeled his horse and rode south, covering three rough miles in a quarter of an hour. His horse was nearly lamed.

He stood at the door of the chapel and regained his composure before entering.

Da la Rivière was an ugly sight, for all the washing and banda-ging. But he remained conscious. The naked boy now twitched and jabbered to himself on the floor. The fairheaded one, the whiteskinned snake, looked him insolently in the eye.

Mustafa said to them, 'The capital of this island is Mdina. This is an Arabic name, the Arabic for "city". You know this, in your hard Christian hearts. And Arabic is a holy language, *the* holy language, the language of the Prophet and the Koran. This Malta was an Arab island once, a Muslim island, and Mdina was a city of Islam.'

'Things change,' whispered De la Rivière, his voice as dry as sand.

Still insolent, still defiant. Curse him. Would these knights never yield?

'It will be a Muslim island again!'

'How was the assault on Castile?' asked the boy.

Mustafa did not even strike him. It was useless with such a one. He ordered all three dragged outside.

The naked acolyte was mad. The knight was almost dead with his injuries, he would not make it through another night. Mustafa ground his teeth. Though the fairhaired boy was the most insolent, the most unbreakable of all, with his eyes like blue ice ... it would have to be him.

A Janizary dragged Faraone forward and drew his scimitar. The boy's lips moved but they could hear no words.

'He is only a boy,' whispered Da la Rivière.

'Old enough to die,' said Mustafa.

The scimitar flashed down, and Faraone's head rolled in the dust. Nicholas had never seen a sight so pitiful. But he did not look away. He commended his soul to heaven.

De la Rivière was beaten slowly to death with fine rods. It took a long time. He never begged for mercy nor made a sound, but Nicholas knew he was praying in his heart. Perhaps in those last minutes, God in his mercy reached down and took away his pain. And that moment before, when he had broken under torture, in the chapel, and cried out ... He had been acting all the time. The slim, aristocratic Frenchman, the elegant swordsman – he was made of something harder than steel.

Even Mustafa had enough chivalry in him to allow a man a last few words. The beating paused.

'For our three deaths,' De la Rivière said, his mouth drooling spittle and blood, but smiling, teeth gleaming through the blood.

'You have lost two hundred men or more. At Castile. This is how it will go with you. A prophecy of what is to come.'

The soldiers raised their rods to finish him, but at last Mustafa stayed them. The courage of this flint-hearted infidel touched even him. Let him die a man's death, at least. He gave the order, and a scimitar blade came down.

Mustafa bent his dark eye on Nicholas.

'Alone of all his tribe,' he sneered.

'Be quick about it then,' said the boy.

The Pasha smiled. 'It tastes foul in my mouth. But it is you who will ride back alive to your comrades, and tell them all. Wear this around your throat and my men will not molest you. Let your comrades know everything. Be sure to tell them of the horror that awaits.'

Nicholas took the decorated green cloth with distaste, tempted to drop it to the ground. But he would never pass by the enemy watchmen without it. He knotted it round his neck.

His horse was brought over, the wound in her belly sewn with strands of her own mane and daubed with turps and earth. He mounted up.

'I wonder if we will meet again before you die,' said Mustafa.

'Once is enough, I think. You filthy mule-fucker.'

Then saving his spurs on the animal's wounded flank, he lashed the reins and trotted north.

Mustafa cursed himself for not cutting off a hand or a foot.

His head still hurt, his vision shimmered, and not only from the afternoon heat haze on the earth. When he reached a spot of shade beneath a carob, he dismounted and was suddenly overwhelmed with grief and revulsion. The dead boy Faraone, an innocent heart, and the horrible torture of De la Rivière. The butchered peasant woman … He leaned and spewed, bilious spew upon the baked ground. His stomach was void, his throat more parched than ever. Mustafa had refused him even a mouthful of water. Only this accursed Mohammedan token about his throat. It burned his skin.

He remounted and sat a moment in the shade. He must have water soon or he would be pissing black. Yet he felt a little better. Things were clearer. Some things. His ardent heart, his fierce loyalty to his father and his sisters and his name, even to Hodge; his love of comradeship, his appetite for glory, and for righteous vengeance. Now he had an object for his temper and his many passions. Of course he had come to Malta to fight the Mohammedan. But now he would fight them with savage joy in his heart, and absolute conviction. For his father and his mother, his sisters, for England and St George. For Christendom, for the Knights, for the magnificent, defiant scornful peasant woman beheaded by the Turks. For Copier and Faraone and De la Rivière, and all the tough soldiers and gallant knights yet to die.

He screwed up his eyes and heeled his horse gently forward into the white blaze.

For all of them.

'Open the gates!'

A party of Turks watched from the heights of Santa Margherita not half a mile off, their muskets trained on his back. But he wore the green neckerchief of protection. The drawbridge swung down, the gates of Birgu swung open. Nicholas stopped his horse on the narrow drawbridge and tore off the neckerchief and looked back at them, unsure if they could see. In case they could, he leaned back and made as if wiping his horse's arse with the cloth, embroidered with the sacred names in Arab script. Then he dropped it in the dust behind him and walked his horse in. A shot rang out wild. The gates slammed shut.

Stanley came running, and also Hodge.

'God's mercy, boy, you're alive!'

'Alive and well,' croaked Nicholas, slithering from the horse and finding his legs didn't work. Hodge held him.

'Water!' bellowed Stanley.

The boy drank.

'Slowly.' After only a few tantalising glugs, the knight pulled the flask away. 'The others?'

Nicholas shook his head.

'Copier too? De la Rivière?'

'They all died fighting. We faced two hundred or more. We charged them … Copier gave the order. They had murdered a woman.'

Stanley gripped his sword hilt. 'This is a sad loss. A bitter loss.'

'I was no hero. I did not break free, the Turks let me go. The tall fellow in the black robe, their leader.'

'Mustafa Pasha himself?' Stanley's blue eyes were round. 'La Valette will want to speak with you. When we've got you bandaged.'

'I'm fine,' he said. 'I only took a blow to the head.'

The knight of the lost English langue looked almost guilty. 'You've not looked in a glass of late.'

'The Turks offered me none. Nor roasted mutton, nor sherbet, nor harem girls. The uncouth barbarians. More water.'

He gave him the flask again. 'Then to the infirmary with you.'

6

They weren't called the Knights Hospitaller for nothing.

The Sacred Infirmary was one of the most beautiful buildings Nicholas had ever seen. A different world from the heat and blood and dust outside, it breathed the spirit of gentleness, expertise and monastic calm. The great dormitory where the sick lay was a vast, high-roofed hall, blissfully cool, with arched windows down the east and west side, admitting only the soft golden light of morning and evening. The walls were plain whitewashed, the smell clean and soothing. Slop buckets by beds were emptied instantly. Alcohol and turpentine and other disinfectants were widely used. All dishes and instruments were made of silver. The ministering brothers wore white. Forty beds lined each wall, well spaced from each other. Most lay empty for now.

Nicholas lay back on cool white sheets and a young brother, Fra Reynaud, washed his face. He kept dabbing around his nose.

'It was the back of my head they hit me hardest.'

Fra Reynaud sat him up again and looked. 'Your skull's thick.' He washed off the crusted blood and dabbed on brine and alcohol. Nicholas gritted his teeth and made no sound.

The knight returned to washing his face. He rinsed the cloth in a shallow silver dish, silver being the miraculous enemy of infection and putrefaction. The water spiralled with red.

'They must have kicked me in the chops or something,' said Nicholas. 'When I was out cold.'

'They slit your nose.'

'They *what?*'

'Just a nick. They might have cut off your nose entire, so give thanks to God. It's only your left nostril. Not bad, but it's bled a lot. I'll put a fine stitch in it. Mostly you need to drink water and then some salted bread. Tonight you'll get meat broth.'

'*Slit my nose,*' repeated Nicholas, still indignant. 'When I was out cold? Damned barbarians.'

'Mind your blaspheming tongue,' said the Hospitaller mildly. 'Most knights have suffered a lot worse in their time.'

His hands were huge and strong, yet his touch precise. It was said that a good chirurgeon should have the heart of a lion, the hands of a lady and the eyes of a hawk. This one's mighty sword-hands were hardly those of a lady, but they were as gentle. He had battle-scars on his face. Over his white soutane he wore a silver cross. Warrior, healer, monk.

Nicholas's eyes roved over the cool white arches and crossbeams of the lofty infirmary roof above him. Like a cathedral. A refuge, a holy place. What men they were, the Knights. How he was beginning to love them.

La Valette rested grave eyes upon him. 'Why were you riding with Copier?'

'As a volunteer.'

'And only you lived?'

'Yes, Sire.'

'The history.'

Nicholas told him.

La Valette studied some papers, then looked up. 'You give a good account. Yet it was a grievous loss. Copier died like a young hothead.' He looked out of the window. 'But the Turks attacked Castile on De la Rivière's advisement. Now that I like. Their loss was greater.

'When the Turks are defeated, we will recover our brothers' mortal remains and give them good burial. Now go to the church and confess. Your soul is stained with blood, though infidel.'

The Conventual Church of St Lawrence was the church of the knights, filled with their escutcheons and tombs. A church full of noble blood-lines. In the crypt lay the bodies of the former Grand Masters of Malta.

Nicholas took his place in the confessional.

He said he had had lustful thoughts.

'Was she married?'

'No, they were—'

'You have had lustful thoughts about more than one woman?'

'Yes, Father. Many.'

'You are young. It is but colt's evil, and the weakness of youth. Yet lust becomes a habit, and habit becomes character. Pray to God for grace.'

'Yes, Father.'

'You're certain they were not married?'

'No, they were young. There was one in a tavern, in Cadiz, and there is one on the island here. She is very beautiful.'

'Think not on her. This is hardly the time for gallantry anyway, not with the Turk upon us.'

'I have killed men. On a ship, and here on the island.'

'You have already killed a Turk on Malta?'

'Yes, Father. I rode out with Marshal Copier's troop. I cut one open across his flanks. I doubt he lived.'

There was a kind of hiss from the other side of the grille. It sounded like exultation. Then sober silence.

'Also Father – I blasphemed and used foul language.'

'In the heat of battle.'

'No, Father. In the cool after. In the Sacred Infirmary here, I said *damned barbarians*. And before the Turks, as I rode away at their bidding, I ... I called their leader, this Mustafa Pasha, a bad thing.'

'To his face?'

'Yes. It was dishonourable, and very foolish.'

'You have insulted Mustafa Pasha of the Ottomans, to his face? And lived?'

'Yes, Father.'

This time, the sound of exultation was unmistakable. With ill-suppressed excitement, the priest said, 'What did you say to him? The exact words, boy. I need to know, so I may pronounce appropriate penance.'

Nicholas hesitated, then took a deep breath. 'I called him a filthy mule-fucker.'

There was silence, and then the unmistakable sound of laughter being poorly stifled in a cassocked sleeve.

Finally the priest controlled himself and said, voice shaking a little, '*Te absolvo a peccatis tuis,* et cetera.'

'No penance?' said Nicholas with some surprise.

'No penance. The Holy Mother Church absolves you of all, though it is God's to forgive you. And no more lusting either. Now go and do some work. *Laborare est orare.*'

'Yes, Father.'

He felt exhausted then, and longed for sleep. But it was yet only late afternoon of a very long day. Everyone worked. Everyone looked exhausted.

'There will not come a day for another month when we do not feel exhausted,' said Smith.

'What encouragement he speaks,' said Stanley. 'A natural leader of men and rouser of spirits!'

'I speak the truth. You speak like a bilge-pump.'

Stanley blew him a kiss.

Towards evening a message came for Nicholas. He was wanted in the infirmary.

Fra Reynaud admitted him. In the beautiful sunset light of St John's ward, there lay a man with his arms and most of his face covered in fresh bandages. Probably the rest of him too, under the sheets. Some bandages seeped a little blood. It was Marshal Copier.

'You survived!' He felt at once overjoyed and stricken with guilt.

'You too,' whispered Copier, barely audible.

He communicated with his eyes. Nicholas drew up a stool beside him.

'They let me go. I didn't fight free.'

'You fought, boy. I saw you. You fought.'

'I am deeply sorry I left you there. I thought you were dead.'

'So did I.' Copier's eyes smiled, since he could not. 'Better, so did the Turk. I crawled by night, found a horse, rode in under dark. The Baptist himself lit the way, I tell you.' He paused for rest, swallowed. 'The starlight was of Christ and the Virgin. It shone like day.' His eyes settled on the boy with his head bowed in shame. 'Your help was not needed. You were right to ride back alone.'

Nicholas could have wept. The Marshal was deathly pale with blood loss, even his moustache hanging weakly, beaded with sweat. Yet he lived. His eyes flicked at the silver cup of watered wine by the bed. Nicholas held it to his lips and he drank.

Copier's head sank back and he closed his eyes. 'My leg is off.'

Nicholas could think of nothing intelligent to say. Any condolence would sound fatuous.

'But I have another that will serve.' His eyes opened again. There was even a soft sparkle in them. 'They will make me one of best olive wood. Most elegant, and shaped to fit the stirrup when I ride.'

'You are not finished yet, Sire.'

'No, indeed. Nor you.' He breathed deep and painfully. 'Leave me now, lad. I tire.'

He stood.

'We fought well though, you and I. All of us.'

Nicholas nodded and went.

He found Hodge and made for the home of Franco Briffa.

'I could sleep for twelve hours,' said Hodge. 'Which is how long I been lugging rocks.'

As they walked back down Margherita Street, someone cried out,

'Hey! See the Inglis! Insulter of the Pasha!'

Two more cried out in Maltese they did not understand, and then there was a crowd of little barefoot boys and girls running after them. Mateo and Tito, the young sons of Franco Briffa, were running with them.

'The hero Inglis! The hero Inglis! He lives in our house!'

Women looked out from the balconies above and lifted their veils. 'It is the fearless Inglis, he escape from the Turks and kill twenty men! Come and see! Hey, Inglis! I kiss you! I kiss you for nothing! You are my hero, my young husband!'

Nicholas and Hodge turned and stared up at them, and back at the clamouring children, their tired minds struggling to comprehend. The children skidded to a halt before them, and Mateo said in macaronic Italian, 'Is true, Inglis? You are the Inglis insult the Mustafa Pasha to his face?'

Slowly it dawned on Nicholas. Evidently the privacy of his confession had not, in this case, been strictly regarded.

In fact, it was all over town that the young English volunteer, the blue-eyed fairhead handsome boy with no meat on him, the one living with Franco Briffa, had defeated many Turks on his own, and saved a maiden's life and virginity, and finally called the General of the Ottoman Army, the terrible Mustafa Pasha, hater of Christians, a *filthy mule-fucker*. To his face! And lived to tell the tale! Nor did he boast of it, but only told the priest in the confessional. He was unbelievable, this Inglis boy. As brave as a lion and as cool as a cucumber.

'I kiss him!' cried the girls in Birgu's brothel. 'I kiss his Inglis cucumber!'

'Franco Briffa should look to his daughter,' muttered an old widow, sitting at the fountain outside St Lawrence Church. 'That pretty Maddalena. All girls love a hero, and *then* there will be trouble.'

'Franco Briffa should put a lock on her loins,' said another.

Nicholas said to the children, 'Other men fought more bravely than I. And they died.'

'Yes,' said Mateo eagerly, 'but you called the Pasha a dirty, you know ... you said he is a lover of mules.'

Nicholas, tired as he was, couldn't resist it. He smiled and slowly turned away. 'Well ... maybe,' he murmured.

'You're a one,' said Hodge.

The children danced in the street.

Franco Briffa's adulation was exhausting.

'Tell me again, my beloved Inglis friend, my sworn brother!' he cried for the umpteenth time. 'Tell me what you said, and then tell me the look on his face! Was it not as black as the devil with piles?'

'Exactly,' said Nicholas. 'Exactly as black. As that. And now I've really *got* to get some sl—'

'And his famed Janizary guards, they did *nothing*! They were too afraid of your lightning sword arm!'

'Mm.'

On the bench opposite, Hodge was already asleep. They must get to their room.

'I bring more wine!' said Franco, staggering to his feet and heading for the cellar.

The moment he was gone, a slim figure in a pale blue dress darted into the courtyard. Nicholas raised his weary head.

She stopped before him and leaned down.

He stared up at her.

She held his gaze with her great brown honey eyes, gleaming with light, and then took the edge of her face-veil and drew it down. Slowly. Her lips were full and ripe, and her eyes were laughing.

Nicholas couldn't move.

'*Hero,*' she whispered. Then she leaned close and touched her soft lips to his. They breathed each other's breath, their lips pressed harder. Their mouths opened. She put her slim hand round the back of his neck. He reached out and slid his fingers up through her long black hair. It was scented with oil of orange blossom. There was no one more beautiful in the world.

And then the door to the cellar slammed, and she fled.

'More wine!' roared Franco.

She stopped briefly in the doorway opposite and glanced back over her shoulder, her long dark hair half covering her face. His heart might break, she was so beautiful. And how she knew it. He could not look away from her, her face, her dark burning eyes, the way she stood, half twisting, looking back at him like that, showing the swell of her small breasts and her slim hips under her dress. Then she smiled, a quick flash of a smile, and drew up her face-veil again, and was gone.

It was good in a way, he thought, that the priest who heard his confession hadn't been entirely discreet.

'Just one more cup,' he said to Franco.

Hodge snored.

Then both boys staggered to bed, Hodge hardly waking between bench and pallet. Nicholas, exhausted as he was, lay on his back with his mouth dry, his heart hammering. How in the name of all the blessed saints and martyrs in heaven was he supposed to avoid having lustful thoughts *now*?

Part III

ELMO

1

In the morning Nicholas was called to another audience.

'I am a busy man,' said La Valette. 'I have four hundred knights under my command, Spanish soldiers, citizen militia, there is Holy War to prosecute, and yet for some reason I continually find myself speaking with a single young English commoner and volunteer. Is this a right use of my time?'

It was always hard to know whether La Valette's sense of humour was very dry, or he had none at all.

'You spoke foul language, I hear. In Turkish captivity.'

Nicholas bowed his head. 'I am sorry for it, Sire.'

'Are you? Are you indeed?' He drummed his fingers on the desk. 'It is between you and your conscience how you pollute your tongue. But for the morale that you have given the city with that juvenile insult, the courage you have put in their hearts, even the coarse laughter you have provided for these earth-born peasants – here is a gift.'

A servant came forward holding a complete steel breastplate. Nicholas was speechless.

The servant placed the breastplate on Nicholas's chest and he held it there while the fellow laced it top and sides to the backplate. It was very comfortably wadded with felt and leather. Hot, for sure. You'd keep out of the sun if you could. But not heavy, not really. Beautifully balanced fore and aft.

'German,' said La Valette. 'Belonged to a young novice who died of a fever last year. It will not stop a musket ball at short range, naturally, but even that will be slowed. Which might make the difference between a wound and a mortal wound. Otherwise it will save you from many a cut and thrust. You have no helmet?'

He shook his head.

'Well, there are none to spare. But there will be. When knights and soldiers being to die, you will have a helmet of your own.'

'And Hodge?'

'Hodge?'

'My companion.'

'Of course not. He may wear a leather breastplate if he finds it. Fine armour hardly befits the lowborn, any more than fine manners or high duties.'

'He has a noble heart.'

'Perhaps.' La Valette's eyes were steely. 'Now assemble the rest of your possessions, your valued Hodge, and be ready at Galley Creek within the hour. You are crossing to Elmo this morning. The fight is about to begin, and you will be worthy.'

Nicholas ran back to the house in the Street of the Bakers and Maddalena was there, and Hodge ready with his pack.

She looked admiringly at his gleaming breastplate.

'You go over to Elmo?'

'Yes,' he said hurriedly, bundling up his cinquedea and wallet in his blanket roll.

'The guns of the Turks will fire on us soon.'

He turned and looked at her. 'I know. I can hardly bear – How will I know ... you are alive?'

Hodge stood and mumbled, 'I'll wait for you outside.'

She smiled.

'No, truly, I must know. How will I know that a cannonball has not—'

'By pigeon? No, you will not. I cannot go up on the walls nor parade about on the parapets of San Angelo waving to you.'

He seized her thin shoulders and almost shook her, his grip so tight and his eyes burning so ardent that her heart burned within her likewise, though she did all she could to keep her smile cool and composed. 'My father ...' she said, glancing over her shoulder.

He let her go. '*I must know.*'

The flame in his blue eyes was so devouring, so beautiful.

'Each evening …' she said slowly. She thought. 'There is a low wall above Kalkara Creek, by the ditch over by San Angelo. You can see Elmo from there, so you can see there from Elmo. When I was younger, before I wore the veil, I used to go down there with Mateo and Tito and they'd catch little fish, and I'd beg them to put them back in the water. Sometimes I will go back there, at sunset. Not every day. But sometimes at sunset, look for me there.'

'In your blue dress?'

'It is my only dress,' she said a trifle haughtily.

'You promise?'

She kissed him swiftly. 'You should go now.'

He pulled her to him, her father in the house or no, and kissed her deeply. They kissed for too long, and she pushed him away. He grabbed his blanket roll and looked once more at her and said, 'At sunset. Be there.'

'Go!'

As she watched him down the street and round the corner, Hodge stepping out from the shade to meet him, she smiled at the thought of his last kiss, the feel of him, and touched her fingers to her lips.

Captain Miranda stood at the head of his troop of thirty tercios, and among the thirty or so more knights with Stanley and Smith, Nicholas recognised the talkative Chevalier Lanfreducci of the Italian Langue, and the young Chevalier Bridier de la Gordcamp of France, no more than twenty years of age.

They greeted him and Hodge with nods.

'The Turkish cannon will soon be roaring at Birgu,' joked Lanfreducci as they boarded the boat for the half-mile crossing. 'For pity's sake, let us flee to Elmo and save our tender skins!'

In the boat across, Bridier de la Gordcamp looked hard at Nicholas. He was a gentle-looking knight, almost girlish, with waving fair hair and blue eyes, and a voice so soft and low that one had to strain to hear him. Stanley had said that he was one of the holiest and most innocent-souled of all the brothers, and kept vigil entire nights long in the conventual church, his knees upon the cold flagstones, sword upturned in the shape of a cross clasped before him, eyes fixed on the great crucifix over the altar. He would pray for the salvation of his soul, and for Christendom, and for all the generations of his noble forebears who had fought Moors and Saracens at Tours and Antioch and Jerusalem, and who had died for the faith at Jerusalem and Acre and at the Horns of Hattin, in the lost Judaean wilderness. It was Bridier's deepest prayer that he be worthy of his ancestors.

Now the young knight said quietly to Nicholas, fixing him with his innocent blue eyes, 'You were the one who insulted the Pasha to his face?'

Nicholas looked uncomfortable. The Chevalier de la Gordcamp was no earthy peasant, to find such obscenities humorous. 'I am sorry for it.'

Bridier said nothing, but gazed out to sea, the wind flicking his fair locks across his face. Then he looked back and said a most uncommon thing. He said, 'All will be forgiven us, I think, in what is to come.'

Nicholas frowned. It seemed strange theology.

Bridier saw his frown, and said, 'You remember the woman in the Gospels who had committed adultery. Our Saviour said, *Though her sins are many, yet they are forgiven her. For she loved much.*' He looked out to sea again, and smiled a strange smile. 'Almost as if it does not matter what we love. As long as we love much.'

The Commander of the fort was Luigi Broglia, another Italian. Lanfreducci and he greeted each other like blood brothers.

A great lover of pageantry, with a round smiling face and equally round belly, Broglia looked to Nicholas more like a cook than a commander. In the parade ground, a small band blew trumpets, banged martial drums and waved banners to herald their arrival.

'What does Broglia think this is,' growled Smith, 'the carnival of Venice?'

They were each given tiny, cell-like quarters off the parade ground, truly monastic cells, and then shown the fort.

St Elmo was built of cheap limestone blocks on a star-pattern, and consisted of the small inner parade ground, a chapel, barrack rooms, some stores, and a single narrow keep as part of the western wall. There were no cellars or subterranean tunnels, no sally ports in the walls from which to burst out on attackers unexpectedly, or clear and burn the ditches of any infill.

'And no defensive lines to fall back on,' growled the burly Spanish soldier, Captain Miranda. He gestured around. 'This is it. This is all we have.'

The knights said nothing. St Elmo was not the proudest of Malta's fortifications.

The single line of defence was the outer walls, surrounded by a deep ditch. The flat-top walls lacked even battlements and embrasures, they had been so crudely and hurriedly built.

'A good thing the Ottoman fist is to fall on Birgu,' said Miranda. 'This place wouldn't last two days.'

'But come come, we are men of stout hearts!' said Luigi Broglia.

His words fell flat. Even Stanley looked uncharacteristically gloomy. Now he examined the Order's only outlying fort, under hard clear sunlight, it did indeed look a pathetic piece of military architecture.

The only flourishes were the tall cavalier on the seaward side, a form of free-standing keep connected to the main fort by a narrow drawbridge across the ditch, and the outlying defence or ravelin built to La Valette's orders, capping one of the star's points and offering a small platform for enfilading fire down one side.

'If we should face any Turkish attack here,' said Broglia, still trying to sound optimistic, 'we will have full supporting fire from our brothers across the water. San Angelo's guns are less than half a mile off.'

'San Angelo's guns will have other targets to aim at,' said Smith so savagely that Broglia's round, boyish face fell abruptly.

Aside from the seaward cavalier and the hastily added ravelin, there were no towers, no high places or vantage points, and the heights of Mount Sciberras rose like a gaunt backbone of rock to the west. Turkish guns and musket barrels might point straight down into the fort.

'They'll never lug their guns up onto Sciberras,' said Broglia.

'Pray it be so,' said Smith. 'As defensive positions go, we might as well be sitting in a cherry tree.'

*

They prayed that night, and in the morning saw with obscure shame and guilt that the guns had indeed been drawn up against Birgu.

Nicholas could think of one thing and one thing only. A beautiful young girl in a pale blue dress, the most beautiful girl in the world. Her kiss. And the black muzzles of the Turkish guns pointing straight at her.

After the farce of the initial assault on Castile, Mustafa had given the order not to hold back.

'Let the first salvo be the basilisks,' he told his gunnery master. 'Two at once. Let them know the power of our siege guns, let them be dismayed, and let them know we are here to win.'

The Turkish gunners wadded their ears with cotton. The moment the long fuse was lit, they scurried back for cover and huddled near the earth, a good distance behind the beasts. There were numerous tales of those who had remained too close, novices who had taken shelter only just behind the earthed-up wheels of a gun, only for the massive recoil to cause the wheels to erupt backwards, and cut them clean in two.

The detonation was an obscenity even to the gunners themselves. It rattled your very skeleton, hollowed in your belly, stunned your heart and brain. But experienced gunners knew an ominous silence was even worse. It meant a faulty fuse or bad powder, and they would have to return to the breech. It was like going up to the flanks of a sleeping dragon, never knowing when it might awake and devour you.

But the first salvo of the two basilisks fired true. The roar was unbelievable in its power. Even across the water at Elmo, the roar of those bronze monsters was terrible. Nicholas prayed with all his soul.

The waters of the Grand Harbour rippled and stirred, the earth shook, and some inland swore they saw birds flying high overhead knocked senseless and falling to the ground. Others clenched their fists and their jaws, fearing their teeth would shatter in their skulls.

In Birgu it was as if hell was erupting.

In the houses, jars smashed to the floor, plaster flaked from the walls, wine barrels wobbled where they stood. Dogs howled, horses reared and tore at their tethers, cats went stiff and wide-eyed and then crept away into corners, children sobbed, weakened roofs fell in. In Sicily, sixty miles north, they heard the noise a few minutes later and thought at first it was Etna.

The massive balls thumped into the southern landwalls, and when the huge plumes of dust finally settled or drifted away, the besiegers saw that one of the two hits had already caused an ominous crack from battlement to midway down.

'Hit them again,' said Mustafa. 'With all the guns, all day long. Never stop except to rest and cool the barrels. Balls of iron then stone then marble, in steady rotation. You know the drill. Give them hell.'

'Sire, crack opened up below the post of Provence!'

'Then bag it up, man. Fortify it with everything you've got.'

'We have done, Sire.'

'Good. What else?'

The soldier looked around uncertainly. 'Nothing else, Sire.'

'Then back to your position.'

La Valette looked out grimly from the post of Castile. How he longed to sally out and cut down those infidel gunners where they worked. Faces already black with powder and smoke, slaves of the Sultan, enemies of Christ. Such lightning sallies by the besieged and beleaguered were always good for morale, and for denting that of the enemy. And morale was of incalculable value. The Turks would never know when the next attack might come, in darkness, or the low grey light just before sunrise ... But the knights were too few in number. They could not afford it. And any captive the Turks took, they would torture for information, like De la Rivière. Yet who else would be so brave as he?

He squared his shoulders. They would only win through defence, and faith in Christ.

It was growing dark when the Turkish guns finally fell silent.

The sudden silence was deafening, almost worse than the eight-hour barrage. Ears rang. Women sobbed. Babies cried.

And then the work of rebuilding began.

None of Birgu's walls was down, but many were shaken, and

cracks had opened up in several places. La Valette seemed everywhere at once, inspecting damage, prescribing repairs, his calmness and confidence infectious.

An hour later a messenger found him.

'Sire, the Turks are retreating.'

He frowned. 'You are mistaken.'

'They are pulling back their guns.'

The Grand Master ran up the stone steps to the south wall like a thirty-year-old. It was true. By torchlight and lantern light, the Turkish army was undoing its own vast labours, and pulling its guns back from the heights of Santa Margherita.

Some of the younger knights were foolish enough to begin celebrations, but this was no time to celebrate. La Valette silenced them with a word.

This was no retreat. His eyes roved across the land. This was only a change of plan.

The four Englishmen at Elmo were eating simple rations at dusk when the cry came from the walls above them. It was a cry not of triumph but of desolation.

They immediately ran up the steps to the parapet, Stanley and Smith both carrying scabbard and swordbelt. Nicholas arrived first and looked out.

The Turkish army was clearly visible, moving round the head of the Marsa. It made no sense. Not a gun was being left on the Heights of Corradino or Santa Margharita for the bombardment of Birgu. They seemed to be pulling back. And then as they rounded the calm waters at the end of the great harbour, the mounted Sipahi vanguard turned their horses and began the ascent of Mount Sciberras.

'So,' said Smith softly, 'the Ottoman fist is to fall on us first after all.'

'What will we do?' said Hodge, wide-eyed.

'What we always do,' said Smith. 'We will fight.'

Stanley already had his hand on his hilt, his customary stance. 'Come, brothers,' he said, 'let us finish our last peaceful supper.'

*

When they had eaten, Smith wiped his mouth, cleaned his knife on his sleeve, returned it to his belt and looked keenly at Nicholas and said, 'I have asked you before, boy, but I ask you again – you do not fear to die? For there may still be time to return over the water beneath the headland.'

Instead of answering directly, Nicholas only said with slow reflectiveness, 'I came here for reasons I do not fully understand.'

'I fear to die,' said Hodge bluntly. 'I do not wish to. I dream of home.'

'Hodge,' said Nicholas, turning to him. 'I will go home with you when this is done.'

Hodge looked at him and said nothing. He knew it was a promise that his master and companion could not keep.

Even La Valette's flint heart was moved when he understood what was coming next. The citizens of Birgu, the women and children and the innocent, would not be under attack tomorrow. Instead, against all his best predictions and the dictates of military science, the Turks would fall first upon Elmo. Presumably so that they might have free access to the northern harbour of Marsamuscetto. And all Elmo's defenders would be killed. Within two or three days.

For some reason he thought of that ardent-hearted, insolent English boy. The Ingoldsby boy, only son of his old comrade-in-arms, Sir Francis Ingoldsby. They had fought side by side on the walls of Rhodes over forty years ago. Now his son would fight on the humbler walls of St Elmo of Malta. It was a strange sad tale, how the last of the Ingoldsbys died. But all of them. It was a sad loss. They had already gone to their deaths.

He sent orders for there to be no idling on Birgu's landward walls. Everything must be brought up for bulking and repair. This respite would be brief indeed, and it was bought with their brothers' lives, across the water. Let them use it well. The Turks would be back into the main attack within three days.

As he watched the torchlit advance from the walls of San Angelo, looking out across the Grand Harbour, a stooped, hesitant figure beside him said, 'I fear they are in terrible danger, our Elmo volunteers.'

It was his Latin secretary, Sir Oliver Starkey. La Valette grimaced into the dark. The scholarly Starkey had never quite understood the exigencies of war.

'The profession of our oath,' said the Grand Master, 'is to sacrifice our lives for Christendom. Those at Elmo must hold it as long as they can.'

Starkey glanced at him in the darkness, and saw that familiar face worn and lined with suffering and – far more wearing – ceaseless responsibility for other men's lives and deaths. It takes courage to die. But it takes still greater courage to send other men to their deaths. In La Valette's features were all the signs of sorrow strongly mastered, and also a strange serenity. They said that some men and women found serenity in the most adverse of circumstances, especially the great of soul; that serenity is the attribute and accompaniment of true power. Certainly to think the Grand Master a man lacking in passion was grossly to misunderstand. He was a man of the deepest passions, most powerfully mastered and directed. You could feel that power in his presence. Like a flow of lava just below the surface of the earth.

'But they will all die there,' said Starkey sadly.

'Yes,' said La Valette. 'They will all die there.'

2

In the pavilion of Mustafa Pasha, there had been a brief council.

'I dislike the main fleet being anchored in the south, in this Marsasirocco,' Admiral Piyale had declared. 'Better to keep our forces together, better to anchor in Marsamuscetto, close to our main encampment.'

'But you feared the havoc the east wind, the *gregale*, would cause,' said Mustafa.

'I believe it will not,' said Piyale shortly. 'I believe I was misinformed.'

Mustafa's eyes glittered with cold amusement. It was as he had said to the aristocratic young admiral, but Piyale had refused to listen to him. Now he was humbled before him, and Mustafa was content.

'And what of that small fort on the headland?' said the Pasha.

Piyale said, 'We will have to reduce it.'

Mustafa nodded. 'We will flatten it. It takes a decade or more to make a good fortress, but this one is of a sorry build, and can only be thinly defended. It will be taken in a day or two.'

Seeing that they were shortly to be under attack, there was no sleep that night in Elmo. The place was a frenzy of activity. And though he never lost his cheery smile, Luigi Broglia suddenly showed himself a very determined commander indeed.

He appointed Medrano to succeed him should he be killed.

'Broglia will survive longer than any of us,' said Lanfreducci. 'That belly of his would stop a ball from a basilisk.'

The jokes grew blacker and blacker, and ever more frequent. Imagining the very worst horrors, and laughing at them, inured a man to real horrors when they came. Between the joking, every man prayed with all the serious fervour of his faith.

'*Dear Christ and Blessed Virgin,*' prayed Nicholas. '*Be with us in our fighting, and in our dying. May we fight with justice and honour.*' He paused. There was no praying for health and long life, nor even an easy death. The suffering were closest to Christ, and the suffering of the dying purged their souls in preparation for the sweet afterlife. A worldly fool prayed for an easy and painless life, a simple peasant prayed to the Almighty Creator to look down and cure his rheumatic aches. But he added, '*If it be God's will, may Hodge survive. May he make it safe back to England after. Amen.*'

And like all those who worked and prayed, he felt the presence of the Father and the Son and all the Saints, looking down in sorrow and compassion upon this bitter and bloody little human drama.

From the ramparts of Elmo, fewer than fifty knights and a hundred infantrymen watched in awe as the Ottoman siege train moved out onto Mount Sciberras. The bump and rattle of war wagons on the stony ground sounded across the peaceful waters all night long. Wagons piled high with tents and provisions, cannonballs and best corned gunpowder, lead musket balls, arrows, helmets, entrenching tools, picks, shovels, staves, ropes, iron bars, timbers, pre-assembled wooden frames for breastwork, lightweight latticed fences for cover and shade, hides, woollen sacks, sail canvas, casks of flour, rice, lentils, dried fruit and dried meat.

All drawn by donkeys and mules, horses and oxen, vast numbers of draught animals, all needing to be fed and watered. The iron laws of the material world applied to the Ottomans as much as to any Christian army. Every 1,000lbs of ordnance required a pair of draught animals to shift. So those 20,000lb basilisks alone each required a team of a staggering forty beasts. All requiring fodder, on this bare, stark, grassless island providing none. Could the very size of the Turkish forces prove a weakness? How many provisions had the Ottomans brought, even in that huge flotilla of ships? How long could they hold out?

But it was foolish to hope. The organisation of Suleiman's armies was legendary. They would be able to wage full war all summer, there was no doubt of that. Three or four months. Against them, Elmo could only stand for three days at best, and then Birgu, by some miracle, perhaps a couple of weeks. And then the slaughter would be terrible.

No, it was foolish to hope. The men of Elmo breathed deep on the morning air and squared their shoulders. Nobility is greater than survival, went the Hospitaller saying, as honour is greater than wealth, and virtue than cleverness.

This Great Siege was not a war that could be won. It could only be a glorious war of sacrifice. And in their sacrifice, the dying knights and the people of Malta might yet bring all of Europe to unity and to arms, to rouse itself against the oncoming Armies of Islam.

Every arquebus was brought up to the walls and stacked, pouches were filled with powder and wallets filled tight with lead balls. Helmets, shields and armour were checked, swords, halberds, half-pikes and glaives given a final whetting, the sharpened edges stropped off and hardened on taut leather belts.

Smith clutched a squat, four-foot half-pike in his meaty fist, and eyed the fearsome blade at the end, half axe, half spear, with a thick spike on the reverse for good measure. 'When the guns overheat and the powder runs out,' he growled, 'it'll be these that keep 'em off the walls. A half-pike may blunt, but it never wears out.' He tossed it at Nicholas. 'Remember that.'

'But meanwhile,' said Stanley firmly, 'you and Hodge are in the role of squires and servants, not front line fighters. You will serve the guns, bring up munitions and stores. You will leave your sword below, it will only hinder you.'

'I will not,' said Nicholas.

'You will.'

'No. You cannot command me, any more than Copier could.'

'That I can. You are now in Elmo, in a fort of St John, and so directly under the command of the Order. Unless you wish to leave, and reside elsewhere.'

Nicholas felt a welling of angry frustration.

'There may yet come a time to fight,' said Smith. 'But there's much to be done besides, and you and Hodge will be more than useful that way.'

'I spent most of my life humping stuff,' said Hodge. 'Hay bales, wattle fences, sacks of dung for the cabbage patch. So I s'pose it won't hurt me doin' some more, even under this sweatin' hot sky.'

Nicholas bit his lip and gave in.

'Your sword?' said Stanley. 'It will only hinder you.'

'But keep on that breastplate,' added Smith. 'It's a fine piece, and would stop all but a close shot.'

Nicholas unbelted the Italian short sword that they had given him on the ship, and left it on his pallet.

'Now to the walls. There's work to do.'

Elmo's crude paparets were attacked with mallet and chisel to make some sort of crude embrasures for musket barrels, crossbows and the small field guns, repositioned now on the landward walls and up on the bastion. They were served not with smooth iron balls meant for holing incoming ships, but with chain shot and grapeshot, for wreaking atrocious damage on close-packed men at short range.

Equally fearsome were the weapons of wildfire: stacks of fire hoops the size of cartwheels, soaked in oil and wrapped in cotton bandaging, dipped in more oil, saltpetre, tallow, more cotton, rope, grass ... Whatever would burn and scald and melt the fat off a man's bones. These would be lit and blazing in an instant and then hurled out over the walls with tongs, to set alight the robes of any assailants. They had been used at Rhodes to devastating effect. There were also flame throwers, long brass pipes that could be poked out over the cracked embrasures, or even through low ducts and vents in the walls. Each pipe had a bowl at the end, something like an ale-yard, and in the bowl, a scorching mix of oil, naphtha and turpentine would be lit, often with some kind of jelly added. Even a minor explosion would erupt in a long gouting tongue of superheated flame. The admixture of the jelly – honey, date wine, anything sugary and sticky – made the flame stick to a man's robes, his flesh, his hair, and not be put out. It was a form of the ancient terror called Greek Fire.

Butts of water were brought up with scoops tied to the rim-hoops, but food was all kept below in the stores. They would eat in the evening, when the guns went quiet.

In the largest storeroom, dimly lit with rushlights, four chaplains of St John did what they could to ready the few beds and their store of bandages and medicaments. But for the best treatment, the wounded would need to be shipped back to the Sacred Infirmary after dark. As long as the Turks left the Grand Harbour ungunned, that might still be possible.

'Though the infidels will fire on a wounded man as readily as a fighting man, I suppose,' said one chaplain.

'Though infidel,' said the Chevalier Medrano, 'the Turks can be just as chivalrous, or as cruel, as any other men.'

The infidel too worked on through the night beneath the brilliant moon. Turkish sappers and trenchers established their forward positions, throwing up earthen ramps, great rocky barricades and defences, gun platforms growing steadily out of a flat and barren promontory. Far beyond them, nearly a mile off, the new permanent Turkish encampment spread out over the low land at the head of the Marsa.

And over on Senglea and Birgu too, the reinforcing of all defences continued. When they saw that Elmo was to be destroyed first, the knights said that the daughter was buying the mother fort precious time by her own sacrifice.

Finally a chaplain, Fra Giacomo, came round and gave them all the last rites. The wine on Nicholas's tongue never tasted so sweet, the bread never so white and pure. Still, despite his careful prayers, not asking for health or life, as a boy he still believed he would not die. Or he feared it, but did not believe. His father used to say a man's heart could easily hold two contradictory things true at once.

They would fight the Turks gloriously on and on until eventually they fell back, or the army of Spain would arrive from Sicily, or La Valette would send reinforcements over and drive them off. Or he and Hodge and the knights would take flight in a longboat by night, or he pictured himself diving into the sea and swimming away with the water around him whipped to a storm by musket balls. He would not die. You could not die as young as he. There was too much ahead, waiting for him. There was a girl waiting for him.

Smith and Stanley saw his lack of fear and understood. They had been young once, and thought they would never die.

Hodge was less deluded, and braver. Racked with fear, often trembling, white-faced, yet he mastered his fear. That was true bravery. He worked like a mule shifting munitions and sandbags, and if the fighting came to him, he would fight as stoutly as any.

A scout from the forward trenches came to Mustafa's pavilion, where general and admiral sat late, eating by lantern light.

'A priest is giving them bread and wine.'

'They eat the body of Christ,' said the Pasha with distaste.

'I think it is the Last Rites,' said Piyale.

Mustafa raised a black eyebrow.

'You remember the ancient tale of Thermopylae,' said Piyale. 'When the Greeks fought the Persians in a narrow pass. A tribe of Greeks called the Spartans, much outnumbered.'

'Persians,' sneered Mustafa. Almost as inveterate enemies to the Turks as Christendom itself.

'But a spy brought news to the Persian generals,' said Piyale, 'that the Spartans were combing their hair for battle. The Persians laughed at such women. Then the spy explained that Spartans comb their hair when they are preparing to die. And the Persians stopped laughing.'

Mustafa regarded his admiral, his stony eyes glittering. 'I have heard this tale,' he said. 'The Greeks of old were not all women.'

'It is the same with the knights,' said Piyale. 'These Last Rites of theirs. They are Spartans combing their hair.'

'Preparing to die,' said Mustafa. His thin lips twitched with a smile. 'And so they should.'

At last it was done. They had made all the preparations they could, they snatched a few hours of sleep, and then dawn began to grey the sky.

The conical tents of Central Asia spread out over the narrow rocky peninsula of Sciberras: the tents of the East at the gates of the West. St Elmo, small and squat, stood against them. Silent and waiting. It looked trapped, like a creature driven to the end of the promontory from where it could go no further and must turn at last and fight.

The Turkish artillery squadrons had twenty-four guns in place already, protected behind wooden battlements and earth ramparts. They also brought up squat, open-mouthed mortars and bombards, crude but effective devices which looked like little more than fat flower pots. But with enough charge they could belch out stone balls high into the air, over Elmo's walls and straight down onto parapets, roofs and walls, doing much damage.

As the sun rose higher over Gallows Point, expert Ottoman and Mameluke engineers were already adjusting gun platforms to steady the guns and achieve the highest accuracy, earthing up ramps further for better trajectories, doing calculations by arithmetic and rule of thumb, squinting, holding up their fingers, surveying, checking the length of shadows.

Meanwhile slave gangs were set to digging trenches down the scarp towards the fort. The ochre earth was all of an inch or two deep before they hit solid rock. After that it was pick and mallet. Sometimes foxholes were blown out with carefully placed packs of gunpowder. Other teams of slaves were ordered to bring up sacks of earth from the lowlands or pebbles from the beach for extra cover.

Everything proceeded swift and orderly and with an absolute sense of mastery. It was an awesome and dismaying sight. Ottoman siegecraft was, as reputed, the finest in the world. They had laid waste to the greatest fortresses from Persia to Hungary. The idea that Elmo might stand against such expertise and determination was almost laughable.

The moment the first transverse trenches were deep enough for a man to crawl in, a crack company of Janizaries was sent up at the run. They carried long, slender decorated muskets. Snipers' muskets.

Smith took up his jezail.

'Let us at least have first blood.'

His posture at the wall reminded Nicholas of nothing so much as his own stalking a hare or a partridge on his father's lands. The silent waiting for the single shot that must count and kill, the infinite patience, looking out for the smallest movement, the stir of a leaf, or of a feather above the Ottoman trench line.

A single blurred movement of that white feather and Smith was onto it. He shifted his muzzle a fraction left and dropped it another fraction and fired a ball into the soft, loose earth that banked the top of the trench, aiming it just a couple of inches below where he had glimpsed movement. There was a cry and a Janizary fell against the inner trench wall, white headfeather sprayed with his own blood, his turban rapidly staining. The ball had holed his turban and cut a groove across the top of his skull.

'Bravo!' called Chevalier Lanfreducci down the line. 'A fine shot – for an Englishman!'

'Damn!' cried Smith. 'Had I another jezail readily loaded I could take him now where he's slumped.'

Then hands pulled the lightly wounded man down into cover and angry cries rang out.

'Nevertheless, first blood is ours,' said Stanley. And he cried out in Turkish, *'Baş kan!'*

More angry cries, screams of vengeance, and throughout, Smith furiously reloading his jezail. In less than a minute he had the barrel back in the rough-hewn niche and was waiting for another vainglorious Janizary to stand and hurl abuse, and then he would have him clean. But none did. The Janizaries were as disciplined as any soldiers on earth.

'God, let it begin,' muttered Smith.

He was furious to fight, and Nicholas knew how he felt. He too longed for it, ached for it, with an ache as deep as love. It would be terrible and bloody and glorious, and after you might be dead or crippled or limbless, but if alive you would never know such glory again as in that wild heat of battle, and the rest of life would taste like stale bread beside it. From only that brief murderous skirmish aboard the *Swan*, and the mad charge on the plain with Copier, he had learnt so much already, about war, and about himself. Princes and kings, sultans and emperors, talks and treaties would come and go, but men would always fight. Only let the fight be just, and let it come soon.

For the Lord has given the horse his might, has clothed his neck with strength. He paws in the valley, he smells the battle from afar, the thunder of the captains, and the shouting. For the Lord is a man of war ...

3

It was late on the morning of May 20th 1565 that the guns of the Turks began their bombardment of St Elmo.

The Ottoman guns were so near that the watchers on the walls could glimpse the gunners moving behind their ramps and earthworks with their linstocks, even the flare of the matchcords as they put them to the powder. Then it was time to duck back down and pray.

'Coming in!' roared Captain Miranda.

There was nothing they could do but sit and huddle behind the walls and wait, and hope that a ball did not come straight through the wall that sheltered them and blast them through the air in pieces, like red rose petals on the wind.

But this first was ranging fire, only one ball struck home near the central wall, while two or three more hissed overhead. There came a pause while the gunners adjusted their trajectories, and Smith was up with his jezail in an instant. Answering shots rang out immediately from Turkish snipers in the forward trenches, under strict orders to keep the enemy pinned down behind his walls, and not let him harass the gunners. But Smith took the risk, keeping low and taking his time, sighting on one of the big guns. Men moved round her breech, mostly out of sight, but here and there was an obvious movement.

The jezail cracked out almost the same instant a Turkish musket ball hit the stonework inches from Smith's face.

'Damn!' he bellowed, turning away from the splinters, but too late. A sliver had lodged in his cheek – but no real damage done.

He glanced back. A flurry of panic around one of the guns. He clenched his fist and dropped back down behind the wall. He'd hit.

'You're cheek's bloody,' said Stanley.

Smith grubbed in his beard and pulled out a half-inch splinter and tossed it over his shoulder at the Turks. 'The other fellow's worse off.'

'How that'll mar your boyish looks,' said Stanley.

'You'll not praise me for my marksmanship? That was a master engineer I just trimmed of his head.'

'I won't. You might grow proud.'

'Coming in again!' came Miranda's cry. 'On target now!'

Knights bowed their heads and crossed themselves. The air erupted.

The Ottomans knew exactly what they were doing. The basilisks were not used. There was no need against so feeble a target. But the biggest field guns alone threw balls of eighty pounds, striking the walls of Elmo in a relentless barrage, and soon the lime and sandstone walls began to flake and crumble. With expert eye, the master gunners had ordered concentration on the points of the stars themselves as the weakest salients.

But the noise was the worst. Nicholas and Hodge were sent crawling about giving out cotton wadding for ears. Still, by the time the hand-to-hand fighting came, they would all be half deaf.

It seemed like hours that they huddled in what shade they could, taking the inescapable punishment, the untroubled sun rising above them in the clear blue sky. Peek out over the eastern walls and the sun glittered on the sea, you could snuff the sea breeze, and there were still birds flying and dipping out there, catching sardines, as on any other day. Then look back west and there were forty thousand men come all the way over that Orient sea to kill you.

It was late afternoon when the guns fell silent. Perhaps Mustafa hoped that the day would be cooling now, but no luck. It burned as hot as ever. The two forward corners of Elmo were beginning to collapse into rubble ridges, overtopping the deep defensive ditch below. Yet that ditch at least still seemed like as much of an abyss as ever. It was their first and now best line of defence. A mere ditch. But the Turks would have to bring up wagonloads of fascines and infill to get across that barrier, or else wrestle with unwieldy bridges and scaffolding. The defenders would yet have time to wreak some damage on them.

It seemed only seconds after the great guns fell silent that a great wave of sound arose as if from the ground itself, rising and rising in volume behind the hanging white curtain of dust and smoke. It was the Bektaşis coming in first, thirsting for Christian blood and crying the names of God.

Along the walls the knights were looking out. It was crucial to see the plan of attack.

'Charge and die,' muttered Smith, 'they're fanatics.'

'No,' said Medrano softly. 'It's more planned than that. They're bringing bridging platforms.'

Nicholas couldn't swallow, and his ears rang dizzyingly from the five-hour bombardment. He gripped the arquebus he held ready-loaded for Stanley, the wooden stock absorbing his sweat, as he looked out and saw, through that immense curtain of dust and smoke, the first ranks of the Bektaşis come howling through. A surge of white robes and turbans and flashing blades, thousands of them it seemed. They moved out wide around the far end of the Janizaries' forward trench, to attack Elmo on her northward side.

'Not foolish at all, you see,' said the sinuous Medrano. 'To our north, they cannot be fired on from our brothers in San Angelo. Fort Elmo itself protects them.'

Stanley grinned. 'Very *fort*-unate for them.'

'Please,' said Smith. 'Not now.'

'Move forward!' roared the voice of Luigi Broglia. 'Barricades on both eastward points, where the parapets are already shot out. Gabions and cordonniers chest high, they'll be across in minutes. Arquebusiers, not till I give the word! And the King of Spain's daughter to any who destroys a bridge!'

Medrano was right. As the Bektaşis came nearer, they could see teams of twenty or so carrying narrow wooden footbridges at the run, and others carrying long firwood scaffolding poles.

'Arquebusiers, at the ready! Shoot the porters, anything to slow 'em down! Brothers, look to your fire hoops! Fire the bridges if you can. Arquebusiers – *fire!*'

The guns cracked out, yet made dismayingly little impact on the vast surge of attackers a hundred paces off or more. Here and there one fell beneath the winnowing volley of loosely arcing arquebus balls, but numberless more came on behind. Nevertheless it was good to have begun, as Broglia understood. His men needed action. Now their fear and trembling began slowly to subside, their battle fury to arise, even as they scrabbled about the mundane task of cleaning out and reloading their gun barrels. Keep 'em busy. God knew they'd be busy enough in the hours to come.

Yet reloading was a slow business. By the time they were ready for a second volley, the Bektaşis were only the other side of the ditch and screaming at them. Nicholas peered out and stared aghast. The cut-throats aboard the *Swan* had been one thing, and that glorious cavalry charge of Copier's. But these ...

He saw eyes reddened and rolling with hemp-induced madness, he saw that some wore not white robes but torn and ragged animal skins, and engraved steel helmets instead of turbans, bearing in flowing Arabic lettering protective Koranic runes and ancient Dervish charms. They carried scimitars and small round shields, their lips shone with spittle, and their dark faces were raised to the sun in ecstasy. Some wielded short curved knives in their fists, scything them through the air and then down into the flesh of their own arms and torsos, slashing themselves like the priests of Baal in their demonic rapture. Cutting their own flesh, as if in ravenous preparation for cutting the flesh of others.

Nearby, Bridier de la Gordcamp, still smiling his soft smile, said, *'Thou shalt be cut down, O Madmen; the sword shall pursue thee ...'*

Nicholas felt hot fear then. Spiritual madmen were ever the most terrifying, and they were so close and so many. How could he and Hodge ever survive this? It would be a massacre. They would fall in minutes. Suddenly it was all very close, and very real. He saw their flashing eyes, their white teeth, their smiles, and he had to fight very hard within himself at that moment not to give in to the deep cowardice that lies in the hearts of all men, even the bravest; to leap up and cry out, and throw down his weapon and flee, and hurl himself from the fortress walls and try to swim to safety. But he mastered himself, and even managed a slap on Hodge's shoulder.

'Ready, Master Hodge?'

'Ready, Master Ingoldsby,' said Hodge with a croak.

218

The two boys waited in agony. Their only task now to clean and reload guns as fast as humanly possible. Their nostrils filled with the sharp, biting odour of burning matchcord.

The Bektaşis howled and milled and jostled, eager to be across and finish this. The second volley slammed into them at brutal range, and thirty or forty were hit, some toppling forward into the ditch, red staining their white robes, some falling back into their brothers' arms as if merely weary. Nicholas's eye caught one whose left arm seemed simply to explode in a cloud of red. Yet there was no reaction among them. There was no cover, and no plan, but to wait for the bridgers to cross the divide.

The simple but tough wooden walkways rose high in the air, ropes attached to the forward arms, and began to fall slowly over the broad ditch, the front measured to hit the corners of Elmo's fort. They were dropping two bridges at once and then they would be across.

A distinctive shot rang out, and a man on the lead rope tumbled back and fell. It was Smith's shot. The bridge skewed slightly.

'Again!' cried Broglia. 'Send those bridges into the ditch, or fire 'em up! Don't let 'em land!'

Then many things were happening at once.

Either in their battle madness, or more mundanely, shoved from behind by their eager comrades, some of the front ranks of the Bektaşis lurched forward and tumbled into the broad ditch. From the outer side it was but a drop of eight feet or so, although the walls of Elmo across the ditch arose a good twenty feet or more, sheer and shadowed. One or two cried out as they fell, and legs were broken, ankles twisted. But most rolled and were on their feet nimbly enough, and seeing this, many more began to jump down after them. Even those who were injured staggered upright again, their pain numbed with hemp and opium. Besides, pain was but a foretaste of death, and death of Paradise, and the fountains, the maidens, the wines promised by the Prophet, which intoxicated and hurt not. Then forward, with that black angel Azrael, *Malak al-Maut,* at their side. For was not the Angel of Death truly the greatest friend of mankind? Their Guide to Heaven. The Angel of Mercy in disguise.

Few of the Bektaşis had brought scaling ropes or grappling irons, but those that had now threw them. At the same time the first bridge crashed down upon the north-east corner of the fort, and then the second upon the north-west.

A quick-witted Ottoman commander ordered wooden scaffolding poles and ropes passed down to the men in the ditch, who might at least begin to erect some kind of supports before they were shot down. Amid the gunfire and the arrows, they set the scaffolding poles upright and tethered them tight with crossbars, and soon a structure arose. Though the knights did their best to fire on them and kill them before they could finish the work, yet they themselves were already too thinly stretched to permit a sustained volley, and pinned down by withering crossfire from beyond the ditch.

'Janizary snipers still in the forward trenches!' roared Smith. 'Watch your left!'

Almost as he said it, one of the Spanish infantrymen grunted and clutched his left shoulder. A Janizary sniper had hit him full on. He lurched into Nicholas and sank down. Nicholas knelt swiftly beside him.

He blasphemed, and blood seeped out between his fingers.

Nicholas said, 'Lean on me to the hospital.'

'Shit no,' said the soldier, 'it's my arm that's shot, not my leg. I can get there well enough.'

He flexed his left hand and his fingers moved freely, though more blood was pumped from his wound at the movement.

'Not paralysed yet,' he muttered. And he crawled back from the cordon and in through the low door of the central bastion and was gone. Yet he was the kind who would be bandaged and back soon enough. The Spanish tercios were the finest infantrymen in Europe, finer even than your Swiss pikemen. No wonder the vast empires of the New World had fallen to them.

Then the outlying ravelin over to the right was under severe attack, there was enough scaffolding in the ditch for Bektaşis to begin climbing, and more still pressed over the two bridges. With typical ruthlessness and unpredictability, half a mile behind the fray, Mustafa Pasha then sent out the order for the Turkish guns to begin pounding the unmanned south-west salient of the fort simultaneously. There were no Ottoman troops attacking there yet – and if there were, well, a few such losses would be well worth the demoralizing force of the renewed cannon fire. Let the attack come from all sides. Soon they would be exhausted. Let those crawling dogs of the Jewish Christ know there was to be no respite. Not enough for them to take a breath.

And indeed, many a knight's head turned, with an expression of dismay, as the guns roared out and the first balls began to strike and reduce the third of Elmo's four star points.

'Ignore it!' yelled Broglia. 'Hold the cordon!'

Attacked from all sides, with the unnerving feeling that they were almost surrounded, they huddled down behind their hastily made cordons of chest-high gabions, heavyweight wickerwork baskets filled with earth, reloaded their guns and bows, and unleashed merciless volley after volley of arquebus balls and crossbow quarrels. From the remaining walls they fired down into the ditch at those who had tumbled and were trapped there, trying to scale the wall with their bare hands. It was like shooting rats in a tunnel, and there was no glory in it, except the glory of victory, and the knowledge that the Turks would count their losses heavily tonight.

From the opposite salient too, there came vicious flights of enfilading fire, and from the upper bastion in the west wall, the fort's only commanding position, field guns began to gout flame and fire into the main body of the Turks clamouring across the ditch. Broglia had one small field gun, no higher than a man's waist but heavy to move, dragged across to the opposite salient and loaded with grapeshot. At a single cry his men ducked down below the cordon in perfect unison, and the gun was fired across at head height.

The damage wreaked on the enemy was atrocious. Five hundred lead pellets flailed into the mass of humanity as the Bektaşis surged over the walls and packed onto the tiny rubble-strewn star point. Within half a minute, that point was so laden with the dead that others trying to come on behind were climbing over them, or shoving them back into the ditch. No need to bring up infill of wicker and bound brushwood. The ditch was already filling up with the Ottoman dead.

Nicholas kept moving, ducking, bobbing. Out in the forward trenches, the Janizary snipers were expert at picking out a man who stayed still too long, aiming in on him, and taking the killing shot in their own good time. Yet as he moved among the men of Elmo, he sensed an exhilaration of spirits. Some punched the air with their fists in between taking their shots, or shouted words of triumph. The Turks fell below like mown wheat. And the defenders were barely scathed.

They could do this. They could hold Elmo.

4

There came one more brief and testing assault, on the post of the Chevalier de Guaras, beaten back with an aggressive counter-charge by the Spanish infantrymen, packed shoulder to shoulder, pikes lowered. Then the fighting tailed off for that first day, and there looked like being no night attacks.

'But they will come,' said Smith. 'For now, boys, get some food and sleep.'

With the soldiers, they squatted in the inner yard and ate quantities of bread soaked in wine, and drank as much water as they could hold down.

'That will suffice for today,' said one soldier. 'But for tomorrow, I expect a fine linen tablecloth and a chair, and candlelight, and a couple of roast quail.'

'Partridge,' said another. 'And dark Tempranillo.'

'Asparagus. In butter.'

'Ah ...'

They were silent a while. Then the first said, 'But bread and wine it is, boys. It was enough for the Saviour's Last Supper, and it may be our Last Supper too. Good appetite.'

Prayers arose from both sides at dawn, and then the defenders hurriedly took their posts, relieving the night watch, and formed up. Where manpower permitted, they formed groups of three, with two pikemen protecting a central arquebusier while he reloaded. Broglia also positioned small squads of reserve troops to rush into any breach.

And then the very élite of the Janizaries were coming in. They wore eagle headdresses, carried bullock-hide shields decorated with verses from the Koran, saying that Paradise lay in the shade of swords, and cried out 'Death to the Infidel!' They howled to Allah to bring down fire and brimstone upon the unbelievers. For did not the Holy Koran say that He had prepared a place for them? A place of burning ...

From the walls of Elmo, the Christians called upon Christ and the Virgin, St James, St George, St John their patron, and St Michael the warrior archangel to fight with them now.

Then the Turks made an unexpected diversion, passing by the bridges and the ditch for the rear of Elmo and the squat cavalier, which guarded the only gate of the fort. As they tried to bypass the northern walls they suffered lacerating flanking fire, and many stumbled and fell, but more ran on. Broglia sent every other man to the rear walls to destroy them.

It was a close-packed and milling confusion. Fire hoops as thick as a man's thigh, as big as cartwheels, rolled heavily down, slow and blazing and inextinguishable, and black spouts of boiling tar. The robes of the besiegers went up well, men screaming in the midst of the crush, burning like flaring white cypress trees.

'They burn as nicely as ashwood, these Mohammedan dogs!' cried a soldier.

Then came volleys of grapeshot and chain shot from the guns steeply tilted on the cavalier roof, and the effect was slaughterous.

'The more that come, the more we can kill,' cried the soldiers.

After only a short time, the curved battle-horns of the Ottomans sounded from the heights, and the attackers fled.

A soldier whistled. The ground was strewn with the dead.

'That,' said Broglia, 'was a poor decision. When they come again – unless they are being commanded by a secret sympathiser of ours – they will concentrate on crossing the ditch. A much wider front, where their numbers will tell.'

Broglia was right.

The attack on the cavalier was but a test, and results were poor. Soon the Bektaşis, not the Janizaries, were coming in again, and bring more bridging materials.

In no time at all, every man on the walls was fighting in the midst of furious incoming fire, showers of arrows, and a third bridge was waving about in the air above the Bektaşis' heads, ready to slam down upon a central section of the wall where the attackers might dash straight across onto the unbroken parapet. Such a bridge would test them sorely, opening up a front behind them where they crammed towards the star points, so they would be truly encircled.

Then Bridier de la Gordcamp crossed himself and arose behind the parapet and turned, fully exposed to the fire of the enemy.

He walked slowly, as if in a dream. He took up a smaller fire hoop in his left hand and in his right he took tongs and he extended the hoop towards a crouched arquebusier without a word. The arquebusier held out his matchcord and Bridier touched the rim of the fire hoop to the smouldering end and the hoop sizzled and sprang into dancing flame. Then he took it in the tongs and stood high on the walls as the bridge wavered in the air before him.

Voices cried out, 'Brother, stay down!'

But the knight was not within hearing or caring.

An arrow from a compound bow thocked into his shoulder through the chainmail with tremendous force and the fair slender knight turned a little under the force of it. Then he turned back, the arrow stuck deep there. Another clanged off his helmet. He was utterly exposed. The fire hoop burned and smoked enormously, black smoke roiling into the air around him, and through the black smoke Nicholas could still see his face, waiting patiently, his expression as serene as a painted medieval saint. The tongs themselves were heating up fast, and a few seconds later they were burning the flesh of his hand. In his dreamy determination he had not worn gauntlets or he might not have suffered, but there was no time. He waited, the bridge descending above him, and the hot metal burned into his palms as the nails had burned into the palms of Christ crucified. His brother knights watched, paralysed. It was like seeing a child stepping out before a pack of wolves.

The bridge was coming down, casting its shadow over the solitary young knight, just as Bridier leaned back and hurled the fire hoop high in the air. It was a perfect cast, the hoop turning and turning in the air, flinging off burning jellied sparks from its rim as it spun, any one of which could have stuck to his flesh or hair and burst into an inextinguishable blaze. But he never turned away, he moved not an inch, waiting again as still and silent as an alabaster statue while the fire hoop spun like a Catherine wheel and then hit the down slope of the bridge and rolled forward into the oncoming dervishes.

Then the slender knight drew his long sword from its scabbard in his burnt hands and raised the blade to his lips and kissed it and then leapt onto the forward end of the bridge, following after the fire hoop, his sword cutting through the air like a whip.

Springing up from their stupor came running Smith and Stanley, Medrano and Lanfreducci, and Nicholas and Hodge ran too. Hodge grabbed a short billhook as he ran. Nicholas thought of his Livy, and Horatius keeping the bridge against Lars Porsena and his army, alone with his two comrades. Yet that had been but schoolwork, and this was life and death.

In the black smoke, the figure of Bridier twisted and turned and fought with all the fury of a Mohammedan dervish himself, revolving in the smoke like a demon, fair hair flying. The howling Bektaşis tried again and again to rush him, to over-run him with sheer weight of numbers, but again and again they fell back, blinded by smoke, howling not in religious ecstasy but raw pain as their clothes turned to liquid fire on their flesh, and that Christian sword sliced through limb after limb.

Broglia on the bastion turned the field gun and loaded it with a single fine iron ball, grapeshot being too diffuse at this range. He blasted it across into the far end of the bridge where the infuriated dervishes crowded, and it drove a platter-sized hole straight through one man's belly before ploughing on into others behind. The gunners sluiced water on the barrel and cleared out the last wadding and loaded another pack of powder and a ball, and Broglia ordered the trajectory lowered to hit the bridge itself.

Bridier cut and thrust and slew, and the bridge being only wide enough for two men at a time, or a twin file of men to surge across in an attack column, none could get past him. Blood coursed over his fine silver breastplate and from around the arrow shaft stuck in his shoulder, he was cut across the cheek and over the eye, yet he seemed oblivious. Nothing could stop him. Nicholas suddenly realised where he had seen such a thing before. A wall painting in a church, that showed the warrior Archangel Michael treading down Satan on the day of wrath. That same slender figure, with hair as fair as the sun, the expression so lacking in hatred and serene.

Then a pistol cracked out and Bridier was suddenly no such immortal archangel but mortal flesh. He sank to his knees, and a great dervish, naked but for grubby white *şalwar* trousers, raised a huge curved sword over the exhausted knight's bare neck. The sword was descending as Smith and Stanley came racing to Bridier's side, Smith raising his shield over their wounded brother and fending off the mighty stroke just as Stanley drove his long pike straight through the fellow's belly. Smith extended his other arm and loosed his horse pistol, at such short range that it blasted the huge Turk back again off the end of Stanley's pike, and sent him crashing into his fellows behind. Then Smith and Stanley, with Lanfreducci and Medrano close behind them, pressed on forward, trying desperately to drive the enemy from the bridge.

At the Elmo end, the quick-witted Hodge was down on one knee, the billhook rising and falling rapidly. Woodcutter's son. Nicholas stood over him, shield raised as if shading him from the sun as he worked. Two more soldiers came running up with smoking fire hoops, freshly dipped in tar, understanding that the black smoke would give the battered defenders vital cover at this critical time. They tossed them down over the posts of wooden scaffolding below, and flames roared up. Beneath Hodge's beefy blows with the billhook, a brummock he'd call it, the first of the bridge's two thick oak foresprits was quickly being cut through. The broad heavy blade fell again and again as with expert eye Hodge cut hard, left angle, right angle, a notch appearing, another left, another right, a bigger notch, and then straight down in a flurry of blows. Though the sprit was as thick as man's thigh and seasoned hardwood, yet it was quickly going through.

'The bridge is going down!' yelled Nicholas. 'Pull back!'

A further supportive shot from Broglia's gun crew and then the knights, dragging Bridier with them, fought their way back, the dervishes snapping at them like a pack of wolves.

Behind the dervishes were coming four men with long muskets, marching in orderly fashion.

'Take out the Janizary marksmen!' roared Broglia. 'Arque-busiers!'

From the north-west star point, some ragged fire came in on the four approaching musketeers, and they had to duck for cover, buying the retreating knights a few precious seconds.

Then the first foresprit suddenly cracked and the entire bridge gave a lurch and sagged to one side. Hodge in a trice was onto the second sprit, attacking it with scowling concentration. The knights came back at a shambling run, Bridier's arm looped around Stanley's broad shoulders, more dragged than walked. They hurried onto the stone parapet and down, and the sprit gave as the dervishes swarmed across. A last volley of arquebus fire slammed into them broadside and then the bridge fell seeming slowly into the great ditch below. An explosion of flame as the fire hoops flared up and the tumbling white robes caught alight. The knights stood back from the parapet at the blast of heat and the sound of agonised cries. The sound of the damned being hauled down to hell, the flames gouting up in leaping tongues around them. To complete their damnation, a group of Spanish infantrymen stepped forward and with the utter ruthlessness for which they were famed and feared, tossed down a couple of packs of gunpowder, three or four wildfire grenades and a couple more brass grenades, packed with a lacerating mix of gunpowder, naphtha, nails and shards of flint. All stood back and shielded their ears as the terrific explosion filled the ditch.

Afterwards, Nicholas glanced over the parapet. A field of white flowers mown flat, wide-spattered blood and dark gleaming puddles. A head sliced into two halves like a melon, dispossessed limbs. From both sides of the ditch, from Turks and defenders both, a moment of stunned silence. Nothing but the soft crackle of small fires below, and the drifting smoke between them.

They laid Bridier down and removed his breastplate.

'Just a scratch or two,' he whispered. 'I'll be back on the wall by nightfall.'

'Silence now, brother,' said John Smith, as gently as a nurse-maid.

The pistol ball had gone deep in his side, perhaps into his lung, though the blood in his mouth showed no bubbles. The arrow was lodged still deeper in his shoulder, his face and arms were badly cut about, and his left foot was mangled. His face was paler than ever. They eased him onto a canvas stretcher and took him below.

'We held the bridge though, did we not?' he said, with great effort.

'We did,' Stanley nodded. 'We did.'

The other bridges were both so thoroughly blasted by cannon fire that though they still lay across the moat, they were too weakened and shattered for further crossings to be attempted. The Turks pulled back into their forward trenches and there was a brief respite. The knights emerged with big axes and finished the bridges off, sending them collapsing down into the moat and then strewing them with pails of oil and setting them alight so they could not be used again.

The flames leapt up and mingled with the golden sun going down over Malta. The defenders felt some cheer. Yet the Turks knew they had already subjected the enemy to a savage bombardment, as well as a day and a half of furious hand-to-hand assault. They must be badly weakened, and tomorrow they would fall.

'Tomorrow?' said Mustafa Pasha. 'We do not have time to wait until tomorrow.'

He considered.

The plan had been to give this wretched little fort no respite at all, simply to press on hard until it fell. But the loss to the Bektaşis was great, even if they were joyful about the prospect of death, and he had reckoned on their dead bodies filling up the ditch for his Janizaries to cross more easily.

'How many dead?' he demanded

'Some three hundred,' said Işak Agha, Commander of the Janizaries. 'Perhaps four hundred.'

'And they are little more than a hundred in all. They have lost ten, twenty?'

'Fewer than ten, I fear.'

It was bad. It was too costly a ratio.

'We want it taken but we want no more losses on such a scale. It looks ill to the men. You will send in the Janizaries once more, and hold back the Bektaşis.'

'Pasha.'

'And you will send them in tonight. Under cover of darkness. They will have no rest. They will have no sleep again until the grave.'

5

Hodge unbuckled Nicholas's breastplate and they went down into the yard and splashed water on their faces and drank deep at the huge wooden butt.

Two of the Spanish tercios came up behind them and Hodge silently passed them the scoop. They were the dark-burned men under Captain Miranda's command, brought back to Spain from the Americas. They tipped the cool water back down their parched throats without touching their mouths to the edge.

Almost shyly Nicholas said, 'So you are come from the Americas?'

The men removed their helmets and stroked back their sweat-plastered hair and leaned against the wall. Like all old soldiers, they liked to talk of their deeds to wide-eyed youngsters, as long as the youngsters looked suitably impressed by their tales, and didn't ask too many damn fool questions.

'What age are you? And what is your accent?' demanded one.

'I am sixteen, an Englishman. My name is Nicholas. This is Hodge.'

'What are Protestant Englishmen doing in this slaughterhouse?'

'We are Catholic. My father was an English Knight Hospitaller, until his langue was disbanded.'

'Ah. By your fat redbeard king. The one with as many wives as an Arab.'

'King Henry. Father of my Queen.'

The soldier nodded, a faint smile. 'Well,' he said. 'You have chosen a pretty place for your foreign travels. I am told the wild-flowers here this time of year can be a picture.'

The other guffawed and produced a rock-hard stick of salt pork.

Nicholas waited patiently.

'I am García,' he said. 'This is Zacosta.'

Nicholas bowed his head a little. Hodge didn't.

Then the first, García, said, 'I was a youth little older than than you, and like you a stranger in a strange land, when we first rode out with Vasquez de Coronado, out of Mexico and across the Rio Grande. We went looking for the Seven Cities of Gold. For you know that Hernan Cortés himself said, *I suffer from a disease of the heart, which can only be cured by gold.* But along with our swords and our guns we also took our priests. To save the souls of the *Indios*, you understand?'

The other, Zacosta, smiled and sliced through the salt port and handed him and Hodge a slice on his knife.

These were dangerous men, their jokes as dark and secret as the grave. Yet they were good to have on your side.

'It's our souls need saving now,' said Zacosta. 'We have been sent to Elmo to die.'

'Not me,' said García. He hefted his sturdy arquebus, and he did not indeed look like a man whose time had come to die. 'I'm here to kill some Turks, take some Mohammedan scalps, dry 'em out nicely in the sun and decorate 'em with beads and quills the way the Indios do.'

Zacosta laughed.

'Then I'm off back to old Spain, to find me a pretty young wife and good vineyard, somewhere along the green banks of the Ebro. And I'll hang up the scalps of the Mohammedans on the door of my house, and sit out of an evening and toast 'em with my own wine, with my pretty young wife in my lap, as the sun goes down over the mountains of Old Castile.'

They were reckless and hard-hearted men, yet they were Christians, and on the right side, and there was something in their wild and savage humour and their sheer carelessness that was consoling and fortifying after the atrocities of the day.

The sun going down ... pretty young wife ...

Suddenly Nicholas tossed the scoop back in the butt and muttering, 'My pardon,' raced away across the yard, and up the steps to the southern wall. Hodge and the soldiers looking bemusedly after him.

The sun was already below the horizon. He stared and stared across the grand harbour into the fast-gathering gloom, cursing himself. How could he forget? But it was too dark. He could not see.

Yet others walking the twilight streets of Birgu saw the young girl in the pale blue dress in the dusk, the daughter of Franco Briffa, down below the fort of San Angelo, looking out over the water, without a chaperone and her face unveiled. *Escandaloso!* And she was singing an old song:

'*Come no musket, come no blade,*
Come no steel and come no flame,
Through the gun smoke flies the dove,
And you will be my own true love ...'

They had just enough strength to eat some bread and a little more salt meat, drink more wine and water and crawl onto their blankets. They were hardly lain flat before exhaustion took them.

It seemed only a few minutes later that Nicholas awoke to a soldier's cry. He had been dreaming of sword blades and his sister Susan dying in his arms, and he awoke to think he was in a dark church, and Christ was looking over him. Yet his sleepless exhaustion soon gave way to new heart-pounding fear as he heard more and more soldiers' cries, and running feet, and then the renewed boom of guns.

No, no, not again, for pity ...

He and Hodge struggled upright.

'I can't take much more of this,' said Hodge.

Nicholas shook his head. 'Neither can I.' He rested his hand on Hodge's shoulder. Hodge was trembling. 'Are you well?'

'Aye,' said Hodge. 'Just weary.'

His face was pale and pearled with sweat.

'Come then,' said Nicholas.

Hodge put on his breastplate for him and they reeled out under the starlit sky and made for the steps.

It was not yet midnight and they had slept for barely two hours and their every muscle ached, their heads throbbed with tiredness, and now they would have to fight again for many more hours, against odds of three or four hundred to one. In a battle they could not hope to win, only lose as fiercely as possible.

6

It was the Janizaries who attacked this time, swift and orderly, dropping two new bridges over the moat and onto Elmo's battered points with little fuss, and beginning to move across as if on night exercise. More ranged round to the rear of the fort and began to try the strength of its only gate and the cavalier in the safety of darkness.

Yet whether it was some unexpected effect of tiredness, or some strange blessedness, the knights and the Spanish infantrymen ranged on the walls of Elmo fought like veterans of a thousand wars yet with the fire of fresh troops, and the Janizaries themselves could not make headway far over the two bridges nor up the fort's sheer walls. Cannon fire continued to erupt out of the darkness, huge tongues of flame blaring suddenly out of the blackness that cloaked Mount Sciberras, and balls hurtle into the southern walls, yet to little avail if no men could follow it. The Spaniards formed close shoulder-to-shoulder ranks of long pikes and halberds, and the Janizaries repeatedly fell back, once their muskets were fired, saying that to run on was to run onto a dragon's teeth. They themselves had always despised the pike as the weapon of the peasant, and refused to use it. Now they were paying for that arrogance.

The Turks were driven back from both new bridges, and once they had lost those, they made a swift and typically orderly retreat to their forward trenches to regroup. In the command tent of Işak Pasha, Janizary General, there was talk of bringing up one of the siege towers with its tall drop-bridge. But it could be moved only slowly over the rough ground, and the Christian guns would have

235

plenty of time to blast it apart before it reached the edge of the ditch.

Then from beyond the forward trench there came a wild hubbub and howling.

'What in Shaitan's name ...' said Işak Pasha, standing.

It was Lanfreducci who led the crazed counter-attack, the Italian Chevalier shouting volubly and swinging his great Milanese two-hander over his head all the while. The Janizaries, pulling back, were astonished to see a small group of knights, red surcoats dark in the night, pursuing them out over the bridge.

'To the trench!' cried the Turkish officer. 'Recharge your muskets and be ready for those mad dogs of Christendom!'

What hornets' nest had they stirred up now?

Other knights paused only to rub their faces with earth and coat their armour hurriedly as best they could with more earth and spit to dull the gleam. And then within moments of their being under attack, they were dashing across the open ground to the right-hand end of the Janizaries' forward trench. Luigi Broglia sent more after them.

Smith and Stanley went with Lanfreducci, firing on the flee-ing, bewildered Janizaries, and then slamming down into the dust at the run, skidding forward, reloading their guns as fast as they could, before getting up and running again. Others brought brass firebombs and hoops, and coming to the head of the trench, fired them up and tossed them down upon the startled upturned faces of the Turks. A knight was shot at short range and spun and fell down into the trench, and then Smith and Stanley, the first knights with muskets to arrive, knelt swiftly at the head of the trench and shouldered their guns and let them loose. Medrano and De Guaras followed, firing the same, and instantly the Janizary trench was a shouting chaos, men scrabbling back into each other, knocking their comrades down, suddenly outflanked, all order gone and their trench being rolled up by these crazed, vastly outnumbered Christian musketeers.

'Form a caracole!' roared Stanley. 'A levasse! The infantryman's formation, be not proud, brothers! Leave your swords at your sides and keep reloading!'

Faces black with gunpowder, clambering awkwardly over the slain in front of them, the knights continued their extraordinary progress down the forward trench, in a repeated volley and pair formation. There was no room for them to retreat to the back of the column once they had fired, as was usual, so Smith and Stanley simply dropped down, and Medrano and De Guaras ran forwards over their prostrate bodies, knelt and fired. Only twenty feet away, two more Janizaries died, and another behind was disarmed by one of the balls continuing on. Never expecting such a counter-attack, they had built their trench dead straight, meaning there was no cornering for cover, and making this enfilading fire doubly murderous.

Medrano and De Guaras lay flat and two more arquebusiers moved over them, firing from the hip. Lanfreducci bellowed somewhere behind that he hadn't brought a gun, and then in the brief moment that two of his fellow knights were reloading, he dashed onward and dropped down into the trench only two or three feet behind the scrabbling Janizary fugitives, sheathed his two-handed sword in the scabbard strapped across his back, and snatched up one of the guns of the fallen. One turned and hacked angrily at him, but he butted him hard in the face with the Turkish musket and clubbed him to the ground. Then he vaulted out of the side of the trench and sprinted back to his comrades. The moment he was out of the trench, there came two more shots and the Janizaries continued to be mown down.

Fire, drop, reload, fire, drop. Ramrod, wadding, powder, ball, ramrod. Check your matchlock or blow your wheel lock clean again, shoulder arms, brace, fire, hear the steel wheel whirr and fizz, the powder crackle and then bang, feel the big gun rear and recoil against you. Ignore your bruised shoulder, feeling like steak under a hammer. And no time to see who you hit. Drop, get walked over, kneel up. Ramrod, wadding, powder, ball, ramrod ...

The advancing column, spitting out two arquebus balls every three or four seconds, was like a lethal snake uncoiling down the trench, and even a soldiery as fine and disciplined as the Janizaries reeled and broke and struggled to regain order. Their officer had been one of the first to die, which didn't help. They piled back against each other like rats, and every shot could not fail to find a mark in Turkish flesh. Soon the knights were wading through a mulch of red earth.

Yet the resilience of the Turks was extraordinary, their capacity to take punishment and then hit back never to be underestimated. Some gallant souls who tried to run at the smoking, spitting guns of the knights with swords drawn, or paused to reload their own muskets, were quickly targeted and shot down. As they had always known – numbers aside – these accursed Knights of Saint John were every bit a match for them, in every respect. In cunning, ruthlessness, stark courage, there was nothing between them. In religion only did they differ from each other.

The moment of crazed counter-attack could not last.

A cry went up. It was Lanfreducci who first spotted the ominous white wave arising out of the darkness to their right. Coming up from the second trench in strict order, muskets held at hip height, and advancing through the night. A drum beat began to sound the slow, sonorous, unnerving dead-march rhythm of the Janizaries, feared from the windy plains of Hungary to the palm-fringed shores of India.

For a moment the knights were undismayed even by this prospect. Twelve of them in a trench with two hundred men ahead and another three hundred approaching from the right. Smith and Stanley took another shot forward, Medrano and De Guaras turned their guns over the back wall of the trench and fired into the oncoming line. One fell, one turned, but the rest continued at their steady march, implacable, heads held high, muskets lowered, only to fire when the order came. Truly princes among men, for all their infidel faith.

'Time to pull back!' cried Lanfreducci. 'We are nearly surrounded!'

How they made it back out of the trench and over the rough ground and across the cavalier bridge into Elmo without another loss seemed afterwards a miracle. Reloading and ramming as they ran, turning and dropping to one knee, firing into the oncoming horde, as if a single ball could stop that mass of hundreds, now at a battlefield run. Smith pulled his horse-pistol from his belt where it sat pre-loaded and the wheel spun, sparks flew and the huge handgun roared. A Janizary fell to the earth clutching his thigh, spouting bright gore from a severed artery. Another stumbled over him but more came on.

Lanfreducci turned and swung his great two-hander over his head in the face of the approaching horde and cried out, 'For San Marco and the Two Kingdoms!' and a ball cut through his mail and grooved his upper arm. Another kicked up dust between his feet and he turned and ran on, cursing this first time in twenty-eight years he had ever shown his back to the enemy.

Somehow they all got home alive, Lanfreducci and De Guaras both hit but neither fallen.

Panting and grinning, Lanfreducci tore off his bloody tabard and breastplate and padded shirt and stood there on the walls, naked to the waist, his great muscled chest bare, his handsome face thrown back, his thick dark hair curling down his neck, teeth gleaming in the moonlight. Entirely exposed to the Janizary muskets and utterly unafraid, laughing down at them ... Nicholas saw him then as some ancient hero, Hector or Sarpedon on the walls of Troy, casting mockery down on the foe, magnificently careless. Not even glancing down at his own bloody arm, the Italian knight took a strip of clean white linen in his teeth and tore it in two and tossed the narrower strip to Nicholas. He extended his muscled, blood-slathered arm.

'Tie me up tight but not too tight, boy. You know the drill.'

Nicholas did his best.

'Hm.' Lanfreducci eyed the reddening dressing. 'Not so bad. You are the English boy, the Insulter? You tie a good bandage. You've done this before.'

'First time.'

Lanfreducci grinned. 'Well, good enough for first time. Come, let us drink some wine, and the wound in my arm may have some too. We have earned it, little English brother. They say your father was a Hospitaller, is this so?'

Exhausted and still terrified and now elated all at once, Nicholas bowed his head, near overwhelmed with emotion, as the Italian knight laid his good arm over the boy's thin shoulders and they went down to the inner yard to drink wine.

*

A hospital chaplain came to urge Lanfreducci inside the store too, to lie down so he could dress his wound.

''Tis done, Fra Gianni,' said the knight. 'But a splash of brandy ...'

He drank wine while his arm was doused in brandy, and showed no reaction until the chaplain had gone back inside. Then he screwed up his face. 'By the arse of Mohammed, that stings.'

Nicholas grinned.

'So you wish to become a brother too, to follow after your father?' said Lanfreducci. 'You know about the rule of chastity?'

He looked away. 'I will not be a knight, I think.'

'Then why are you here? There is no compulsion. And you know we are in terrible danger.' He hesitated a moment. 'Indeed, most of us here will die.'

He passed Nicholas the cup of wine and he drank.

'I suppose,' said the boy, wiping his mouth, 'I think I won't die. And I am here because of my father.'

Lanfreducci nodded in the darkness. 'The Blessed Virgin look over you, boy. There is no need for you to fight. Bring up water, wine, casks of powder. Bulk the walls. Help the chaplains here. Tie a good bandage. Keep your head down, and keep away from the front line. My heart would be heavy if boys like you died here.' And he hugged him hard.

They might snatch a couple more hours' sleep before dawn. But first Nicholas needed a word with someone.

'Stanley?'

'Hnn.'

'*Stanley.*'

Stanley snorted and stirred. 'What is it, boy?'

Nicholas hesitated.

'For all the saints. Be quick. I was dreaming of roast beef.'

'It's about Lanfreducci.'

'What of him?'

'Forgive me, only I need to ask you ... he's not ... he's not, is he?'

'Not what?'

'A ... *un sodomità*?'

Stanley said in a tight voice, 'Lanfreducci?'

'Yes.'

'No.' He gave a strangulated laugh. 'No, the Chevalier Francesco di Lanfreducci is most certainly not *un sodomità*.'

'Only – he kept putting his arm around me, and then he hugged me.'

'Ay. And soon enough he'll be telling you he loves you,' growled another voice out of the darkness. It was Smith. 'It means nothing, boy. He's just *Italian*.'

'In fact,' said Stanley, 'Brother Francesco is one of our order who is most troubled by the vow of chastity.'

'He's not troubled by it at all,' said Smith. 'He's quite happy with his mistress over in Birgu.'

'Mistress?' said Nicholas.

Stanley nodded, looking serious. 'We are knights, boy, not saints. Though it is a shameful thing for a knight to break a vow. Yet the Chevalier Lanfreducci fights as valiantly as any knight in the Order – you have seen – and besides, it must be said, he has the looks of some ancient god, and the women will pursue him to exhaustion, like hounds after their quarry. And he is too lazy and smiling and—'

'And *Italian*,' said Smith.

'And Italian,' said Stanley, 'to say no. Hence the mistress – the very pretty mistress, I acknowledge – in Birgu.'

'And the one in Naples,' said Smith.

'And in Messina,' said Stanley.

'The *two* in Messina.'

Stanley looked over his shoulder. 'Two?'

'Ay. The Contessa as well.'

Stanley looked back, reflective, his eyes distant. 'Well,' he said. Then he focused on the boy again. 'Unseemly talk for your ears, boy. Get some sleep. And have no anxieties about Lanfreducci that way. He is not interested in you for your – fleshly configuration. But you might pray for his soul. He needs it.'

7

From San Angelo, La Valette and Starkey looked out at the beleaguered fort, silently smoking in the night.

'The banner of St John flies yet,' said Starkey, 'though they have fought there two days and two nights.'

'And will be fighting all tomorrow too, no doubt of that,' said La Valette. 'Against entirely fresh troops. But they have withstood well so far, and Birgu is grateful for it. Not a minute has been wasted.'

In a courtyard in a quiet backstreet, a mother said to her daughter, 'What is it, child?'

The girl said nothing.

'Is it the English boy?'

Then tears came to the girl's eyes, and she stood and ran into an inner room.

'You know it is the English boy,' said Franco Briffa, throwing another wad of dried brush in the brazier. 'Leave her be.'

The woman bent over her sewing again. 'How it hurts to be young and in love.'

'Love,' sighed Franco. 'Ay, I remember that word. But as to its meaning ...'

His wife smiled in the firelight and pricked him in the leg with her needle. Franco chuckled.

The Turks fell on Elmo again the next day, and the defenders fought from dawn till dusk, and then the next. The high confidence of the first day and the blistering counter-attack began to wane. In their weariness they began to make misjudgements, and Smith stood to move along the line just as new gunfire poured in upon them at close range.

He was struck in his broad bullneck by a musket ball. He fought on, blood slowly drenching his throat and shoulder, before he suddenly weakened and tottered, and then said with great dignity, 'Brothers, I must leave you,' and went below.

Stanley rammed a fresh musketball home with vehemence. 'He'll live,' he said. It sounded as much a prayer as a prediction.

Nicholas glanced after Smith, Sir John Smith, the indestructible, knight of both England and Malta ... And Hodge, too, was not well. He drank excessively, and ate little, and looked wan, and struggled to bring the smallest sacks of powder and ball up the steps to the walls. But Nicholas would not let Hodge die. He had decided that they would fight the good fight as long as they could, but then somehow make their way back across the water before Elmo fell, to Birgu, alive, to fight again.

Men's plans are not God's plans.

Hodge dropped down beside Nicholas with a grunt, the sack of balls hitting the ground and the dull leaden spheres rolling away over the stone.

'For God's sake boy, pick 'em up!' roared a nearby soldier.

But Hodge could not. He lay back sickly, lips thin and drawn, eyes barely open, trembling. Nicholas scrabbled around gathering up the musket balls again and passed them up to the soldier on the wall. He ducked as another explosion went off overhead, and more masonry tumbled down and hit the yard below.

'Master,' whispered Hodge, 'I am going.'

'I'm not your master, Hodge,' said Nicholas fiercely. 'Master no more. And you're not dying. You're fevered, and tonight you will go—'

'Fevered and hit too,' said Hodge. He moved his left arm slightly across the stones, and it was limp, and left a slather of blood in the dust.

Nicholas in dismay sliced open Hodge's sleeve and saw the horrible sight of a white splintered arm bone gouging up through the torn flesh of his forearm, the flesh around it blown clean away, more white bone showing, and blood leaking everywhere.

'O sweet Jesus, sweet Jesus, look down ...' gabbled Nicholas, tearing off the band of cloth around his head that kept the sweat from his eyes and trying to slip it under Hodge's shattered arm. Exhausted and near delirious as he was, Hodge arched his back at the merest touch of the material and screamed. Nicholas felt the agony, his very arm throbbed in unison. And the worst thing, panic began to set in.

The soldier above them gave a grunt and stepped back, the soldier to whom he had given the fresh bag of musket balls. Then he fell across them and crashed down. He was already dead, half his head gone, his helmet rolling clumsily away across the parapet and over the edge. Another man was screaming with madness, and there were more shouts of sheer desperation,

'They're coming in! We can't hold them!'

Nicholas held onto Hodge's other hand, stricken helpless. A shadow fell across him from behind, and he knew it was a Turk up on the cordon, yet even then he could not look round. Smoke and dust blinded his eyes, his eyeballs stung with grit, his ears were stunned and deaf, his throat like sharkskin as it had been for days now. Yet he could not look up, could not move, and the cries of despair around him seemed even now very far away. There was only him kneeling there in the dust below the half-shattered parapet, and Hodge lying before him, near dying, to be buried here in this stone-hard fly-blown island, forgotten and far from home.

'O sweet Jesus ...'

Then two more Spanish infantrymen were fighting behind him. It was García and Zacosta, thrusting over the cordon with fantastic savagery, their half-pikes dripping, and there was another man kneeling beside the boys, keeping his head low. It was Lanfreducci. You beg of Jesus, and a mortal man comes. But that is how Jesus answers. With practised skill he held Hodge's shoulder in one hand, and then swiftly but gently drew his hand up and across, ignoring the boy's cries, so that the shattered forearm lay across Hodge's own belly. Then he scooped Hodge up in strong arms, keeping him prone and motionless, and carried him down to the stores for the chaplains to tend. They were so low on medical supplies, they were splinting with scabbards now.

Nicholas ran down after them. His every desire was to go with

Hodge, sit with him, be with him. But that was worthless, and not his duty. He was urgently needed on the walls. He seized more bags and powder packs and ran up the steps once more. Sweat immediately began to pour into his eyes again in the atrocious heat, salt to sting his cracked and sunburned face. The sun was a living fire, but it punished all equally. He paused half-way up to tie the cloth around his forehead again, for without it he could barely see to crawl along behind the cordon, handing out the bags and packs.

Behind him came another knight up the steps, his throat wrapped tight with a white bandage, limping badly, his face deathly pale. The rest of his wounds and his half-destroyed body were hidden by his fine suit of armour. He raised his vizor and smiled at Nicholas above him. It was Bridier de la Gordcamp.

'Brother!' called one of the chaplains from the yard. 'You cannot—'

Bridier raised his hand without turning. 'Later, brother, later.'

The situation on the walls was desperate. The Janizaries were pushing with vast concerted force now to finish this damned fort and be done, knowing that the defenders had been fighting for close on seventy-two hours, with barely a rest. That lunatic counter-attack of theirs must have boosted their morale, yet still they must be near finished.

The heat was terrible, and while they in their white silk robes had it better, the Christians in their suits of armour must surely be dropping of suffocation and thirst if nothing else. A quarter of them were dead already, and the rest must surely be destroyed soon. And yet those dogs of St John fought on, like men who did not know when their appointed time was come.

Not twenty men stood behind the north-west cordon, locked in struggle with the packed Janizary assault. Though distant Turkish snipers might try to pick off isolated defenders, yet guns were in the main useless in this mêlée of swords and half-pikes, deteriorating into the crudest blows with shield boss or butt in the face with armoured head.

Through the ranks of the soldiers and his brother knights, not one of them unwounded, slipped the slender Bridier. He stepped up onto the cordon of barrels and bales, drew his sword and cried out the name of the Saviour. Then before the astonished eyes of all, attackers and defenders both, he flipped his grilled vizor down, dropped in among the Janizaries themselves and began slaying.

For a moment it seemed like he was a man enchanted, or a demon come from below. His armour was of the very finest, of the workshops of Brescia, and even the most powerful cuts and thrusts made no headway against him, while his own long lean blade sliced cruelly through Turkish flesh without ceasing. The attack began to fail, some Turks fell away, some retreated. Then a veteran Janizary sergeant aimed grimly and stabbed the point of his scimitar straight at the exposed underarm of the fair-haired knight and drove it in deep.

Bridier pulled himself back from the scimitar and swung his sword and missed and staggered and fell. Janizaries crowded vengefully forward, but from the roof of the bastion came a command to his own men to duck down, and then a perfectly timed volley of crossbow bolts under Luigi Broglia's all-seeing direction. They flew in hard and hit the close-packed Turkish soldiery while the prostrate Bridier lay safe below them. Half a dozen more Turks fell. In the pause, Bridier climbed to his feet again, leaning on his sword, and then raised it once more, beyond exhausted, just enough to drive it low into the sergeant's belly. The Turk leaned forward and vomited blood over the weapon that had killed him. Bridier pulled his sword free and sank to his knees. The sergeant knelt with him, facing him. They appeared like men confessing their last sins to each other.

But it was enough. The drum retreat had already sounded. The Janizary captain across the ditch saw that his sergeant was dead and order among his men once more lost. The shattered, exposed, bitterly contested star point was once more abandoned, and the damned fort of Elmo lived to breathe another hour.

The knights at the barrier cheered their brother Bridier, but the older knights looked grave as they cheered, knowing he must now be wounded to death.

Nicholas wanted to run out to him and help him in, but he froze. With implacable calm, beyond the ditch and safely behind a forward breastwork, half a dozen Janizary marksmen were now taking aim on the lone, broken knight, standing isolated out beyond the defensive cordon.

Bridier turned and walked slowly back towards the heaped barrier of barrels and gabions and stone blocks, his vizor raised, his head hung down, his long girlish locks plastered to his pale cheeks. He could no longer lift his sword enough to sheathe it. Its point dragged in the dust behind him.

'Run, brother, run!' cried his comrades.

The marksmen took aim at his back, not forty paces off.

Knights began to climb up onto the cordon to dash to his rescue. But that was precisely what the Janizary captain had foreseen. Such foolish nobility in those Christian dogs. Yet such nobility, a true Muslim might yet admire it, even though it must be destroyed. He dropped his arm, and his marksmen's muskets cracked out a hard unwavering volley.

Two of the marksmen had aimed at the cordon iself, and their shots smacked into the gabions and the stones and sent chips flying amid the whine of ricochet. The knights ducked down.

The other four marksmen had aimed for Bridier's heart.

The young French knight, almost the last flower of a thousand years of Frankish chivalry, barely twenty years of age and beautiful still like a boy, took a staggering step forward. Then with great effort he raised his head and gave his brothers a sad smile and they knew he had already been shot several times and enough had gone through his armour to kill him.

They could hear the Janizary captain's cry clear across the field. *Shoot him down! Shoot him down!* This enchanted one could not be allowed to live.

A different shot rang out, and Nicholas turned his head sharply. It was Smith's jezail, but Stanley taking the shot, putting one of those precious lethal *stuardes* straight through the Janizaries' forward breastwork, to their astonished horror, and sending one of their invaluable highly-trained marksmen staggering back and dropping in the dust, clutching his belly.

The momentary confusion among the other marksmen was enough for Bridier to be brought home, arms reaching out for him, half lifting, half dragging him over the broad cordon to safety. An arrow clanged off Stanley's plated arm even as he dropped back, laid the jezail down and drew off Bridier's helmet.

The young knight breathed with deep pain. Blood dappled his

face and ran from his ears and a thin trickle from the corner of his mouth. By God's grace alone did he still breathe at all. His sword lay at his side and still he wore that serene saint's smile.

'I am struck very near the heart, I think,' he whispered.

Stanley said, 'It's a mighty heart.'

'Leave me be. Prepare to fight again.'

Then the burly Chevalier de Guaras said, in the old-fashioned idiom, as seemed only right before this unearthly knight from out of the old tales and chronicles, 'By the fair fame of France I shall not quit you.' And he pulled him upright.

Bridier de la Gordcamp looked at the thin English boy who knelt in the dust nearby, and perhaps saw something of himself there in that young, torn, passionate face.

'Here, boy,' he said weakly. 'Take my sword, guard it. Bring it to me in the evening.'

Nicholas took up the fine long sword.

'God bless you, little brother,' murmured Bridier.

Then De Guaras took him on his shoulder and carried him below.

The crude, four-bed hospital was filled with the wounded and dying, the air filled with their groans. Flies buzzed expectantly, and the stench was terrible. Smith, his neck bandaged, lay on his side on a pallet on the floor, and breathed badly.

'Leave me here at the door,' said Bridier.

De Guaras ignored him. 'In the name of pity, see to our brother.'

The chaplain did not even turn, and his arms were red to the elbows. Another knight bucked underneath him as he tried to draw free an arrowhead from his guts, the cavity of his abdomen welling out blood. 'As soon as I can.'

'Now!' shouted De Guaras. 'This brother of ours, this hero—'

Only then did the chaplain glance back over his shoulder. It was the imperturbable Fra Giacomo. 'All heroes here, brother. Do not shout, not even in this extremity.'

Bridier clutched De Guaras about his thick wrists. 'I sit and sun myself here, Fra Melchior, and bide my time. Now go and fight for the faith.'

How they fought through a fourth afternoon under that burning sun, they hardly understood nor remembered. Many were wounded, and more fell not to rise again. Yet still the Turks could not break in. Towards evening the attack faltered, and finally the mournful blast of the Ottoman curved battle-horn sounded over the wreckage of the field, and the Janizaries pulled back. From now on into night, they would fire only from a distance, sniper and cannon.

'We will bring up field guns and blast that wretched cordon to pieces across the ditch,' said Işak, Agha of the Janizaries. 'It is only a *cordon*, in the name of the angels. It is only a rough mound of earth and stones that holds us back. It is a disgrace.'

The captain nodded. 'Yet they rebuild it every time.'

The Agha refused to hear. 'Then at dawn the infantrymen will go in again, and surely they will finish it.'

Nicholas drew out Bridier's sword from the shadows inside the door of the bastion where he had carefully stowed it, and went down to the hospital.

Inside it was so dark, and his eyes so blinded with glaring day-long sunlight and smoke and dust, that he could see nothing for a long time. Then a throaty voice said, 'He is not here.' It was Smith. 'Bridier. He is gone.'

Nicholas was all confusion. He knelt at Smith's side. 'How is it?'

'I have been better. The ball's stuck in my throat, and the chirurgeon says' – he gasped, went on – 'says, he cannot dig it free without making me bleed like a stuck pig.'

Nicholas felt close to tears. A man like Smith could not die.

'Stanley keeps trying to dose me with more opium, but I know his game. He thinks to send me to sleep so I can be shipped back over to Birgu and out of the fight. But he'll not.'

He laid a great hand on Nicholas's head. It felt like his father's.

'But your gallant friend needs to go over, boy.'

'Hodge!'

Only then did he see the racked, stretched body of his companion through all. Hodge on his back, delirious, drenched in sweat, muttering, eyes roving through the darkness of the roof above. Then Nicholas wept without shame, kneeling at his side. *'Hodge.'*

Hodge did not know him. Hodge knew nothing, but in his fever-dream saw only the woods and hills of Shropshire, the hedgerows white with may.

'The chaplains in the Sacred Infirmary will mend him,' said Smith. His voice was thick with pain, his throat with blood and swelling. But he must tell him. 'You go back too, boy. You return. This will be the last boat. It'll not come again. Go with Hodge. Your time is done here.'

Nicholas said nothing, bent and kissed Hodge on his burning forehead, prayed that God have mercy on Smith's soul as he stepped past him, and went out.

He still held Bridier's sword. Where had he gone? Cast himself off the wall into the sea below? So as not to be a burden to his brothers even in death. The boy stood in a daze. Weak with hunger but sick at eating. A Spaniard infantryman went by him. It was García.

'You sicken, boy?'

Nicholas shook his head dumbly.

'Battle sickness. The stench, the flies, the ruin of men's flesh. Hope bleeding away too. Drink my wine.'

Again he shook his head.

'*Drink it.* To show you're not a damned Mohammedan dog if nothing else.' García shoved his wine cup to Nicholas's lips and almost forced it down his throat. It had a bitter tang.

He coughed and swallowed, wiped his mouth and said, 'There's opium in it.'

'Ay. Just enough so you sleep through the night. Else the horrors of your mind will frighten sleep away.'

The drugged wine warmed him and softened something hard and painfully knotted within him.

Barely conscious of his way, he went over to the little chapel of St John, up the three shallow steps. There on the stone lintel was blood. Blood was everywhere. The whole of Elmo was bleeding.

He stood while his eyes adjusted to the darkness of the little chapel. It was empty, and blissfully cool. He approached the high hanging crucifix over the altar. The stones beneath his feet were slathered in blood. In his exhausted delirium he thought it was Christ's blood, streaming down from the crucifix, to cleanse Elmo and all the word of its manifold and numberless sins.

A figure lay at the foot of the cross, motionless, suited in armour. His hands were clasped in prayer.

It was Bridier.

Nicholas knelt by his side. He would have wept, but he was beyond tears. He laid his bare hand on the fallen knight's breast-plate, like the rest of his armour dented and dusty and cracked and half ruined. What blows it had taken. At last the steel was cooling, after the hot fury of battle and the Mediterranean sun. Bridier's cheek too was cold, alabaster-cold to the touch. He scraped back the plastered hair from his cheek. His eyes were still open, but the light was out in them and the soul was gone. Very gently Nicholas drew down first one eyelid and then the other with the trace of a forefinger and Bridier slept in the arms of God. Never had he seen an expression so at peace.

With his very last strength he must have left the field hospital and crawled into the chapel, unseen by any. He had crawled up the aisle to the foot of the cross, dragging himself with his bare hands, his blood shining behind him on the stones. Neither wine nor opium for him. Only the wine of faith, the opium of the divine. His life was done, only his soul mattered now. Here he had made his last confession, begged for God's mercy on his sinful soul, and quietly died.

Nicholas laid Bridier's sword down beside his lifeless body. Untenanted flesh. All flesh is grass.

Someone came into the chapel. It was Edward Stanley.

'That is of no use to him now,' he said gently. 'No swords where he has gone.'

Nicholas stared dumbly down. He was so tired.

Stanley said that the Chevalier Bridier de la Gordcamp had had the tranquillity of a great soul, a noble heart. Such a man never loses his temper or becomes angry, not even in the heat of battle. He is only an instrument in the hands of God, a feather on the breath of God, and he accepts everything appointed for him as God's will.

'Our brother Bridier died on the fourth day,' he said. 'Yet Christ rose again from the dead on the third day, in glorious foreshadowing. Or rather, the precedent light to this shadow. There is a pattern to everything. Now take up his sword.'

Stanley himself took up the body of the knight, and walked away down the aisle.

He laid him in a side room of the cluttered, fly-blown chamber that served for a hospital, where the chaplains would do their best amid the attacks and the explosions to wash him down and scent him and wrap him in linen cloths in the hope that he and all the dead might yet have a decent and Christian burial. *Deo volente.* Then Stanley removed Bridier's armour, piece by battered piece, inspecting it closely. At last he passed Nicholas his helmet, his two arm vambraces and mailed gauntlets, and his sword-belt and scabbard.

'I am to fight?'

'No. You are exhausted.'

'We are all exhausted. You know I fight well, how fast I am.'

'You may need to fight to save your life soon. But now you are returning to Birgu with Hodge and my brother John.'

Nicholas bit his lip.

'Yet this armour may save you. It is meant. Bridier had your frame to an uncanny degree. And he gave you his sword.'

'Only to guard till evening.'

'No. He knew he was dying. He meant you to have it.'

Nicholas eyed the edges, badly toothed and dented.

'Find a whetstone, do what you can to the edge. Wear it with pride.' He smiled a soft smile, his eyes shining with a proud sorrow. 'I do not need to tell you to be worthy of it. You are worthy already.'

8

The death of Bridier affected them all deeply, for in it they saw the longed-for type and template of their own. Already their numbers were deeply winnowed. Whatever they did cost lives, whether they counter-attacked, fell back, dug in. De Guaras was sorely wounded to the head, and wore a bandage tight around his temples, deep dyed. Smith was badly hurt though he denied it angrily, still unable to rise from his pallet. Bridier was dead, Lanfreducci's arm wound was not healing well, though he hid it as best he could.

The one shred of good news for Nicholas was when Hodge suddenly appeared at his side. He looked very pale, but not fevered. His injured left arm was in a thick stiff plastercast made of cotton bandages and white clay.

'What ... How fare you?'

'Alive,' said Hodge. 'So it seems.'

'You'll not go back to Birgu?'

'Will you?'

Nicholas shook his head. 'Not yet.'

'Then me neither. Bugger Birgu.'

Of the fifty knights, twenty were dead or wounded beyond fighting, and of the one hundred soldiers who supported them with such stubborn and dogged courage, fewer than sixty still stood. They were less than a hundred. Maybe a thousand Turks had died before the walls of Elmo, maybe more. But there remained tens of thousands more.

Yet they fought on. Another day, another night. Another day, and the assault seemed to falter a little, as a bewildered Ottoman high command pulled back to count their losses, and to consider. Day followed night followed day, the days lost their names, the dead piled up, and they fought on. They slept a few minutes at a time, whether light or dark. Small, delicate tasks became difficult, as if their very fingers longed for rest. The buckling on of armour, the reloading of an arquebus took longer and longer. Yet they fought on, more and more exhausted, uncertain even how long they had withstood the army of Suleiman the Magnificent ...

In the gathering dark they huddled in the inner courtyard and ate what rations they could of bread and biscuit and salt pork, and drank watered wine. They could hear the distant shouts and orders of the Turkish medical corps, coming forward as darkness fell to rescue the wounded. They did not fire on them.

'Not out of mercy,' growled Zacosta. 'Out of bone tiredness.'

'He hates those Mohammedan dogs,' said García, jerking his head at his comrade. 'They raped his sister.'

Nicholas looked horrified.

García nodded gravely. 'They mistook her for a camel.'

Zacosta gave him a thump.

These soldiers' humour took some getting used to. Yet perhaps it was the best defence against despair.

And then in the midst of their laughter, another of the soldiers came running from the south wall to say a longboat was coming in below Elmo. Perhaps a messenger from La Valette, it was hard to see in the moonless night. The Turks could not seal off the crossing from Birgu to Elmo even now. They couldn't seal off the Grand Harbour without first taking Elmo. And after ten days – *ten days* – against all expectation, they still couldn't take Elmo. The paradox was becoming agonising.

A second soldier came panting into the courtyard. His face gleamed in the firelight, his eyes danced. Nicholas held his breath. Relief forces from Sicily?

'Speak, damn you,' said Zacosta.

'Our brothers have come out to us,' said the soldier. 'Fifty or more reinforcements!'

All of them, soldiers and knights, dashed to the south wall and looked down, and their hearts swelled in their chests. Climbing up the steep rocky coast beneath the walls of the fort, unseen by any Turks, was a column of fifty, perhaps sixty more veteran tercios. They trod softly, their boots bandaged in cloth, every inch of steel about them dulled with mud.

'God be praised,' breathed Stanley.

'And La Valette,' said De Guaras. 'He has not abandoned us yet.'

They hurried to open the gates.

Although the reinforcements might seem pitifully few, when faced with an army of thousands, none of them felt that way. Instead a newly indomitable spirit stirred within them, steeled once more for the fight. Perhaps it was La Valette's plan, for the Turks to waste themselves and bleed away bewildered before this wretched little fort, while Elmo itself was constantly resupplied from Birgu under cover of darkness, without the Turks even knowing. If so, it showed masterful tactics.

The fresh troop of soldiers were led by the powerful Captain Miranda himself, and had been guided across by a local fisherman: Luqa Briffa, the celebrated scoundrel, the greatest swimmer of the island, suspected 'liberator' of various jewels and costly trinkets from the houses of the Maltese nobility in Mdina, and older brother of Franco Briffa himself.

Miranda saluted smartly. Broglia returned the salute. 'By God, you are welcome here, Captain, more welcome than a hundred of the most beautiful courtesans in Venice.'

'We fight better too,' said Miranda dryly.

'Which is the Inglis, the Insulter?' demanded the short, bandy-legged, loosely turbanned Luqa Briffa. 'It is you, is it not?' He prodded a stubby forefinger in Nicholas's chest. The boy nodded. 'My brother sends greetings, and his good wife. He says God bless you and keep you. You are a crusader for the island. He prays you come home.'

Nicholas smiled forlornly. Sick and dizzy with tiredness, muzzy with opium and wine yet his parched gullet still sore, his mind still full of pictures of atrocity from the past days, made bearable only by those rare, brief lightbeams of heroism he had seen ... he felt like no crusader. He felt like an unwashed, exhausted fugitive wretch and exile, trapped here in a war to the death with an enemy never to be defeated. Yet it was good to hear of the family across the water, and good to see the grimly determined tercios come to join them.

'You also have a cake,' said Luqa Briffa. And to general surprise, he brought out a small, beautiful white cake wrapped in a clean white cloth.

'Cake,' said Stanley close by. 'Just what we need most. Not musket balls, powder, medicines or bandages. Our greatest need is for cake.'

Luqa Briffa shrugged. 'This is not my brother. If Franco bake a cake, it come out looking like a donkey's pat, and tasting much the same. This is baked by his daughter, my niece. Maddalena. For you, Inglis.' He eyed Nicholas sternly under his bushy eyebrows. 'Especially for you. Yes?'

'Yes.'

'You understand?'

'Yes.' He could think of nothing to add except, 'Thank you. Say thank you.'

Stanley said, 'Tell us some good news, Captain.'

'The news,' said Miranda, 'like life itself, is good and bad. The Spanish relief force for Malta is now being fitted out in earnest, in Barcelona. But meanwhile another relief force, ready to sail, is being held up by rough seas in Genoa.'

'That is reasonable,' said a hoarse voice nearby. It was Smith, on his feet again, quite expressionless, using a broken pikestaff for a crutch. His neck wound was making him feverish, dizzy, and he swayed abominably without support.

'For all the saints,' muttered Stanley, trying to look annoyed and failing, 'is there no putting the man down?'

Smith went on, 'It is reasonable that our comrades in Genoa should not wish to come and fight beside us, for fear they might feel a touch queasy on the sea crossing. That is understandable. They should wait for seas as smooth as glass. We are happy to fight on here without them, outnumbered as we are by a mere four hundred to one. We will be pleased to see them when they can finally make it over.'

The sarcasm was hardly subtle, but the tercios guffawed. Zacosta slapped the knight on the back, impertinently. They had taken to this gruff blackbearded Englishman like one of their own.

Luqa Briffa was heading for the gates. 'As for me, I go back. What more can I say? You are men among men. You are as stout as Maltese. There, there is a blessing. May Christ and the Virgin watch over you, St Michael and all angels fight for you.'

From the rocks below the south-east point, scrambling down to his fellow rowers in the longboat, he called back, 'Enjoy the cake!'

Nicholas passed it round. It was very fine, filled with almonds and honey.

'And made with love,' joked García.

Nicholas flushed, looking down.

Behind him, Stanley touched García on the shoulder, to silence his mockery. He said no more.

When they had eaten, many fell asleep where they sat. For the first time in days they felt some contentment, some hope. Another fifty fresh men on the walls tomorrow would tell significantly. They would fight on, good for another week perhaps. Then maybe they would never eat cake again, never taste honey. Some thought they would never taste a woman's lips or lie between a woman's thighs again. Some thought in silence of far families. All prayed. Even García and Zacosta prayed, to whatever God made sense to them.

The mood was different in the pavilion of Mustafa Pasha.

He said to Işak Agha, 'Why have you not taken it?'

Işak looked riven with shame. 'They are few, Pasha, but they fight like lions.'

'And the Janizaries fight like, what? Like women? Like girls? Like lambs?'

Işak Agha bowed his head.

Suddenly Mustafa's infamous, furious rage rose up in him. He strode towards Işak Agha, almost into him, put his hands around the Agha's throat and shook him, raging, 'Tomorrow is the eleventh day. *The eleventh.* And still not a single Janizary has stood inside that fort, even to die there like a hero. Take it! Allah damn you and your seed and your family for ever, if you do not soon take that accursed pox-ridden Christian nest of snakes!'

Işak had his hands on Mustafa's hands, his eyes bulging, the words squeezed dry in his throat.

Mustafa raged, 'For more than a week now that cesspit of a fort has stood against us, the dogs of St John in San Angelo looking on and laughing. *Laughing!* Have the Janizaries no sense of shame, of dishonour? Two thousand of my men, *two thousand . . . !* Shit on them, rip them apart, rip their livers out! Rip their hearts out of their splintered ribs, do you hear me? Kill them! Take that place NOW and KILL THEM ALL!'

And in his fury he hurled the muscular Agha of Janizaries backwards out of his tent as if he were a wrestler of twenty-five.

Smith was on his feet the next day at dawn, his whole neck and throat swollen and sore beneath the linen wrappings, his left arm strangely numb and tingling and stiff to move. But it could clutch his broken pike-crutch well enough, and he swung his right arm, his sword-arm, vigorously, readying for the fight.

Stanley said wonderingly, 'I have given him enough opium to put a draught horse to sleep.'

'How?' said Nicholas. 'He suspected you. He'd drink nothing that tasted of opium.'

'I had one of the chaplains steep his fresh bandage in opium and brandy. Straight into his blood that way. A slight risk, it might have proved too much.' Smith was swishing his sword now sharply left and right, parry and thrust. 'Yet clearly not enough. The man would have outwrestled the angel at the Brook Jabbok that defeated Jacob himself.'

Smith stumped over and glared down at them.

'What are you two idlers gossiping about, like women at a well? On your feet.'

They stood.

'Strike me,' said Stanley, 'but you've a broken fingernail, Fra John.'

Smith stared down. Amid his multiple wounds and bruises, and a lead ball festering in the muscles of his mighty neck, he had indeed broken a fingernail half through, leaving a small scab of blood.

Stanley clucked like a hen. 'That must sting painfully. You should see a physician.'

Smith growled like a bear and stumped off.

How could they joke like this, with death imminent? wondered

258

Nicholas. Yet he had seen enough jesters going up to the gallows in Shrewsbury Town. Laughing at death as they went. Perhaps it was the best that man's wisdom could do.

Will I die? he asked inwardly. Lord, will I die today? Or will I live to see England again? My sisters? Even my estate restored?

The answer came as usual. A silence, filled with a presence, and with wordless consolation.

Minutes later a cry went up from the bastion. A new flag was flying on the lookout of San Angelo.

Many rushed to the top, straining to see, desperate for the rapturous sight of the black, two-headed eagle on a yellow ground: the standard of Christian Spain, showing that the longed-for relief of King Philip had come.

The flag showed a ship and a lightning bolt.

'The banner of Saint Elmo,' said Lanfreducci.

Stanley stared and then said, 'They are telling us it is the Feast Day of Saint Elmo.'

Neither knight allowed a hint of disappointment in his voice.

Stanley stared around. 'June 3rd.'

Eleven days.

The Turks were moving guns about busily, carefully. They were not attacking yet. Everything suggested absolute determination to finish this. When they came in, it would be very hard.

Commander Luigi Broglia moved about busily too, as yet unwounded, marshalling soldiers and guns, an energetic and expert leader of men. At last the eight-barrelled organ gun had been made serviceable, a small-bore field gun that nevertheless wreaked bloody attrition on close-packed men. He set it low on the bastion, ready served.

Even among the dark pools of dried blood, the mangled bodies dragged into shade and roughly covered with sacking for decency, and the severed limbs, discreetly gathered up by the medical chaplains, Broglia retained his optimism.

'I admire good spirits in a man,' said Smith. 'But Commander Broglia, do you not think there comes a time when sunny optimism, in certain circumstances, can seem like nothing but sunstruck lunacy?'

Both ducked as a cannonball whistled in. An initial ranging shot, but a good one. It struck the parapet of the south wall and sent splinters flying. They would be coming soon. Smith held his sword unsheathed.

Broglia grinned. 'Ah, Fra Gianni Smit! Come come, my morose and melancholy English Brother, be of stout heart! And I will be of stout belly, though I fear it is diminishing daily on our paltry rations.'

There was something grotesque about Broglia's high spirits amid the strewn limbs, the sun-crusted pools of blood, the flies sipping and fattening at their margins, and worst of all, the ubiquitous, slaughterhouse stench rising from the moat beyond. Yet Smith couldn't help but smile likewise, revealing a split gum and a gap where yesterday two teeth had been.

'*Ecco!*' cried Luigi Broglia. 'Just so! *Coraggio e Allegrezza*, Courage and Jollity, the ancient motto of the Broglia family, ever since I made it up five seconds ago!'

Smith went up to the north-west cordon. A soldier was just lugging a fresh earth-filled gabion onto the pile, heaping it as high as a man's head, when a single shot rang out and he fell back. Shot clean through the heart. Behind their breastworks, fresh and well slept, handsomely breakfasted and full of confidence, with limitless supplies of powder and balls at their disposal, the Ottoman snipers were working.

Cursing, Smith clambered up after him to bring him down where he sprawled.

'Brother!' cried out Stanley. For the soldier he had gone to rescue was dead already.

Then a second shot rang out – timed with ruthless perfection – and it hit Smith sidelong the moment he was exposed, by damnable luck at the join of breastplate and backplate, passing clean through and slicing up into his belly. He fell back, clutching himself, exhaling hoarsely.

'No!' cried Stanley, coming at the run.

Not even Smith could take such a second wound. He lay in Stanley's arms. 'Brother, my brother,' he murmured, his eyes closing. ''Fore God, I am undone.'

9

'Your time is finished here,' said Stanley to Nicholas urgently. 'You and Hodge and my brother John. You have shown yourselves not boys, but men. Now, though the cause is far greater – yet the life of this my brother John Smith matters to me as much as the war itself, though it should not. As much as you do to each other. I charge you with this. Do not fail me, brave Hodge and Ingoldsby.'

Nicholas scrambled into the tiny rowing boat below the rocks, Hodge close behind him. They looked over their passengers, taking up their oars, Hodge rowing with his right arm only. Smith, barely conscious, but still clutching his precious jezail. Two badly wounded soldiers, and two dead bodies sewn into rough shrouds, one of them Bridier. Though it wasn't fighting, yet here was a job to be done.

'We'll get them there,' said Nicholas, pushing off the rocks. 'If that Sacred Infirmary cannot cure them, nothing can. Then I will come back.'

'You will not,' said Stanley. 'The Turk must surely blockade us fully soon. But you will be under La Valette's orders. Now row. With all your might.'

Their hands blistered, eyes stung with sweat, rising up from the rowing bench with the force of each pull, legs straining as much as their arms, they rowed. The weight of the boat was considerable, two rowers but seven men, dead and alive. From the half-delirious Smith and the wounded soldiers came dazed groans, and worse, the stench of sickness and the fetor of decay. Yet they crossed over the eerily silent half mile of harbour in minutes.

As they neared the Birgu shore, hands came down to help. Questions assailed them on every side, until a quiet but commanding voice took charge. It was Fra Reynaud, who had tended Nicholas before in the infirmary. He protected the boys from the jabbering questioners, had the three wounded lifted carefully onto the wagon, and ordered the shrouded bodies taken to the cool crypt beneath the Conventual Church.

'The Chevalier Bridier,' said Nicholas, still gasping from rowing, indicating the lighter body.

Fra Reynaud looked grave.

'He fought and died like a ... like a—'

'Like a Knight Hospitaller?' said Reynaud.

Nicholas nodded, eyes almost closed.

'You come with me.'

'No need.'

Reynaud was astonished. 'You are quite unhurt?'

'Yes.'

He reflected. 'You were not meant to die there. Your story will go on. For those left at Elmo ...' He looked just once, swiftly, across the water. 'Maybe their earthly pilgrimage will end there.'

Nicholas and Hodge could now see Elmo and the Ottoman camp as Birgu saw it. The camp so vast, proud, magnificent, its numberless cohorts spread out at ease across the mountainside, vast enclosures of horses and draught animals, its great field-hospital pavilions so tall and airy, its war banners gleaming in green and gold. And at the tip of the headland, a hundredth of its size, what looked like little more than a circle of smouldering rubble.

La Valette would see them that evening. They returned to the house of Franco Briffa. Franco was away with his brother Luqa, fishing down on the rocks below the town, while they still could. Maria wept when she saw them and bowed her head and showed them to their room. Hodge lay down and closed his eyes.

'And the cake,' mumbled Nicholas, his tiredness now breaking over him like a great grey wave, 'the cake was very good.'

Maria smiled through her tears. 'Maddalena will return this evening too.'

He lay back and slept almost immediately, woke some hours later, slept again. Dreamed of Elmo, of the horror. Woke and thought of how he would never more see smiling Ned Stanley. Of how they were still fighting over there, at this very minute, while he slept in a bed in a comfortable cool white chamber. Numb with sorrow, guilt, exhaustion, he slept more.

When he woke it was dark, and Hodge was making a strange noise, breathing like an old man with congested lungs. He peered over to him and saw with a chill and sinking heart that he was sweating heavily. He placed his palm over his friend's forehead and it was steam-hot and clammy.

In a whirl he ran into the street, seized a two-wheeled wooden barrow from a passing street seller and, jabbering, made him help carry Hodge out and wheel him to the Sacred Infirmary.

'Is it grave?' he asked desperately.

'All fevers are grave,' said Fra Reynaud. 'Marsh sickness, sweating sickness, camp fever ... but thank Christ he is here now, and not still at Elmo. He is young and strong. We will do all we can.'

Nicholas walked slowly back to the house, and thought that Death walked with him.

In the courtyard, the family were gathered for evening. Franco embraced him like a son, and talked ceaselessly of his heroism. He told them about Hodge, and Maria said quietly that their prayers would save him.

With Maddalena he exchanged secret looks. How he longed for her. He would be healed that way.

But he was not a hero, and he was not healed. He had left too many of his friends and comrades over at Elmo, and Hodge was sick, and maybe his whole left arm would have to be cut off. And though Elmo was hell, and would only get worse, he longed for it too, and felt he could hardly talk to this loving new family of his. For he spoke a different language now, and had seen a different world.

It was late when La Valette saw him.

'Again, an audience with the English boy,' he said. A possible smile. 'You give a good report of a battle. Now tell me of Elmo.'

So Nicholas told him, of Broglia, and Bridier, and Lanfreducci, and Smith, the counter-attack on the trench, and the many deaths. He did not tell him about Hodge. The Grand Master was little interested in peasants.

Yet at the account of Elmo, La Valette, impassive as he was, could not hide his sorrow and pride.

'And their spirit?'

'The same as ever, I think. They were much gladdened and strengthened by the reinforcement of Spanish infantry. They will fight on to the end.'

La Valette stroked his beard. 'I am glad you have come back, boy. I did not see that Elmo would become such a battleground. I would not have allowed you over there.'

'I – I want to go back.'

'No.'

'I cannot sleep. I have bad dreams.'

'You are not alone in that.'

Without further conversation he led him up onto the roof of San Angelo. Even as they were ascending the steps, a servant carrying a rushlight behind La Valette, Nicholas heard the sound of cannon fire across the water and impulsively ran ahead. Out on the flat roof he looked north and gasped and leaned on the battlements, almost crumpling. La Valette was at his side immediately.

'Bear up, my son.' For once there was real tenderness in his voice.

In the night, Elmo looked like a little volcano, huge gouts of smoke roiling ceaselessly into the dark heavens above, lit from below by leaping hellish flames. It was under attack tonight as never before. This must be the end. Nicholas's tears fell on the stone.

'Bear up,' La Valette said gently again. 'Every night I have stood and watched this scene. Soon the same inferno will be visited on Birgu, and then it will not only be my beloved brother knights dying, but the people of Malta, old men and women, children, infants in arms ...'

Nicholas cried angrily, 'How can you bear it?'

La Valette said, 'With God's grace alone.'

Another day and a night, Nicholas still slept. Every time he awoke he asked after Elmo, and then ran out onto the walls. The banner of St John still flew. Every morning, every evening, people said it was a miracle. Then he worked hard on the walls, bringing up the materials for the coming storm, shaping stone missiles, cutting staves. Yet he felt as miserable as he ever had in his life. Whether Elmo stood or fell, he was wretched.

Maddalena found him when her mother and grandmother were not near.

'If you go back you will die.'

He looked startled. 'What do you mean?'

'I see it in your eyes now. Now that you are no longer so tired and withdrawn from us. You want to go back to Elmo.'

How could she read him so close? 'I—'

'You want to go back. And if you die I cannot live.'

Her eyes blazed from such depths. Then she held him and kissed him and the kiss lasted long, and neither of them saw her grandmother appear from the kitchen, and stare a moment, and then retreat inside again without saying a word. There were kisses and kisses. And this was a kiss not to be interrupted, and a love not to be stayed. Only let them be married, before . . .

She pulled away. 'You think you cannot die.'

He floundered hopelessly. 'No, I . . .' He tried to kiss her again as if that would be answer enough but she would not let him.

'You think I cannot imagine what a hell it is over there at Elmo,' she said. 'What a hell on earth you have walked through, eyes wide open. But I have a heart, and I can imagine. And men can fall in love with war as with women. I have seen this. My love, my life, you are falling in love with war.' Her eyes were full of light and tears but her voice was steady. 'Even Christ passed through hell only once. You do not escape from such a hell as Elmo twice. If you go back, I do not think we will ever see each other again.'

In the afternoon he went to the infirmary, and Fra Reynaud admitted him.

Hodge was sitting up, his colour returned.

'His fever is broken,' said Reynaud. 'Opium stilled his bowels, and then he needed to drink water, and salt bread. And he drank like a thirsty elephant.'

The boys hugged and then looked awkward.

'His arm is without infection,' said Reynaud, 'and the bones knitting fast.'

'Take more than a funny foreign fever to see off Hodge,' said Hodge. 'I'll be out again in a day or two. I'm as thin as a straw though, straight up and down.'

'Where's Smith?'

'You cannot see him,' said Reynaud. 'And he would not know you.'

'He's still alive?'

'Yes. But very sick. He has had Last Rites. Pray for him.'

The dizzying joys and sorrows Nicholas felt were soon shared by the whole town.

The following morning, two knights from Sicily somehow managed to run any Turkish patrols, and came with dramatic news. The relief force would be arriving very soon, perhaps only three or four days now. Those mighty Spanish galleons with their great guns, supported by more gilt and stately galleons from Genoa and Venice, also heavily gunned, would sail in and attack the Turkish fleet at anchor with all force. They would also land an army of at least fifteen thousand of the finest Spanish infantrymen. With their naval support under threat, and fighting on two fronts, the Ottoman land forces would feel dangerously isolated, and surely have to abandon the siege.

The town erupted in frenzied celebration.

La Valette gave orders that the news be carried over to Elmo with all speed. If the defenders there heard it, it would be wonderful for their morale. They might yet hold out, and Birgu itself, with its vulnerable population of women and children, be saved from the Ottoman flames entire, not an innocent life lost.

Yet even before La Valette's order could be followed, another piece of news came through, and reduced their brief joy to ashes of sorrow, and far greater fear.

An armada of thirty more galleys had been sighted, and a force had indeed landed, at St Paul's Bay, and was already marching south towards the main Ottoman camp. Yet it was not the relief sent by Christendom. These galleys had come from the south-east and they carried another army of Mohammedan warriors. The news spread like a bitter plague. Hassan Ali was come, the Viceroy of Algiers, with an army of five thousand Algerian cut-throats, bent on holy war, rapine and loot. Women wept and shook their heads and said the North Africans were worse, far worse even than the Turks. Fears grew hysterical and evil rumours abounded.

There also came Candelissa, the vicious Greek renegade, Christian-born but now one of the most savage of Islam's generals – if you could attribute any religion, even Islam, to that monster of cruelty. With him came two or three thousand more corsairs and cut-throats, not ashamed to march in the army of such a villain, but proud.

But worst of all was the name of the man who headed this vast new force. Dragut.

Dragut was come.

10

To call Dragut a mere corsair, a pirate captain, was gravely to under-estimate him. He was an engineer, cartographer, strategist, and the greatest naval commander of the age – as well as the most savage. Even Mustafa Pasha would never cross him, would bow before him. They said he had once ripped the tongue out of the throat of a Christian captive with his own hands, and eaten it before his eyes. An apocryphal tale, no doubt, but people believed it.

Fourteen years ago his brother had died on the neighbouring island of Gozo in a clumsy slave raid. In revenge, Dragut came and carried away the entire population of the island into slavery.

'Not a man nor woman on this island but lost some cousin in that enslavement of Gozo,' Franco Briffa told Nicholas. 'We were the same people. What Dragut did in that island is beyond words. Those he did not enslave, whom he judged worthless to be sold as slaves – the sick, the very old or the very young, the suckling infant – what he did to them is beyond words. How he ... *disposed* of them.

'Knowing this, Inglis, we Maltese will only fight the harder.' Franco looked dark indeed. 'When Dragut comes to Birgu, he will know our anger.'

Yet Dragut came with his own fifteen hundred fresh fighting men, veterans of bloody battles and encounters numberless, and in overall command of close on ten thousand. They brought cargo ships of fresh water, barrels of balls and powder, gleaming new weapons and guns from the armouries of Tripoli and Algiers, flocks of fat-tailed Barbary sheep for fresh meat, and fresh fruit from the

African shore. Luxuries indeed. His men joked that they would eat ripe figs, suck sweet oranges below the very walls of Birgu, so that the infidel wretches within could see how they were cursed and abandoned by their false god.

La Valette responded to the dreadful news as curtly as ever.

'Send out messengers by night. Let all Malta know that it is against Dragut we now fight – as well as the most powerful Empire on earth. Make sure the nobility of Mdina know. And ask of them about cavalry. Have Don Mezquita ride out with his cavalry and demand of them, when will they begin to harry the Turk in chevauchées from Mdina? Tell them that we would be happy to hear that such operations had begun.'

'And what of the message to Elmo?'

La Valette considered hard and long, in inward agony that all could see. 'Tell them nothing for now.' His brow was deep furrowed with anxiety and grief. 'Perhaps tonight, tomorrow.'

In the Ottoman camp, Dragut immediately assumed overall command. He was especially contemptuous of Piyale, the palace-born Admiral Piyale. He heard a full report from Mustafa.

'So,' he summarised when he had heard. 'The knights are still sending out and receiving intelligence. The Maltese cavalry at Mdina, few though they are, may still strike at our flank or rear at any time. You have not taken any harbour near to Birgu. You have not rolled up the island with any consistency, but attacked one small target at a time. St Elmo you could have ignored. But not now. Now you have attacked it, you must finish it, or it would look like weakness. This wretched fort must be taken, and quickly.'

He squinted through an eyeglass at the smoking ruin. 'A hundred and fifty men or so defending it, maybe fewer. And this has gone on for ten days now?'

'Thirteen or fourteen.'

'Which? Thirteen or fourteen?'

'Fourteen,' said Mustafa through gritted teeth.

'Hm. And this is the sacred army of the Lord Suleiman, son of Selim Khan, son of Bayezid Khan, son of Mehmet Khan who conquered the City of Konstantiniyye and the Eastern Empire of Rum. And you cannot capture this – witch's tit of a fort!'

He slammed the eyeglass down so hard the lens dislodged.

'Get that mended,' he said, striding from the tent.

'Sire,' Sir Oliver Starkey reported to La Valette, 'there's a new Turkish gun emplacement being built. With all haste.'

'Where?'

'Across the harbour, below Sciberras. At Is-Salvatur.'

La Valette ran up to the lookout. Had he been a man who cursed, he would have cursed.

'And what of eastward?' he said.

Starkey squinted. 'I cannot see, Sire. Years of study ... Is there movement on Gallows Point?'

'There is. That too will soon be a gun emplacement. A second upon Is-Salvatur. And I would guess another beyond Sciberras, across Marsamuscetto, at Tigné perhaps. The guns will be ready to fire by tomorrow. Elmo will be completely surrounded by a ring of fire, and with the battery at Is-Salvatur, cut off from us for good. There will be no more crossing the Grand Harbour then. Any here can no longer go over. And any who have gone over cannot return.'

Starkey crossed himself. 'Our poor Brothers.'

'Ay,' said La Valette. 'Dragut has most certainly taken command.'

A moment later he said, 'A last message must go over to Elmo, to steel them unto the last. Write to them that King Philip's relief force is now very close.'

Two Maltese volunteers came. Sturdy brothers, fine rowers and swimmers both.

'It is late afternoon,' said La Valette. 'You may either row out now in daylight, under the noses of the Turks at Is-Salvatur – but knowing their guns are not yet ready. Or go over tonight – but it is a clear night, there is more than a half-moon coming up already in the tracks of the sun. The harbour will be bright till near dawn, and by then the enemy guns may be ready.'

'We go now,' said one, Paolo.

La Valette handed them the brief, vital message, carefully sealed with wax in a brass case. 'This will work wonders for the morale of Elmo,' he said. 'Much depends on it. Do not fail us.'

'We will not.'

People watched from the walls in speechless anguish as the little blue-painted boat moved out across the still, empty harbour. It was like a crowd watching over an arena. Many could hardly breathe. Over on the spit of Is-Salvatur near the water's edge, it seemed the Turks at work paused momentarily, observing this crossing. Then they resumed.

They had two breastworks in place already.

From Elmo itself, as usual, came the continual sound of cannon fire and gunfire and muffled explosions.

The little boat moved fast, the two men side by side on the narrow mid-bench. It was already half-way there. Three-quarters.

People held their breath.

Behind the nearest Turkish breastwork, not two hundred yards off now, something was stirring.

The two rowers gasped and pulled as never before, not even when trying to outrun a summer storm back into harbour.

Suddenly the air erupted with a deafening explosion away to their right, and a ball struck the surface of the water just yards ahead of the little boat, sending a huge white geyser spouting high, showering down over them. They glanced over their shoulders and saw the ball itself pass on behind them and then sink below the surface.

At least one gun was already in place, and ready served. Dragut meant there to be no more crossings.

'Row! Row!' cried Paolo frantically, drenched, wild-eyed, shaking the saltwater from his eyes.

With his usual cunning and foresight, even while his men were still building up the earth ramp for the main guns to cover the harbour from mouth to Marsa, from Birgu to Elmo – the work of several more hours – Dragut had covertly taken down to the water's edge a single, elegant long-barrelled culverin, firing through the crevice between two boulders. For as he well understood, when they saw the emplacement being built, the Christians would want to send along their last message of hope, perhaps some last reinforcements to their comrades in Elmo. Sidelong fire from Is-Salvatur would soon bring to ruin that little ruse.

The culverin was cleaned, swabbed and reloaded with lightning efficiency, and served with another fist-sized four-pound iron ball: quite enough to hole a small rowing boat with a single good shot, and take a rower's leg off with it. From his pavilion on the all-commanding heights of Sciberras, Dragut ordered another team down to the shore. Half a dozen Janizary marksmen, each served by two more re-loaders. Over two or three hundred yards was a long range. But then they were very good marksmen.

From the walls of Birgu, some people could hardly bear to watch. They held their hands to their mouths, gnawed their fists. It was like watching war for the sake of amusement, as mere bystanders, and they were ashamed.

The two rowers floundered at the oars for a few seconds at the shock of coming under fire. At such a low trajectory, a short ball could easily have bounced onward over the surface of the sea and smashed into them still. Mercifully this first shot was wide before the bows. The next shot would be on target.

They had just regained their control and were rowing hard again, rising up on the oars, when a cracking volley of half a dozen long Turkish muskets rang out over the still, tense water.

They were very good marksmen.

Paolo turned his head suddenly as if looking out to sea, and when he turned back his brother saw with sick horror that half his face was gone. Another ball had struck him in the upper arm. He fell forward.

'No!' cried Marco, reaching for him. 'Paolo!'

The Janizary marksmen were already levelling the next six muskets handed to them.

On the walls, people whimpered. Franco Briffa turned his back and sank his chin into his chest. In the close-knit community of Birgu, the two fishermen were like brothers to him.

Nicholas could barely tear his gaze away. But as well as the grim execution being done out there to the two poor valiant Maltese, his eyes darted back and forth across the calm water. The distance, no more than five hundred paces ... on the diagonal, from the low walls below Angelo across to the rocks below Elmo, eight hundred paces, nine? The sea warm and flat calm. No powerful tides or contrary currents here, not like the strong Severn flowing down to Shrewsbury from the dark mountains of Wales, where he had swum since he was a small boy. Sea-water stings the eyes, is denser, lifts you more. How deep would a cannon ball or musket ball sheer through that water?

With a ruthlessness that seemed almost gleeful, the battery at Is-Salvatur loosed another six musket balls, peppering the side of the boat but seeming not to strike Marco, and then there came a third tight volley, followed almost immediately by another boom of the culverin. The little rowing boat spun on the surface of the water and the bow was blown away in a shower of shattered timber. Marco, the brass case clamped between his teeth, was seen to dive off the fast disappearing boat, curving down into the sea.

He surfaced again and seized hold of Paolo and cried out his name, and saw that he was dead already. He let him go with speechless grief and began to swim the last hundred paces to the rocks below Elmo. For a moment there was hope. But the Turks would not give up now. This had become a small but significant skirmish, this one man's life of considerable significance.

Musket balls spattered into the water around Marco's head. The watchers on the walls in their agony saw the drift of smoke from Is-Salvatur, heard the report of the volley a moment later. There was a deathly stillness, and then a low, collective groan, the keening of a crowd already in mourning. The fisherman Marco lay on his back in the sea, face lit by the setting sun, his legs curving down into the depths. Between his teeth still glinted the brass letter-case.

There was a heart-searing cry and it was Franco Briffa, animal, inarticulate, knowing he could do nothing. Then he swore that he would kill many a Turk with his bare hands in the doomed days to come.

There was a single splash from the walls below Angelo, and someone, a single figure, was swimming out after Marco and Paolo, into the murderous heart of the Grand Harbour. People murmured and stared.

Few of the Maltese swam, and fewer knights and soldiers. Now another was going out to him, and he swam smooth and fast. A solitary hero or madman.

He was slim. His hair was fair.

They began to say it was the Inglis, the Insulter of the Pasha, he who had already fled from Elmo. There came a girl's cry from the walls, and a girl racing down the steps below Angelo. There she saw a pair of battered leather boots pulled off and dropped in the dust, and on the low wall she found a torn patched shirt that she knew, and she took it up and held it to herself weeping, as if it was the most holy relic of a saint. As if it was the hair shirt of the Baptist himself.

'Is that him?' said La Valette. 'My eyes tire.'

'I cannot see, Master.'

La Valette demanded urgently, half turning, 'You, Fra Girolamo, tell me – is it the boy?'

'I believe so, Sire.'

'He has gone out there to die,' said La Valette. 'The Maltese are dead already.'

Nicholas swam out fast to where the last few broken splinters of the boat still floated, and then came to the body of Marco, lying back, staring into the sky. He swam in close behind it, using the corpse as a shield. No shots came from Is-Salvatur, but the marksmen were surely watching, waiting. There could be no doubt of that. He tried not to think of the people also watching him from the walls, or of the girl. He tried not to think of why he was doing what he was doing, or what would come of it, of tomorrow, or the next minute. There was only now.

The afternoon sun burned down hard, low and blinding if he looked westward. The rocks below Elmo were a warm gold, and from up above he could hear the sound of relentless and desperate gunfire from the dying fort. That was where he was taking the message. That was where he was returning. *Do not think. Do not ask.*

He kept his head high in the cover of the floating body, treading water, listening. How long did a dead man float? The moment he heard a crack it would be too late, the musket ball would already have ploughed into him. Or they might blast a culverin ball at him. A culverin ball at a single swimming man.

Marco's eyes were open and he was quite dead. The boy reached up and twisted the brass case out from his teeth and tucked it tight into his waistband under water. He hoped the wax seal was good. Then he took hold of the dead man's shirt collar and began to drag him slowly back to the Birgu shore.

By the time he came near Kalkara Creek, there were as many as fifty people there, weeping but cheering him on. No shots were fired from the Turkish side, and now he was out of range. They had failed to get the message to Elmo, but a slain gallant son of Malta had been brought home with utmost bravery and daring. Dragut must be cursing. The strange little drama, a family's tragedy, had been a commanding triumph for neither side.

Nicholas stopped twenty yards out and trod water. He was exhausted, his muscles burned. People crowded the shore, two or three fishermen waded in, everyone shouted praise and cried vengeance. He did not take in the words. He turned the body of Marco around, head towards the shore, and gave him a gentle push. Then he turned and swam out again. Cries went up behind him as they hauled in the dead body of the fisherman. A girl's voice cried out, No! No! as he swam away. The people on the shore carried Marco to his mother where she lay kneeling and howling and taking up handfuls of dust, and they laid him at her feet, the very tableau of Mary and the dead Christ that they saw daily in the crude, heartfelt carvings in their mean island churches and chapels.

Nicholas did not see or hear. His attention was all turned towards the battery of Is-Salvatur.

In the glorious light of the setting sun, the people watched and thought they were witnessing something out of ancient myth. A dragon stood guarding the evil shore opposite, a fire-breathing dragon, and the fairheaded boy, as thin as a child, swam nearer and nearer beneath its black mouth. Prayers went up from a thousand witnesses. His courage was dauntless, the strength of his heart was beyond reckoning.

And where he was gone, they said, there would be no returning.

A girl wept and sank to her knees, and a woman helped her away from the walls where she could watch no longer.

A volley of Turkish muskets cracked out, and the water about the fair head of the boy spat up white. When the water had settled, the people groaned. There was no swimmer to be seen. Surely he had not gone below so easily, that fair handsome head split open by a gobbet of lead?

They waited in despair. The sea returned to its implacable silence. The sun shone down.

And then twenty yards ahead, he surfaced again and swam smoothly on. Slowly, slowly, his arms rising and falling so slowly now. But he swam on.

Behind the wicker breastwork, the Janizary corporal swore and ordered his men to fire again. He bawled out for more men down at the run. This swimmer must not get through. He could only picture the scenes of rejoicing on the walls of Birgu, and within Elmo's stubborn, fire-blackened ruins.

11

The sea erupted more and more. The boy curved and dived down like a dolphin. There were twenty, thirty musketeers trying to hit him at no more than a hundred and fifty paces now. A hundred and twenty. It was a crazy waste of powder and ball, but a captain, and then Işak Agha himself, had taken command. Dragut's word was plain. Kill him.

The cursed Christian swimmer swam on, though it was like swimming through hail now, where every hailstone was a lead bullet that could take your head off.

Eventually in exasperation, Dragut himself came thundering down on his white charger to the headland above Is-Salvatur. He dropped from his horse and strode down to the hapless battery, his voice like the cannon's roar. He had not even troubled to don armour or a helmet. There was no time. That damned swimmer must be stopped.

His lungs were in agony, his arms would barely rise and pull again, and yet he continued. There was no other way. Already he had registered two fresh things, both bad. How long did a dead man float? Not long. The body of Paolo was already gone below. He had hoped to use it as a shield while he paused, trod water, took fresh lungfuls of air. Perhaps even drag it along through the water with him, keeping low behind it. It would have been horrible, a kind of grim sacrilege, the poor brave fisherman's body steadily shredded by incoming musket fire, his corpse at last dragged up onto the rocks below Elmo like a flayed and bloody sandbag. Yet it might have saved him. But Paolo's body was gone below. Like his soul, it was already departed into another silent world, unimaginable to men.

But there was worse. Out to sea beyond Gallows Point, he had glimpsed over the blinding sparkle of the water, a small low Turkish patrol boat coming in. It had seen what was happening and understood, and was racing in to cut him off and kill him in the water, in case the efforts of the musketeers failed. And he could not outswim what looked like a four- or six-man galliot.

Yet he swam on. He could see the rocks below Elmo, the heaped and tumbled sandstone boulders, and he knew exactly which outcrop he must reach to be round the corner from the battery of Is-Salvatur. He must not lose concentration, he must mind his breathing, and he must swim below the surface often, pulling himself down, two feet below, five feet, breathing out to let himself sink though the heavy saltwater, so much heavier than the fresh flowing waters of his native Severn.

Then he must come up and take breath, his lungs burning, in air that exploded around him. Soon the Janizary marksmen would get the rhythm of his descent and rise again, and they would be ready for him, so he must break his rhythm, and he must try to stay down as long as possible.

Now he must come up, and when he opened his mouth there was a gout of water that dashed in his face. A ball had struck the surface of the sea six inches in front of him. He took another deep breath and sank down. He was so tired, and his heart hammered in terror beneath his ribs. He could swim no further, yet he could not stay under either, nor curve out of range to sea, for there the lean galley was coming in like a shark.

Something seethed in the water to his left and his elbow sang in sudden agony. He rolled and looked down and there was blood spiralling round his left arm. He had been hit, and his uncertainty as to how far through water a musket ball might go had been answered. Far enough.

The low galley was very near now. A man stood in the prow, naked but for a loincloth, a Barbary corsair, teeth showing in a grin, holding a forked weapon you might use to spear tuna.

Nicholas raised his left arm and there was no strength in it. The elbow felt smashed. He could have cried out for mercy, but the sharpshooters on the spit were not men to give mercy, nor the man who commanded them, nor, least of all, the coming corsairs. No mercy to this impertinent wretch in the water, swimming doggedly on before the eyes of all the citizens of Birgu.

His lungs were screaming at him now and he came up again. The Turks knew exactly where he was heading, and at what pace. He rolled and tried to get just his face, his mouth, above water, and his lungs exploded out and then sucked in again. He took two more breaths and he heard the crack, but it was too late. By the time he heard it the balls had already struck. Yet by some miracle none hit him, and he thought that there would be a few seconds while the next guns were passed to the marksmen and they could fire again, enough for two deep breaths, he thought, no, three. He forced the air out of his lungs and in and out and in, he thought of bellows, his head was dizzy, the blood pumped with sudden air, the vessels in his head throbbed, and then he sank below the water as it hissed in white trails above him. Perhaps one tickled through his hair, he couldn't be sure, and that was the next volley. Now he could swim another ten underwater strokes again, perhaps more, before he needed air. Yet his arm hurt abominably. He didn't look down. Occasionally he saw from the corner of his salt-stung eyes a trail of blood in the blue sea, but he did not want to see. Not a wound like Hodge's, please Christ, a white shard of shattered bone jutting out through his water-whitened flesh.

He came up again to the brilliant sun and the blue sky, his cheeks blowing out with the pressure of air rushing to escape his lungs, and then sank to see the deep cobalt-blue abyss below him. Little bright-coloured fish darted about, and below that, hundreds and hundreds of feet down, miles down, a dizzying nothing. Nothing but that deep blue abyss over which he floated like a mere speck of flesh.

He rose to the surface with his hair plastered over his face and scooped it away. There was the lean shadow of the narrow rowing galley almost upon him, cutting straight over him, and the lean naked corsair raising his forked spear to strike.

He gulped in air and dragged himself down and the big shadow passed over him. He was blinded with the surge of bubbles it dragged up through the water, yet he reached out and his right hand caught the slender keel. He gripped it with all his might and was wrenched through the water with it. Then the boat slowed and stopped.

The Janizary gunmen on the shore ceased their shooting. Dragut yelled out in fury. They could not fire and hit one of their own.

In the shadowed darkness beneath the boat, clutching the keel, his lungs burning and the light of his conscious mind failing, Nicholas saw that forked fishing spear stabbing down again and again into the water all around the boat. He saw the light green ripples, and the sun itself, a scribble of burning light through the water above him. His lungs would tear open in his chest, his gorge felt swollen with air, he would not have the strength to do anything, and if he came up they would kill him. For men like these, killing him was like killing a fish.

Yet he must come up, wounded as he was. He must try and take one of them with him at least, though it was not the end he had hoped for. With his very last strength he clawed his way through the dark water to the rear of the boat, some twenty feet in length, and with the last shred of his discipline, he rose to the bright surface as slowly as he could, to break through it in near silence. He lay back with his face just above the surface, exhaled and inhaled with agonising slowness, aware of nothing else, expecting to feel the searing stab of the forked spear at any moment. Nothing. He pulled upright and turned his eyes away from the sun and opened them.

He trod water behind the stern. In the boat above, none looked down upon him. They looked over the sides, the bow. The water cleared from his ears and the air was filled with noisy chatter, angry shouts. More angry calls over the water from Is-Salvatur, and always in the background, the grim, ceaseless music of the Elmo guns. Their noise had covered him.

He could turn and swim on unnoticed. He turned himself about very slowly, silently in the water. The shore was no more that fifty yards off. He might yet do it.

There was a sound above his head. He glanced back and up, and a naked corsair was standing in the stern, towering over him, face dark-shadowed but visibly grinning, and stabbing a long-handled, narrow-tined fishing spear down into his upturned face.

He thrashed violently and somehow the forks missed him. When the corsair pulled his spear back to stab again, he found he could not. The boy had seized hold of the shaft. The corsair gripped tight, and Nicholas, the pain in his elbow dulled and distant in his surge of fighting fury, curled himself up in the water and planted his bare feet against the flat stern-board and pulled himself up on the spear. He rolled in over the stern, crashing into the corsair's legs, and they both sprawled to the floor of the boat.

The bright sun and the upper air were like the taste of resurrection to him, and that inner fury and that uncanny speed again possessed him. In the time the lean young corsair took to leap nimbly to his feet, the leaner boy had snatched up the spear and flipped it round and driven the twin nine-inch prongs deep into his chest and then kicked him overboard to die.

There were five other men in the galley, two still on the rowing bench, staring at him. He moved forward and drove the fishing fork in long clean strokes deep into their chests, one, two, pulled it out, stabbed them again in the neck, and then as they slumped down he jumped up onto their prostrate bodies, his feet bare on their flesh.

On Is-Salvatur, the marksmen sighted down the lengths of their barrels and saw the dancing figure against the darkening sky and waited for the order to fire anyway and finish this farce. A single raking volley would kill them all. Dragut ordered the culverin hurriedly reloaded.

Flailing and thrusting with the long forked fishing spear, Nicholas fell on the last three men who were still gaping in amazement at this creature in human form that swam beneath the water, and erupted from it like a flying fish. The men of Barbary knew every island and inlet of the Western Mediterranean, but like most fishermen of Malta, they did not swim. It was an unholy mystery to them.

They were only lightly armed with daggers, one fumbling with a pole, and with his quick dancing movements, his lightning thrusts, Nicholas had stabbed all three of them before they fled this crazed idolater come from the deep, and threw themselves into the water, there to thrash and scream and perhaps drown.

He had despatched six men in under a minute. From Is-Salvatur, Dragut stared out. What in hell was this thin white djinn?

Even as he was driving the last of the corsairs into the water, Nicholas heard a volley of musket fire and the bellow of culverin. It was not finished yet.

He heard a harsh voice – it was Dragut – ordering the culverin reloaded fast. One of the gunners said the barrel was heating up, but Dragut struck him a mighty blow across the face, and he got to reloading.

He might shelter behind the boat, but there he was trapped, and the culverin would soon blast it in pieces. He could not row it alone. There was nothing else. He must swim again. But it was with a savage elation that he flung the fishing spear high into the air towards Is-Salvatur, like a javelin, then ran the length of the galliot and hurled himself off the prowboard and cut into the water. He felt invincible as he ploughed on, the sheltering rocks below Elmo only forty strokes away now.

Then something hit his head. It was like he had been cuffed. He saw blackness, and then blackness starred with pinpricks. He slowed and stopped. There were cries about his ears. He wanted to shake his head but it hurt too much. He gasped and sputtered, limbs flailing without control, musket balls sizzling around him. The distant roar of the culverin, followed by a silence and then many anguished cries. He should duck down but he could no longer. His left arm felt useless again. He ducked his head underwater and there was a great cloud of blood. He tried to drag himself onwards with his right arm and kicked his exhausted legs. Face turned into the dying sun, not seeing, blind with salt and inside his head only black space. No longer knowing where he was or who, not even his name. Only the sun beat down, nothing else lived nor would outlive it, not he, not she, there was only death and the sea and the sun.

12

The overheated culverin had split at the last shot and the ball had erupted at a sharp angle out of the barrel. It sheared into the water not twenty paces off. But as it went, it chipped a sharp blade of stone off a boulder, and the stone flew through the air and struck one of the men at the base of his skull, just beneath the wrappings of his turban.

It was Dragut.

The great corsair commander was stretchered over to the Ottoman field hospital at the Marsa, men jabbering. They said that the gun had overheated, they had worked it too hard and had neither water to cool it nor time to piss on it. The medics said that a stone shard might not be too serious, but Dragut's eyes were closed, his face sickly pale, and he was beyond speech, his breathing deep and stertorous. When they unwrapped the turban, they found to their horror that the skull had been severally shattered, and a dribble of grey brain was oozing through the fine silk. It was accursed luck that so small an accident should wreak such damage. But it was as Allah willed it.

Three hours later, as the secretary wrote in elaborate Turkish fashion, in the letter that would be hurried back to Suleiman with galley slaves lashed to ribbons all the way, 'our noble Dragut drank the sweet nectar of martyrdom, and forgot this vain world.'

The nectar of martyrdom did not always look so sweet up close, thought the Ottoman medics, swabbing up his brains.

*

Nicholas lay on his back in a small room, his head heavily bandaged. He stayed still for a time, trying to gather his thoughts and senses. Then he tried to move his left arm. The elbow felt terribly bruised, but he could move it, and with gritted teeth, flex it a little. It too was bandaged. He moved his right arm, his legs. He breathed deeply.

He had survived. How, he didn't know. He stared up at the roof of the cool and peaceful Sacred Infirmary. Fra Reynaud was somewhere near, that strong and comforting presence. He gave thanks.

Then the walls, his narrow bed shuddered with a monstrous explosion, and he knew he had been deceiving himself. He was not in the Sacred Infirmary. He was at Elmo. He was back in the hell of Elmo.

Stanley stood by him, bloody and cut about. His head too was bandaged, his left arm was in a sling, a different look in his eyes. There were no more bad jests. There was an edge of anger in his voice when he spoke.

'You have come back to your death.'

Nicholas was still confused. He could not remember what he had done, or why.

Stanley said, 'La Valette cannot have sent you.'

'What I have written, I have written,' he said incoherently.

'I cannot believe you came back to us.'

'To bring the letter,' said Nicholas, light dawning. 'Did you find it? How long have I lain here?'

'We found it. We are now in our sixteenth day of fighting. Or perhaps seventeenth. In truth, I no longer know. Does Smith still live?'

'When I left, yes. Very sick, though the chaplains can work wonders. But the armies of Spain have come now?'

Stanley's blue eyes were flat and without hope. 'Alas,' he said. 'No. It may be that hearing of Dragut's arrival with a fresh army, King Philip has decided to hold back again.'

Nicholas didn't know whether to laugh or weep. 'All that struggle, the deaths of the fishermen, for nothing. To bring a false message.'

'A false message that lifted us up for a time,' said Stanley. 'You were not to know.'

Nicholas's heart thumped with anger. '*Help must come from Christendom* – from Spain, from Venice, the Papal States – after all we have suffered.'

Stanley shook his head. 'King Philip must look to defend Sicily and Spain afterwards. The armies and navies of Suleiman are greater than those of all Christendom combined. It may be that Malta is only the first chapter in a far longer war.'

'Then we will be destroyed. And – Birgu.'

'I cannot say, little brother.' Stanley's voice had a crack in it. 'Truly. But we fight on.'

'I will fight with you.'

'Your arm is damaged and your head wound was bad enough when we pulled you from the water.'

'But I can still fight.'

Stanley could have wept. In all the sorry siege and fall of this island, he doubted if there would be a hero greater than this skinny boy from Shropshire. Blast him for returning.

'You are your father's son,' he said softly.

Another explosion came from above. Stone flaked from the walls, Nicholas closed his eyes, fine sandstone showered down on his upturned face.

'Rest,' said Stanley. 'I must go.'

He lay back and tried to rest. He would be killed in his bed, skewered by some raving Bektaşi. Or enslaved. Or held as a pretty captive by some senior Ottoman. Held in chains, naked, visited daily … Then Birgu would be attacked and taken, and she would suffer the same fate. And this but the first chapter. Smith had said that in capturing Malta, the Turk would acquire the finest natural harbour in the Mediterranean for his Grand Fleet. And Rome itself then lay not four hundred miles away …

One of the chaplains, it was Fra Giacomo, came and gave him water and some bread. He was very hungry, and ate all he gave him. Drank more water, slowly and steadily, until he was full to bursting, then struggled upright and sat on the edge of the pallet. His head throbbed painfully, his eyes didn't seem right. He named the six planets in order. He counted backwards from twenty to one.

'You are going to fight?'

He nodded.

'There are few left. And the dead are no longer shrouded. You will find plenty of armour there.'

It was like a dream to be back at Elmo. Like one of those dreams of being back at school again, studying Latin grammar under the harsh eye of Master Elliott –but a dream of darker hue. In a dream he found himself scuffed boots, a shirt and jerkin, back and breast-plate, stripping them from a dead young soldier of his frame, and a close-fitting steel morion that he tugged down over his bandaged head, relieved that but for a dim throbbing at the back of his skull, he felt no pain. His left elbow was damnably stiff where the ball had struck the knuckle bone there, perhaps chipped it, sundered the skin and flesh but done no worse damage. It flexed awkwardly, hot and swollen, but had enough strength to bear a shield. Then he lifted a half-pike. The grim stabbing weapon for close-quarter fighting. Yet it felt too heavy to him, the evilly spiked head alone weighing twelve or fifteen pounds. A weapon for a man with two strong arms.

He knew his advantage was in fleetness of eye and foot, not muscular strength. And he had already lost blood, flesh, strength again over the last days. Instead he found himself a sword, regret-ting that the sword of the Chevalier Bridier was left over in the house of Franco Briffa. But may he fight with the spirit of Bridier nevertheless.

Here was a long slim sword, finely balanced, the hilt butted with a fat leaden sphere to make the lean furrowed blade feel almost weightless.

Then in the charnel house of the inner yard, surrounded by the dead, he flexed and moved and eased himself into fighting.

From the walls above came cries and shots, yet they seemed thinly scattered.

He whipped the blade through the air before him a couple more times. Took one deep breath, kissed the blade, said a prayer. And then went up the steps, now rust-brown with old blood, to join his brothers.

He came up into the midst of a new attack, with barely time to register the situation of the fort or condition of the men. He saw through the black smoke-laden air that all four of Elmo's star points were now reduced to promontories of rubble. The single high bastion was half blasted away, and almost the entire parapet along the northern and western sides had been reduced, to be hurriedly bulked by sacks of earth, stone blocks and wicker gabions. Most calamitous of all, the main northern wall teetered dangerously out over the ditch, ready to collapse, filling the gulf with its own bulk, and leaving the fort exposed along far too long a front for the defenders to save. Yet still it held.

As for the men still fighting, there remained perhaps fifty or sixty. So few.

There was Lanfreducci, his face pale with siege fever and blood loss, yet he cried out and grinned when he saw Nicholas through the black fog, and called him a damned young fool.

There was Stanley, and Medrano, and De Guaras, and Luigi Broglia still in command, and fighting as an unbreakable pair those two Spanish soldiers, García and Zacosta, and Captain Miranda too. Every one of them loading and firing his arquebus with fanatic swiftness, screaming through his teeth, hair plastered across his cheeks. Broglia heaving the organ gun around on the crippled bastion roof, single-handed because his four-man gun crew all lay dead or dying around him, bringing it to bear once more on the section under attack, loading each of the eight barrels himself with dogged determination. His eyes shone from a face powdered and sooted like an Ethiop's.

Random fires blazed and billowed, the walls were smoke-darkened, and above them on the last few feet of high bastion, the flag of St John, ripped and frayed, still flew.

The smoke and dust were blinding but the heat was worse, and the noise worse still. For a few minutes the infantry attack was held once more, and another lacerating volley of cannon fire came in. Defenders sank down behind the improvised ramps and bulking, gulped foul water, loosened helmet straps and dropped their heads as the iron and stone and marble balls hurtled in yet again. Such a volley that at its height, Nicholas could not distinguish one blast from another, only a continual roaring wave that did not cease.

His eardrums fluttered in his skull, he bent his head and cradled it in his right arm, and a hand was laid on his shoulder. Lanfreducci.

'Brace up,' he shouted through the storm. 'Soon you'll be as deaf as the rest of us!'

The Italian knight had a bloody rag stuck in one ear.

Worse than the rolling thunder of the guns was the dread pause between. He lay side on, favouring his good elbow, and glanced through a crack between two sacks. Not three hundred yards away, with sweat dripping down from his bloody head bandages, already saturated, he saw with blurred eyes a hot bronze barrel being rapidly cleaned and reloaded. Then the agonised moment of silence, the muzzle seeming to gape directly at him. The black muzzle like a lightless evil eye. The gunner lowered the smoking rope to the hole and in the instant of sizzling burn, on an impulse, he rolled a few yards to the left, until he bumped up against García.

The next moment a thirty-pound ball erupted through the sacks where he had just lain. They were blasted high into the air, ruptured into tatters, the contents falling back over where he and García huddled. But it was only earth, it could have been worse. He opened his eyes. The ball had gone on and destroyed yet more of the bastion, then rolled down into the inner yard, bounced over the hardpacked earth there and ended pummelling into a mound of heaped corpses.

Another ball hit two men crouching along the barricade not twenty yards down and they flew high into the air, limbs flailing, both dead already. One fell in the yard below, one landed stretched limp and near naked over a torn, toothed section of wall, his body obscenely elongated, innards spilling.

More balls came in, many marble. The deafening bang, the whine, eardrums batting and pulsing and nerves shredded. Splinters of hot stone shrapnel shearing through the tremulous heat haze of summer air, billowing clouds of soot-black dust, and then a volley of defiant musket fire from the defenders kneeling up once more, trying to take out any gunners careless enough to show themselves above their own breastworks. And everywhere gunpowder smoke bitter on the parched dry tongue, and so dense that the enemy might advance through it at a slow march and not be seen.

The enemy were advancing again.

The last defenders of Elmo dragged themselves back to the cordons of rubble, spat out gobs of cartridge paper, teeth blackened with cordite, reloaded, wondering how much powder and ball remained to them. They gulped down scoops of wine and water, wiped trickles of sweat-diluted blood from their eyes, spat blood and teeth, cried out to each other last words of encouragement and defiance. Lanfreducci even yelled out, seeing another movement among the Turks as they reformed beyond the bridge, 'Aha, we've got 'em on the run now, boys!'

His forehead streamed with fresh blood from a shrapnel splinter, and he was dragging one leg behind him, but he seemed oblivious.

He would die laughing in the teeth of the enemy. They would kill him but they would not break him.

Nicholas gripped his sword hilt. Now let it come. He hoped to die like this if he must die, on the barricades, sword in hand. Let it be quick, but let him take some with him.

The Turks came swirling through the smoke of their own cannons, over now-toughened, scaffolded and reinforced bridges made of hardened Turkish pine from galley masts, lashed thickly together with ships' rope. The last few battered defenders had no hope of firing and collapsing them as before. There were too many and they were too few.

Nevertheless a last gallant knight went down on a rope to try. He was shot by a Turkish marksman and left hanging there. They could not retrieve him.

Another fellow next to Nicholas was hit, an unlucky shot that ricocheted off his steel gorget and ploughed up into his throat. He gagged and fell backwards. Another shot whined off the stones nearby. Nicholas seized the man's arm and hauled him back into the cover of the cordon.

'Cursed luck,' gurgled the soldier. 'The ball's just under the skin.' His throat was filling with blood, but he seemed not seriously hurt. He pulled off his helmet and then one glove and groped about with his bare fingers. 'I could almost pull it free myself.'

And then a heinous brass firebomb came arcing in over the cordon and exploded right above them. In the random way of such cruel weapons, not a splinter touched Nicholas, but four or five broad shards of ragged, superheated brass drove into the back of the fellow's exposed head. He simply sat forward, the bloody mess of his head in Nicholas's lap. The boy screamed despite himself. Then Stanley was beside him and taking the dead man by the shoulders and laying him back on the ground. Bullets and arrows and cannonballs seemed to fill the air around them as if they were in a storm, yet Nicholas was aware of nothing but the dead man, the back of his head blown away, the light in his eyes gone out.

Stanley shook him. 'Get below, boy. Have some water and wine.'

Nicholas shook his head dumbly.

'Get below!' shouted Stanley, as belligerent as any master-sergeant. 'And keep down!'

Nicholas crawled for the low bastion door.

He glugged down a scoop of water and wine, shook his head and breathed deep. He had no cloth he could use, and it was wrong to waste water. So he took a handful of dust from the ground of the inner court, and cast it over the front of his breeches. The dry dust quickly soaked up the black and purple mess of blood and brain adhering there, and he brushed it off with his sleeve. Then he crossed himself and prayed for the passage of the nameless soldier's soul, and took another scoop of wine and water, and finally stopped shaking. He set back his shoulders and thought of his father, and then went to climb the stone steps back to the firestorm above.

A fine Janizary in tall white hat and scarlet waistcoat, wielding a mace, its wings deep-toothed, came dashing up the rubble of the shattered point, urging on those behind, slipping over the blood-slathered bodies of their fallen comrades. Stanley stood swiftly and shot his arquebus from the hip but it misfired and the imposing Janizary came on. He rested his left hand on the rubble barrier and leapt over in a clean vault, pirouettting and expertly swinging his mace, which struck Stanley, slow with exhaustion, a ferocious blow which met the knight's ungauntleted right hand.

He reeled in agony and stepped back, the Janizary raising his mace for another swift and decisive blow. Nicholas raced up and thrust from behind and his blade glanced off. Beneath the Turk's scarlet waistcoat was evidently a very fine steel breastplate. The Janizary turned, his eyes dark-browed and flashing with strange pleasure. He stepped back and forth. Nicholas hesitated. Here was one of the finest soldiers in the world, veteran of a hundred battles on three different continents. Guns roared about his ears, desperate cries that sounded like the last cries of men. Perhaps this was the end.

Stanley had collapsed back against a wall, clutching his hand to his chest, his face a rictus of pain.

Nicholas weaved left and right and then wide aside and raised the sword before his eyes as if sighting down a musket barrel. He saw the mace rise high in the air, but by that time he had already thrust forward and the blade was through and a foot of it out of the back of the Janizary's throat. He pulled it cleanly out again and the man fell, blood pumping rhythmically from the front of his throat, and Nicholas finished him with another sharp stab straight through his broad forehead.

Onward surged the mix of Janizaries and less disciplined auxiliaries, Moors and Algerians. A dark fellow straight out of Ethiopia or the Nubian desert, barefoot and wearing bells on his anklets, a white wrap around his forehead and a loincloth, naked otherwise, came at him babbling and whooping. Nicholas wrong-footed him, leaping high onto the barrier and stuck the lean point of his sword straight through his heart. He pulled it free and leapt back again like a cat, the fellow falling dead against him, almost knocking him down.

'Bravo!' cried Lanfreducci.

He steadied himself. Never stop moving, never stop to admire your handiwork, fight on. Hit first, hit hard, and carry on hitting. Remember Smith's lessons. Never look back. And get over there to Stanley.

Another younger Janizary, in a green tunic and white hat, carrying a long musket, died at a long broadsword backslash from Lanfreducci, and another Nubian, finely arrayed in leopard-skin topped with a leopard-skin hat stuck with orange feathers, was torn open by a close-range blast from a squat-barrelled arquebus packed with the devil knew what, for it was no clean ball that made that carnage. He flopped limp over the barrier and Nicholas pushed him clear, his tattered lungs dragging out on the sandbags. The attack began to falter, the shouting died down, the survivors retreated back across the bridge. There were more distant shouts of the Ottoman captains, lambasting their fleeing men.

Nicholas ran to Stanley, who was trying to bandage up his shattered right hand with his teeth. He was finished fighting.

'You fight like a devil still,' he said. 'Bandage my fingers. Tie them tight.'

'Your hand's ruined,' said Nicholas.

'Do as I say,' he rasped. 'Tie forefinger and middle tight together, and the other two likewise. I will hold a sword that way.'

So he tied his right hand into a bandaged white claw, and helped him to his feet. Stanley's left arm hung down loose now, useless, the sling torn away, and Nicholas could see with dismay how badly it was wounded, dark oily blood oozing down over his forearm. But Stanley said no more, took up his sword in the bandaged linen claw of his right hand, and went back to stand beside Medrano, looking out over the piled dead, the groaning dying below.

'As they say in the Turkish *orta*,' said the tall Spanish knight, 'the body of a Janizary is but a stepping stone for his comrades behind.'

The last thirty or so Spanish soldiers went their rounds. Some collected musket balls where they could find them. They collected the very grains of powder out of the pockets of their fallen brethren. At least, those that were not sodden with blood.

Word went round that Luigi Broglia lay dead in the inner yard, beheaded by a culverin ball. They bowed their heads and crossed themselves.

One by one they must fall.

A knight slumped near, he seemed to be singing a low song. He held out a flask to the English boy and it was full of black gleaming powder still. He gave him a pouch of twenty or thirty more balls and his arquebus. Nicholas did not ask why he could no longer shoot himself. Instead he asked, taking the gun from him, 'What day is it? Stanley does not know.'

The knight raised his eyes to the sky and they were maddened. 'Nor do I know,' he said, and began to laugh. It was fearful that he should laugh so, his head back, eyelids half lowered. The loss of control was shameful. And worse, Nicholas was afraid he might start laughing with him.

'I do not know!' cried the knight. 'How long have we been here, how long have we been fighting! Perhaps a month? A year? Are we old men? Elmo will never be done. We have been fighting here now for thirty years, and our hair is white – but we do not know it because we have no looking-glass!'

Nicholas tucked the arquebus under his arm and went below to drink more water and snatch a handful of bread and wine, and pray for his soul that would shortly stand in its sinful nakedness before the Throne of Judgement. Yet surveying the last of the defenders, he began to understand that those who had survived thus far – maddened and wounded as they were – had also toughened like old leather under the sun. And he too. Already they understood now how to duck and run, how to use cover, how to listen out for the whistle of incoming cannonball, how to spy on cannons and estimate trajectories, all without conscious effort. Many had died in the first few days. But more recently, the Turks had killed fewer, not more.

He reloaded the arqbuebus swiftly and deftly, and looked around. No one had seen him do it, and he mocked himself inwardly for his vanity at wanting to be seen. In this slaughterhouse. But he knew it was very quick.

There came a distant, juddering bang, and the noise of something blustering through the air, and he stepped smoothly into an open doorway. A cannonball from a long-range gun sheared in low over the remains of the north wall and ploughed deep into the ground of the inner yard, gouging a long groove of earth before it, settling up against a barrack-room wall. In the following silence he darted over and touched the cannonball's iron surface. Still hot. If only they still had men enough to serve their own guns, it might be re-used, and sent back to its makers with vengeance written on it in blood. But a single gun needed half a dozen men. They didn't have half a dozen men.

At Angelo, La Valette asked about the rumour that Dragut had been injured on Is-Salvatur. Some were even saying he was killed.

'It is not credible,' said the Grand Master.

'It would be by the grace of God,' said Sir Oliver Starkey.

La Valette said slowly, as if picturing it, 'The boy swimming past them ... he made them work too fast. They misfired, hit their own breastwork, or a barrel cracked ...'

293

Starkey nodded. 'Dragut has not been seen out on Sciberras for a day or more. No sighting.'

La Valette clasped his hands, as if in prayer that it might be so. It would be their first good fortune in months. Though it was too late now for the news to be carried to Elmo.

The knights tore up the shirts of the dead to wrap around their heads, or to staunch their wounds, the white turning red to match their surcoats. Bearded and exhausted, snatching mouthfuls of bread, minutes of sleep when they could.

'If a man can stand,' said Medrano, 'he is not wounded.'

The Spanish knight, their new commander now, addressed them all in the precious lull, his face lean and intelligent, his eyes hooded and fierce.

There were no more elaborate fire hoops or exploding brass grenades left, and too little powder for cannon, even if they had the crews to serve them. They would fight on with notched and broken blades and muskets, and when the powder ran out, they would use their muskets as clubs. They would fight with stones. They would fight with their bare hands.

'How bitter it will be for the Turks when they understand that every inch of wall, every stone, must be fought for, bled for. Nothing will be given to them. Nothing!'

The last knights began to nod and raise their weary arms and cheered.

Not an inch of Elmo would be given away, said Medrano. Not one shot-splintered stone. They would fight unto the very last. And the story of how they fought at Elmo would be told forever after, till world end.

13

A bird cried out to sea.

Scribbles of cloud in the fading sky like Arab script.

A lucky Turkish shot took down the banner of St John itself, smashing through the flagstaff. Lanfreducci somehow managed to scramble back up there, insanely exposed, one of his legs a mere burden to him, and raised it up again on a pike, half as high again as it had been before. Shots whistled round him. He grinned and taunted them.

Nicholas could not move, his eyes black and hollow, staring at nothing. Blood and spittle drooling from his lips, leaning on his gun, looking at the ground at his feet but seeing nothing, the ground itself swaying and tilting under him. Then he knelt and fell sideways without a sound. Looking out on nothing but emptiness with the hollows of his eyes. The face of war. Beyond exhaustion, mind reeling, then floating away in white smoke, body incapable of stirring another inch.

Then the call went up, Medrano's even voice. The Turks were already re-forming.

Around him where he lay, men who looked beyond the last stages of war-wounded, far beyond mere field casualties, were stirring and dragging themselves to their feet where they had fallen.

Wounded man knelt beside wounded man and held a flask of water to parched lips. The wounded drank, hands shaking, neck straining, lips split and bleeding with the sun. Then wounded man helped wounded man to his knees, his feet, leaning on shattered pikestaffs and gunstocks for crutches, thighs bandaged, arms in slings. One man loaded up an arquebus and handed it to another, who took it unsteadily in his left hand. His right arm dangled down useless at his side, hand severed above the wrist.

Stanley was beside him and holding out his great crushed bandaged hand, saying with his sad smile, 'Come then, little brother. Come with us to our deaths.'

He heaved himself to his feet on his arquebus, butt in the dust, one hand gripping Stanley's rock-like arm. He took a breath and stood swaying a moment until enough blood coursed again through his veins.

He followed after Stanley to the steps.

De Guaras was lying in the dust of the inner yard, trying to push himself up where he lay on his belly, only to collapse again.

'Brother,' said Stanley gently, halting beside him and seeing the extent of his wounds. 'Lie still.'

'I cannot,' he gasped, almost sobbing. Bravest of the brave, weeping in the dust. 'God forgive me but I cannot. My strength is all gone, my sword arm …'

'Here,' said Nicholas, and he pulled up a lump of shattered stone and put it at De Guaras's head, and drew a cloth over it and the knight's face so that he should have shade a few minutes, as he died there.

'No,' said De Guaras, pushing the cloth away again. 'Let me burn. Let me not be covered, not even from God's midday sun. Let me die hearing my valiant brothers fighting to the last.'

Then he held Nicholas's hand and Stanley's and there was no more to be said, not another word.

Nicholas lifted his arquebus onto his shoulder and followed Stanley over to the foot of the steps. He looked up. Eighteen steps to the parapet. He thought of the climb up the Stiperstones and Long Mynd, and the rapturous views west over the mountains of Wales. But that climb of his boyhood, made so many countless happy times, was as nothing to these eighteen steps. These would exhaust him beyond any hill in England. Yet he climbed slowly up, legs burning, head thumping, to crouch behind the low barricade at the top.

In the door of the bastion behind appeared another figure. It was Captain Miranda, head bandaged, arm and leg bloody. But the worst wound was in his side, hidden and cinched in beneath a tightly laced jerkin.

He growled, 'All that's holding my guts in is my belt.'

Men leaned on their elbows, sighted with tired eyes, past all anxiety in a world falling almost silent around them with tiredness.

The Turks were coming again.

They could not go on.

They would go on.

The Janizaries came running with eager tread, a new regiment, like men just sprung from bed, in their first youth, at dawn. They came brimming with murderous energy, some grinning beneath their black moustaches. Surely they would be the ones who finally stormed this wretched fort, and won the glory!

The knights waited, the distance closed.

Here came death, beautiful under the sun, in ranks of fanatic hordes from a foreign land. The knights swooned and dreamed. Here came death in white silk robes, scimitars sailing overhead, crying of Allah and Paradise. And the knights too, bowed down beneath the burden of their wounds and their exhaustion, longed for the Paradise of their faith. They dreamed of green grassy ways and the shade of fruit-laden trees, the golden city of Zion amid the gardens, and their wounds cleansed and healed, their love unto death requited.

The air was splintered with cries and howls. Shots rang out. The bridges were crammed, fresh scaling ladders knocked against unmanned walls to the south. The cannonade of Smith's horse pistol rang out, in the hands of Miranda now, and a besieger flew back off a ladder, hitting the rocks hard below.

Medrano alone saw that another, smaller group of Turks, carrying heavy backpacks, were moving out wide and at a run, towards the rear cavalier and the gate. There was not one defender left there to shoot them down.

Nicholas raced over to the south wall and raised his sword, his every fibre burning and crying out, and was fighting again.

He stepped aside and brought his sword down hard onto the nearest Turk's shoulder. A clumsy stroke. The Turk turned it easily with a swipe of his small round shield and stuck his scimitar in Nicholas's breastplate. But even in his last exhaustion, the boy stepped back with his instinctive grace of movement and the sword point did no more than punch the air from his chest, its power lost.

In the same instant, never hesitating, never stopping, whilst the Turk drew back his sword for another stroke, the boy spun and drove his sword forward under arm, and the Turk was skewered, falling back off the ladder. His fall dragged the boy with him. He twisted and slammed against the broken parapet and only held onto his weapon by a whisker, the hilt so slippery with blood. Another Turk hacked down to slice through his arm but he rolled away and the Turk was in over the parapet and standing before him hollering. They ducked each other's blows and the Turk slithered and slipped and the boy slipped too in the shambles of the strewn and crumpled bodies. Sitting up, Nicholas aimed at the fellow's armpit where it was uncovered by breastplate, and stuck his sword awkwardly in. A horrible stroke, a crude stabbing, like that of a backstreet thug.

The Turk howled with pain and his sword fell. He clutched his armpit, blood seeping through the white silk, and Nicholas was back on his feet and had stabbed him long through the throat and out the back of his neck before he could do more. Then he knew that these were no longer the best regiments they were sending in. So much for his white Janizary silk. This man had fought with all the experience of a ploughman or wagoner, conscripted only last week.

What butchery it was. The fellow lay back gargling blood. Nicholas turned and almost toppled off the wall, so clumsy with exhaustion, but still fighting, still killing. Anointed in fresh gore with each new enemy, each new encounter, morion and breastplate and blade agleam with a new red sheen of slaughter every time.

A lull. García gave the English boy a glug of wine from his flask. It was nearly gone. The boy went back to the south wall and waited. He was a boy with a man's heart.

Zacosta shook his head. 'How can men fight in this heat?'

García said, 'They're not fighting, they're dreaming. None of them knows any more who he is or where he is.'

'Or what he's fighting for.'

'That least of all.'

Nicholas knew. He fought for one thing and for one thing only. He had forgotten that this was a Holy War, or he only remembered nightly when he came to pray, to ask for God's blessing, and for- giveness for blood shed. He no longer thought of this as some vast historic struggle between rival Empires, enemy civilisations, Cross and Crescent, true faith against false. Such abstractions meant little in a charnel house like this. They melted away in the red heat of battle. He no longer fought even for his father's memory and his family's pride. His father was dead: he had seen him die and spoken with him as he died, and he saw his face and heard his voice still daily. But let the dead bury the dead. It was the way of all the earth. One day he would return, to find his sisters, fight to win back the name and honour of his family.

But for now, he thought of one thing only, as he fought, reloaded, fired, struck, stabbed, buffeted, reeled back. A thing still closer to his heart. He fought not for his father or his sisters or his name, not for St George or England, the Knights or the Cross. He fought for her. Maddalena. He fought ferociously, and for the simplest reason. The harder he fought, the longer Elmo held, the longer it would be before the Turkish guns turned back on her.

They attacked Elmo by night, the exhausted sleeping knights stumbling to their feet to a weary trumpet call. The Janizaries' white robes gleaming by moonlight, sweat-slicked skins orange by torchlight. The attackers fired flares and firebombs and in a scene from hell, wheeled up a wagon holding a brass barrel with a long spout that looked like some gleaming brass-winged insect, hugely fat-bellied. They lit a touch-hole and the spout shot forth thirty- foot flames in an angry animal roar. Two knights were caught by that burning tongue and turned into living torches, yet even in their death trance they ran out across the bridges and hurled themselves burning into the midst of the enemy, who were aghast at such colossal courage even in the agony of death. The defenders were equally astounded that they still had strength in their arms, blood still swelling their hearts.

In a small but concerted pike charge, masterminded by Medrano, the Turks were driven off again, with great slaughter.

The stench from the ditch below was almost enough to knock a man senseless. The flies buzzed and gorged and laid their eggs day and night, through all gunfire. It was terrible to sleep through such a stench, it infected one's very dreams. But when the sun came up at dawn and burned down on the rotting bodies, it was worse.

It was the Valley of Gehenna spoken of in the Scriptures, said Fra Giacomo, outside the walls of Jerusalem, where the wicked in ancient times offered up their own sons and daughters in sacrifice to their false gods.

'See,' he said. 'See where Suleiman the Magnificent and the Lords of the Ottomans have offered up their children to their false god likewise, and lain them out upon the altar of death. How the sacrificed sons of Suleiman are to be pitied. How the stench of his vainglory and wickedness rises to Heaven.'

The cannons continued to roar all night, but no more attacks came.

In the leaden light before dawn, they saw with grieving eyes and heavy hearts that a green banner of Islam hung limp but unmistakable on the roof of the ravelin. Turkish snipers, well defended, now looked down on them from less than fifty yards away.

It was a cruel error. Desperately short of men, Medrano had left a single watchman there, and at dusk some knights had checked and seen him lying patiently on lookout. In fact he was already dead with a shot to the heart.

The Turks had followed up under cover of darkness. Mustafa Pasha sent out a small team of his élite night warriors, who wore black robes, and nothing on their feet but black cloth wrappings so that they might move silently over any terrain. They blackened their faces, and carried no weapons but black-metalled knives. And in the night they had successfully climbed the outer walls of the little ravelin, ready to cup the mouths and slit the throats of any weary watchmen leaning on their pikes there. But there had been no need. As the Janizary musketeer had boasted, he had taken out the single watchman there with a single shot.

The Ottomans were now in possession of an outlying corner of the fort itself.

The knights could also see their slain comrade, the watchman, one of the tough veteran Spanish soldiers. One of the last. As a powerful signal that this was indeed *guerre à l'outrance,* Mustafa had ordered him tied by the ankles and then suspended head down, sliced throat exposed, and hung out over the wall of the ravelin so that the last of the stubborn defenders could see what fate awaited them.

Yet the sight of the atrocity made none quaver with the fear that Mustafa intended. Some wept, some sickened, some grimaced. But all felt the steel of righteous vengeance in their bellies.

From Angelo, La Valette could discern the green banner through an eyeglass.

'Take it back, my Brothers,' he urged under his breath. *'Fight.'*

'Sire,' said Oliver Starkey at his side, quiet and steady. 'They have fought as few men have ever fought before.'

La Valette lowered the eyeglass. 'I know,' he said. 'I know it.'

He ordered a last desperate attempt to help them.

He spoke to a master gunner on the east wall of the castle and asked him if he could fire a shot high over the Grand Harbour and hit the Turkish lines.

The master gunner shook his head. 'As I said to you before, Sire, at this range we might hit anything.'

'Try it, man. Do your best. God will guide.'

The master gunner was as experienced as any, and yet the first shot he fired curved right as it flew over the harbour and struck an unmanned section of Elmo's wall itself. A few yards' difference and it could easily have killed the defenders.

A look of agony crossed La Valette's aged face. Then he turned away.

'We cannot help them,' he said. 'They are truly on their own.'

In the brief silences between the roaring of the guns, there came another sound. Far quieter, but to the ears of siege veterans, far more ominous. The steady, rhythmic chink chink of pick axe on solid rock. The Turkish miners were at work down in the great ditch below, now working quite free of enemy fire, since they had possession of the flanking ravelin. The defenders could no longer fire down on them, only hear them at their relentless task. Soon the walls would be down.

Yet they could only imagine what it must be like to work down there in that reeking netherworld, amid the heaps of dead bodies and the clouds of flies. The flesh of the dead around them turning green and then black with putrefaction, sliding off bones like soft cheese.

'They'll blow them in a day or two,' said Zacosta. He grimaced at Nicholas. 'Do not be taken alive by these unbelieving dogs, lad. Find some way. For they have a taste for boys, for fairhead boys like you. Or they will torture you for information, with the very worst tortures they can devise. They will torture you simply for amusement. In celebration of Elmo's fall.'

'Hold your tongue, man,' growled Stanley nearby.

'You know I speak the truth,' said Zacosta.

Nicholas glanced at Stanley, his ravaged and sunburnt face, lips and cheeks blistering through the black mask of powder soot. He said no more.

At dawn the snipers on the ravelin began to fire down on them in earnest, at the slightest movement behind the cordons. They bulked up the defences as best they could, but the ravelin's height placed then at a grim disadvantage.

Sheltering behind a low barricade, the ridge splintering in a cease-less hail of bullets, Medrano shouted to Stanley, 'The Venetians at Padua, half a century ago – 1509, the Italian Wars. Under severe siege. They mined their own walls!'

Stanley frowned.

'When the French took them, the Venetians lit the fuse.'

'Padua fell?'

'For sure Padua fell. But a lot of Frenchmen died taking it.'

Stanley shouted, 'It would be good if we'd thought to mine the ravelin so.'

Medrano's lean face split in a rare grin.

'We did?'

'It's beyond the next star point, right below the ravelin.'

Lanfreducci insisted on going.

'You can hardly walk, Brother.'

The Italian just grinned his broad, handsome grin. 'But I can crawl excellent well. And this is a job for a crawler.'

'It's a very long powder trail,' said Medrano. 'It may not go, and if it does, it'll take minutes. Meanwhile the snipers will be after you all the way as you crawl out below the parapet.'

'It's in God's hands,' said Lanfreducci.

A sniper observed the wounded knight clawing his way behind a near-flattened section of parapet almost immediately, and took aim. That sixth sense of the veteran soldier told Lanfreducci that a musket muzzle was aimed straight at him, and he curled himself into a ball behind a single earth-filled barrel. His face creased in agony as he bent his wounded leg, and he could feel fresh blood seeping from the split crust. But he hauled it in close by the ankle, numb below the knee, all pain above it, and lay there curled up as best he could.

A sniper musket wavered over the ravelin wall. He held his fire.

A few moments later a helmeted head appeared round the side of the barrel and a single sniper bullet put a hole clean through it.

The helmet rolled away. It was a feint, a helmet of one fallen, held out by the trapped knight.

As the sniper angrily set himself to reload, and called up his fellows to take the shot, the Italian set off crawling like a lizard along the wall, weight on his forearms, working forward rapidly, one leg dragging behind him.

Now he would not stop. A musket cracked out, yet it missed him. He crawled on. The Turks knew now that something was up. He must be stopped. Another musket shot, and a small plume of blood rose from his shoulder, but he crawled on without slackening his pace one iota. Then a dreadful sound: the spattering bark of a cannon loaded with grapeshot.

Grapeshot from the roof of the ravelin, fired down on a single wounded man.

Medrano lost his cool composure then and cried out in anger. He fired an angry shot up at the ravelin, but it was wasted.

The smoke drifted across the ditch from the fired gun, and Lanfreducci's prostrate form was momentarily lost to view. In the moment before, Stanley thought he had glimpsed the terrible sight of the knight arching up from the ground, head thrown back, as the balls spat into him. But then the smoke finally cleared – and he was nowhere to be seen.

His brother knights clenched their fists.

On the ravelin, another sniper took careful aim. The Turks could see what they could not. He was in no hurry. Then the muzzle flared and a shot rang out, and distraught, they heard the sniper crew erupt in a great cheer and saw them exchange a flurry of shoulder slaps.

Medrano and Stanley both crossed themselves. Fra Francesco Lanfreducci had left Elmo far behind. It was but consummation.

Nothing more came. The ravelin remained. The snipers looked down on them and reloaded their fine bore muskets.

Then they all suddenly looked back aghast.

The defenders peered out.

Round the corner of the shattered point came a figure dragging his leg. His breastplate and backplate so pocked and ruptured with lead that he looked squilled like a porcupine. He was grinning.

'My God is a burning fire!' he cried out.

He was hit again where he stood, and calmly sat down against the back wall, in full view of the ravelin. He removed his helmet and set it by his side, and leaned his head back like a man tired with a hot morning's walk. Eyes crinkled in the sun, white teeth showing in a smile.

The Turks took aim again.

He called out to them with tattered lungs, 'More haste, more haste, you uncomely sons of Oriental whores! I tire here. You must be using mouse turds for balls!'

Then there came a full blast of half a dozen muskets at no more than twenty yards' range, and the Hospitaller slid sideways to the ground, a smear of blood on the wall at his back, eyes closed in peace.

The Turks did not celebrate this time. It had been a man among men they had killed, whatever insults he had hurled at them in dying, and he had a contempt for death as fine as any Janizary could muster. Let him lie there and sleep undisturbed.

The world was ruptured by an explosion so vast that it was some time before any there, defender or attacker, could shake his thoughts into sense. With animal instinct, Nicholas simply cowered behind the cordon, his face pressed so hard against the wickerwork of a gabion that it left an imprint on his cheek, his arms over his head, lumps of rock and stone showering down around him. None struck him, mercifully. One alone might have broken his arm.

A long time passed. The darkened sky gradually cleared, the ringing in their ears slowly subsided. There was stunned silence from all sides.

They squinted out. Clouds of dust and smoke hung like ragged veils over the ravelin. Or where the ravelin had been. As the veils slowly cleared they saw nothing but a field of rubble. They could not even discern any human remains.

Medrano said, 'When we laid the charge, as you see, we still had plenty of powder. In those far-off days.'

The water itself was now foul to the taste, but men's tongues and lips were black with thirst. There were no more frontal attacks that day. Medrano thought he knew why, but he said nothing to the men.

Stanley understood too. He said quietly, 'They are confident of breaking in soon another way.'

Medrano's lean, sallow face looked at its most grave and composed. 'I think they will soon blow the main gates at the cavalier. A mining gang was round there. Then they will be in. There is no more we can do.'

'But look what we have done,' said Stanley. 'How many days did we win for Birgu?'

'Many,' said Medrano, and his sweat-streaked, dirt-streaked face showed a distant smile. 'We lost count how many. But many days we bought for our brothers over the water. Our Grand Master will have made sure Birgu is now defended as best as it can be.'

'And we died honourably, did we not?' said Stanley, his voice soft and low.

Medrano liked the past tense. 'We died honourably,' he said. 'As at Acre, as at Jerusalem. As Knights Hospitaller should die.'

14

Before a huge column of Janizaries, fresh and armed and bathed and scented with rosewater for the fall, Mustapha Pasha strode and screamed derision. They shifted with painful discomfort, looked down at their feet and bore it in silence as they must.

'So-called Sons of the Sultan!' he raged. 'You have fought these last days and weeks like women! The dogs and pigs of Christendom, they laugh at you, they call you little girls, daughters of Eve, of Lilith! They think you are men with breasts, fit only for sewing and baking!'

The Janizaries glowered and clutched their sword hilts tighter.

'Now go out and destroy them, your most ancient enemies! They who have killed so many of your beloved brothers. Instruct them in the way of the Janizary, teach them that there can never be forgiveness and mercy between Islam and the Cross, and show them that you are men, not women, and understand how to kill.'

Dusk fell on Elmo, and with it an ominous, oppressive sense of expectation. Now they were only waiting for the end.

Stanley spoke to the boy. 'You are not mortally injured.'

'I'm bad enough.' He hurt all over. Even tiredness could not dull it.

'The Turks will be in very soon now. I think tonight. You must escape. Go over the south-east wall and down to the rocks. I know you can swim.'

'I go if you go.'

'I can't swim. And I will not abandon my brothers. I am a knight, you are—'

'Just a vagabond orphan and exile.'

'No.' Stanley smiled gently. 'You are a deal more than that.'

'So you'll not try to come?'

He shook his head. 'It is not the way for me.'

'Smith still lives, but mortally wounded.'

Stanley looked enquiring.

'If he set eyes on you again, lying there in the Sacred Infirmary – you know he would rally. That would be better medicine for him than all the skill and art of Fra Reynaud. You know how he would come to himself then, fight off his sickness and fevers with all his strength. And then you could both join in the fight for Birgu. You know you will be needed there.'

'You argue with all the guile of a Vatican cardinal, boy.'

'Besides, La Valette will want to hear of the Battle of Elmo from survivors.'

'You will survive. But not I. As I say, here is the way to death for me. Here at Elmo.'

The boy looked so haunted and sad in the gathering darkness, fitfully lit by guttering fires. Stanley knew that he and Smith be-tween them were something like fathers to him now. And he would only lose them again. Yet a knight's duty was not to his fellow men, but with all stern unbending piety towards God alone.

'When the Turks come in, you will go,' he said. 'I will give you the shove myself. Return to Smith, and to Birgu. The family, and – the girl.'

Nicholas looked at him sharply, but Stanley was beyond teasing now.

Nicholas said, 'If you look out from the south-east wall – what's left of it – on the rocks below you will see a broad flat timber washed up. From the boat of the two fishermen, destroyed by the guns of Is-Salvatur.'

'Yes?'

'Immediately below on the rocks,' persisted the boy. 'You say you cannot swim. Wood floats. Do you follow me?'

'I follow your meaning,' said Stanley. 'Surely you should be a wily diplomat for the Vatican when you are grown. But—'

It was not a big explosion, but measured just sufficient by the expert Mameluke engineers to blow open an entrance below the cavalier, and then swiftly another charge was placed at the foot of the stout wooden gates into the fort. One or two knights hauled themselves to their feet where they lay in the inner yard, and tried to make it up the steps to fire down on the miners. But it was hopeless. The Turks proceeded with ruthless speed and efficiency, knowing that the defenders were now too reduced and exhausted to pose a threat to them as they worked, and the snipers and gunners out on the ravelin gave them added cover. There came a muffled crump from beyond the gates and the gates shuddered. Another few moments and they would be in.

From the north wall a cry went up. An immense column of Janizaries was moving fast and wide round the back of Elmo, a captain at their head bellowing out to the engineers to get that gate down now, they were coming in. The miners worked frenziedly, packing up another pile of powder below the hinges of the right gate.

With the Janizaries came a rabblement of Bektaşis, daggers clutched in their fists, howling the ten thousand names of God, eyes bloodshot and deranged. Some split off and came rushing the bridges to distract the last of the defenders from the main gate.

'Kill! Kill! Kill in the name of Allah!'

At last their time had come.

'What is my strength, that I should hope?' murmured Stanley. *'And what is mine end, that I should prolong my life?'*

It was the final moments of Elmo.

'The last stand!' bellowed Captain Miranda with bitter humour, crawling out into the yard dragging a stool with him. He could no longer stand. He dragged the stool up in front of the wooden gates and hauled himself into it, and then there he sat – Nicholas would never forget the sight of it – amid the blackened ruins of the fort, eerily lit by the dancing orange flames that still burned. Miranda drew his great two-handed sword from his scabbard and held it out in front of him. Since he could no longer stand, both his legs wounded and half eaten away with black infection, he would fight his last battle sitting down.

His men, García and Zacosta, stood beside their captain to the last. The night sky serene above them. All around the inner yard, and on the walls above, men lying dead under wooden beams, men slumped over barrels stuck with feathered arrows, men standing impaled by spears, men burned beyond recognising, half buried in rubble and shattered stone.

Fewer than thirty remained to fight, some gathering close round the seated Miranda, and others pulling back to the steps of the little chapel with Medrano, their backs to the wall, there to finish their lives and the human pilgrimage.

Fra Giacomo, the only chaplain who still lived, burned the few sparse tapestries, icons and furnishings within the chapel, so that the heathen should not desecrate them. Then he kneeled before the altar, his back to the doorway through which they would come, and bowed his head in prayer.

Another muffled explosion, and very slowly, as if in a dream, amid soft billows of pale dust, the gates fell in and hit the ground, and the Janizaries swarmed over them.

Miranda was shot dead in his chair, still swinging his sword. García was hurled to the ground but picked himself up and managed to seize a pike, before he was beheaded with a scimitar. The others were cut down on the steps of the chapel, and Fra Giacomo slain where he knelt, his lips moving in prayer to the last. One by one they perished.

Medrano died lighting a beacon fire to tell Birgu that Elmo was lost. But as he lay dying on the bastion top, he saw the fire blaze up, and saw the Janizaries let it burn. Let them know across the water that Elmo was lost. Let them know that now it was Birgu's turn.

The flag of St John, what remnants remained of it, was hauled down and the crescent moon of Islam raised in its stead, to a mighty cheer of *Allahu Akhbar!*

A Bektaşi dervish hurled himself down onto Stanley from the walls above, a twenty foot drop, and both tumbled into the dust. They rolled together until the knight caved his windpipe in with a blow of his forearm, and leapt to his feet again, unhelmed. Then several shots were fired and either a ball itself or a chip of stone struck the side of his head and he careened running into Nicholas against the wall. He slumped back, eyes closed.

Holding his sword in his right hand, Nicholas hooked the knight's right arm over his shoulders and put his left arm around the knight's waist and seized hold of his broad leather sword belt for better grip, dragging him back into the shadows of the colonnade below the south wall. Stanley's head was rolling alarmingly, he was badly concussed and muttering. Blood streamed from his head wound over Nicholas's shoulder.

Nicholas dragged him to the foot of the steps under the colonnade, expecting at every moment to feel long cold steel thrust into his backbone, and he prayed with desperation, sweat pouring down his face, prickling his armpits, trying to ignore the dull throbbing ache of his deep-bruised left elbow. The knight might have weighed twice as much as him in full armour, yet he dragged him along, gasping, muscles tearing.

'Move your legs,' he hissed.

Stanley mumbled, *'This is the beginnings of sorrows...'*

Nicholas kicked him violently in the side of his calf and Stanley began to take some of his own weight on listless legs.

The boy glanced back out into the moonlit yard and saw Zacosta struck down and on his knees, gouting blood, yet still sweeping his sword wide and low before him, cutting clean through a Turk's leg just above the foot. He toppled forward and five more swords were raised over him.

He looked away. They came to the foot of the steps and somehow, God alone willing, he half walked, half dragged the bewildered Stanley up them. They emerged onto the height of the ravaged south wall and without a moment's hesitation, knowing that this was probably when they would be killed, Nicholas broke into a low shuffling run, dragging along the man beside him, thigh muscles screaming, to hurl themselves over the wall. Yet the Janizaries were there already.

Fighting against every base natural instinct to turn Stanley as a shield, he thrust his right side forward and stabbed at a Janizary, who laughed and said something in mocking Turkish about how he was too burdened to fight a good fight. But if Nicholas let Stanley drop, he would never get him up again. The Janizary switched left and right, eyes gleaming, the sea brilliantly moonlit behind his dancing silhouette, and then Nicholas lunged so fast and unexpectedly that he drove the sword point low under the Turk's waist-sash and he gulped and bent double. He pulled his reeking blade free and left him there, and hauled Stanley onward, the knight muttering that he was blinded by the moon.

Something thumped them from behind, Stanley taking the blow. It was a musket butt, the concussed knight felt little. Nicholas, already bent at the knees, swivelled round as hard as he could, sword out wide, and sliced into the fellow's hamstrings. There was no time to finish him, but he hoped that would stay him enough. They staggered to the brink of the parapet flattened by cannon fire, he dropped his sword to the ground, more dangerous to take than to leave, and dragged them both over the edge.

Like a drunk man, Stanley hit the steeply sloping rocky ground twenty feet below and rolled on down without apparent injury, coming to rest entangled in the last clumps of brushwood before they gave out to bare sea-washed rock. Nicholas screamed out in agony, he couldn't help himself, landing with hands outstretched, palms scraped raw, one knee feeling as if it had fully shattered, hipbone bashed, feet curled up and red with pain. But of course the Turks had the fort surrounded by men, and some were already running over to where they lay to finish them.

Stanley flopped over onto his back, his wounded arm useless, gazing up at the dark Mediterranean summer night with his blue English eyes, murmuring softly to himself words Nicholas could no longer understand. The air was filled with the sweet aromatic smell of crushed thyme, the first sweet smell they had known in weeks, and Stanley smiled.

Only the boy could save him, the knight was finished.

He came to his feet, snatching the dagger from its sheath on Stanley's belt, and closed tight into the nearest Janizary, to the soldier's surprise. Well inside the sweep of his sword, almost embracing him, Nicholas butted him in the face with the top of his head and then stuck the dagger into his side rapidly, four or five times. He pushed his lifeless body away, gasped at the fresh hot stab of pain in his knee, eyed the two other Janizaries circling him warily. One glanced across at Stanley lying murmurous amid the thyme, carolling, smiling at the stars, and went over quickly to despatch him with a sliced throat while his fellow Janizary dealt with the boy. Nicholas cried out and moved faster than even he knew he could move. He slashed the nearer man across the face and hurtled through the bloody spray to fall on the fellow kneeling beside Stanley like a ministering angel of death. He clamped his left hand over his mouth, wrenched his head back and pulled the dagger hard across his muscular throat, slitting the windpipe. The air whistling free from his lungs, still redolent of tobacco smoke.

He turned back and the fellow with the slashed face was swinging wildly, half blinded, but he was big and strong and had been cut many times before, and now he was angry. He swore and shouted, and more troops were coming round the starpoint to the west, along with a couple of stark naked Bektaşis, who seemed to be carrying severed heads as well as narrow spears.

He could not fight them all. It was a wonder he could fight any. There was one last trick. He dropped to his one good knee and bowed his head in weary surrender, and the Janizary stepped up to behead him, and seeing his red leather boots in the dust feet before him, judging his stance and position, in a flash Nicholas drove the dagger sharply upwards into the man's groin. He felt the white silk wet with blood and urine, clinging hotly to his hand as he snatched it away. The Janizary screamed in agony and something like terror, unmanned.

The boy did not wait to finish him, but hauled Stanley along by his belt. Twenty yards away came on a dozen men at the run to kill him, fresh and eager. And yes, those were severed heads that the Bektaşis clutched, their bloody fingers plaited in dark matted hair, babbling and singing of Allah and his works.

He raised Stanley under the armpits now and hauled him, heels in the dust. They went down half crawling, half falling over the heaped sandstone boulders below, a bloody dagger clamped between Nicholas's front teeth, the Janizary's hot metallic blood running from the blade over his own lips like those of some Carib cannibal. They flopped into the lapping shallows and Nicholas heaved the knight out on his back into a larger deep-water inlet, the pursuers gathering immediately above them. None had musket balls left in their pouches, they had wasted them all in joyous firing into the air at the fall of Elmo, or he and Stanley would have been dead by now. They jabbered on the rock and began to clamber down, blades glinting.

There was the flat timber from the smashed fishing boat where he had observed it and planned it days before.

A skin-and-bone Bektaşi scrambled down to him, eyes rolling, naked but for a sheen of Christian blood in which he seemed to be slathered from crown to toe, as if he had anointed himself in bloody baptism. Nicholas pushed Stanley back against a rock, eyes closed but mouth open, still breathing, and turned on the dervish as another jumped into the water the other side of the rocks. Nicholas waded forward and smacked the knife out of the Bektaşi's hand with his forearm and then grabbed him by his bony shoulders and unbalanced him by pulling him abruptly forward into the water. The dervish came up spluttering, the blood of his enemies washing from his dark skin. It was horrible to feel the weight of the fanatic buoyed in the water, as light as a child. For many years he had fasted his frame down to nothing but skin and bone for the love of Allah, and so it was with ease that Nicholas gripped his head under the chin and smashed it back against the boulder once, twice, three times, until even his fanatic arms had no strength, and his skull no longer knocked on the stone but made a wet, soft noise. The dervish never gave a blow with his long thin axe.

The other was swimming round to him but frenziedly, flapping like a dog. Nicholas swam out to him and took the dagger from between his teeth and raised it high and stabbed down into the floundering swimmer's skinny back. The dervish's head went below the water. He stabbed and stabbed and stabbed until the white sea foam turned pink in the sinless moonlight, and he knew he had lost all restraint and become merely murderous and all his boyhood innocence was gone.

The air was filled with shouts, they were calling urgently for musketeers to come up and kill these two fugitive wretches. But he paid no more heed to the bloody wreck of Elmo behind him, nor the blood-stained promontory of Sciberras. He pulled Stanley out into the water and draped him on his back over the middle of the spar. The spar sunk down only a little, Stanley's fair locks trailing in the water, his beard beaded with pearls, eyes closed, but breathing, still breathing.

Then he pushed the weight out over the water, and gripped the near end, and began to kick.

At any moment, another might have been swimming beside him, slicing into him. Or musket balls peppering the water around him, and then his world going red and then black. But it never happened. He never knew why.

The Birgu shore seemed as far distant as some uncharted coast of the Americas.

He would never know how long he kicked, panted, rested, sometimes flopped over onto his back and lay floating in the salt sea of the great harbour, unable to move either himself or his friend another yard. And then after perhaps five minutes, the stars moving visibly overhead, and shouts and cries still coming from the inferno of Elmo, he would roll over again on his front and rest his chin on the half-submerged spar of timber, seawater flowing over his face, and kick forward that way, arms draped without strength, turning his face aside to take breath, stopping more and more frequently, kicking less and less, drifting often.

Lights twinkled on the Birgu shore, but they seemed more like a taunt than comfort. So far away.

Where the water streamed past the jagged ends of the spars as they inched forward, he saw clouds of glowing green phosphorescence. Drowned stars.

The five hundred yard crossing took him perhaps two or three hours. At any time a sharp-eyed sniper on Is-Salvatur might yet have tried to hit him in the water by moonlight. But he felt strangely past caring. He rested and kicked and rested. What would be would be. He could do no more.

A little later as he lay on his back, and Elmo looked a little further off, the high walls of San Angelo loomed a little nearer, he sucked in air and began to feel light-headed. Almost as if he might start to laugh. He knew it was only exhaustion.

On the heights of Sciberras there was immense activity by torchlight and lantern light and the bright aid of the moon. Not at Elmo, but westward at the vast Ottoman camp, and around the trenches and gun platforms. They were already being dismantled. He tried to see with his tired, salt-bleared eyes. The tents and pavilions were being taken down, the great guns roped and craned onto the massive wheeled wagons. He could hear the oxen bellow and low as they were driven into their teams and the thick leather yokes set on their muscled backs once more. He could hear the roll of the heavy ironbound wheels, perhaps even the ground and the water trembling under that massive weight. And many men marching away by orange torchlight, a drum sounding, standards raised high in the night. Then he could have laughed.

They were breaking camp already. The moment Elmo fell, Mustafa Pasha had given the order. They were already pulling back off Sciberras, returning past the low-lying Marsa, and over the Corradino Heights to Santa Margherita and the ruins of its ancient monastery. They were coming back to Birgu, the greatest prize, and the key to the island of Malta.

It could be as soon as dawn tomorrow that the great brazen guns would begin to roar again. Elmo would lie deathly quiet, smouldering, forgotten. And he and Stanley had escaped the quiet of that grave, to swim back into the cannon's mouth once more.

He could have laughed.

With the last defenders tortured to death or beheaded, none having uttered a word under torture, Mustafa Pasha rode back to make a final survey of the paltry ruins. As he sat on his white horse in the moonlight, he revolved in his mind the figures: eighteen thousand cannonballs used, some seventy thousand pounds of gunpowder. About a fifth of their supplies. Cannonballs could be retrieved and re-used, some of them. But they had no access to more gunpowder except from Stamboul herself, nearly a thousand miles away. Worst of all was the cost in Turkish and allied dead. The siege of Elmo alone had consumed nearly a quarter of his forces. Some eight thousand dead or wounded beyond fighting more. Against some two or three hundred defenders. It was scarcely credible.

Then he lifted up his stony eyes and gazed across the Grand Harbour.

From Birgu rose a great curtain of silence, high into the starlit sky. In response to the tragic spectacle of valiant Elmo, valiant beyond words, now fallen at last, and with the banner of a false and arrogant religion polluting its walls, there came only a grave and mighty silence.

In the heart of the night, many brothers and citizens gathered on the walls of the city to witness the death of the little fort that had died for them. And as often with the death of a loved one, relative or friend, silence was the truest expression of grief.

Even Mustafa Pasha spoke little as he surveyed the devastation, the bodies, and eyed with distaste the various mutilations practised on the corpses by the laughing, maddened Bektaşis.

'In the name of Allah,' he was heard to murmur, looking across to Birgu once more. 'If the son has cost us so much, what will the father cost us?'

Part IV

THE CITY

1

Nicholas came back to Birgu as he arrived at Elmo before, not knowing when or how. The two broken refugees were hauled from the water by stout fishermen on the Kalkara shore, just below the walls of San Angelo, and given watered wine to drink. Nicholas knelt, for he could not yet stand, and put the trembling cup to his lips and gulped it down. He thought he was at the Mass. Then he handed the cup to the figure beside him. His eyes and understanding were so blurred, he did not know exactly who it was.

The fishermen helped them and they both stood upright with great effort, swaying, barely seeing or hearing, their senses far way. But exhausted as they were, something fresh coursed in their veins, along with the wine and water. They were back in the city. Birgu. They had escaped Elmo. Their brothers were all slain there.

Stanley said, his voice his own once more, *'And we only are alone escaped to tell thee.'*

The wound to his head ran with fresh blood thinned with saltwater, his fair hair was darkly plastered, his wounds too many to count, his clothes like Nicholas's own a disgrace of blackened and bloody tatters. Yet they both lived, and with their full senses. The healing power of seawater was deep and mysterious. Along with all the deep sorrow of Elmo's fall, and the bitterness of this war that had barely begun, they felt a surge of powerful contradictory joy: the ancient primitive joy of the survivor.

Around them the people and then more and more knights came to greet them and look on with wonder and relief. Young boys ran off to spread the word that though Elmo was indeed fallen, yet

319

two had escaped alive, and before long the word was all over the town. La Valette was immediately informed, and according to his prompt orders, in the heart of the night, aged sacristans shuffled up darkened spiral stairways in cobwebbed towers to ring solitary stark iron bells. It was the second time the bells of Birgu's churches had rung tonight, the first time with a more direful peel. The two fugitives had not heard that earlier peel across the water, their ears deafened and bleeding with the roar of cannon.

In response to the joyful tolling of bells, heads turned and glared across the water from the Turkish column. Mustafa's eyes burned black. What were the slaves celebrating now? No help had come. No help would come. Ottoman intelligence was sure. The Christians had as much sense of unity and brotherhood as weasels fighting in a hole.

Nicholas and Stanley looked at each other and then embraced. Two figures that might have come up from the deep ocean, or from another world imagined by the poets. A man and a boy, who had that look in their eyes and that strength in their bearing, however weakened their frames, of two who had walked with death for many days and weeks and not been destroyed by it.

The scene was unreal after the abattoir of Elmo. People lined the streets and cheered as if in nocturnal starlit fiesta, torches blazing, faces smiling and people calling out blessings on the heroes and curses on the coming Turks, arms raised, fists clenched. The streets eerily untouched as yet by cannon fire and war.

The two went down the Street of the Knights unwillingly in the role of returning heroes, still feeling themselves to be but the last pitiful pair of refugees from a grievous loss. But to the people they were warriors from the ballads and stories, and women sang and cast flowers, rose petals and sprigs of rosemary, and men clapped their shoulders and hailed them as brothers.

Nicholas could have fainted, or dropped to his knees and sobbed, but he and Stanley walked steadily thorough all the magic and the unreality of the moment, nodding graciously, knowing that for the people to celebrate now, with such zeal, was far more important than their own private sentiments. An ancient Jewish fiddler pushed forward through the crowd and walked along behind them in their torchlit procession, playing a stately Spanish dance, a courtly pavane. The two of them, knight and boy, stained with blood and salt and exhausted beyond speech, had spoken barely a word since crawling ashore, not a word in reply to the clamorous questions and the showers of praise, but gazed mutely with surging sorrow and remembrance of horror and comrades lost, and of the great wordless gulf that separates those who have lived through war from those who have not.

But now all around them and their sorrowful silence there was laughter and music and dancing as if this night was fair day or high holiday. Maidens crying to see such heroes among men, men admiring, and the two of them stepping forward to the tune of this sweet melancholy pavane, all passion under immaculate restraint and formal ceremony, like all courtly dances, and walking in measure to the music. More street musicians joined the aged Jew, and the music swelled.

Then through the crowd which shimmered and moved apart, there came a figure, and she reached out towards the boy. Like two of the courtliest dancers in all of Europe, a gentleman and his fine lady, she held out her slim hand upward, palm outward, and they touched palms as pilgrims do. She wore a pale blue dress, her only dress, and amid all the laughter and folly and rejoicing around them, as if the worst was not yet to come, her dark eyes fixed upon him with deadly seriousness, and no one else was there. There was only the battered bloodied boy soldier and the slim virgin girl. Their palms touched, and they turned and danced, moved left and then turned and back, to the slow stately pavane, the Jewish fiddler and his fellows picking up the time. The boy's exhaustion was great, he moved slowly, and the fiddlers played with it.

All the people looked on at this strange sight, falling quiet. It was the Inglis boy, the Insulter, come back from Elmo to dance in the street like a prince with the daughter of Franco Briffa. She was still a maiden pure, you could tell, but in the expression of each of them there was such a love that burned, and in the deadly seriousness of their young eyes, his a Northern sea blue and hers the colour of Malta honey.

Franco Briffa also saw, and his jaw fell open. These two loved like none other. '*Dios mio,*' he muttered. There had never been such love as theirs. Some looked on and remembered the love they had known when they were young, and some longed to know such love, and some felt the most aching regret that they would never know such a love as this of these two stately dancers, the slim Malta girl and the bloodstained boy, dancing in the Street of the Knights, as if no one else lived in the world with them but they alone.

Only hours later, soon after sunrise the next day, guns booming, banners flying, casting giant crinkled shadows over the sea before it as it came, the Ottoman fleet sailed safe at last into harbour in Marsamuscetto. The Turkish force, with all its supplies, munitions and material, was now on the very doorstep of San Angelo and Birgu.

Another departure was little noted, and went without gun salutes and fanfare. A small galley departed for Tripoli, bearing in a casket the corpse of Dragut Rais.

Nicholas slept a day and a night in the Sacred Infirmary, given drugged wine, barely conscious of the chaplain physicians ministering to him. When he came to, Smith and Hodge were by his bedside.

'You're …'

'Both still in the land of the living,' said Smith, a faint smile showing through his black beard. 'God wanted me here still.'

'Right as rain,' said Hodge equably. His arm was still in plaster.

'But what about—'

'He's fine,' said Smith gently. 'He needs a lot of rest. But he'll mend. He's made of ox leather and oakwood. Here' – he fumbled for something in his jerkin – 'you know that in the days of ancient Rome, a man who saved the life of a fellow citizen, such as Coriolanus, was crowned with the oak-leaf cluster. Well, I could find no oaks on this blasted island. So,' he tossed something into Nicholas's sheeted lap, 'I give you this.'

It was a lemon.

'I am honoured,' said Nicholas gravely.

'The honour, though, is all real,' said Smith, and he was serious again. 'You saved Stanley's life.'

'He wanted to remain at Elmo. To die there.'

'He was wrong. As was I. We are needed here.' He looked about the beautiful hall of the infirmary, but seeing things far off. 'Or we soon will be.'

Fra Reynaud said he could leave that evening.

'You had more than one interesting wound that could have killed or unlimbed you had it been half an inch different. That musket ball that ploughed across the back of your skull when you were swimming. Impressive. Perhaps you ducked just in time.'

Nicholas felt gingerly. There was a wide crust of scab across the back of his head.

'How you went on from there, I do not know. But I have seen many wounded men perform miracles of endurance. You are among them.'

He felt himself colouring with pride, and to cover it he asked, 'What else? My elbow?'

'Otherwise cuts and bruises. A wide cut to your flank that you probably never even noticed.'

He shook his head. 'No, I—'

'Sewn with six stitches and healing well. And your elbow, another very lucky strike indeed. Another half inch in and you'd have lost your arm. As it was, the ball took a flap of skin with it, a chip or two of bone, and drove another chip far under your skin as it passed. Still there.'

'Really?'

'Butcher surgeons always go digging around trying to get things out of a man's flesh,' said Fra Reynaud dryly. 'Often better to leave them in. Many's the time I've wrapped up a knight with a musket ball still in him. It does no harm. It's your bone, isn't it? It'll dissolve away eventually, I expect. No point digging you up and you losing more blood, is there?'

'But – it can strengthen a man to lose blood, can it not? Balance his humours? I thought Galen—'

'*Galen,*' said Fra Reynaud with a sudden flash in his eyes. '*Hippocrates.* Don't speak to me of the Greeks, the theory of humours, miasmas, all those notions of theirs.' He leaned close to the boy and whispered, as if passing on the direst heresy, 'All the best of the Hospitallers' knowledge of medicine, *we learnt from the Saracens.*'

Then he stood swiftly, appeared to give just the faintest wink, and departed.

'Fra Reynaud!' he called after him.

Reynaud stopped. 'I am busy, boy.'

'Just one thing. What is the date?'

He looked back. 'You have no idea?'

'None.'

'It is now the Eve of St John, the 23rd of June. Elmo that should have fallen after two or three days at most, stood for one day short of a month.' He smiled.

Nicholas's head sank back. Thirty days. Sweet Jesu, it felt like it.

He walked south through the narrow, deep-shadowed streets of the little town, and to the steps below the great curtain wall, three times the height of Elmo's defences. Vast quantities of earthen sacks, backed with huge timber props and well-placed stones, bulked up the walls from behind, so that even a direct hit with the biggest ball in the Ottoman artillery might be absorbed and do little damage. Such was the hope.

From the top of the walls, he greeted the soldiers there and they did not know he was from Elmo so he said nothing. Looking out towards the stony heights south, golden in the setting sun, he saw a horribly familiar sight. Great gun emplacements and platforms being erected, well shielded and protected, and the smaller guns being craned into place already. Between the guns and walls, ominous gouges and mean trenches beginning to run through the rocky ground, where the Turkish forward troops and the miners were creeping up to the base of Birgu's walls. Over before Senglea, it was just the same. They ran through the earth like the cracks of some slow motion, infinitely sinister earthquake.

That evening there washed up on the shores of Kalkara a horror unspeakable.

Word was sent to La Valette, and he came running down to the harbour wall. There floating below were three great crucifixes made from lashed spars, and tied to them in savage mockery of the Passion were the naked bodies of three Hospitallers from Elmo. They were headless, mutilated and degraded beyond recognition.

The people of the town looked down aghast at the nightmare

scene, their hearts chilled within them. Was this the fate that awaited them when the Turks came? Was this what they would do even to their children? What kind of an enemy were they facing? Even the warm and passionate blood of Malta ran cold. How could they fight such devils, and so many? Their faith faltered.

La Valette himself seemed frozen in horror for a moment. He was heard to mutter just two words under his breath. *'Christ re-crucified.'*

Then he gave angry orders that the foul flotsam should be brought up with all care and reverence, the bodies untied from the spars and washed and censed and prepared for burial. The spars should be burnt.

His white silent rage was terrible to behold. His lips worked as he watched the blue bodies carried away, signs of the cross carved into their bare chests with daggers.

Then he gave a further order. None dared to question it, for to do so was to break their vow of obedience, though it went against the old rules of chivalry. Some said that this was no longer a war that could be fought to the old rules of chivalry, and others said that without such rules to ennoble and purify it, the business of war was but the business of butchery, and there was no choosing between good and evil.

They brought up the eight Turkish prisoners that they had already captured in the last few days in sallies from Birgu, careless scouts, and one prospective miner who had foolishly been surveying the walls a little too close. They came up from the deep dungeons of San Angelo, blinking even in the dimming twilight. The guards led them in chains up to the gun platform and unchained and beheaded them, despite their pathetic last pleas, and then their still-turbanned heads were rammed into the mouths of the guns there and fired across the harbour towards the Turkish encampment.

Curious what this seemingly random cannon fire might be, the Turks sent down slaves to see, and minutes later they dredged from the waters of Marsa the eight tattered heads and brought them to Mustafa's pavilion. He set down his cup and nodded. He understood.

La Valette further ordered there to be no public display of grief for the fall of Elmo nor for the mutilation of these knights. 'Neither grief nor surrender,' he said harshly to the captains of the langues, his fists clenched on the tabletop.

Since all proceeded as appointed by Heaven, why should they grieve? Their brother knights had done their duty, they had fought most valiantly, and died in the service of Jesus Christ. Grief and tears were a womanish insult.

'Let the bodies be laid to rest with all due dignity,' he said. 'Then let us return to our posts, and be ready to fight and die as they did.'

2

The bodies of the unknown knights were placed in caskets and laid to rest in the crypt of the Conventual Church, to be properly buried at a later date. A less urgent time.

Meanwhile the Feast of St John the Baptist, the patron of the Order, proceeded with all due and solemn ceremony. No gunpowder was wasted in fireworks, but bonfires were lit and church bells pealed, and a general air of rejoicing began to fill the streets. For the Baptist had announced the coming of Christ, and with the coming of Christ they were saved.

Nicholas went out into the evening streets, wearing the fine sword of the Chevalier Bridier de la Gordcamp once more at his side, and gravely conscious of it. The little town was alive with light and life, and even though the vast Turkish encampment that now spread out threateningly across the whole of the heights of Santa Margherita was many times larger than Birgu and Senglea combined, and existed solely for the destruction of the town, hearing the distant shouts and sounds of rejoicing within the Turks must have wondered what these people under desperate siege were made of.

The Feast of St John, as La Valette intended, restored order and confidence after the horror of the crucified knights.

The indefatigable priest, Roberto di Eboli, preached a sermon to a packed town square, his voice even and resonant, his dark eyes burning with the faith, and his words put new strength into the people's hearts. He spoke of the loyalty unto death of the Baptist

327

himself, and of that evil eastern tyrant, Herod. He conjured for the illiterate people vivid images of how the Baptist had been captured by that accursed Oriental potentate, and mutilated and beheaded, and they felt how eerily full of meaning and symbol it all was, on the very night that the three crucified bodies had washed ashore from Elmo, similarly mutilated and killed by this new and godless eastern tyrant, Suleiman and his hordes.

Someone tapped Nicholas on the shoulder. He turned, a smile already spreading over his face, and there was Stanley. Pale and gaunt, but a bony, sinewy strength still in his tall broad frame. He was freshly bathed and his beard neatly shaven, and he wore the long black robe of the Hospitallers, emblazoned with a great white cross on the chest, that made him look startlingly like the monk he was. It seemed wrong to embrace a monk, so Nicholas seized his hand. Stanley clapped him on the back.

'My one regret,' he said, 'is that though I am told you saved my life, I have no recollection of any of it. By the way, Dragut is dead.'

Nicholas looked startled.

'His mortal remains gone to Africa, his soul down below. Apparently there was a hubbub at that battery on Is-Salvatur, as they tried to hit some impudent Christian swimmer crossing the harbour right under their noses. Dragut took charge, and in the haste their gun misfired and he was struck in the head by a piece of stone. He died soon after.'

Nicholas clenched his fists in front of him.

'It could be said,' Stanley whispered, 'that the swimmer killed him.'

'Well, I ...'

'But that seems an exaggeration, does it not?' His eyes twinkled. 'We should be listening to the words of Fra Roberto.'

Roberto di Eboli said, 'The martyrs of Elmo too were beheaded for their faith, crucified for their Lord, on the very Eve of St John. In everything there is a pattern, to those that see with their eyes unclouded, and understand with their hearts. In everything there is the Hand of God.'

He spoke of how the Baptist today sat at the right hand of God the Father himself, as you could see in many of the paintings in the churches, his lean figure and coarse camelhair garment unmistakable. And most inspiringly of all, he reminded the people on this lonely and beleaguered island that all of Christendom this night was celebrating the same Feast with them. From Norway to Spain, from Spain to the borders of Russia, their fellow Christians were lighting bonfires in the streets to celebrate the Baptist, patron of the Knights Hospitaller. Looking down from the walls of heaven tonight, the angels would see all of Christendom as nothing but a great starry floor of bright and burning bonfires.

A new fire was kindled in their hearts at that wonderful image. The people cheered, their dread and loneliness falling away, the sound of their cheering like the cannon's roar.

A French knight, the Chevalier St Aubin, out patrolling near the Barbary Coast, had tried to run the Turkish blockade recently and failed, and so fallen back after gallant engagement to harry the Turkish ships as best he could in a single galley. The Chevalier Romegas, too, still roamed the seas like a wolf.

So it was with surprise and delight that another Christian vessel managed to arrive in the Grand Harbour that night, flying the flag of St John. On board were a number of knights and soldiers come from Europe, including a young French knight, Henri Parisot, La Valette's own nephew.

'Reinforcements,' said the Grand Master. 'You are welcome, even at this late hour.'

To Sir Oliver Starkey he said privately, 'Ten thousand are needed, and some seventy have come. Yet we should welcome them with grace. They have come here to die for us.'

Early the next morning, La Valette called his closest to him: Smith and Stanley, the captains of the langues, Don Pedro Mezquita, and young Parisot. Nicholas was permitted too, but not to speak. It was hard when another figure entered the room: Marshal Copier, now one-legged, but supported on a very fine olivewood peg-leg. He eyed Nicholas, seeing the boy's pleasure at his appearance, and winked.

La Valette said it was as Mustafa Pasha had foreseen. 'Despite the great spirit and faith of our brother Roberto di Eboli,' said the Grand Master, 'and his picture of all Christendom standing shoulder-to-shoulder, worshipping as one – you know this is not so.'

'No relief is coming?' said Smith.

La Valette shook his head. 'Apart from the gallant few who sailed in last night – no relief is coming. Other kingdoms may burn bonfires like us, but they will send no ships. And we will hear from Venice sooner or later, I have no doubt, that the bankers who run that serene Republic' – his voice was corrosive with bitterness – 'ordered great celebrations when they heard of Elmo's fall. St Marks' Square will look like Carnival time.'

Nicholas looked baffled and agast.

Stanley said to him *sotto voce*, 'To assure the many Ottoman diplomats and spies in Venice that the Venetians value peace and trade with the Empire above all else, and have no love for the Knights of St John. They say we are no more than troublesome pirates, causing wars and ruining Mediterranean trade.'

Smith growled, 'A Venetian would sell his own daughter for a ducat.'

The stench of politics was worse than corpses under a midday sun.

'No, gentlemen.' La Valette spread his hands on the tabletop. 'We fight on alone, as God wills it. Dragut's ten thousand are now under Mustafa's command, of course, making a total still of at least thirty thousand in all. And there are the cut-throats of Candelissa and Hassan, itching to get into the city and loot and … worse. Remember that Hassan Ali is the son-in-law of Dragut himself. So for him, it will be vengeance. And for the Mohammedans of North Africa, to fight against Christendom is always vengeance for the loss of Spain. For seven centuries, their beloved Al-Andalus was their home, and then the Catholic Kings cast them out and they were exiled to the barren African shore. They became corsairs with all of Christendom theirs to sack, sailing out in their low galleys from their lairs at Tlemcen and Tenes, Bizerta and Susa, Djerbah and Monastir, to fill their pockets and honour Allah simultaneously. If they break into the town, it will be terrible.

'We lost nearly two hundred at Elmo, nothing to the Turks but a great deal to us. We are left with fighting men but two or three

330

thousand in number. You know I like precision, but do I count fourteen year old Maltese militia boys, armed with butcher's cleavers, protected by nothing more than jerkins wadded with sheep's wool?'

His face was heavy with care. The burden of responsibility, thought Nicholas, for the lives not only of his soldiers but of all the people of Malta, nursing mothers and eager ignorant boys and babes in cradles – it must be well-nigh more than any man could bear.

La Valette said, 'Elmo was a month of heroes, and sheer bloody attrition. Janizary faced knight across a single ditch, and both died. It was a simple affair. The siege of Birgu will be very different. More mobile and varied, fought over a much wider front, and I do not doubt that the wily dog Mustafa will try many tricks to break in on us. We have tricks prepared too. But – we also have women and children. It will be a very different battle in this never-ending war. And you will see not only your fellow knights and soldiers maimed and killed. Be ready for it.'

He gestured to his secretary, and Oliver Starkey spread a map over the table.

'We hold Birgu and Senglea, both promontories largely surrounded by water, and protected on the landward side by their curtain walls. The Turkish fleet still cannot sail into the Grand Harbour itself, or they will be blasted in pieces by the guns of San Angelo. I do not expect any attack over the water.'

'But then you should expect the unexpected,' said Mezquita, stroking his fine moustaches.

'Quite so. Every gun on the harbourside is primed and ready, manned day and night.'

'Senglea,' murmured Don Pedro, waving an aristocratic hand over the map, slender fingers gleaming with jewelled rings, raising his delicate eyebrows. His bloodline went back to the Visigothic kings, it was said, and even to the Spanish Emperor Hadrian. Yet he was a very fine soldier. 'Is it worth holding?'

The others could see what he meant. Birgu was a populous, tight-packed city, the beating heart of Malta. But the neighbouring promontory of Senglea was thinly inhabited, with a few mean houses and some creaking windmills, and the little fort of St Michel at its tip overlooking the harbour. To defend it was to stretch defensive lines thin indeed.

'You mean pull back, consolidate? Abandon Senglea, defend only Birgu? Yet you see that Senglea is already conjoined to Birgu in three ways, by the great chain across Galley Creek, by a pontoon bridge behind, and by an inner chain boom we have laid across as well.' La Valette's voice was steely. 'No. We surrender not one inch, no matter what the military textbooks and manuals might advise. As at Elmo, we give not a handful of dust away. The Turks must fight and bleed and die for every forward footstep.'

He indicated again. 'The Turkish main camp and field hospital remain at Marsa. The forward camp is here, on Santa Margherita, and their biggest guns. They have further gun emplacements on the Corradino Heights, on Mount Salvatore across Kalkara – very close indeed to your post, Don Pedro – and also on Gallows Point, and across at Sciberras, albeit at long range.'

'That is truly a ring of fire,' said Smith softly.

'The main attack will come from land, against our walls. And no matter how many tens of thousands Mustafa commands, only a wave of a thousand or so can attack at a time. They will also try to get miners in close as soon as possible – as they are already. They may attack across the creeks in small boats. They will try everything. But we will be prepared.'

They stood and shook hands.

'To your posts, gentlemen. And God go with you.'

After he had spoken with them, La Valette had a private matter to attend to, and he could not bear that any man should even know of it. He had assessed the amount of food left in the city, and it was not good news. There was no choice.

He buckled on his dagger, opened a door in the corner of the great state-room, and two lean and beautiful hunting dogs bounded out. They leapt at him with joyful little yaps, licking his hands in panting excitement. It had been so long since they had hunted out over the island. Surely today was the day. La Valette fondled their silken ears and they playfully bit his hands, their great jaws as gentle as a maiden's handshake.

Everything about a dog was noble. Its candour and affection, its love unto death, its freedom from words, and therefore from lies.

Dogs knew everything about loyalty and fidelity, the beauty of running with the wind, the joy of the world. And they knew nothing of princes and politics, bankers and gold, treachery and war. He embraced them around their powerful necks and lean ribbed sides in a manner that was strange to them, and gazed long at them, and they saw it in his eyes. They looked uncertain, crestfallen, knowing there was to be no hunt today. But there was something else. They snuffled at him pleadingly, tails curling between their legs. And when he came to lead them down the steep stone stairs to the cellar below – they followed him obediently, of course, to the very end – he had to go slowly, holding on to the rail, for his eyes were so blurred with tears.

3

'Can we truly defeat such an army?' asked Franco Briffa. 'We have seen the numbers of the Turks, and they are as numberless as the sands of the shore. Their guns are like dragons, a child could curl up and sleep in the mouth of one. Their trenches advance daily to our walls like snakes. We are so few, mere people of the land and the sea. You believe we can defeat them? You who survived Elmo?'

'Yes,' said Nicholas. 'Yes I do.'

But the boy looked away as he spoke and did not meet his eyes. And Franco Briffa knew he was lying to him, though it was a noble lie.

That night, Franco Briffa held his wife very close to him. In the morning, she watched him go over to the cradle and take up the bambino and hold the gurgling smiling infant very close to his chest, tears running down his face, and she went and held them both in a human trinity.

'When will they come?' people asked. 'When will the guns start to roar?'

They kept looking out to sea, for the sight of Spanish or Papal galleys. None came.

The waiting was terrible, and though the preaching of Roberto di Eboli had put fire in their hearts, yet it was beginning to die again. They were trapped in their little town, surrounded, and no one was coming to help. The villages beyond were laid waste and desolate, and the size and number of the Turkish guns, glimpsed from the walls, ranging up against them line on line, was truly terrifying. Elmo, that had seemed such a heroic tragedy lately, now seemed like the stirring up of a hornet's nest. There would be no mercy.

La Valette and the more experienced knights knew why the guns were still silent. It was not only them that would begin the battle. Mustafa was preparing other means. When it began, everything would come at once. And the three thousand fighting men, knights and soldiers, bakers and shoemakers and apprentice boys and urchins – they would not be enough.

It was to people's amazement then that news spread that Mustafa Pasha had sent a messenger to parley. He was proposing terms.

It was an old Greek slave who came and stood before the post of Provence, carrying a white banner. He was led to La Valette.

'Mustafa Pasha,' he stammered, 'Supreme Commander of the Ottoman Forces of Suleiman, Lord of the Universe, Possessor of Men's Necks, Viceroy of Allah, Master of the Two—'

'Suleiman's nicknames do not interest me,' cut in La Valette icily. 'What is your message?'

'My, my master,' faltered the poor Greek slave, as old as La Valette but a good deal more decayed, 'decrees that if you depart from this island as you once departed from Rhodes, without further resistance, you would be granted free and unmolested passage to Sicily. Not a shot will be fired, not a man, woman nor child harmed.'

'Let the people know this for certain,' said La Valette, turning sharply to Oliver Starkey. 'The Turks want terms. It means they fear they may not be able to beat us. Let the town know. Let it put the fire back in their hearts.' He snapped back to the slave. 'And if we do not depart from this our island, gifted to us by the Emperor Charles himself?'

The slave looked anxious in the extreme. 'Then, then your fate will be that of your slaughtered comrades at Elmo, now,' he gulped, 'now in the hell of the Unbelievers.'

La Valette towered over him. 'Where?'

'In the hell,' he stammered, 'of, of —'

'You say that our Christian brothers burn in hell?'

The old wretch fell to his knees, whimpering and cowering, well used to heavy blows. 'Not I, master, I beg you, not I, I but carry the message ...'

La Valette turned from him in disgust. A man whose spirit had leached away with his youth.

'And then what?' he murmured, more to himself than the slave. 'The Turks will come on to Sicily soon enough, and then that island too will be a part of the Caliphate. As Rhodes is now.' He turned back. 'And then Rome, yes? Venice, and Genoa, and Marseilles, and inland, all of Western Europe. Another army will swarm over the Danube frontier, and all of Christendom will be a part of the Empire of Islam, and Christians once more reduced to servile *dhimmi* status, taxed and spat on and beaten in the streets, as Jews and Christians are today throughout the East.' His voice trembled. 'Where then will we go with our Bible and our Cross? Will the Turk gracefully allow us to depart for the New World, do you think? Or perhaps the Moon?'

The slave trembled and said nothing.

'I reject the offer of Mustafa Pasha,' said La Valette. 'Here we take our stand. On this bare rock.' He tapped the stone flag with his foot. 'Here.' He flicked his fingers at a soldier. 'Take him away and hang him.'

'No, master, mercy!' cried the old wretch.

Even the soldier hesitated. It was a cruel order.

La Valette considered, his thoughts dark and labyrinthine, comprehending the power of every threat and counter threat, every gesture, small and great, and above all, the desperate straits of Malta.

'Bandage his eyes and lead him back to the Gate of Provence,' he said. 'Take him up on the walls. I will follow.'

The old slave was dragged back to the walls and held at the very tottering edge, in sight of the Turks, and the bandage torn away. He stared down into the deep ditch far below.

'Mark it well,' said La Valette.

The old man looked up the Grand Master with his wrinkled toothless mouth agape, and then down again into the ditch.

'The Turks will never take this place,' said La Valette. He fixed his ice blue eyes on the shaking slave, gripped by the arms between the two soldiers. 'Return to Mustafa and say this. Tell him he may have possession of the ditch below, with our most heartfelt blessing, to lay the dead bodies of his Janizaries in. Beyond that – he will have nothing.'

The slave went back to the Ottoman camp, walking awkwardly, for he had dirtied his breeches.

Mustafa's anger would be terrible. But not so terrible as the ice blue eyes and the even voice of that Grand Master. A sincere madness burned in him.

Mustafa heard, rolled up a map, looked out of the door of his pavilion and said, 'When we capture Birgu and Senglea, every man, woman and child there will die. La Valette has sentenced them to death.'

Among the townspeople there was murmuring and lamenting, but no revolt. They had always been governed by distant aristocrats, Maltese and Spanish and now Hospitaller. And the Grand Master had now decreed that they must fight.

With all their ancient peasant fatalism they sighed, 'So be it,' and set to sharpening their billhooks and scythes.

Out across the island, over the arid plateau, in the coastal ravines and in the shadows of the devastated and fire-blackened villages, the people of Birgu heard rumours that their brothers were already waging war. The magical, talismanic name of Tonio Bajada, folk hero to some, bandit to others, was leading a group of partisans, harrying the Turkish patrols wherever they could. Rumour said that another band of partisans had caught one Turk, isolated from his squad, cut off his head and replaced it with that of a pig. They had left him sitting up against a dry stone wall for his comrades to find. Minutes later the Turkish patrol came by, and their howls of execration were a delight to the ear.

In another village, still sparsely inhabited, they caught an Italian renegade who was working for the Turks, keeping lookout on the headland. They tied him to the tail of a mule, and some children beat him to death with sticks. Even as he lay dying in a pool of his own blood, he told them, 'If not today, tomorrow will be your last.'

'Yah! Yah! Yah!' the children sang round him.

'This will be a most brutal encounter,' said Franco Briffa, head

337

bowed. 'I will kill Turks with my bare hands if I have to. They have come to my island, I did not invite them, and they have come bearing arms. Yet already my islanders are turning brutal, recounting such tales with glee, of pigs' heads, and desecrations, and child executioners. Already my friend, the bastard Anton Zahra, talks of how he is longing to take Mohammedan scalps, and show them to his grandchildren one day. Even if we do survive' – he looked up and fixed his eyes hard on Nicholas – 'like any who engage in killing, we will leave something of our Christian souls behind us. In ashes and tatters.'

La Valette had been uncharacteristically hesitant about giving another defensive order, in case it struck dread into the people. But then he decided it must be done, and he ordered all streets nearest to the landwalls to be barricaded at regular intervals, and cul-de-sacs formed as entrapments. The people understood immediately what it implied. The Grand Master and the knights were expecting the Turks to break in through the walls soon enough, and desperate hand-to-hand fighting to take place in every street.

They did not lose heart. Nicholas and Hodge watched, deeply moved, as the people of this poorest, most barren of islands dragged forth from their houses what little furniture and possessions they had, chairs and tables and ancient linen chests, smashing some of them into spars and timbers. Then they nailed them up into makeshift fencing, preceded by sets of three or four spars lashed together in the centre with strong rope to form a kind of jack or caltrop, of the kind used to trip up horses in former times. Some even took picks and poleaxes to their own outhouses and piggeries and stableblocks, and dragged the stones into the street to make further barricades. They created narrowing funnels into squares and courtyards without exits. They worked through the heat of the midday sun, half naked and sweating, coughing, plastered in dust, without one murmur of complaint.

Knights watched them at these peasant labours, and said among themselves that these low-born people over whom they had haughtily ruled for decades, barely noticing them, were in some ways as brave as crusaders. They began to say that it would be an honour to fight for them.

338

'To fight with them, you mean,' said Stanley. 'To fight alongside them.'

Nicholas was in the courtyard, sewing up his battered leather jerkin. He glanced up and there was Maddalena standing before him, her hands folded. She was annoyed that he had not paid her more attention.

'In my country,' she said, 'girls must insult the boys they like very strongly. It is a custom.'

He looked down again at his work. 'Flirting, we call that,' he said. 'The village girls do that in my country too.'

'The more they like him, the more they must insult him. In the street, before all his friends. Especially the boy they would like to marry.'

'So what would you say to me?'

She clapped her hands. At last she had his attention. 'I would say you are puny and feeble, and as thin as an anchovy!'

'Thank you.'

She giggled, the tip of her tongue between her teeth. 'Your clothes are dusty and torn like the clothes of a vagabond—'

'I *am* a vagabond.'

'And your nose is red because of the sun, and peeling like the bark of a sickly tree – but otherwise your fair skin is pale like a woman's. Like a spoilt princess's in a palace.'

'Hm.'

'And also your nose has a white scar down the side, where the Turks slit it when you were captured. And you have bruises all over you and scars like an old fighting dog.'

He looked up. 'But that means I'm brave, doesn't it?'

'In my country, it is not the custom for a girl to say nice things to the boy she likes. We should be cold and haughty, and throw insults in his face, to test him.'

He tried to take her by the hand, but she slipped away and twirled, laughing again. *Flirting.*

'When a girl insults a boy like this,' she said, gesturing dramatically, 'if he becomes indignant and angry and sulks, then we know he is a weak man, with the heart of a little boy still. A real man will just laugh at the insulting. He will toss back his head, and put his hands on his hips like this' – she tossed back her long hair which she knew to be so lovely, and imitated what she thought was a manly stance – 'and he will laugh aloud. Because a real man has greater things to become angry about. We say, *an eagle does not catch flies.* A real man does not trouble himself with petty things.'

'Such as what women say to him.'

'You are wicked!'

He laughed. She wanted to kiss him again. He was an eagle. But her mother came with the washing, and they looked away from each other with faces lowered, and did not see her mother suppress a smile as she reached down into her basket.

'Nicholas,' said Maria, 'go and find the boys. They are playing out in the street somewhere. It is time to eat soon.'

Nicholas found Mateo and Tito play-fighting in the dust, rolling into a pyramid of small cannonballs, and yelled out to them. One of them had a little dagger, and when Nicholas yelled out, he cut his brother on the arm and the other boy howled. Nicholas seized them both by the scruff of their tattered shirts and dragged them to their feet. He kicked the wicked little dagger from the first's hand, none too gently, and trod on it.

Tito nursed his cut arm.

'Little idiots,' rasped Nicholas. 'You think the medical chaplains haven't enough to do without stitching up urchins like you?'

He grabbed Tito's thin arm and examined it. It could have been worse. 'Now home and ask your mother to douse it in vinegar,' he said.

'Will it hurt?' said Tito, looking up at him wide-eyed.

'Like hell,' said Nicholas unsympathetically.

'Will I die?'

'One day.'

'But we are going to have to fight, aren't we?' said Mateo.

'No you are not.'

'We are. We are too few. Or we will be made slaves in Algiers, and I have heard stories of that.'

Not as bad as the truth, Nicholas hoped. Stories of boys as young as these two, held in the boy brothels of that fetid pirate port, their arms and legs amputated, for the sick pleasures of their captors.

Boys held in Istanbul in 'peg-brothels', waiting for their customers, seated naked on wooden pegs for ... ease of access.

'Come home,' he said.

'Can I have my knife back?'

He kicked it over to him.

Mateo said, 'I'll need it when the Turks come.'

'Home,' he said again wearily. 'And stay home.'

After supper Nicholas went up onto the walls again, and found Smith and Stanley beside the Post of Germany. They were listening to the Turks singing and chanting in the forward camp, not four hundred yards off. They could have tried firing cannonballs into them from the bastions even now, but La Valette had said hold. Time enough to fire when they came.

'They are singing like they sung before Elmo,' said Nicholas. 'The night before they attacked.'

Smith nodded. 'It will start very soon.'

The voices of the imams rose and fell, the guttural flowing Arabic phrases for the ninety-nine names of God. The stars shining, the fires burning. It had a strange beauty.

Later Nicholas heard a faint lone voice in a forward trench, and to his surprise, almost amusement, the sound of a stringed instrument. Some homesick soldier singing an old song.

'A poem by Ibn Zaydun,' murmured Stanley. 'A poet of Moorish Andaluz, centuries ago.' Nicholas looked at him startled, but he did not explain further. Rather he translated.

'Two secrets in the heart of Night
We lay, until the light
Of interfering Day
Gave both of us away.'

Smith harrumphed, but Stanley's expression was distant.

'Aye,' he said softly, head tilted back against the low ramparts, eyes half closed. 'They are men much like us. They bleed red when cut, they grieve to grow older, they sing verses, they fall in love ... Hard it is to fight them, when you understand this much.'

4

It was as an hour before dawn, only four or five hours after midnight, when Mustafa first unleashed hell.

The biggest Turkish guns, the bronze basilisks, had not been used on Elmo. They were not needed, and they consumed gunpowder with a gargantuan appetite. But they were used now.

They could hear the rumble of gunfire in Syracuse and Catania, one hundred and twenty miles to the north. It seemed like the whole world was trembling. Fourteen batteries of sixty-four guns opened up simultaneously, along with four monstrous basilisks each firing a ball weighing a scarcely believable two hundred pounds. They had reduced the Walls of Theodosius, that defended Constantinople for a thousand years. It was foolish to think they might be held back by the small walls of Birgu.

Yet the blood of Elmo had bought the defenders so much precious time, an entire month, that these modest curtain walls were now massively reinforced along their entire length. Mustafa had no doubt that his basilisks would soon bring them crumbling to the earth. But La Valette, ceaselessly walking on his rounds of inspection, instilled confidence in every defender's heart.

'Let the Turkish guns fire,' he said. 'Our walls can take it.'

Mustafa also had the master gunners of the leaner, longer-range culverins triangulate their guns to fire clean over the top and hit the town itself at random.

'Churches, fine houses, knightly auberges, paupers' hovels, dog kennels!' he said. 'Flatten them all!'

And from the forward trenches came the muffled thunk of

fat-bellied mortars, belching out coarse-shaped, short trajectory missiles high into the air, crashing to land with equal, random destruction.

Cannonballs from the culverins bounced clear down narrow streets until they smashed into low walls, demolishing mean house-fronts in seconds. Pigs squealed, geese honked and raised their wings, a barrel of wine burst open on a cart and flooded a street claret-red, the cart exploding in splinters. The pigs twirled their tails and drank the spilled wine, then ran off screaming down the street as another ball crashed into a nearby well and destroyed it.

Women and children gathered at the base of the shuddering walls, handing up stones in lines to continue the bulking. La Valette ordered the rest of Birgu's Mohammedan prisoners up from the dungeons of Angelo, to work on the most exposed parts of the walls at the end of a whip. Messages were sent back from the Turkish trenches to tell Mustafa. He dismissed the news with a single wave of his hand, and told them to keep firing. It was war. Men died.

In desperation, two of the Turkish captives were seen to raise their still-manacled hands, loosened only enough to let them lift rocks, and cry out the ancient formula of Muslim belief, the Shahada, *Lâ ilâha illallâh, Muhammadu rasûlullâh!* to show that they were brothers in the faith. But a work-gang of Maltese women heard them and believing that they were crying out secrets to the enemy, reacted in fury. Like maddened bacchantes, throwing back the veils in which they worked even now, and hitching up their long black skirts, they clawed their way up the wreckage of rubble and scaffolding to where the two unfortunates stood, and dragged them down to the square below. There they beat them to death with fistfuls of rocks. Children beat their bloody corpses afterwards with canes, and a wandering madman thrust sharp wooden sticks into their mouths and drove them hard down into the back of their throats to stop their traitorous speech.

It was a cruel fate that the culverins kept succeeding in hitting the Sacred Infirmary, which soon threatened to be rendered a bloody chaos. Panicked medical brothers hurried to and fro bearing bowls of water, bandages, flasks of turpentine, tripping, slithering and yelling out. One of them already wore his own wounded arm in

343

a sling. But among them strode the tall, imperturbable figure of Fra Reynaud, determined that through sheer willpower, the chaos should not take hold. He forbad a single brother to raise his voice, though the wounded being stretchered in through the door in a stream made noise enough. Groans and screams rose to the high rafters.

Explosion followed explosion, almost as if the Turks knew where the infirmary was in the town and were targeting it deliberately. Jars of precious ointments trembled and jerked off the shelves, smashing to the ground, until Reynaud ordered all breakables stored on the flagstone floors, wadded with whatever they could find. Supplies were low enough, they could not afford to lose more. Then began the grim business of triage, moving from bed to bed, each already occupied by a dying man, determining who might be saved and who was already lost. A chaplain followed in Reynaud's wake, administering Last Rites to those deemed beyond help. Dust cascaded down from the ceiling, already zigzagged with cracks, settling on bloody wounds, helping them clot. A woman screamed. She had gone into labour early, having seen her husband killed in front of her.

'A wall is down on Senglea!' someone cried. 'The wall over French Creek, opposite Corradino!'

'Rubbish,' Reynaud said evenly, never lifting his head, attention fixed on the scalpel in his hand and the dying knight beneath. 'Hysterical rumour. And do not raise your voice, Brother.'

The knight's belly was ruptured within by shrapnel from a devilish exploding ball. Reynaud placed his fingers on the knight's sternum and sliced quickly downward through the skin and muscle layer as far as the umbilicus. He carefully opened the cut. The belly's organs were further encased in a translucent layer called the peritoneum, and now beneath it he could see the welling blue-black shadow of the blood that filled his abdomen. Cut open the peritoneum and that blood would flood out like water from an overfilled bucket. And a good operation should lose your patient no more than four ounces of blood. The knight was wounded deep in the spleen or liver or both.

Sweat dripped from the chaplain's face onto his hands. He drew the cut to and sat back and covered the man's belly with a cloth that seeped red instantly.

'In the name of Christ,' he said gently, 'your time here is done.'

The knight closed his eyes. 'I am glad of it, Brother.' A minute later he died.

Reynaud stood. 'Carry him out. Then see to that man there. And do not be too tight with the tourniquet. Enough to give the blood time to clot, that is all. Apply egg white, and bring me more alcohol. Now, Brother. This will hurt. Bite down. The stick is soaked in Alicante wine, so savour it.'

As the day went on, the medical chaplains began to see more and more burns victims. Burn wounds were the worst, the skin falling away like the skin of rotted fruit, flesh slithering off the bone, and the smell horribly like cooked meat. It had been a long time since Fra Reynaud had been able to eat roast pork. Fires raged from Ottoman incendiaries, firebombs, even mortar balls evilly laced with Greek fire that erupted in great clouds of inextinguishable flame as they struck home.

Reynaud called for more precious ointment of aloe and onion to reduce burns and blistering, and for an amputation, a caudle of alcohol, opium and hemlock. He sawed fast through a man's leg bone, cut away the muscle and fat to leave a bone stump but with plenty of loose skin, applied a styptic, and tied up the skin and laid over it a wet ox bladder which would shrink as it dried. The fellow would probably live, though he'd be unlikely to run again.

He called for a count of how many ounces of opium remained to them. The count was not good, but his face remained impassive. He also demanded regular reports from the walls, and his firm, clear voice rang out across the infirmary ward at intervals.

'The walls are still holding well! This town has not gone the way of Jericho just yet! So work on, Brothers, work on, and keep a steady hand.'

Word went round that a deserter from the Ottoman camp had revealed Mustafa's terrifying intentions: not to enslave, but to slay every living thing within the town – every man, woman and child, every dog and chicken – except La Valette. He would be taken in chains before the Grand Sultan himself, and tortured to death at his pleasure.

Hearing that they were under sentence of death only steeled this steely people further.

La Valette vowed publicly that he would never be taken alive. 'Though I plan to take some considerable killing.'

Such grim humour and granite resolution were much to Maltese taste. They began to say that this Grand Master of the Knights was not all bad.

'Perhaps,' said Franco Briffa, 'he is the kind of cold-eyed bastard you want in command, during a little crisis like this.'

'This deserter from the Ottoman camp,' queried Smith. 'Deserting already? Seems unlikely.'

'It does,' agreed Stanley.

'Has anyone *seen* this deserter? How did he enter the town? What is his name? His reasons?'

'Brother John,' said Stanley, his ingenuous blue eyes wide with shock. 'Surely you are not suggesting that there *is* no such deserter, and that this reported sentence of death we are all under, knights and citizens both, is merely a rumour circulated by the Grand Master himself, to put more strength in our backbones?'

Smith grimaced.

Stanley laughed.

Darkness falling on the second day revealed a new front of attack, and it seemed momentarily to strike dismay into even the heart of La Valette. It was a front he had truly not foreseen.

The Turks had observed that while the walls of Birgu still remained steadfast, cracked and battered but far from fallen, the walls of Senglea over French Creek were indeed beginning to crumble. They would be coming in over the water after all.

From the Turkish main camp over at Marsa arose vast sounds of shouting and rumbling, a great weight being hauled over the stony ground. And then across the harbour, the besieged saw trains of oxen, horses and mules, and hundreds, even thousands, of naked men, sweating in the flickering orange torchlight, men and beasts all alike under the lash, whipped onward, dragging behind them over the hill some mighty load. Finally their burden appeared, little by little. A beaked prow rose up into the starlit sky, high over the hill and then tipped down again. The dark hull of a galley, dragged along on greased timber rollers. They were dragging their boats overland from Marsamuscetto, directly into the Grand Harbour, evading the guns of San Angelo altogether. Then they could row out from the Marsa and attack Senglea and Birgu unopposed.

Flanking them marched hundreds of Janizaries, resplendent in damask and gold and silver, scimitars encrusted with semi-precious gems, beads of coloured glass and turkey-stone, muskets superbly damascened, and carrying high above their heads green banners embroidered with the sacred letter *Aleph*.

They were to attack on two sides at once. From land and sea.

La Valette clenched his jaw and called himself a fool. At his age. There was only one way into the harbour? But no, boats could always be carried overland, with enough manpower and determination. Had the Turks not done the same at Constantinople, a hundred years ago?

It was then that La Valette showed what a commander can be. His moment of paralysed shock lasted no longer than a bird's call. *'Hit back, hit back,'* he muttered to himself. *'Every time, in every place, hit back.'*

Then he rapped out his orders.

'Mezquita to assemble a cavalry column with grenades! Ride out on the guns of Santa Margherita. The citizens to make up a volunteer force of the best swimmers, to cross the harbour under cover of night, and harry the Turkish column coming over with the boats. We will not sit and wait for them. We will attack on all fronts!'

The gates of the post of Provence thudded open and Don Pedro de Mezquita with forty armoured knights rode out at full gallop, swords raised over their heads. The Turkish gunners gaped. So confident had they been, so unsuspecting of anything so crazed as a counter-attack by the vastly outnumbered defenders, that they hadn't even any armed infantrymen around to protect them.

The knights were upon them in a moment. Many fled in the darkness, and many more were cut down by the scything blades of the furious cavalry charge. Gunners collapsed back against their own guns, feeling the heat of the massive brazen barrel burning through their robes, as huge half-armoured chargers reared terrifyingly above, and long cavalry swords drove into them. Other cavalry men milled about before the guns and tossed grenades with smouldering fuses into the barrels. One or two even dismounted and began to pack the guns with all the powder they could find, while others wedged great rocks into the muzzles and hammered them home with mallets.

Don Mezquita himself had galloped up high onto Santa Margherita's top, alone and exposed, to keep lookout.

'Remount NOW!' he cried, galloping back.

A large column of well-armed Ottoman musketeers was already swarming out towards them, the glow of their matchlock ropes like dancing fireflies in the dark.

A young knight – it was Henri Parisot himself, La Valette's nephew – hurriedly lit the fuse at a gun's breech. He then hauled himself up onto the gun barrel itself, about to explode, using it as a mounting block to get back on his horse.

'A somewhat risky manoeuvre!' called Don Pedro. 'I advise you to trot away quite briskly from that gun now.'

The young knight spurred furiously and the horse veered sharply away just as the gun exploded. The great bronze barrel reared and then slewed hard to the right, spewing up dust and stones over the fleeing Parisot. When it had settled again, a black hairline crack had appeared along its side. Other grenades were detonating in the barrels with muffled booms, and then came a more ominous volleying crackle of musketry behind them, not three hundred yards off. All ducked in their saddles.

'Open the gates!' yelled Mezquita.

He needed to give no order to his cavaliers. They galloped back down from Santa Margherita in a cloud of dust and even as the gates were slammed shut behind them, the wood splintered with the incoming musket fire.

They dismounted and celebrated wildly in the street. Not a man was hurt. They must have slain forty or more trained gunners. As to how many Turkish guns they had successfully spiked, it was not certain. Perhaps no more than three or four. But the effect on the spirits of both besiegers and besieged was invaluable.

When they next looked out, the guns were being rapidly checked, or withdrawn to the armouries at the main camp for repair, and a

sizeable detachment of well-armed infantrymen was now perman-
ently stationed on Santa Margherita.

Any further cavalry sorties would be purely self-sacrificial.

The native Maltese volunteers knew exactly where to swim across
the harbour, but they were few in number, just eight men, since so
few of Malta's fishermen had that strange art of moving through
water like a fish. Those that could came up silent and dripping from
the still water, daggers between their teeth, unseen and unheard by
the enemy.

How many of the Turks hauling the boats they fell on and slew
before they themselves were killed was never known. None of
those men ever returned. It was a suicide mission. But for a while,
from the tower of San Angelo where he kept watch in hawk-like
vigil over the unfolding siege, La Valette could see clearly that the
ominous procession of hauled galleys had slowed and stopped,
and the column of orderly marching Janizaries broke into panic as
they came under ferocious and unexpected attack from maddened
knifemen, vaulting out of the dark from behind the heaped rocks.

Again, the moral effect of such an attack was considerable. The
Turks had now been twice surprised and dismayed by the defenders' aggression. Not for one second, though they were a force of
many thousands, would they be safe from these Christian wolves,
pouncing out of the night and falling on them with cold bloodlust,
as careless of death as their own Janizaries.

The Grand Master said to Sir Oliver Starkey, 'They were brave
men.'

'Sire? You mean – the natives?'

'I do.'

'The poor, low-born, barefoot, ragged-trousered native militia?'

La Valette looked at him. Starkey was making a mocking point.
'I concede it,' he said at last. 'They fought and, I think, died, as
bravely as any high-born knight of Europe. This peasantry that we
rule over here – sullen, uncommunicative, dirty, dishonest, super-
stitious, forever quarrelling and fornicating among themselves as
they are – I am beginning to think that they are not all bad.'

Starkey smiled to himself. From La Valette, it was high praise
indeed.

But there could be no extended rejoicing or self-congratulation. Despite the defenders' gallant sacrifices, by the following afternoon the Turks had thirty or forty lean galleys jostling together at the far western end of the harbour, well out of reach of the guns of San Angelo.

La Valette ordered the post of Senglea to ready themselves. He sent reinforcements across the pontoon bridge of boats behind the great chain, though only a hundred. No more could be spared. They were to hold out in St Michel, Senglea's tiny fort. Marshal Copier commanded, and among the reinforcements went Henri Parisot and Nicholas.

'If the pontoon falls,' said Nicholas, 'I can swim back again.'

Parisot grinned. 'You seem to like being at the heart of things.'

5

At dawn they heard the sound of drums across the still water. Nicholas awoke in a panic before understanding where he was, and threw off his blanket. He had been dreaming he was trapped at Elmo, but with his sisters.

There was a thick summer mist on the water. But the drums meant one thing only. The galleys were coming.

They crept down below the walls of Senglea and took cover, hiding behind the shoreline rocks, old timbers, even upturned fishing boats. And there they waited, breathless, hearts thumping in time to the Turkish drums. Nicholas clutched his sword, and thanked Christ that, exhausted though they were, they had worked all night under cover of darkness to build the primitive, bristling new defence in front of them.

For with the precious few hours they had, the defenders of Senglea had improvised a spiked palisade, some five yards out in the water, made up of roped and nailed staves joined to deep-sunk piers and ships' masts, further reinforced with anchors and chains. It didn't look like much, a messy assemblage, but it would halt the Turkish galleys offshore, and mean they could not leap onto land and start fighting. They would have to swim in. Then the defenders would attack.

He felt cold. That was impossible. The sun was already burning off the mist, the July Mediterranean sun. Or was it August now? Soon it would be as hot as a blacksmith's forge. He straightened his helmet. His face ran with sweat and still he shivered. He knew once the fighting started, he would change. He would become a different person, and fear would give way to fury. He wished Stanley and Smith were here, but he had volunteered. They were needed on Birgu's walls. The sound of the drums came nearer, and through the thinning fog, he could now make out the dark, drifting shadows of the approaching galleys, hear the soft dip and drip of the oars.

Then the relentless barrage of guns started up again from the heights of Santa Margherita behind them, hitting beleaguered Birgu, and Nicholas saw the very surface of the water in the harbour tremble at that monstrous sound, like water in a cup. The guns drowned out the soft noise of the approaching galleys, and the barrage continued as the deafening background music throughout the chaotic fighting of the next hour.

The Turkish galleys surged forward at ramming speed, appearing suddenly very stark and clear out of the last veils of mist, and crashed hard into the spiked palisade amid a furious exchange of gunfire from the galleys and the walls behind. Yet the vessels could not crash through the barrier, and were now dangerously held and exposed, when their whole plan had depended upon being able to slip in fast, scale the walls and attack.

The defenders rose up from their cover and those that had arquebuses fired a murderous close-range volley, and then all gave a cry and waded out to the palisade.

The Turks saw immediately that they must attack with all force or back-row in dismal retreat, and with their characteristic bravery and zeal, they attacked. Janizaries stood and stripped almost naked, realizing their fine robes would only be a hindrance, while light-clad marines and grinning Barbary corsairs, well used to such fighting, plunged off the sides of the galleys and swam up to seize hold of the palisade, trying to haul themselves up and over. But the defenders were already out there, the palisade their defensive wall, to which they clung like monkeys in a tree. Guns were useless in the watery, close-packed mêlée. It was sodden and bloody fighting, hatchet and club, dagger and sword.

Some Turks tried to swim around the palisade underwater, but were clearly visible from the walls of St Michel above, and shot in the back as they swam. They turned over, the air stopped in their lungs, and floated dead in spirals and coils of their own dilute blood.

Others came with hatchets and hacked busily at the ships' ropes that held the rough palisade together. There came a single cannon shot from the Corradino heights beyond, perhaps trying to show support and hit Fort St Michel, but it misfired badly and hit one of the Turkish galleys. By double misfortune it ruptured the galley's powder store, and the entire sixty-foot vessel reared up like a mule as its stern was blown apart like a black exploding star. Some men closest were deafened for life, staring around open-mouthed and dazed in the soot-laden air, treading water, until the splintered timbers began to rain down about them, some big enough to brain a man.

Nicholas squatted on a cross-bar of the palisade and clung left-handed to a well-roped stave, the sword of Bridier de la Gordcamp in his right. He saw a shaven-headed corsair, a gold ring in his nose, make for the ropes with a hatchet, and swung ape-like down on top of him, driving the sword through the back of his neck. The fellow turned in the water, even as he was dying, and struck out with the hatchet. Nicholas blocked it with his left arm and fell into the water beside him. He came up spluttering and the fellow was dead, his hatchet turning and sinking slowly to the bottom of the creek. Nicholas tried to haul himself back onto the parapet but a very fat Turk, as at home in the water as a whale, dragged at his legs and tried to drown him. He revolved underwater, refusing to panic, sword still in his hand, and drove it long into the Turk's broad belly, a white bloodless mound seen underwater. The gush of blood and matter was horrendous, and Nicholas erupted out of the water gagging and spitting, hurriedly clambering back onto the palisade, shaking with disgust. The slaughtered Turk floated just below him, obscenely ripped, eyes open.

All along the length of the palisade it was the same grim tale of stabbing, hacking, splashing, floundering, screaming, drowning, the once crystal-clear blue water now pink and foaming, the galleys crowded and bumping helplessly behind. The Turkish attack on Senglea had stalled.

In his pavilion, Mustafa heard of Mezquita's cavalry sortie and of the palisade and the stalled attack on Senglea in almost the same instant. Only moments later, another obsequious and trembling messenger came to tell him that one of the four biggest basilisks on Margherita had exploded, killing the entire gun team of master and eighteen men. Evidently it had been damaged by the Christians, but the master had not realised, nor seen the damage before reloading and firing.

Mustafa's mouth worked furiously beneath his moustache. The days went by, the guns roared on, from the heights of Sciberras and Corradino lookouts reported that Birgu appeared to have been half demolished already. And still the Christians fought back unrelentingly, with one trick and ruse after another. There was even some roving regiment of boy slingers working on the walls of the town. In the name of Shaitan and all his devils.

In his dreams now, Mustafa saw himself receiving from the Sublime Porte the silent but eloquent gift of the Black Kaftan. The Sultan's way of saying that he was relieved of his command, and must return immediately to Stamboul, where worse might await him.

'Ready the Janizaries for the frontal assault,' he snapped.

'Honoured Pasha,' said Işak Agha, 'the main walls of Birgu, though ruptured and part-fallen, still present a formidable obstacle. The townspeople within must be helping, they rebuild them all the time, as fast as we—'

'Do not insult me with your objections. Ready them. What of the mining engineers?'

'They dig through solid rock. It is slow. They work day and night.'

'Tell them to work harder. Tell them the walls of Birgu must fall soon.'

A curved Ottoman horn sounded across the waters before Senglea, and some of the attackers fell back and swam to the galleys, leaving the left-hand section of the palisade unmanned. The defenders were barely aware of what happened or why, as they moved along to help their struggling comrades further down, where the attack still came on thick and fast. They fought desperately, vastly outnumbered but with the single advantage of defence, holding their position with bitter determination, clinging exhausted and soaked to sodden timbers, eyes half blinded with sun and salt and sweat, flesh turning white and ridged in the water. Wave after wave of corsairs continued to come at them.

Then bow guns roared from the galleys not fifty yards off, a dozen guns in grim unison, all aimed at that unmanned section, some of them so skilfully levelled that their shots were perfect *tiro di ficco*, the Portuguese speciality denoting a ball that bounced shallow over the water and hit the hull of a boat low and hard, with devastating effect. Now it did the same to the wooden palisade. It was a cunningly judged manoeuvre. Iron balls passed over the water faster than the eye could see, left a single slash of white foam across the surface, and then the hastily improvised spars and staves of the barricade were smashed in pieces, flying into the air, a hail of splinters, long timbers wheeling and turning and falling, the defence in ruins.

Nicholas clutched an upright pier, shuddering under the impact, and glanced round in dismay, hair plastered to his cheek. He understood at once. The palisades had been smashed down just below the most damaged section of Senglea's walls.

The galley drums beat, the slaves heaved under the lash, the oars creaked against the roped tholes. Gunners rammed fresh powder and ball into the muzzles. Even in the few moments it would take to cross the water, they could loose another volley.

Firing as they came, demolishing the very last of the palisade that held them back, or even firing directly into the walls of Senglea, the low galleys surged forward. The corsairs attacking the rest of the palisade fought with renewed ferocity, hacking and slashing blindly. The last surviving defenders gulped deep breaths and hurled themselves from the tottering barrier into the water. Formation lost, many more were killed as they fled. It was impossible to get back onshore fast, even though it was but five yards behind. There were too many dead bodies, thickly strewn. The once clear sea was a swamp of saltwater and blood and corpses, already softening and bloating under the sun.

The bedraggled remnant crawled out onto the narrow stretch beneath the walls, smashed and jagged behind them like the teeth of some aged giant. Nicholas was one of the very few young enough, with enough strength remaining in his aching limbs, to haul and clamber up the walls into Senglea. Clutching the great sandstone blocks, his skin cracked and stinging with salt, he wondered if he had been wounded anywhere. He paused to glance back, vaguely conscious of random arrows clacking into the stones around him. Only twenty feet below, corsairs were seizing kneeling men by the hair, pulling back their heads and cutting their throats. He flopped over the wall and fell at the feet of an armoured soldier who shoved a half-pike under his chin.

'For God and Sant'Iago,' he gasped.

One hundred and twenty fresh fighting men from each galley leapt directly onto the collapsed rubble of Senglea's wall further along, and stormed into the little settlement.

A beacon fire was lit on the bastion of St Michel, and La Valette ordered axemen on the Birgu side to be ready to destroy the pontoon bridge that crossed Galley Creek.

'Senglea will soon be lost,' he said, his face grey. 'God help the defenders.'

The last of them there must get back across the pontoon ahead of the Turks, or they would be caught there and massacred.

6

The Turks surged victoriously over the bare promontory of Senglea, firing the few mean huts and the windmills with glee, and hacking down anyone who opposed them. They opened the gates of the settlement to their forward trenches and gunnery teams, who dragged in smaller guns by hand immediately, and set them up on the east side of Senglea, turning on Birgu at short range just across Galley Creek. After nightfall they would drag up the bigger guns.

The panicked defenders felt as if all Christendom had shrunk back to just Malta, and now Elmo and Senglea were lost too, all that remained of the island was huddled Birgu itself. A trapped animal, surrounded by hostile guns: the last redoubt and stand, the tattered remnant of the once vast domain of the Knights of St John. A few mean streets, churches, a fort, a half-wrecked hospital. Barely two hundred knights still able to fight.

The forces over-running Senglea were jubilant and numerous but ragged in formation. Suddenly the gates of the tiny single-square fort of St Michel slammed open, and out marched a small but close-packed column of armoured men. Perhaps no more than thirty in number, they bristled with pikes and swords, and in a cold, efficient silence, they began to slice through the milling, rejoicing Turks and corsairs.

At their head was a heavily armoured knight who sliced and slashed with wordless slaughter, uttering never a sound, a terrifying steel automaton amid the flames and gun smoke. It was the Marshal Copier himself, and by his side fought Henri Parisot. Seemingly invulnerable, Copier cut down half-naked Turks to left and to right, moving slow and implacable amid the carnage, his fine fluted greaves and cuisses gleaming silver and red, his olive-wood peg-leg thumping over the dusty ground. Steadily the column cut a swathe across Senglea promontory. The Turkish commander, Yacoub Agha, saw what was happening and called his men back into some kind of formation. The last few ragged defenders, Nicholas running among them, all youthful dreams of glory gone, had their chance to dash for the pontoon bridge on the eastern side, and flee across to Birgu.

The armoured knight and his closest comrades held the head of the pontoon now, and the Turks came against them in far stricter order. Behind them, St Michel was already fallen, the last defenders there beheaded and tumbled over onto the rocks below for the gulls. The standard of Suleiman flew from the bastion.

The moment St Michel was fallen, her captured guns were turned back to fire across at San Angelo, and long lean rowing boats nosed out round the end of Senglea. Well bulwarked with pavisades of wool and cotton bales, men crouching behind them, muskets smouldering, they made for the great chain across Galley Creek. Now La Valette could see them himself, he needed no reports. The battle spread out below him. Birgu, the last isolated outpost on the tiny island that still held out against the might of the Ottoman Empire, was now truly under attack from all sides.

He knew who that was coming round to the chain. It was Candelissa, the Greek renegade, and his band of cut-throats. They held half the Aegean throttled in a reign of terror, and none were more savage in their cruelties. If anyone on some small, sparse island resisted paying them their 'taxation', Candelissa had no hesitation in having the population of the entire island killed. Their heads were collected in sacks and sent to Topkapı Sarayı for the Sultan's approval. They had opposed his God-appointed rule, and were therefore heretics as well as rebels. It amused Candelissa to have the sacks of heads carefully labelled by age and sex. 'Old men.' 'Crones.' 'Women expectant.' 'Suckling infants.'

La Valette sent out his orders.

Standing at the back of his galliot, Candelissa cried to his corsairs that Birgu itself was already taken from the landward walls, and they would soon be in for the loot. A lookout heard his lie from the battlements of San Angelo, and La Valette promptly had a gigantic banner of the Cross raised over the post of Germany at the landward end. The corsairs saw it going up and looked puzzled.

A Spanish soldier with a fine musket said, 'I could hit the swine even from here, Sire, I'm sure of it. Top him off like a nettle in the field.'

'No,' said La Valette. 'I want them in closer.'

Candelissa and his men could do nothing against the great chain or the massive posts at either end, sunk into the rock and thickly mortared. The Sultan's flagship herself couldn't drag them free. His galliots drifted uncertainly. No one fired down on them from San Angelo above.

'The scum are almost out of gunpowder!' yelled Candelissa. His men grinned.

La Valette looked across to the ruins of Senglea.

Yacoub Agha strode into the turreted gun room of St Michel, eyeing the guns turned on San Angelo just across Galley Creek.

'None of them spiked, you are certain?'

'None, Lord,' said the master gunner confidently. 'They never had time.'

Yet Yacoub Agha felt uneasy. Something was wrong. He wished he was far away from this gun room, from this accursed island. Something prickled on his skin.

'Shall we fire?' said the gunner.

Suddenly he knew. 'No gun has been fired yet?'

'No, Lord.'

'Then why can I smell burning matchcord?'

The gun team stared around. Then one of them glanced down and saw the corner of a trapdoor to the stores below, just showing beneath a piece of sacking. Laid across the trapdoor just recently, to hide it.

'Allah,' he murmured.

One of the men leaned down to move the sacking.

'No!' cried Yacoub Agha.

Six fat barrels of gunpowder detonated in deafening unison. The wooden platform of St Michel's gun tower, heavy Sicilian oak though it was, virtually vapourised in an instant. The tower

359

erupted like a small volcano, entire stone blocks thrown into the air in a huge black spout of earth and smoke and cindered mortar. In the heart of the dark fountain, to the music of that deafening roar, dead bodies turned and flailed like burnt and ashen children doing cartwheels in the sky.

At the pontoon bridge, men on both sides stopped and stared, mouths agape. Then battle was rejoined, the last few armoured knights standing their ground and hacking furiously at the vast press of enraged Turks, while their brethren fled back to Birgu behind them across the rocking pontoon.

Candelissa too looked back at the tatters of St Michel and then stared up at the high battlements of San Angelo. They had known. Those Christian dogs had known.

Another figure appeared on the battlements of San Angelo, too dark against the bright sky to see his face, but distinctively tall and wearing an imposing plumed helmet. It was La Valette. For a moment, Candelissa and he seemed to lock their gaze on each other. Then the figure raised his arm, and another shout went out, and Candelissa felt a shadow fall across him.

Almost at the water's edge, from the heart of the solid rock below San Angelo, the muzzles of cannon appeared where no cannon should be. They poked out through tiny, rough-cut wooden-shuttered niches. Black, unblinking eyes. Most of the corsairs did not even see them. They had been thinking of climbing over the chain and swimming in below Birgu. The battle must be almost over now, depsite that last little kick of resistance on Senglea. Some even had their knives between their teeth, ready to go.

Then they saw their bearded commander, the dread of the world, Candelissa. His hands were outstretched as if to ward something off, and his eyes were wide with terror.

No more than twenty yards away, those black unblinking muzzles flared out in flame, the concealed battery below San Angelo opening up with all four guns firing as one. They fired grapeshot and chain shot, packets of jagged steel and nails, spiked balls and bags of sharp stones, and the lacerating cloud flew out across the water like a storm of hellish insects and tore into the faces and flanks of the half-naked corsairs and turned the very air to a bloody mist.

The guns reloaded.

One or two boats at the back still had enough oarsmen alive to try a desperate retreat.

Other torn survivors leapt or rolled almost paralysed with wounds into the water. Some fainted with shock and pain at the salt. The guns roared a second time, and the boards of the crowded galliots were swept almost clean of life. Snipers on Birgu's walls finished off the few who continued to swim.

La Valette sent not a word of congratulation. The waterline battery had simply done as commanded. Perhaps two or three hundred assorted Turks, Saracens and Algerians had been killed in a minute or two. The explosion in St Michel had killed at least another fifty.

An hour later, Mustafa Pasha learnt of the figures, and that both Candelissa and Yacoub Agha were dead.

'What of the attack of the Janizaries on the land walls of Birgu?'

'Beaten back, Pasha, with great loss of life.'

'Numbers there?'

'A wave of one thousand went in. Many fewer returned.'

'How many fewer?'

The messenger looked at his feet. 'Perhaps two hundred.'

Slowly his vast army was bleeding away. No, not even slowly. He had lost well over a thousand men this morning. The people of the town were evidently fighting shoulder to shoulder with the knights whom, his intelligence had told him, they despised as their arrogant overlords. Mere low-born fishermen, barefoot and ragged, they now fought on the walls with those pork-eating Crusader dogs as valiantly as any. Curse them.

A thousand of his men slain since dawn. Forty more days like today, and the entire Ottoman army would be exterminated. Not a single soul would return alive to Stamboul.

It was not credible.

Mustafa turned back into the shade of his pavilion. A long looking-glass leaned against a post, and he stood before it and stared long and deep into his own fathomless black eyes. The distant noise of battle rumbled over the sunblanched hills beyond, men screamed and fought and died. But in the looking-glass he saw only himself.

Nicholas reeled and clutched tight the sword of Brider de la
Gordcamp, the crude pontoon bridge on its mix of boats and
wooden barrels rolling underneath him. Arrows hissed in the air,
shouts came from the Birgu side. They were already cutting the
ropes. They could not allow the Turks across to form a bridgehead.
The pontoon must be destroyed.

But Henri Parisot leaned on his left, a gaping wound in his neck,
and he struggled forward, legs shaking. Behind him the last of the
heavily armoured knights, half a dozen of them, still held the bridge
against the howling, frustrated hordes. Then the sounds of muskets
cracked out at short range, and a heavy splash told him that bullets
this near were armour-piercing. He heard the deep roar of Copier
behind him.

'St Elmo's wages!' he cried, and there was the sound of a slicing
sword, and guttural cries.

The bridge rocked, his eyes were blinded. The pontoon was as
slippery as fishskin. And now there were dark-skinned corsairs diving into the water and swimming round the last of the armoured
knights to scramble up behind them. They would be trapped. And
it was Maddalena he thought of, even now.

'Get back, lad!' roared Copier. 'Or I'll brain you and drag you
back myself!'

More musket fire, more arrows hissing into the water. A corsair
arched out of the sea in agony, an arrow from his own side stuck
in his back. From the walls of Birgu, knights and townsmen were
witnessing in anguish this last desperate act of Senglea's fall.

Parisot's grip on Nicholas's left arm suddenly lightened, and
there was a great whooping expulsion of air from his lungs. A blade
jagged out of his chest, and then vanished. He collapsed to the
roped boards.

Nicholas ducked instinctively and turned as something swished
over him, and there was a heavy Turk in baggy red breeches standing before him. Small eyes twinkling, huge bald head shining, his
sword dripping with Parisot's blood. Behind him he could only see
Copier still standing, another knight lying at his feet, and a dozen
Turks pushing forward. More dived into the water.

Nicholas looked over the Turk's shoulder and grinned and nodded, and the Turk turned for a startled moment, expecting the heavily armoured knight to be upon him from behind. But it was a feint of the boy's, and by the time he realised it the boy's sword blade had run through his ribs. Air rushed from his lungs through the small puckered wound as the boy whipped the blade back again, and the heavy Turk thumped to the deck, blood bubbling on his lips.

Nicholas glanced down at Parisot and he still breathed. But now there was an Egyptian corsair ahead of them, his dark skin half-blue with many tattoos. He crouched low and slicked the dagger from between his white teeth and tossed it back and forth from hand to hand. These two boys would be easy to finish, one lying mortally wounded, the other a thin shrimp with fair plastered hair, struggling even now to lift his wounded friend to his feet once more. Such chivalry. The boy's knees almost buckled under the weight of it.

The corsair moved in for the snakelike kill, thinking to seize the wounded helpless one and push him forward hard into the other as his shield, sticking the white shrimp in the ribs below the wounded fellow's arm before cutting his throat and tossing them both over the side. But first for amusement he jumped and came down hard and the pontoon rippled and rolled on its wooden barrels. The boy staggered and leaned, nearly slipping on the wet planking. Then Parisot with his last strength pulled away from Nicholas's grasp and sank to his knees before the corsair. He was deliberately freeing the boy to fight, though it might mean his own death. Unburdened, Nicholas sprang forward like a cat, the corsair open-mouthed with horror at the sudden agility of this blood-streaked infidel, who seemed to be flying through the air towards him. He heard the whip of his sword blade rather than saw it, and then he was cut open once, twice, a deadly flurry of slashes and then a long clean thrust to the heart.

Nicholas pulled back and whipped the blade once more through the air to clear it of blood. The Egyptian was still standing, looking shocked, as men eerily may who do not realise they are dead yet. Then he fell sideways into the water, and it seemed to Nicholas that dead men made less splash than the living, their bodies already lightened by the flight of their souls.

'The bridge is going!' they shouted from the Birgu side.

If Copier went in the water he would drown, heavily armoured as he was. He stepped backwards to Nicholas, the Turks pushing forwards. Copier hauled up Parisot and Nicholas whirled his sword through the air in front of the oncoming enemy. They saw something crazed in his eyes and hesitated. He glanced back and the powerful Copier was hauling Parisot fast, almost carrying him under one arm, his peg-leg clomping. Nicholas hurried after, knowing that if he slipped, the Turks would be on him and he would die. But as soon as a gap opened up, an order to fire came from the Birgu shore and a murderous volley of arquebus hit the nearest Turks without risk to the last fugitives. Amid the volley sounded the deep distinctive crack of Smith's jezail. Bullets sang, the bridge rippled under the footfall of numerous Turks, the thump of bodies, cries and splashes. And then someone was dragging Nicholas onto the stone creekside. Another volley came, a grenade exploded far behind, the pontoon was cut loose, and sank under the weight of men a fathom deep.

7

Nicholas came in under the steep shadow of Birgu's cracked western walls after Copier and Parisot, the youth unbelievably carried slung over the Marshal's shoulder. Then Nicholas was half pulled up a ladder. A soldier took the sword from his tight fist firmly and encouraged him in over the parapet. A fair-haired sunburnt giant was clapping him on the shoulder and saying in a voice he knew well, with inimitable humour, 'Late again, Master Ingoldsby. Why so tardy?'

He grinned and reeled and nearly fainted, and Stanley held him upright.

'And why so weary? Anyone would think you had just run a mile, lad.'

'Give him some water,' growled Smith, busily cleaning the blackened barrel of his jezail. 'He's done more good works than you today, you fat tallow-haired lummox.'

When he had wet his throat and could speak again, Nicholas asked weakly, 'How's it been with Birgu?'

Smith said, 'Busy.'

They moved at a crouch along the parapet to the post of Provence, and the stench that arose from the ditches below the riven walls was the stench of Elmo. Janizaries, Bektaşis, Sipahis, Berbers and corsairs lay in indistinguishable heaps.

'We held the walls,' said Stanley, 'while the townsmen mounted charge after charge into the breeches in support. They fought with long-handled billhooks, scythes, fishing spears bound to wooden poles with wet rope, which serve to gut a man as well as a fish. It is good to fight with them.'

'And the women are all turned builders,' said Smith. 'The girls, the grandmothers. All of them.'

Though the walls of Birgu still stood, to the Turks' frustration, the effect of the bombardment took its toll in other ways. The guns raged on and on and never stopped. Every man and woman in the city must hold their nerve. The endless battering explosions frayed the soul. Already the weaker-minded had begun to gibber and go mad, to grip tables and walls, to walk slowly, eyes staring, or hold their hands to their ears and beg it to stop. They began to cry and say that they must get away, they must escape. Some took to the rooftops and gazed up into the sky and prayed to God to take them. And often they were killed there, standing stark and terrified under the cannon-torn sky.

An hour later they were under attack again. A troop of boys came up onto the blasted parapet, and scrambled out onto perilous crumbling heights and fought too. They cried '*Vittoria!*' in high piping voices as they fought with their only weapons, which were birding slings. For the people of Malta were passionate bird-hunters, so much so that few birds survived on the island. The knights martialled the boys carefully and had them loose their stones in a flanking hail at the Janizary onrush as they tried once more to come in over the rugged rampart of the breech.

The Janizaries glanced up and one yelled out, 'We are under attack from *boys!*' As if not knowing whether to be amused or indignant. Yet the rounded stones hurtling forth from those whirring leather straps were no toys. Flying stones struck exposed throats and temples, shattered wrist bones, hands and knee caps, and David slew Goliath once more as he did in the Valley of Elah in ancient times.

Perhaps eight hundred Janizaries had been killed at the land walls, and astonishingly, not one had broken into the town. But the losses of the defenders had been grievous, far worse in proportion, and the little victories of St Michel and the waterfront battery were small comfort.

In the evening, La Valette heard the roll of the dead from Sir Oliver Starkey.

'The Chevaliers Federico Sangrigorio; Giovanni Malespina; Raffaele Salvago ...' The list went on and on.

At one point La Valette interrupted, 'Do you have news of the English boy? The Ingoldsby boy?'

Starkey scanned the list for his countryman. 'No, Sire. He is still with us. I know he fought at Senglea—'

'Did he?' La Valette clenched his mouth.

'He came back almost last, with the Marshal Copier himself, moments before they blew the bridge.'

La Valette's eyes gleamed. 'Continue.'

'Javier, the nephew of Don Pedro Mezquita.'

'What age was he?'

'Eighteen. Don Pedro was wounded trying to save him. Slain Janizaries lay around the boy like mown flowers.'

La Valette buried his face in his hands for a moment and then looked up again. Starkey had never seen him look so tired. How much longer could a man of his years go on, barely sleeping, barely eating, grief-stricken to the heart but refusing to weep? Starkey wished he could take some of the burden from him. But La Valette would not share it. The grief and the burden would lie on his old shoulders until the end.

'The young always die soonest,' said La Valette softly. 'With their brave, reckless hearts. And?'

'Don Federique de Toledo.'

'Slain?'

'Yes, Sire. A grenade misfired, he lost his hand, and still he fought on until he collapsed from loss of blood. The medics could not save him.'

'Age?'

'Also eighteen.'

The son of Don García de Toledo, Viceroy of Sicily. How would that help or hinder the relief plans? It was a sad loss. They were all sad losses.

Names piled on names. Starkey's voice grew more and more strained. At last he hesitated. He could not finish.

After a time, La Valette said quietly, 'My nephew is dead. Henri Parisot is dead.' He nodded almost imperceptibly. 'Also eighteen.'

'Sire—'

'They have only gone along the road we all must follow soon. And every knight is equally dear to my heart as if he were my son.

367

The loss of Javier de Mezquita moves me no less than the loss of my beloved nephew.' His voice was very even and calm. Starkey could not bear to look at him. More quietly still, he said, *'A little while, and we shall not see them. And then a little while, and we shall see them.'*

His grace and greatness as a leader, his natural authority, his sad nobility, were never more evident to his secretary than then.

He stood and turned his back on Starkey and went over to the window and looked out across the harbour. Dying sunlight bright on half-drowned coloured banners and sundered timbers, flags of gold damask, corpses lining the shore, shields washed new and cleansed.

'Leave me now,' he said.

As he bowed out, Starkey saw that the Grand Master's shoulders were shaking.

Under cover of moonless nights, the women crept out through small postern gates and culverts in the walls, veils over their faces, as much to shield themselves from the foul stench of the dead than out of modesty. The men kept watch from the walls, in case of further attack, while their womenfolk went among the enemy fallen with knives, cutting the throats of any they found still moving. They killed them, they said, for the sake of Christ and their children.

Stanley watched over them. Of all battles fought, this was the most merciless. Yet he could not doubt that at the last, when the Turks captured the town, in their vengeful fury they would kill and crucify every living thing within. He foresaw scenes of women cut in two, boy slingers nailed to parodic crosses all along the walls.

No, this was not a battle that left room for mercy. He cradled his gun and waited.

Two hours or more into the night, he woke Nicholas with a whisper, shaking his shoulder. 'I need your eyes, boy. Out there, just this side of that sand ridge, see? I thought I saw a spear.'

'What do you mean?' he mumbled, still rubbing sleep away.

'Just watch.'

Nicholas stared another minute, and then to his amazement saw what Stanley had seen. A spearhead, bright in the moonlight, suddenly appeared eerily out of the ground itself, and then vanished.

He stared at the knight, not understanding.

'Miners,' said Stanley. 'Testing their progress. But they have given themselves away, still twenty yards out from the walls.' He squared his shoulders. 'Time for the counter-attack, I think.'

The Turks had found mining through the solid rock of the island a terrible labour, and the defenders did not attempt counter-mines. Instead Smith and Stanley led a small, swift party out through a small postern gate to the place where the telltale spear had been glimpsed, and with ferocious rapidity, simply gouged their way down through the earth into the tunnel from above. They dropped down into it and penetrated some way along, until they were surprised by a group of miners.

What an infernal skirmish was fought underground then. In that perpetual subterranean darkness, the Turkish and Egyptian miners fought back with picks and shovels by dim torchlight, choking on fetid air and dust. Eventually they were beaten back far enough for the knights to stack ample explosives about the pit props, set light to the fuses and flee. Moments later, a hundred yards or more of painstakingly built tunnels were detonated to ruins, and many miners buried alive.

Back on the walls, a panting Smith and Stanley grinned when they saw the telltale subsidence in the ground beyond, and clapped each other on the back.

Mustafa heard this latest news in utter silence. He did not even give orders for further tunnels to be built.

The night before, his personal valet had died of camp fever. The night before that, his cook had also died. But they were only servants. The worse news was that a massive resupply ship from Stamboul, carrying much-needed powder, food and medicines, had been sunk by a Christian galley. The galley flew the flag of the Knights Hospitaller, and its hull was painted blood-red.

It was the galley of the Chevalier Romegas.

*

News came to La Valette that the harbour of Marsamuscetto had been blockaded with tethered logs. To stop the Sicilian and Spanish relief from coming in?

'Or perhaps,' said Starkey hopefully, 'to stop the Turkish galleys deserting? Which would show we are indeed winning, would it not?'

'Of course we are winning,' said La Valette. 'We have been winning for four months. Another month of winning like this, and we'll be done for.'

Again the Grand Master's harsh joke spread through the town as fast as a whipped dog. They smiled grimly and fought on.

Tales and rumours had begun to spread out over the wider world also. At last the epic nature and importance of the Siege of Malta began to dawn upon Christian Europe. The French court stirred guiltily, the German princes uneasily, Philip II continued meditating his private plans, though sharing them with none. The merchants of Genoa and Venice looked to their great galleys and counted their guns and wondered. Even Protestant England said prayers for Catholic Malta. Her cold Virgin Queen demanded intelligence from her exceptional network of informers, questioning her spies with sharp, crisp interrogation, in the six different languages she spoke fluently.

Where would the armies of Islam strike next, if Malta should fall? France and Spain, her greatest enemies. No harm in that. Yet what if the Turk should conquer them, and all their possessions besides? The Lowlands of Holland resound with the cry of the muezzin? What if the divided German princes fell one by one, what if Rome was sacked once more, and Genoa and Venice and the Adriatic bowed the knee to Suleiman? Then England might stand alone, a solitary island in the silver sea, the warriors of the Prophet like a pack of slavering hounds upon the French coast, reaching across, straining at their leash, eyes hungrily fastened on the green fields and woods of her beloved kingdom.

Pope Pius IV, who had shown little resolve in the face of threatened catastrophe, led prayers in St Peter's, saying, 'Almighty Father, we realise in what great peril Sicily and Italy will be, what great calamities threaten all Christian people if the island of Malta should fall ...'

He announced that he would remain in Rome rather than flee, if the Turk should come. But many wondered, was Judgement upon the world?

The politics and prayers were not heard on Malta, exhausted and decimated and deafened by the Turkish guns. None could run the blockades any more. Turkish galleys ringed the island, cannon ringed the last tottering, dust-caked streets of Birgu. Whether or not the Holy Father or the Queen of England was praying for them now, they knew nothing of it. It hardly mattered.

It was August. Perhaps the Feast Day of St Lawrence, the 10th of August, perhaps later. Days had lost their names. There had been no festivities to mark the patron of the Conventual Church. There were no priests left alive. The young priest who had laughed on hearing Nicholas's confession – Nicholas passed him in the street. He lay under a shroud of dust, his black hair now plaster-white, a thin trickle of blood dried at the corner of his mouth, his young face serene.

Maddalena went through the streets with a pitcher of well-watered wine and a fresh loaf, and found Nicholas on the south walls. He hurried her down to shelter again.

'I have brought you these,' she said.

He took them. 'I am grateful for it. But you must return home, it is safer there.'

'Why should I be kept safe? You are not. Many are not.'

He looked exasperated.

She shielded her eyes and looked up at the toothed walls. 'Will they stand? Will we live?'

'Yes. I think so. But pray for it.'

Suddenly she raised her arms above her head, stretching, showing off her slim figure, and pirouetted, there in the ruined street. She said with a smile, 'In November it is St Catherine's Day.'

Girls' minds were so *strange*. 'Your point eludes me.'

'It is Maltese custom that on the feast of St Catherine of Alexandria, a girl can ask a boy to marry her.'

371

'In my country that's on the 29th of February. Only once every four years. A safer arrangement.'

'Well, you are in Malta now.'

'I know that. The cannonballs keep reminding me.'

She looked serious again. 'It will be over soon.'

He nodded. 'One way or another. You should go home.'

She hesitated and then at last she said shyly, 'I think of you ... all the time.'

'I think of you likewise,' he said softly. 'Which is why I want you to go home.'

She turned and went. A little way up the street she looked back, but he was climbing up on to the walls again and did not mark her. Only when he reached the parapet did he look back, but she was gone.

8

All day Nicholas and Hodge had fought on the walls, watched advance and retreat, shaking at the impact of the guns. Day after day. Their shoulders were bruised deep from the arquebus's recoil, their eyes stung, their ears thrummed and sang. Nicholas's elbow still ached, especially at night when he tried to sleep.

Boy slingers were shot from the walls. He helped to bury a ten year old. A woman fell into his arms where she worked, and he never knew what had killed her. He could see no wound. A Spanish soldier was hit in the head and leapt up and ran away down the street like an athlete and then fell to the ground dead.

At evening the guns would fall silent and the attacks fall back. Mustafa had ordered day and night – but it was not possible. The guns must be rested.

Smith said, 'Even Janizaries must rest.'

The late summer sunsets flared more and more resplendent over the island every night, and dawn was like heaven on fire. People said it was all the dust kicked up by the guns. The setting sun bathed the stricken streets in soft gold. The guns fallen silent, old people and cripples and the wounded emerged from the remnants of their houses in their crumpled dust-caked robes, and women and children coming from work on the walls. In black widows' gowns, heads covered, they moved like mourners through the fallen streets of their poor beloved city. Some picked up strewn rocks and carried them as if in a dream, to mend their hearts with mortar and stone. Some wept as they walked, and some women walked steadily ahead with tears running down their dusty faces, for their children were all dead, yet never making a sound nor giving way to a sob. Silent tears that seemed to run in mere accompaniment to their solemn labours as they gathered stones and worked on into the night.

They heaved and rolled aside half-sunk cannonballs, they drew out the dead from beneath the piled walls and from collapsed cellars, passing out infants, crossing themselves, working in absolute silence. An infant half crushed, its body half white with dust and half black with dried blood, was passed reverently along the line of workers and finally wrapped in a clean cloth and laid on the ground for a mother to find if she still lived. Or if her soul had gone before, then the soul of her child had gone with her. Yes, said the women, there was the mother, she had died flung over her own infant, see how the wall had collapsed over her and crushed them both. She died in the pathetic hope she might shield her infant with her own body from the damage wreaked by Turkish guns so huge they were pulled by eighty oxen. Now mother and child had died and gone together to the otherworld, said the women. As it should be. No infant should go alone.

The sun was glorious over Sciberras and inland, illumining the great cliffs of the west copper and gold, the sea barred with burning orange and the sky like red banners streaming in the windless evening sky.

Down the street came the boy, limping slightly, helmet under his arm, his fair hair haloed by the sun, and even in their grief and exhaustion the women greeted him, the Inglis hero, and smiled. His armour barely shone beneath so much dust, the street golden in the evening and light, dust motes dancing, women cooking the evening meal, children coming out to play with hoops as if the siege was all a dream and over now.

Nicholas stopped and leaned against a wall and rested his head and smiled. There beneath a small vine was a wooden cradle with an infant in it, perhaps three months old, left by his mother as she washed clothes round the corner in St Mark's Fountain. The infant looked up through the vine leaves and the warm light twinkled on his face as the leaves moved and stirred, and he laughed and reached out to play with them. He couldn't reach, so Nicholas broke off a leaf with its stem and put it in his pudgy little hand. The baby clutched it wonderingly, his fingers like tiny pink shrimps, and then gurgled with delight at the green waving flag in his hand, and the coming and going of the setting sun beyond the leaves, and the flickering green forest light over his upturned face.

The boy was overwhelmed at the infant's joy amid the horror. Two dead bodies lay only ten feet away, but the baby was oblivious. Nicholas dropped his helmet to the ground and closed his eyes and tried to let his mind fill only with this sound, these chortles of infant happiness. Like water from a well, washing it all away.

He pictured the Turks encamped on their hills, putting their guns away, cooking meat on their rings of mail. Cookmasters slicing onions and simmering rice, cauldrons steaming over dung-fires: a domestic scene. The end of another working day.

He opened his eyes.

Up on the heights as the sun went down and the sky darkened, there was other activity than slicing onions and simmering rice, cleaning swords and settling down to tell tales.

A tall lean man with the face of a hawk walked among the greatest of the guns and gave quiet orders without cease, and against the blood-red sky off Gallows Point, gunners set to work once more, silhouettes against the setting sun, re-powdering and tamping and wadding. Even if the guns needed resting and cooling, tonight there would be no rest. On Margherita, two men heaved up hundred pound balls into gaping muzzles, carved like the mouths of dragons and serpents.

Nicholas kept quite still, the baby gurgling by his side. But a fine muscle in his right hand twitched.

It was coming again.

He looked down the street to where the much reinforced curtain wall still towered. It could not be. As Smith said, even the Janizaries must sleep.

On the heights they were lighting the matchstocks and passing among the guns, the sun now just below the rimmed horizon of the sea, the sky fading into night, the last birds but shadows of scimitars against the deep blue dusk.

His hand twitched. He stared down at it. No, please God, no, not more. Not now. They could not take any more. They would surely fall, they could not hold them back again now, and everything they had fought for would be wasted and lost, and everyone slaughtered in the town like cattle. Let it be evening. Let it be peace for a while, dear God.

He moved down the street a little way, towards the walls, setting his helmet back on his head.

The infant chortled and the last light went. He lay in darkness and the leaves stopped twinkling at him. He turned and stared with his huge baby eyes at Nicholas passing him, no longer smiling. Staring, waiting.

Something was coming.

A matchstock was lowered to the powder.

Nicholas cried out and ran back.

A cannon roared and a ball the weight of a man flew through the darkening air.

'No!' he cried and hurled himself on the infant.

The ball crashed into the wall and came hurtling through as the boy threw himself on the baby.

The Turks had succeeded in mining the walls after all. It was not the renewed bombardment of the guns that had done it. They were merely announcing that they had conquered.

A hundred-yard section of Birgu's landwall was ruptured wide open by the terrific blast from the mines. Sections of wall split from top to bottom and collapsed slowly forward in billowing waves of rubble and shattered stone. The great heaped earthen ramparts and sacks of bulking behind were blown high into the sky, solid earth reduced in a second to nothing but vapour and dust. Bodies of the slain fell flailing through the night air and came to land in a sickening, inhuman tangle. Others lay still convulsing and twitching, legs and arms snapped under them.

A wall of dust and hurtling masonry came surging up the street towards Nicholas like a great wave forty feet high, billowing overhead. Nearby houses shuddered, roofs caved in, and more cannon balls hurtled triumphantly in. The Turkish guns lit up the night sky in a monstrous bombardment. Once more the city dragged itself upright to fight. But this time it would surely lose.

The old and the sick were already defeated in their hearts. Further up the street, torn at by the hail and the dust as if by a storm wind, an old woman fell back against a doorway and raised her hands to heaven and tears coursed down her face. Slowly she slid to the ground, weeping and shaking her head and crying, *no more, no more*, her face crumpled like ancient parchment ruined by time.

Mustafa Pasha raised his arms again and again. The cannons roared, the serpent mouths flared, the balls flew, the ruptured walls shivered and shattered further and bodies tumbled.

Another huge blast and Nicholas crawled free, and then another ball roared into the same place, the Mameluke engineers ensuring that strike after strike hit the same spot on the broken walls, so desperately propped and thinly manned, and blasted into the heart of the city. The wall that Nicholas reeled against began to topple and fold forwards, and then the boy and the infant he was dazedly clutching were buried beneath enough masonry to kill a horse, a sudden white tomb of powder and sandstone dust.

The knights limped and staggered to the massive breach, up onto a ramp of rubble twenty feet high, as the Janizary corps charged down the hill from Santa Margherita. Word went out to the infirmary that the Turks had successfully mined and blown the walls. All able to walk must come at last to fight. Blinded men tapped their way with crutches to the walls, determined to die sword in hand.

The opposing forces clambered up from each side, the breach must somehow be held, and there was La Valette himself, the old man unmistakable. There was a pummelling encounter as the two lines clashed, the rent walls either side of the breach manned by Maltese men and boys, screaming women, black hair flying, stones hurling down. The Janizaries crowded forward in far greater numbers than the defenders, yet were still held back by the line of pitiful rubble and the people, heedless and wild with exhaustion. A last few fire hoops and grenades rained down on the close-packed attackers, a surge of white silks and dark skins, as desperate as the defenders now to be in and finish this.

Then a fresh band of knights came in, heavily armoured, led once more by Marshal Copier. The townspeople parted before them as they pounded up the rampart to take their place and fight alongside La Valette himself.

'Forward! Forward!' screamed a voice from the heights. It was

Mustafa. But his men could not do it. Once more, of the thousand who went into the attack, a third were already killed or wounded beyond fighting. Mustafa held his scimitar aloft as if to slay any who returned, but they would have to fall back in bitterness and shame. They would flee as so many times before, the Maltese running after them in the dark and sinking hatchets into their backs, backs arching, crying out, gross insults hurled over the strewn dead. The rubble mounds slathered black in the night, blood-rusted sandstone when the dawn sun rose.

Then a terrible cry went up that La Valette was hit. The battle-line wavered, Copier himself stopped to help the tottering Master, and was hit in his turn by an arrow to the thigh. The Janizaries sensed that victory was within their grasp and pushed forward with one last mighty heave, maces and swords and axes cutting destruction through the thinned, despairing defenders. Maltese and knights and the last few Spanish soldiers fell back and tumbled down the breach in disarray, Bektaşi howled, Janizaries pushed on, keeping formation. Finally their numbers told.

They were in.

From out of the heart of a tomb of white dust and sandstone in the street behind erupted a plaster-coloured hand. It flattened against the wall, held there. Stones were pulled way and a fallen soldier crawled out dazed, an infant clutched to his chest. The infant was wide-eyed and covered in dust like a homunculus made of all flour, but unhurt except for a small cut on his head, blood seeping through his fine baby hair and turning the white dust red.

But he did not cry. He stared around in his infant amazement at the infinite strangeness of a world that could change so quickly from the sunlight coming dancing through vine leaves to play with him, to burial alive beneath the ruined stones of war. The boy raised him up and wept openly, risen like Lazarus from that abrupt tomb. The boy was bruised and cut about, but his morion was still on his head, or the falling masonry would have killed him.

The boy's prayers of thanks were as fervent as any in his whole sixteen years, or maybe seventeen. His birthday used to be in August. As if it mattered. He knelt in the ruins of the street and bowed his head and prayed over the infant.

A woman came round the corner, still dazedly clutching her washing linens, silently staring at the mound of rubble where her infant had previously lain in his simple cradle that her husband made from olive wood last winter. Then on her left hand a dust-covered knight or soldier was standing beside her, speaking to her. She heard nothing. There in his arms was her boy, her bambino, her first-born son, dusted all in flour and with a tiny red cut on his head. She heard nothing of the soldier's words nor anyone else's, nor even the shouts and screams from behind that the Turks had broken into the town. There was nothing but her son. She took him from the knight's arms, and the infant looked up at her, wide-eyed with amazement still. She bent down, her headdress falling over him, and she kissed the tiny wound on his head. Then she spat on a corner of her headdress and with infinite tenderness wiped away the little blood. The infant never cried, only gazed up at her, and the knight stared too. Never a word was spoken, but he saw the woman and her child like Mary and the Christ child wounded, and Mary herself kissing and salving his wounds with her kisses.

'Get back in your house!' cried Nicholas, coming out of the dream.

She gestured at the mound of rubble and smiled a strange smile.

They were fighting furiously just at the end of the street yet she seemed oblivious.

'Any house!' He shoved her into a darkened doorway. 'The cellar!'

La Valette refused assistance, and demanded that his wounded leg was bound up so he could continue fighting. Copier knelt and tore off his neckcloth and tied him as best he could.

'We must fall back to San Angelo, Sire!' cried another knight nearby. 'Take up the drawbridge, we may still hold out.'

'And abandon the town to its fate?' said La Valette savagely. 'This town of heroes?'

The knight looked ashamed.

'It is too late anyway. As I joined you here, I gave orders for all the precious icons of the Order to be carried from St Lawrence into San Angelo, the fort to be evacuated, and the drawbridge destroyed.

Here is where we take our stand.' He stabbed the ground with his sword point. 'Here is where we die, if we must! With our people!'

The invading Turks soon found themselves lost and divided amid a dense labyrinth of narrow, dark-shaded streets and mean, tight-packed alleyways. The undisciplined Bektaşi, their hearts already set on rape and enrichment, dissolved into a mere horde of frenzied individuals, dashing into houses to find the women and steal the gold. One or two managed to satisfy themselves in the murderous panic, but one found that his woman cut her own throat even as he stripped her naked, and more than one felt himself stabbed to death in the side even as he copulated with his kicking victim. Most other maddened Bektaşi, however, were trapped in small rooms of houses and brained with chamber pots in doorways, tripped up in nets, cut down with knives, run through with pitchforks or garrotted with ropes. Having broken into the city, they believed it was finished, and victory was theirs. They learnt differently.

The Janizaries kept order, better acquainted with the savageries of house-to-house fighting, but they found themselves trapped again and again in cul-de-sacs, behind hastily erected but effective barricades of mere furniture, chairs and tables and bales of bedding. More than a hundred charged into the little square of St Mark, only to find that there was no exit, and quickly blocking their retreat was a line of a dozen or more knights, grim and silent in their battered plate. The Janizaries surged against them but could not break out again, and from above, from the first floor windows and balconies and flat roofs of the surrounding houses, missiles began to rain down upon them. Plates smote bare heads, rocks and stones shattered shoulder bones, and they sank down stunned, grovelling on their knees. They had captured the city, surely. The green banner of Islam and the golden orb of Suleiman now stood on the walls of Birgu above the ruined post of Provence. And yet still they were being slaughtered like dazed cattle, as the shadow of armoured knights fell across them.

La Valette's ruthless preparations had followed every rule of defence in depth. The invaders found themselves faced with one exhausting, attritional barrier after another. Every street, every wretched back alley, was a new battleground. It was a wearying and dispiriting labour. One house after another must be captured, one barricade after another stormed, and again and again they were trapped in small bands, isolated and destroyed.

At times fresh explosions went off behind them as they surged forward through the town, and they were not explosions caused by their own guns, which had fallen silent now. They were charges laid in preparation by the defenders. Houses were carefully blown to collapse behind them as they advanced, another would be blown ahead of them, and yet again they were caught, unable to escape. Yet again missiles rained down from above.

Often at the end of the streets, they glimpsed a tall, ancient figure striding past, grim-visaged with his clipped white beard beneath his high scarlet-plumed helmet, unmistakable yet seeking no cover. Quite the opposite: determined to be seen everywhere. His only protection was his armour and his great shield, emblazoned with the cross and a falcon. His left thigh was bound with a bloody bandage, yet he walked without the faintest limp and directed all operations with a steady energy and tranquillity. That was the Frankish warrior, their Pasha, called La Valette. He had about him an aura changeless and terrifying.

Nicholas and Stanley had chased two Janizaries into a cul-de-sac, and the two warriors now turned like noble beasts at bay and faced them. Four swords and scimitars thrust accusingly towards each other, all four of them panting, exhausted, uncertain. There came shouts and footfalls behind them, a furious exchange of clanking blows of steel on shield. Nicholas fixed his opponent in the eye. The Janizary had blue eyes, fair skin. He had been a Christian until he was seven. Nicholas's sword point wavered with tiredness and doubt. And then a look crossed the Janizary's face. Nicholas glanced back and saw two more of the enemy running towards them. Two tall, straight-backed Sipahis with their long cavalry swords, still fresh-looking and alert.

'Stanley!'

A veteran fighter, Stanley knew from the boy's tone of voice that danger was coming, he didn't need to look. He sliced his sword warningly through the air before him and at the same time seized the boy in his left arm and dragged him back into a doorway just wide enough for the two of them, backed up tight, blades before them. The knight heaved but the damnable door was firmly bolted inside.

'Open up!' he roared.

The terrified family inside remained frozen.

The four enemy soldiers formed a semi-circle around them. This burly blond giant would not be easy. If only they still had guns, it would be like shooting rats in a ditch.

A distant horn sounded, a single long wailing note that sounded like mourning. The four Turks looked at each other. They still did not step in for the kill. Nicholas doubted that his right arm could mete out another convincing blow. His arm muscles burned, his sword point wavered and drooped before him.

'Weapon up, boy!' shouted Stanley.

But there was something about the soldiers' stance that told Nicholas they were not going to close in for the kill. Something had happened.

The horn sounded again afar off. A long lone call, falling away.

Everything was very still. Then the four lethal blades hemming them in, ready to run them through, were let drop. The blue-eyed Janizary shot his broad-bladed scimitar back in its sheath, his jaw clenched but his expression of sad resignation. Then he took one step back, out of range of Stanley's sword, and gave a small, unmistakable bow.

The horn sounded a third time, and then he and his three comrades were striding away back to the breach in the walls, heads lowered, silk robes billowing.

All over the town, the defenders stopped and peered through the dust and the black powder smoke and saw that there were few more Turks left to kill. They patrolled carefully through the streets and cut down those few they could find. It was eerily silent. A cry here, a groan there, the last few Turks being despatched by womenfolk with their knives. A Bektaşi who had tried to rape a girl in an alley was punished appropriately by the girl and her mother, and left in the street to bleed to death.

The little square of St Mark with its precious freshwater fountain was awash with blood and the corpses of a hundred Janizaries. Knights lay slain also. But more still patrolled the streets, or returned to the remains of the walls, barely breathing or daring to hope. The attack had died off.

All who entered had been killed or laid low. And instead of the entire Turkish army pressing forward after them, as it could easily have done ... no more came.

Nicholas and Stanley found Smith among a group standing with the Grand Master at the head of the street, looking down to the rent in the walls.

'Master,' gasped Copier, almost collapsed forward on the weight of his own sword, visibly bending under him. 'What now?'

'Sheathe your sword, man,' said La Valette. 'It isn't a walking stick.'

Very slowly, Copier cranked himself upright again, blood leaking from a dozen wounds. With enormous effort he lifted his sword, his muscles so tired that the blade trembled violently. Nicholas stepped forward and helped him and he managed to set the point into the mouth of his scabbard and thrust it home and then took a deep breath.

By heaven, the Grand Master was a tyrant worse than Nero. But he was magnificent.

'Now, Marshal,' said La Valette, 'you ask what has happened. Can you climb with me to the walls?'

'What's left of them.'

'What's left of them.' La Valette nodded. 'Or can you lean on the boy?'

'The boy will collapse. Won't you, boy?'

'I ...' stammered Nicholas, struck like all the others there with a fatigue like death. 'I ... I'm not sure—'

'Allow me, Marshal,' said Smith, so slathered in blood that barely a gleam of armour showed. 'Lean on me. I have looked from the walls already. It is a fine sight.'

'Who has come?' said Stanley. 'Smith? How do you know?'

'Counsel is mine, and sound wisdom,' said Smith unhelpfully.

'The relief?' said Copier. He looked around with wild hope. 'Spain has come?'

'Not Spain,' said La Valette. 'Come and see.'

*

They leaned on what remained of the walls beside the shattered post of Auvergne. The neighbouring post of Provence, walls and bastion both, were virtually flattened. The Turks could have marched in two hundred abreast. But as La Valette knew, though had passed on to none, everything was against them. Their numbers, once forty thousand strong, were less than twenty, perhaps fifteen. Before Elmo and then Birgu, half of them had died. Another five thousand or more were sick of dysentery and camp fever, sick unto death. He had smelled the foul taint of it on the air across the harbour, two weeks ago now, and seen them burning blankets in desperation. Birgu, meanwhile, had been kept free of any outbreak of crippling disease by the most stringest rules governing wells and fountains, hygiene and sewage. The moment any well or fountain was ruptured by cannonball, it was declared unsafe to use and blocked off. The people had to work harder, walk further each day for their water. But no disease had come on them. And La Valette knew of old that it was plague and pestilence that killed, more than any war.

The Ottoman food and powder supplies were almost gone too. He had noticed days ago that the guns were firing less often. They could no longer afford it. Despite that vast armada that had sailed down the Bosphorus four long months ago, carrying an unimaginable tonnage of provisions and military materials, it was close to exhausted. They might have hoped to be resupplied from North Africa by Dragut. But Dragut was dead. And another mighty supply ship, desperately needed, had been sunk by the blessed Chevalier Romegas, wolf of the Inland Sea.

The Grand Master and his Marshal and knights looked out across the stricken tableland. The main camp of the Ottomans at the head of Marsa was ablaze. Hugely ablaze.

'Who—' muttered Copier.

'Malta,' said La Valette, 'Malta herself has saved us.'

9

As soon as La Valette had heard of the death of Don Federique de Toledo, he had sent news to his uncle Don García in Sicily with all speed. No reply came. He had then sent out as many of his knights as he could spare to Mdina under cover of darkness, a troop of fifty mounted men under the command of the redoubtable Don Pedro Mezquita, to remain at Mdina in its defence.

'At Mdina!' Mezquita had protested, thirsting for vengeance for the death of his own nephew.

'You must bring the Maltese nobility in Mdina to battle,' said La Valette. 'And observe how the camp of the Turks at Marsa will be ever less and less defended, as the siege wears on.'

And so Mezquita and his horsemen had harried the Turks relentlessly from Mdina. At first the Maltese nobility ordered him to cease, but by then it was too late. The Turks were marching on Mdina in punitive mood, knowing it was only thinly defended.

The nobility panicked and begged for Mezquita's advice.

'My advice,' he said grandly, tossing back his cloak with his still-bandaged arm and assuming his haughtiest air, 'is that you appoint me Military Commander of this city. Otherwise you are doomed.'

They agreed.

Don Pedro had the men and women of the ancient capital of the island dressed as soldiers, bearing pikes and lining the walls when the Turks came in sight. A crude and laughable ruse, but it worked. Bewildered at the large number of defenders, the Turks backed off. Mezquita told his anxious hosts that they would return. This was not a battle they could leave to Birgu. This was a battle for the whole of Malta. Indeed, for the whole of Christendom. The older nobles still hesitated, but hot-blooded younger sons begged to join Mezquita's cavalry and ride out against the Turk.

Finally Mezquita could command a hundred and twenty horseman. A small force against an Ottoman army, true. But it could move fast, and must suffice.

It was La Valette's desperate, last-ditch ruse. To fool the Turks, even in their moment of victory, that a mighty Spanish army had arrived.

Mezquita and his cavalry troop rode out in the thick summer mist before dawn, passing silently through the humid night. The horses snorting softly, muffled with cloths, the men not talking. And keeping watch from an outcrop of rocks, they saw the last titanic bombardment of Birgu begin, and the entire Turkish infantry move out from Marsa to the forward camp for the final assault.

Once battle was joined there, Mezquita and his cavalry galloped in behind and descended on the main camp like a whirlwind. They took no prisoners. They slaughtered all the sick and wounded that they found, they fired the tents and the magnificent pavilions, even the pavilion of Mustafa Pasha himself, they ruptured the water butts and burnt the last of any supplies remaining. In less than a quarter of an hour they had wreaked utter devastation, and were galloping back to the safety of Mdina even as Mustafa and his commanders looked over their shoulders towards Marsa, vaguely uneasy, to see black smoke roiling high into the sky.

Not a Turk had seen the horsemen come in secret from Mdina, and so they thought there was only one explanation.

'The Spanish have come, and fallen on us from behind!'

The battle-horns sounded the retreat, and Mustafa ground his teeth and almost wept as Birgu was abandoned at the hour of its fall.

The Turks broke camp and pulled apart or burnt their gun emplacements and, utterly broken in spirit, began the trek north to their ships. Wooden wheels grinding over the stony implacable landscape, past ransacked and ruined villages, the sky hotly burning, shame on their sunburnt cheeks.

Outriders kept lookout for the imagined Spanish army, but saw none. The camp appeared to have been attacked by djinns. Some said among themselves that they no longer had enough food to keep them alive on the three-week voyage home.

As they retreated they looked back and saw with crushing dismay that a triumphant banner of St John was once more flying ... over St Elmo. A mere patch of cindered rubble on the end of Sciberras.

One Turk shook his head. 'Against such men as these,' he said, 'there could have been no victory.'

A strange and unseasonal wind was picking up from the north, a *tramontana*, they said, bringing a thin scattering of rain and turning the thin earth of the island to mud. The guns were twice as heavy to haul, the oxen emaciated for lack of fodder. There were more heavy and ominous clouds to the east: the way home looked rougher each day. The rain came down harder on their sodden backs, their hanging silks, and their muskets were now useless if they should need them.

The news that it wasn't the Spaniards did not bring them to life again. The bitter truth – that their camp had been sacked by only a hundred horsemen or so, riding from Mdina – was even harder to bear. They hung their heads along with their horses and oxen, humiliated to defeat and beyond. Allah had turned against them, and so all was hopeless.

The sky rumbled with late summer thunder. The day was as dark as winter twilight.

'We go,' said Mustafa. 'We are finished.'

But the people of Malta were not finished. Now it was time to punish the Mohammedan invaders with a punishment they would never forget. On the Naxxar Plain, between the saltpans and the sea, it was a bitter butchery. Led by Don Pedro Mezquita himself, resplendent and terrible in his billowing crimson cloak, they harried the retreating army with savage, unrelenting ferocity. Women and children with knives, old men with crutches, falling out of the night and destroying wagons, killing horses, even flinging dead or poisoned rats down on the Turks from the rocks above. In their implacable fury they pursued them all the way to the shores of St Paul's Bay and the waiting ships. Many Ottoman guns were abandoned. Great basilisks sunk half drowned in mud and sand, their heavy breech-ends sunk deepest, their serpent mouths raised to the sky as if gasping for air, for their last breath.

Mezquita's cavalry and the nobility of Mdina and any still with an appetite to fight fell on their rear and slew them in their hundreds. Maltese fishermen rowed out and attacked the waiting galleys, cutting throats and rigging with equal zeal. The rain lashed down, the wind grew, the waves reared up angrily and dashed against the rocking hulls, straining at their hawsers. Mustafa's orders were lost on the wind and he too looked lost.

The embarkation of the Turkish forces, hugely reduced in number though they were, was not the work of an hour. It took three days. During all that time the rain drove down, and the beach and the surrounding fields began to resemble a scene of sodden trench warfare. To defend themselves, the Turks in their turn erected poor and hasty barricades around the shoreline, as the Christians had done against them: overturned wagons, barrels, bales, dead horses. Rats fed among the dead, and bit the living if they tried to sleep. The people of the island returned to their hidden stores across the island and ate well enough once more, but the Turks were weak with hunger and trapped in a hostile land. The first galleys left, but more struggled to follow. Bodies floated in the bay bloated and gaseous, giving off a stench like putrid cheese. The sea was cluttered with wrecked shipping, timber and corpses.

It was too wet for arquebus or musket, but the islanders and the knights fired down on them with crossbows, and the bolts fell ceaselessly with the rain. The sandstone ledges of St Paul's Bay ran red.

10

The Ottoman galleys pulled away into a gale, a churning sea beneath and louring sky above, and few there doubted that Allah was angry with them for having failed to conquer this wretched island in His name. As they left the accursed island behind the seas grew ever rougher. Fighting spurs were ripped from the ships, masts and oars snapped asunder, rigging tore and sagged, men spewed, the wind howled, and rainwater and seawater drenched all. And somewhere out there, they said amongst themselves – somewhere out there, fearless of any storm, there still lurked that most ferocious of all Christian sea captains, the Chevalier Romegas.

On some of the ships a strange light was seen, dancing blue and white on the shuddering mast-tops, hissing audibly and malevolently, a sign that terrified them. A Christian among them who had turned Turk and corsair because it paid better suddenly found that he was crossing himself. His comrades seized him and held knives to his throat and demanded to know what was happening.

'The flames on the tops,' he muttered. 'Among the Christians, it is called St Elmo's fire.'

They let him drop, and stood aghast. Truly they were damned.

The once Grand Fleet slipped into Constantinople under cover of darkness, in silence but for the slow rise and dip of tired oars. A forest of shattered masts, of stinking galleys, ruined and shamed. Of the forty thousand who had sailed, fewer than ten thousand returned. Of the corsairs and cut-throats who had joined from the African coast, from Egypt and Tripoli and Algiers, hardly any returned at all.

Suleiman decreed, as only the Lord of the Universe can, *'Malta Yök.'*

Malta Is Not.

Mustafa and Piyale were removed from their commands, but to general surprise, both kept their heads. All of the city went into mourning. Few had not lost a brother or a cousin in the disaster. A number of Christians and Jews were stoned or stabbed to death in impotent vengeance.

Yet the work of conquest could not stop. It was the Will of Allah that Islam should reign supreme over all the earth. Suleiman vowed – *Malta Yök* notwithstanding – to lead another army the following year, in person, and this time he would slaughter every man, woman and child on the island. He ordered fifty thousand oarsmen and forty thousand soldiers to be ready by the following March.

In time they heard of the news across Europe. Church bells rang out and people danced in the streets of Lisbon and Amsterdam and Munich and Rome and Vienna. In time they would hear even across the great divide of Christendom, and celebrate in Moscow and Kiev. And weeks later, in the old Christian heartlands of the Levant, oppressed now for a millennium, there would also be secret rejoicing at the victory of the true faith, among the Maronites and the Copts of Syria and Egypt. For the mighty sword of Islam had been broken, shattered in pieces by a small, ill-defended but unimaginably courageous Mediterranean rock, no more than two or three hours' walking from side to side. Yet even amidst their celebrations, anxiety would remain. As if they knew the war of the world had only just begun.

Celebrations were more grave on Malta itself.

The guns fell silent, the miraculous rain washed the streets clean, and the people breathed again. They looked around and saw their shattered city as if for the first time, and the farmland beyond stripped of livestock, untended now for four long months under the broiling sun. Any sense of victory was tempered by how much labour would be needed to rebuild their beloved island. There were no dances or bonfires in those rubble-strewn streets, their houses overthrown as if by almighty hand or earthquake, but only humble thanksgiving.

A slow hymn arose from the rubble, at once mournful and yet inexpressibly triumphant. The voices of men and women and children, unaccompanied, singing in their ancient language, voices high and low, young and old commingled. It was inexpressibly moving to hear it arise from the ruins. It was one thing for a people to love their proud and beautiful city, if that city was gilded and magnificent Venice or Genoa – but quite another for them to love this barren rock so deeply. Smith turned to Stanley and Nicholas with tears in his eyes and said, 'If you love a thing, you fight for it. But if you fight for a thing, in time you come to love it.'

And it was true. The knights themselves had so loved their lush and beautiful island of Rhodes, island of butterflies and roses, and so despised this substitute of Malta, so mean in comparison. But now they loved it as ardently as the people themselves. Love grows in the hardest ground.

'Malta of gold, Malta of silver, Never will we forsake you, Never will we forget you, Made precious with our blood ...'

It was the small, weary, steadfast song of a people whom even the greatest army on earth could not break. They came up the street towards their church, where nothing awaited them, no precious paintings or treasures or even a living priest. Only the consoling silence of God. Barefoot and ragged and half starved, skinny arms raised to the sky, they were going to give thanks. They held their heads high and raised their tear-streaked faces to the blue heaven, a dusty black column of old men tottering on olive sticks, widows with veils raised, children arm in arm, helping each other as they limped along, a boy with a bandaged leg, a little girl with one hand. All sang.

The knights thought their hearts would break. And then on impulse one knight sank down on his knees at the side of the street, and bowed his head in all humility to the people passing by. This people with the hearts of lions. The knight was La Valette. Jean Parisot de la Valette, 48th Grand Master of the impeccably aristocratic Order of the Knights of St John.

Then one by one, all the knights did as he did. All down the street, the stony ground rang with the clank of poleyns and greaves as the noblest sons of European chivalry, hair matted, beards filthy, beribboned in bloody bandages, sank down and bowed before a troop of dust-covered peasantry. They closed their eyes and rested shaggy, blood-encrusted forelocks on their clasped fists, holding their swords before them like crosses set in the ground, like knights in midnight vigil before the Cross.

What an Island of Heroes they had fought for and died for. What a high honour it had been. Suleiman should see this, the Magnificent, the Lord of the World, Padishah of the Red Sea, the White and the Black. Then at last he might be humbled. For such a people as this could never be destroyed.

Later that night, a message came from La Valette. The relief force from Sicily, under Don García de Toledo, had landed on the north of the island at Mellieha Bay. They had not been able to sail earlier, because of bad weather.

Then La Valette gave a rare laugh.

11

It was just an ordinary backstreet house in Birgu that had been struck by one of the last Turkish cannonballs fired into the town. The house had a small courtyard where the family used to sit, old Mama and mother and father and their daughter and two boys. The boys slept in the tiny room up the stairs from the courtyard at the top of the house. But some days before, the daughter had looked at the other houses hit by cannonball, and had made her brothers change rooms with her. Her noisy, dirty, scrappy, irritating, beloved little brothers. They said they didn't want to move, they liked their room, but she said they must, it was dangerous. They said but then she would be in danger and she said don't argue, go and sleep in my room. Or we could all sleep in the cellar, they said, but she said that would not be decent as they well knew, for men and women did not sleep in the same room after a girl had become a woman. And besides, cellars collapsed and buried people alive. They wouldn't like that. So the boys grumpily took up their blankets and their thin straw pallets and moved into her room and she into theirs.

Nicholas ran back to the Street of the Bakers, a surge of wild survivor's joy in his young heart. It was over, and he lived. He and Hodge and Maddalena all still lived. Suddenly a future was possible again, after months when he thought he might die here. Images of the green hills of Shropshire flooded into his mind, long distant plans, confused desires, his sisters found and restored, their rightful estates ... Hodge his companion on the hills once more,

393

long fowling pieces over their shoulders, dogs at their heels. And a beautiful young wife, taken back to England with him. How she would complain of the snowbound winters! Suddenly it was all possible. He shivered with happiness.

When he came running pell-mell into the Street of the Bakers, the house of Franco Briffa was no longer there. Just a shattered waste of white stone and dust, a section of wall hanging free in the air above, suspended in shock.

A woman saw him and took his hand and led him to a small courtyard further down the street, and there was Franco Briffa and Maria, her head sunk on his chest, and old Mama, and Mateo and Tito sitting nearby on the ground looking wide-eyed, and beneath a white shroud a slender body covered from head to toe.

Nicholas cried out in every language that he knew, broken fragments of Spanish and Italian and Maltese and English, and he tore off the pure white shroud that covered her and saw what the cannonballs and the falling stones had done to her. Yet her face was untouched and as beautiful as ever in life, and he fell on her and kissed her, until at last gentle hands held him and stilled him and then helped him up.

Franco Briffa was speaking to him, and Maria also, but he could not hear their words. His ears screamed. But then he tried to make himself hear them. Was it not their grief too? He had loved her more than he would ever love another, but her parents too had loved and lost her, borne her, nursed her, raised her. For four months she had been a flame in his heart, a painful beautiful burning flame, but for fourteen years she had been their jewel, and they had lost her. He gulped down his desperate sobs and strained to hear their words.

'You would have been my son,' said Franco Briffa, and held him to his breast. Maria wept beside him and stroked his hair as if she was truly his mother.

'You would have been our son,' she said. 'We would have been proud of you as though you were true-born Maltese, and you would have been our son. For she would have had no other but you.'

Nicholas and Hodge sat out on the headland beyond Gallows Point and watched the sun go down over the island. Nicholas sat with his arms around his knees and his head bowed as if he was praying, but he was not praying. Hodge sat near to him, squinting, pulling a bit of dried grass. It had all been for nothing. The chivalry and heroism and the unimaginable hardship. What was it all about? A few barren miles of island and a dead girl's grave.

Now the world was all before them, and they had nothing but their lives, their limbs and their spirits, wounded deep but not broken. It was more than many. What was next for them? Return to England? For there was business still to be done in Shropshire, and much to be set right there. Or Cadiz? Venice, and the hope of fortune? Or eastwards, to unimaginable adventures? Perhaps they would become wanderers of this Inland Sea, and of the blazing, war-torn borderland between two worlds, the Cross and the Crescent. Nicholas knew he had too great a restlessness, too great a sorrow, for any peace. Would they lose their honour and sink to mere mercenaries, going from war to bloody war, swords for hire, men who have looked on so much horror it has left their souls emptied out of everything once human?

'I'm sorry for it, though,' Hodge suddenly blurted out. 'The girl and everything.'

Without Hodge, he might have chosen to die here, leave his bones here. But he would go on. Hodge made it bearable.

'You have a stout heart and a noble soul, Hodge. For a peasant.'

'That I have, Master Nicholas, that I have.'

'I'm not your master.'

'Just as you say, master.'

The sun sank slowly down.

'I'm glad you're here, Hodge.'

'I'm not. Don't know why I'm here, any more'n you do.'

Nicholas thought he had known. To fight for her. Afterwards to be with her. Just to be with her, just a few years. The tears came.

'Come on then,' said Hodge. 'They're pouring the wine free in all the taverns. We should go back to town and get drunk as badgers. Remember how they used to get drunk at night, down in the cider-apple orchard?'

Long ago, when they were boys. Nicholas raised his head, crying with a smile.

EPILOGUE

Jean Parisot de la Valette was offered a Cardinalate in Rome, but he smiled and gracefully declined. 'For the next few years,' he said, 'I must needs be a builder.'

Money now poured into the coffers of the Order, from those European princes who had been so slow to send help while the battle raged. Their small consciences pricked, they delved into their treasuries and sent gold and silver, food and supplies, fresh livestock, seedcorn, and teams of stonemasons and engineers.

'Birgu will be rebuilt as before,' said La Valette. 'And a glorious new capital will be founded upon Mount Sciberras, called Humilissima. The Humble.'

The first stone was laid on 28th March 1566 by La Valette himself, a stone bearing the impress of a golden lion on a bloody field, his family device. Everyone else already called the city Valletta in his honour, but he always referred to it as Humilissima. He said they should never be too proud of a victory that was ultimately in the hands of God.

A stranger rumour circulated in the ports and harbourside taverns of the Mediterranean at that time. It was said that during the winter of 1565-66, La Valette had sent a covert team of knights, all fluent speakers of Turkish and Arabic, on a mission to assassinate Suleiman. A mission of astonishing daring and danger, which perhaps not surprisingly failed. The Lord of the Universe was one of the most closely guarded rulers on earth.

But it was said that the assassins themselves escaped from the Topkapı without being captured, and instead took another revenge. For in January 1566, the massive arsenals which lined the Bosphorus, where materials, weaponry and powder were already being stockpiled for a second invasion of Malta that summer, went up in an explosion so vast that it sent waves crashing across the Golden Horn and into the walls of Seraglio Point, shaking the very foundations of the Topkapı Palace itself. It was whispered to be a stupendous act of sabotage by the Knights of St John themselves.

La Valette naturally denied it. As if the Knights of St John would engage in such underhand tactics as assassination and sabotage! But he smiled and admitted that such a devastating misfortune for the Grand Sultan had certainly been music to his ears. He thought that Suleiman would probably not attack Malta again soon.

He was right.

With the start of the campaigning season in the spring of 1566, the Lord of the Universe attacked Christendom not by sea but by land, and not Malta, but the hard-pressed marches of Hungary. This time he would take Vienna, the Danube valley, and seize the heart of Europe.

Suleiman himself rode at the head of his army, dropsical, sallow, eyelids sagging, eyes haunted. They muttered that their lord was a broken man. He had seen many of those closest to him die – and worse, he had ordered the deaths of several of his beloved sons, to secure a succession without bloodshed, as was the Ottoman way. His son Mustafa was strangled before his eyes. Another, Beyazid, with four of his own sons, also died choking on bowstrings wielded by deaf mutes. Suleiman's successor was to be the one called Selim, son of the Sultan's favourite wife, Roxelana. Behind his back, he was already called Selim the Sot. He was obese, stupid, vindictive and generally drunk.

That last Hungarian campaign was not a success, the weather was terrible, and the Ottoman army became bogged down in the Siege of Szeged. The fortress was eventually taken, but Suleiman never knew it. He died in his tent the night before, on 5th September 1566.

Jean de la Valette outlived his old enemy, dying on 21st August 1568, at the age of 73. He was buried in the chapel of Our Lady of Victory, in the new capital of Valletta arising on Sciberras, where the

Turkish cannon had roared all summer long, three years before.

Today you can still read his Latin epitaph, composed by Sir Oliver Starkey. In its stern, proud and laconic style, it is the Grand Master to the letter.

HIC ASIAE LIBYAEQUE PAVOR TUTELAQUE QUONDAM
EUROPAE EDOMITIS SACRA PER ARMA GETIS
PRIMUS IN HAC ALMA QUAM CONDIDIT URBE SEPULTUS
VALLETTA AETERNO DIGNUS HONORE JACET

Here lies La Valette, worthy of eternal honour.
The scourge of Africa and Asia,
the shield of Europe,
whence he expelled the barbarians by his holy arms,
he is the first to be buried
in this beloved city which he founded.

La Valette himself insisted on the new capital being so described in his epitaph.

'This beloved city,' he murmured as he lay dying. 'This beloved island.'

TIME LINE

1453: Wednesday 29th May: The Ottoman Turks under Mehmet II capture Constantinople, the last redoubt of the Eastern Roman Empire

1492: Fall of Granada, the last Moorish kingdom of Spain, to Ferdinand and Isabella. Muslim exodus to North Africa, the beginning of the Barbary Corsair kingdoms

1517: Martin Luther nails his famous 95 theses to the door of Wittenberg Church. Christendom slowly begins to break apart into Protestant and Catholic

1519: Charles V elected Holy Roman Emperor

1520: Suleiman becomes Sultan

1521: Pope excommunicates Luther

1522: Turks capture Rhodes from the Knights of St John

1526: Suleiman's Turks annihilate Hungarian forces at the Battle of Mohács, and kill King Louis of Hungary

1529: Turks invade Austria, but fail to capture Vienna

1531: Henry VIII declares himself Head of the Church of England

1537: Turks declare war on Venice and ravage Southern Italy

1538: Turks capture Spanish-held Castelnuovo in Montenegro

1542-43: The French ally with the Turks to attack the coast of Italy and sack Nice. Barbarossa's North African corsairs briefly occupy Toulon

1556: Philip II, son of Charles V, becomes King of Spain

1558: Death of Charles V

1560: Charles IX becomes King of France, with Catherine de' Medici as regent

1562: Massacre of Huguenots in France

1565: Siege of Malta

LIST OF PRINCIPAL CHARACTERS

All those marked with an asterisk were real historical figures

Franco Briffa, Maltese fisherman; his wife Maria, and their
   children Maddalena, Mateo and Tito
*Luqa Briffa, celebrated Maltese folk-hero
*Luigi Broglia, commander, died at Elmo
*Candelissa, Greek Christian renegade turned corsair
*Miguel de Cervantes Saavedra (1547–1616). His father was
   Rodrigo de Cervantes, an apothecary-surgeon with pretensions
   to nobility. Cervantes' early life is obscure, but by 1569 he was
   serving in Spain's Navy's *Infantería de Marina* – the Marines.
   He went on to fight at Lepanto in 1571, where he was wounded
   three times, and in 1575 he was captured by Algerian corsairs,
   and held for fives years until ransomed. Later in life he turned
   to writing, and gave the world his immortal *Don Quixote*
*Grand Marshal Copier, marshal of cavalry
*Dragut (1485–1565), Ottoman corsair and naval commander, died
   in the siege of Malta
*Bartolomeo Faraone, Portuguese novice knight, died of torture at
   the hands of the Turks
*Bridier de la Gordcamp, French knight, died at Elmo
*Melchior de Guaras, Spanish knight, died at Elmo
Matthew Hodgkin, manservant and friend of Nicholas Ingoldsby
Sir Francis Ingoldsby, of the County of Shropshire
Nicholas Ingoldsby, his son
*Don John of Austria (1547–1578), bastard son of Charles V and

his German mistress Barbara Blomberg, and therefore half-
brother of Philip II of Spain. A knight of Malta
*Francesco Lanfreducci, Italian knight, died at Elmo
*Chevalier Medrano, Spanish knight, died at Elmo
*Don Pedro Mezquita, Portuguese knight, Commander of Mdina
*Captain Miranda, Spanish knight, died at Elmo
*Mustafa Pasha (1500–1580), commander of the Ottoman forces
at Malta
*Henri Parisot, nephew of Jean de la Valette, died in the siege
*Piyale Pasha (c.1525–1565), Admiral of the Ottoman Fleet
*Adrien de la Rivière, French knight, captured by the Turks, died
under torture
*Mathurin Lescaut, known as Romegas, French knight, born
1528, and one of the greatest naval commanders of the age. Was
said to have destroyed more than fifty Ottoman galleys, and
liberated more than a thousand slaves. Harried the Ottoman
Fleet at Malta, and went on to fight at Lepanto in 1571
*John Smith, English knight
*Edward Stanley, English knight
*Sir Oliver Starkey, Englishman, Latin Secretary to La Valette
*Suleiman the Magnificent (1494–1566), Sultan of the Ottoman
Empire
*Don García de Toledo, Spanish nobleman, Viceroy of Sicily
*Federique de Toledo, son of Don García, died in the siege
*Jean Parisot de la Valette (1494–1568), Provençal nobleman,
Grand Master of the Knights of St John from 1557 until his
death

AUTHOR'S NOTE AND FURTHER READING

Any keen reader of historical fiction will soon ask, How much of this is true? How much has the author invented? In the case of *Clash of Empires*, the honest answer is that a great deal is accurate and follows the facts closely. If you glance at the List of Principal Characters, you will see that almost all of those in the book are genuine. The main exception is my protagonist, Nicholas Ingoldsby himself. Edward Stanley and John Smith were both there at the siege, although sadly we know little else about these two mysterious figures.

As an English writer, I am naturally proud that a handful of Englishmen, at least, fought at this most heroic of battles, and I have put English characters at the heart of the story; but I wouldn't suggest that this was in any substantial way an English victory. The Siege of Malta, 1565, one of the most extraordinary episodes in the lamentable, 1,500-year conflict between Christendom and Islam, was overwhelmingly a victory won by Italians and Spaniards, Frenchmen and Portuguese – and the staunch, stubborn, often overlooked people of Malta themselves.

If you want to know more of the history, unadorned – or untainted – by a novelist's imagination, and check how much is accurate, then three books stand out. Ernle Bradford's *The Great Siege: Malta 1565*, first published in 1961, will probably never be surpassed as a sober, vivid and gripping account of the battle. Bradford served in the Royal Navy during World War II, and was also a passionate sailor of the Mediterranean for many years, both of which contribute to the power of his narrative.

Three other books I found particularly inspiring were Roger Crowley's *Empires of the Sea: The Final Battle for the Mediterranean, 1521–1580*, a colourful, compelling and brilliantly researched history of the entire period; Barnaby Rogerson's excellent *The Last Crusaders: East, West and the Battle for the Centre of the World*; and *Suleiman the Magnificent: Scourge of Heaven* by Antony Bridge, now sadly out of print, but freely available second-hand, and a wonderfully readable, often dryly amusing portrait of the greatest of all the Ottoman sultans.

Other books to which I owe a considerable debt include *The Shield and the Sword: The Knights of St John*, also by Ernle Bradford; *The Monks of War: The Military Religious Orders* by Desmond Seward; *Victory of the West: The Story of the Battle of Lepanto* by Niccolo Capponi; *Malta 1565: Last Battle of the Crusades* by Tim Pickles and Christa Hook; *The Renaissance at War* by Thomas Arnold; *The Ottomans: Dissolving Images* by Andrew Wheatcroft; *History of the Reign of Philip II* by William H. Prescott; *Don John of Austria* by Sir Charles Petrie; *White Gold* by Giles Milton; *Muhammed and the Conquests of Islam* by Francesco Gabrieli; *Anthology of Islamic Literature*, ed. by James Kritzeck; and *The Janissaries* by Godfrey Goodwin. And keen-eyed readers will recognise immediately that the 'old ballad' quoted on page 73 is of course a straightforward steal from G. K. Chesterton's magnificent poem *Lepanto*.

I would also like to acknowledge the endless help and support of Patrick Walsh, agent extraordinaire; Jon Wood, Genevieve Pegg, Natalie Braine, Jade Chandler and all at Orion, and my eagle-eyed copy editor, Gabby Nemeth; cover artist Steve Stone, and Hemesh Alles for the wonderful maps.

If you tire of reading, then you can always visit the island of Malta itself, so packed with history at every step – despite its very twenty-first century traffic. The city of Valletta remains a splendid monument to a certain stubborn Grand Master. You can walk the narrow, winding streets of the town of Birgu on the opposite side of the harbour, among the people who are direct descendants of those stalwart sixteenth-century citizens, and visit the great fort of San Angelo, parts of which are now leased back by the Maltese Government to the still-flourishing Knights of St John (these days more committed to charitable works than crusading). And you can stand on the walls of Fort St Elmo, much changed and restored though it is, and look out across the sparkling Mediteranean, as one day in April 1565, a small, fearful but determined band of brothers looked out, and saw a vast armada approaching from the East ...

William Napier
Wiltshire, 2010